Janie Crouch writes passionate romantic suspense for readers who still believe in heroes. After a lifetime on the East Coast—and a six-year stint in Germany—this *USA Today* bestselling author has settled into her dream home in Front Range of the Colorado Rockies. She loves engaging in all sorts of adventures (triathlons, two-hundred-mile relay races, mountain treks!), travelling and surviving life with four kids. You can find out more about her at janiecrouch.com

A true Renaissance woman, **Deborah Fletcher Mello** finds joy in crafting unique story lines and memorable characters. She's received accolades from several publications, including *Publishers Weekly*, *Library Journal* and *RT Book Reviews*. Born and raised in Connecticut, Deborah now considers home to be wherever the moment moves her.

Discover more at millsandboon.co.uk

TEXAS BODYGUARD: CHANCE

JANIE CROUCH

CHASING A COLTON KILLER

DEBORAH FLETCHER MELLO

MILLS & BOON

First Published in Great Britain 2023
by Mills & Boon, an imprint of HarperCollins*Publishers* Ltd
1 London Bridge Street, London, SE1 9GF

www.harpercollins.co.uk

HarperCollins*Publishers*
Macken House, 39/40 Mayor Street Upper,
Dublin 1, D01 C9W8, Ireland

Texas Bodyguard: Chance © 2023 Janie Crouch
Chasing a Colton Killer © 2023 Harlequin Enterprises ULC.

Special thanks and acknowledgement are given to Deborah Fletcher Mello for her contribution to *The Coltons of New York* series.

ISBN: 978-0-263-30738-2

0823

MIX
Paper | Supporting
responsible forestry
FSC™ C007454

This book is produced from independently certified FSC™ paper
to ensure responsible forest management.

For more information visit: www.harpercollins.co.uk/green

Printed and Bound in the UK using 100% Renewable Electricity at
CPI Group (UK) Ltd, Croydon, CR0 4YY

TEXAS BODYGUARD: CHANCE

JANIE CROUCH

Since this book is about family, it's dedicated to my Kiddo #4. I am delighted to see the woman you're becoming, but you are, and always will be, my baby. Your artistic talent and bullheaded stubbornness amaze me on a constant basis. Go out and do great things in the world!

Prologue

The moment his alarm rang, despite the fact that the sun wasn't quite cresting the horizon, Chance was up. He didn't have time to waste on snoozing.

He needed to help everyone with breakfast, washing and hair and teeth brushing. Everyone had to be outside for the bus by eight. While the others were eating, he'd check homework and make sure their backpacks were ready to go. Snacks for the younger kids. Change of clothes for the preschool—

"Chance, breakfast is ready!"

Chance froze midway through pulling on his pants and blinked at the darkened room around him.

His room. His alone.

He wasn't in the group home anymore like he'd been for the past four years. There was no small army of other kids around him. No one he needed to help get out the door every morning.

He was at the Pattersons' house. He'd been here for five months now.

He finished getting dressed and walked down the

stairs. He didn't need to make breakfast for a bunch of hungry little kids. Sheila had made breakfast for *him*.

She smiled at him as he walked in the kitchen. "Pancakes. Strawberries on the side for you. The other boys should be up in a minute. Sit and eat."

"Um, thanks." He sat down, still trying to adjust to someone feeding him rather than him being responsible for feeding others. "Do you need help packing lunches or anything?"

Sheila smiled. "Already taken care of. Thank you for asking though."

Right. Already taken care of.

When Sheila shooed him onward, Chance nodded and sat at the six-seater table in the breakfast nook. The room was silent for less than a minute before the others started trickling in.

"Morning, Mom." Brax, Sheila and Clinton's biracial adopted son, kissed Sheila's cheek as he grabbed his plate and sat down next to Chance. "Thanks for breakfast. I'm starving."

"Yes, pancakes!" Luke, their adopted White son came in next, taking his plate and shoving a whole pancake in his mouth before he sat down. Chance winced at the painfully large gulp he took to swallow it, but the others just laughed.

"And that's why I always make yours smaller." Sheila grinned.

The last ones down were Clinton and Weston, who talked quietly on their way into the kitchen. Weston had arrived a few weeks ago, after Chance. The Black boy hardly ever said anything, and worked out in the garden all the time, but Chance liked him.

He liked Clinton too. Sheila's husband was big and Black and funny. He was always respectful to Sheila and didn't yell. He worked as an accountant for some business here in San Antonio.

Sheila joined the rest of the family at the table once they'd all sat down. "Anyone have after-school plans?"

She took a bite of her own pancakes and looked pointedly at Chance's untouched plate. He'd waited for the rest of them too. She didn't say anything, but she didn't have to. With a small grin, he took a bite, knowing it was what she wanted.

What would it be like to have Sheila Patterson as a mom? She was Hispanic like him, so they already looked similar.

Sheila and Clinton had started some of the preliminary paperwork for adopting Chance, but he wasn't holding his breath.

Minds changed. Circumstances changed. Systems changed.

It was why Chance liked to take care of others rather than someone take care of him. That way, if *things changed*, he'd still be okay.

He could take care of himself. He could take care of everyone.

Silence crossed over the table and he looked up, startling when he caught everyone's eyes on him. He'd missed something.

What were they talking about? *Plans.*

"I don't have any plans," he said when the others

kept looking at him. He hadn't realized they'd been asking him.

"Do you want to come hang out with us? We're going to a movie," Luke said, stuffing another pancake in his mouth, only to swallow quickly and painfully again.

Clinton chuckled into his coffee while Sheila pointed at Luke with her fork. "I appreciate that you enjoy my cooking, but you'll eat with some manners at my table."

"Yes, ma'am," Luke said, throwing Chance a wink when she wasn't looking. He laughed under his breath.

"So, movie?" Brax asked.

Chance thought about the cash he'd squirreled away doing odd jobs over the summer. Mowing lawns and whatever side jobs he could get here. He liked having money saved in case he needed it for something.

He did the math in his head. The movie would take a bit of it, but he'd still have plenty left over if he needed to buy new clothes or school supplies once he went back to the group home.

"We're paying for everything, and you could use an afternoon out," Clinton said. "You should go, Chance."

Sheila smiled kindly. "Go be a kid for a change."

Chance wasn't sure he'd ever felt like a kid. There was always too much that needed to be done. Too many people who needed taking care of. Too many bad things to plan for in case they happened.

And in Chance's experience, the bad things always happened.

But he was smart. He knew saying no now would be upsetting to everyone. So he nodded at his foster family. "Okay. A movie sounds good."

The other boys high-fived and started talking about what they would see. Sheila and Clinton smiled at each other.

Chance took another bite of his pancake.

He'd have a good time and enjoy the movie. But despite the happy faces around him, he still knew the truth.

The only one he could rely on was himself.

Chapter One

Abrupt knocking startled Chance Patterson into spilling hot coffee across the back of his hand as he poured it into his mug. He muttered a curse. This wasn't how he'd wanted to start his Monday morning.

The San Antonio Security office—the company Chance had started with his brothers five years ago—didn't open for another hour. He'd come in early in hopes of getting some time to work without interruptions. Obviously, that wasn't going to happen.

Throwing a towel over the puddle on the counter, he pulled out his phone, swiping to look at the doorbell camera.

On the office's stoop stood a man dressed in a suit, carrying a briefcase. Thanks to the HD camera, Chance could see him clearly enough despite the early morning's naturally low light. He had a medium build and was middle-aged and somewhat pale—not unusual for someone who worked in an office full-time.

"May I help you?" Instead of going to greet the man, Chance used the microphone feature on the doorbell. Security Business 101 was not to open the door to just anyone, regardless of how official they looked.

"Is this one of the Patterson brothers?" The man's voice was clipped and his words concise. Like he was used to only saying what he needed to and not a single word more.

"It is, but we don't open for another hour. If you want to come back then—"

"I can't," he said stiffly, not at all bothered by cutting Chance off or speaking through the microphone. "I'm here as a proxy for someone who wants to hire your services. To whom am I speaking?"

"Chance Patterson. Look, have your employer call us, and we can schedule a time to talk."

"I can't do that either. My employer is busy, and the issue is incredibly time sensitive."

Chance barely refrained from pointing out that he was busy too. He ran his burned hand under some cool water at the sink next to him, while pouring a new mug of coffee with the other. "Who is your employer?"

"I can't provide that information until you've signed a nondisclosure agreement." He waved a manila folder in front of the camera. "His need for privacy is very real, which you will understand if you sign. For now, I can tell you that my name is Benjamin Torres and that your business came highly recommended to my employer by Leo Delacruz. Once you sign the NDA, I can provide further info."

Chance turned the water off and dried his hand. Leo Delacruz was basically extended family at this point. The man had hired San Antonio Security—specifically

Chance's brother Weston—to guard his daughter, Kayleigh, to protect her when a merger got dangerous a few months ago.

Leo was a well-known Texas businessman and associated with a lot of people, so knowing he'd recommended their company didn't narrow down who Benjamin worked for.

The man didn't shuffle or fidget in the silence while Chance thought this through. He came across as not impatient, but efficient. He had things to do and needed his answer.

Chance couldn't give him one under these circumstances. "I'm not comfortable signing something that would require me to keep secrets from my brothers."

The Patterson brothers didn't keep secrets from one another.

Chance grit his teeth. Actually, he'd been keeping a pretty damned big one from them for the past few months.

Benjamin shook his head. "The NDA will permit you to tell your brothers anything you deem necessary, but requires you to keep the identity of my employer and anything he discusses with you confidential, even if you choose not to take the assignment."

"Put the NDA through the mail slot. I'll look it over."

A quick read proved it to be a standard document, with the only changes being what he'd outlined. He could share information with his brothers and their employees as necessary, but no one outside the company. There were no penalties or clauses that would make things difficult if they didn't take the assignment either, so he signed it and unlocked the door, handing the stack of papers back to Benjamin.

"Thank you, Mr. Patterson." The older man tucked the contract into his briefcase and stepped back. "Mr. LeBlanc will be pleased. He's anxious to meet with you all to discuss the situation."

"Nicholas LeBlanc?" The Texas real estate tycoon? He was *big* money. "What exactly does he want to hire San Antonio Security for?"

Someone of LeBlanc's stature would have his own full-time security team.

"Mr. LeBlanc would prefer to give you the details himself. If this afternoon works, he has an availability at 3:00 p.m. Top floor of the VanPoint Tower."

"We'll be there."

With an efficient nod, Benjamin left, getting into the back seat of a town car at the edge of the sidewalk. Chance watched him go, then turned back into the office. He needed to find out as much as he could about Nicholas LeBlanc and get everyone into the office stat.

Looked like a quiet morning working on his own was not in the cards.

"Why are we all here again?" Luke asked as they stepped into the glass elevator in the VanPoint Tower's lobby later that afternoon.

Chance looked out at the pristine building. "Because Nicholas LeBlanc is the type of client whose recommendation could set us up for years."

Chance and his brothers had started San Antonio Security five years ago. They'd wanted to work together and, between the four of them, had years of prior military and law enforcement experience. At the beginning of their business journey, they'd had to take whatever assignments they could get, which included a lot of following cheating spouses and hunting bail jumpers.

But in the last couple of years, San Antonio Security had grown to become one of the most respected firms in their hometown. Now they did a lot of personal and corporate security—not only the bodyguarding, but situational awareness and tactical defense.

They were brought in by companies and individuals to find and fix the holes in their security, to stop the bad things before they happened.

But sometimes the bad things were already in motion when San Antonio Security was brought in. Chance was afraid that was the case now with Nicholas LeBlanc.

The elevator gave Chance and his brothers a view of the indoor complex that housed a virtual warren of businesses. LeBlanc Holdings held the top two floors—announcing its prestige and prosperity without ever saying a word.

The elevator doors opened, releasing them into a large lobby. People were everywhere, talking, walking, typing. Phones were ringing all over the place, but there was order even in the chaos.

"Mr. Patterson?"

Chance turned and found the man who had showed up at the office this morning. "Yes."

"I was under the impression that you were bringing your brothers with you, not employees. Security downstairs listed you all as Pattersons."

"That's because we are. These are my brothers—Brax, Luke and Weston Patterson."

It was a common misconception, since none of them looked alike.

"I see. My apologies for the error." Once again, Benjamin was all efficiency. "Mr. LeBlanc is waiting for you. Follow me."

Chance followed behind everyone else, taking in the office and the atmosphere. Though the office was guarded downstairs, he saw a man stationed near the elevator and another near the stairs. Both security guards had a line of sight to the door Benjamin was knocking on.

Was it LeBlanc who was in danger then, or was that standard practice?

"Come in." Benjamin pushed the door open, and Chance found himself in a corner office with more windows than walls. The city was sprawled out, with buildings dotting the horizon and tiny people and cars jostling about like ants.

It was the view of someone who had money and power and liked both.

Beyond that, the rest of the room was taken over by a massive desk covered in neat stacks of paper. Everything else in the office, from the carpet to the chairs to the paintings, was done in warm, masculine neutrals. Deep navy and warm gray mixed with the dark mahogany of the bookcases to create a type of space that fit the CEO and founder of a multimillion dollar company.

"Mr. LeBlanc, these are the Patterson brothers, owners of San Antonio Security."

Nicholas LeBlanc stood from behind his desk. "Thank

you for coming, gentlemen. Leo Delacruz speaks highly of you. Please sit. Benjamin will get you whatever drinks you want."

Chance took note of the expensive watch and tailored suit jacket. Everything on LeBlanc's body—and in his office—was both extravagant and orderly.

Chance had no problem with either. But once again he was trying to figure out why someone like LeBlanc was interested in a security firm like theirs, even with Leo's recommendation.

Nicholas motioned everyone to a sitting area off to the side of his behemoth desk. They all declined the offer of drinks.

"What can San Antonio Security do for you, Mr. LeBlanc?" Brax asked. As the most charming of the Patterson brothers, he tended to do the initial talking. He had a way of making people feel at ease.

Chance preferred to let Brax talk so he could observe.

"Leo told me that you four were the best at what you do."

"Thank you. We work very hard and pride ourselves on our solid reputation." Brax tipped his head in acknowledgment. "Are you needing more personal security? It seems like you've got plenty."

"Not exactly." Nicholas sighed. "My daughter, Stella, is having an issue. She's a social media influencer, and recently she's become the target of a stalker."

Chance leaned forward, leaning his elbows on his knees. "What kind of stalker?"

"At first it was messages on her social media, comments and DMs from dummy accounts. Then it turned into actual letters being sent to the house with no clue how the individual got the address. Recently it has been bizarre gifts and more. She wants to use what she receives to further build her social media following. Obviously, she doesn't understand the severity of the issue."

"Tell us what you perceive that severity to be," Brax said gently, nodding at Nicholas.

If it was just letters, there wasn't much anyone could do to stop them. Even the police rarely prosecuted stalking cases. There was too much ambiguity to make them stick in court.

Gifts were the same, as long as they didn't cause harm. Icky wasn't illegal.

Nicholas rubbed the back of his neck. "The problem is, no matter what our security measures are, her stalker keeps getting through. We've had Stella on lockdown and they've still gotten letters inside the compound to her. We've gone through three security teams and none of them have been able to stop her from receiving the notes. I'm worried that things are going to get worse, and I don't want my daughter caught in the crosshairs."

Brax sat back, resting an ankle on his knee. "So, you want us to bodyguard Stella?"

Nicholas shrugged. "Yes and no. She has guards on her at all times, though she's not often aware of it. Her constant companion, Rich Carlisle, is someone I hired a few years ago as a social secretary/babysitter. He's also trained in defense, although that's not his primary purpose."

It sounded like Stella had a full team. "Where would we come in?"

"While you might do some guarding and security setup, I'd really like you to focus on finding the stalker. Since we don't have proof of anyone physically harming or threatening Stella, the police can't do anything but write reports. I need someone out there looking for whoever is behind this."

Chance caught his brothers' eyes. They all knew how beneficial this assignment could be for their business overall, but for something like this, everyone needed to be in agreement before they took it on.

Things had changed for his brothers over the past few months. Luke and Brax both had wives now. Brax even had a kid. Weston was engaged to Leo Delacruz's daughter, Kayleigh.

Chance was the only one still alone.

An assignment of this magnitude would take a lot of man hours for everyone, even if Chance took the lead.

It would also mean Chance would be spending a lot more time in the office. A lot more time around Maci Ford, the San Antonio Security office manager.

Who he saw every day, while both of them pretended she hadn't snuck out of his bed in the middle of the night a couple months ago.

All his brothers gave him subtle nods, so he knew they were okay with taking the LeBlanc assignment. Chance gave his full attention back to Nicholas.

"If we do this, we'll have to split our time between bodyguarding and investigating. It's going to take a lot of planning and strategy."

"I'm willing to pay whatever it takes. You kept Leo's

situation quiet, and that's what I need—someone with both discretion and skill."

"This isn't necessarily about the money. What about your own security team?" Brax asked. "Will they feel threatened by us coming in here on top of them? That sort of divided energy makes a difficult situation even harder."

They'd dealt with that exact situation with Leo Delacruz, and it had ended in bloodshed. None of them wanted to take that on again.

Nicholas shook his head. "No, it won't be like that at all. I would not even be here talking to you if my team hadn't vetted you. As a matter of fact…"

Nicholas walked over to his desk and typed something. A few seconds later a man walked through the office door.

He was maybe in his late forties, with salt-and-pepper hair styled neatly to match his black suit. It was tailored, but not designer, and the slightly worn quality of his shoes told Chance he didn't sit behind a desk all day like LeBlanc. He was on his feet a lot.

"This is Dorian Cane, my head of security. Dorian's been with me since I started the company, and he's known Stella her whole life. Dorian, these are the Patterson brothers."

Dorian stepped forward and shook everyone's hand as they introduced themselves. When it was Chance's turn, he watched Dorian's calculating eyes run over him, stopping briefly at the places where Chance had a weapon of some sort stashed. He only missed one, which said Dorian Cane was good at his job.

Chance sat and cleared his throat. "In your opinion,

how dangerous is the stalking situation, Dorian? Based on your experience, are these pranks, someone seeking attention or something worse?"

To his credit, the other man thought before he spoke. "It definitely felt like a game at first, but the messages have been getting stranger as time wears on. I'm worried about escalation becoming a very real possibility in the future."

It was one thing for a concerned father to say he thought a stalker was dangerous. It was completely different for someone of Dorian Cane's experience to say the same.

And Nicholas was right. There was nothing about the other man's actions or mannerisms that suggested he felt threatened or angered by their presence.

But Chance asked him anyway. "You're alright with Nicholas bringing us in?"

"My top priority is figuring out who this stalker is. Something about him—although it could be a her—has got all my internal alarms going off. You guys are good. I checked you out myself."

Chance had no doubt that was true.

"I can't let Nicholas's other security concerns fall to the side while concentrating on the stalker. Bringing in people we can trust, who can keep it quiet, is the best solution."

"If we take this job, we'll need to know that Stella will actually listen to us," Weston said. He was the quietest of all the brothers, but he knew from personal experience that trying to guard someone who didn't want to be guarded could be dangerous for everyone. "From what you've said, she may not be interested in that."

Dorian looked over at Nicholas, who gestured for him to go ahead and answer. "Stella is spoiled. She's used to getting what she wants, and she doesn't understand that this stalker isn't something to joke about. It's unsafe and getting more dangerous by the day."

Nicholas adjusted his tie. "Dorian's not wrong. I've definitely spoiled and sheltered her more than I should have, but she's my whole world."

Nicholas reached for one of two framed photos on his desk and held it out to Chance. He took it, nearly doing a double take.

Ah, hell.

"We'll accept the job," Chance said. The picture solidified any doubt he had in his mind.

All three of his brothers looked at him with raised brows until he turned the picture around. Chance wasn't the type to blindly accept any deal without analyzing the details of the contract, but this time was different.

Stella LeBlanc looked exactly like Maci Ford.

And there was no way anyone who had Maci's face was getting stalked on Chance's watch.

Chapter Two

"I've been waiting for this all day."

The soft-spoken words tickled the skin of Maci's rib cage as the feel of warm, calloused hands on her waist made her shiver. She writhed as those hands slid down to her hips, pulling her closer, and those lips climbed to brush her neck and shoulders. She couldn't stop her groan at a soft swipe of a tongue along the hollow of her throat.

"Maci, you taste so good."

Chance's voice was so low it was barely a sound, and the heat of his breath on her skin gave her goose bumps. Threading her fingers through his hair, all Maci wanted to do was feel.

Here in her room there was no work, no clients, no danger. There was only the two of them surrounded by darkness. The pressing weight of him on top of her, the slow glide of their bodies coming together, the touches that anchored them together as they climbed.

Everywhere he touched, her skin burned. It had never been like this with anyone else. She shouldn't have been surprised. There was no one else in the world like Chance

Patterson. Even when he drove her mad, he made her feel more than she ever had before.

It always made her wonder how hard it would be to survive when he eventually got tired of her, when he realized how bad she was for him.

He nipped his teeth against her collarbone, his palm warm against the side of her throat. "Stay with me, Maci."

He knew her. He may not have known the details of her past, but he knew her need to overthink things that could get the best of her during inopportune moments.

She pressed her lips to his temple. "I'm here. I'm here."

He pressed a kiss over her throat, then continued along the side of her neck, driving her higher until she was gasping for breath. Her nails dug into Chance's back as she found herself falling over the edge. He whispered praises with every sweep of his hips until they were calling each other's names.

As always, there was a moment afterward where they clung to one another. Their breaths mingling, their bodies soft and warm and pliant.

Their hearts unguarded.

It was both too much and never enough for Maci when Chance looked at her then. She had too many secrets to guard, and he was too close to discovering them. Too close to walking away once he did.

Sated and relaxed, Chance pressed a kiss to her head, rolled to the side and tugged her into his arms. Maci tried to pull away, to give them some sort of space so the lines wouldn't blur come morning.

She needed a minute. Just one to rebuild the walls he so easily broke through every time they were together like this. Usually, he let her have some space, but this time he was having none of it.

"Stay with me," he whispered into her hair.

She wanted to. How she wanted to. No matter how short this passion with him lasted, she wanted him with a fierceness that made her feel weak.

Maci Ford was weak for almost nothing, but Chance Patterson was the exception to that hard-won rule. It was as surprising as it was oddly delightful.

When he squeezed her tighter, she smiled and let him drag her close enough that there was no space between them. "I'm not going anywhere."

She didn't want to go anywhere.

She wanted to stay with him.

She rested in his arms and let contentedness wash over her.

But as he fell asleep and the darkness around them became heavier, she knew she couldn't stay. Knew she should've never let this happen again, no matter how much she wanted it. Knew she had to walk away from him—from this.

It was the only way.

Wakefulness came in fits as Maci reached her arm across the bed, expecting Chance's warm skin. At the feel of cold cotton sheets, she frowned and pried her eyes open.

She was alone. Of course she was. She hadn't been with Chance in that way since she'd snuck out of his bed two months ago. She'd made sure he'd known the physical aspect of their relationship couldn't happen again. Even though that had been damn near the hardest thing she'd ever done.

Second only to seeing him every day at the office and trying to pretend like she wasn't interested in him. That they were nothing more than professional colleagues.

She peeked at the alarm clock on the bedside table and groaned. 5:45 a.m. Not enough time to go back to sleep if she wanted to get to the office on time. She spent five minutes glaring at the ceiling—frustrated and wishing that dream had been real—before she tossed the covers off her body. She made her way out of bed and to the kitchen and started the coffee with half-opened eyes.

At least the coffee would give her enough energy to get through the day. Another day with Chance.

Maybe she should get a new job.

She shut down the thought almost immediately. She couldn't do that. Wouldn't. She owed the Patterson brothers for being so good to her. Who else would have hired a twenty-five-year-old with a shiny new GED and no experience?

No one. The Patterson brothers were all upstanding, honorable men. Even before she'd slept with Chance and they were bickering all the time she'd still respected him. She respected all of them. She didn't want to give up her job.

She would have to find a way to continue working for San Antonio Security despite her very nonprofessional feelings for Chance. Which she thought was becoming easier until whatever had happened yesterday when the guys went to meet with Nicholas LeBlanc.

Chance had come back staring at her, even more grumpy with her than usual. No explanation, just a demand that she pull everything she could on the real estate tycoon and his company.

It had been all Maci could do not to tap her heels and salute. She was trying her best not to pick fights with Chance. Jabbing at each other at the office had been fun at first but now had taken a turn for a little more bitter since she'd snuck out of his bed.

She took her shower and got ready for the day, washing the memories of Chance down her drain like she tried to do every morning. Some day she hoped it wouldn't be necessary. But she wasn't holding her breath.

By the time she was ready to go, she was already half a coffee pot into her day and desperately in need of some food before the shakes took over. Still, it was nice pulling into the lot of San Antonio Security as an employee. She loved her job. Loved sorting the guys' paperwork chaos into systems that were tidy and manageable. Loved taking things off their hands and greeting and helping customers.

It was nice to be needed and feel like she was *capable*. That was definitely a first.

She turned off her car and glanced at her cell phone. Swiping away the notifications from her calendar and news apps, she froze. Two missed calls and a text, all from her mother. She stared at the phone, wishing she could toss it out the window.

Delete. She didn't listen to the voice mails. Nothing good came from her mother's mouth before eight in the morning.

Nothing good came from her mother's mouth any time of day.

She glanced at the text from her before deleting it also.

Need to talk to you.

"Of course you do." Maci tossed her phone back into her bag, yanked her keys out of the ignition and opened up her car door.

She fought not to let the text ruin a day that hadn't even started yet. Her relationship with Evelyn had been *strained* for years. Suffering from addiction her whole life, Evelyn treated Maci like a glorified ATM, showing up just long enough to get cash for her next fix before leaving again.

Taking a fortifying breath, Maci got out of her car, holding the handle up—the only way to get the door to stay closed on this vehicle that had seen better years. Evelyn wasn't her problem today.

"Hi, baby girl."

Or…maybe Evelyn *was* her problem today. The sound of her mother's voice was enough to snap Maci's spine straight. Turning quickly, she put her back to the car and stared at the slightly older reflection in front of her.

Evelyn Ford had once been the type of beautiful that people gawked after. Long blond hair that hung in silky waves, icy blue eyes rimmed with thick lashes and an hourglass figure that didn't care what she ate.

Back then, she'd been movie star beautiful. Now, she just looked tired. Almost thirty years of addiction did that to a person. Her hair was still long, but fried and stringy, her eyelashes sparse around dulled eyes. Now her body was thin with scabs from itching. It was like the disease had eaten away at her.

It was everything Maci was terrified of becoming. Everything she'd come way too close to becoming.

It was Evelyn who had sent Maci into such a horrific tailspin that she'd ended things with Chance. A single text threatening to show up had been enough to send Maci packing.

Chance didn't need someone like Maci dragging him down. He had a good family, a job he loved and a great life. There was no room for a high school dropout who'd spent her formative years following in her mother's footsteps. The drugs, the men, the mistakes. Not exactly the type of daughter-in-law Clinton and Sheila Patterson were used to.

No, Chance was better without her and her messy history. No matter how painful it was for Maci.

"You can't be here." Maci leaned against the car door, blocking her mother from view of anyone coming into San Antonio Security. The office wasn't open yet, but the urge to keep this part of her life hidden was stronger than ever. The Pattersons—Chance especially—didn't need to know what Maci came from and who she had to fight not to become.

"You didn't answer my calls." As if it was normal for Maci to be on the phone at 3:00 a.m.

"I was sleeping."

Her mother huffed. "Well, I need your help."

Maci stared at her. If Evelyn wanted help in the form

of rehab or counseling, Maci would do whatever was in her power to assist. But that was never the case.

When Evelyn said *help*, she wanted funds to feed her habit, to drown herself in her current drug obsession. "You need money."

Evelyn nodded. She didn't even seem ashamed. Why would she when Maci had been cleaning up her messes since she could hold a broom?

"How much?" It wasn't how Maci would normally handle this but she needed to get Evelyn out of here now before someone saw her and started asking questions. That was the problem with working for a bunch of highly-trained security guys.

Her mother shifted on her feet, now looking sheepish. It was an act, one Maci was all too familiar with. Gritting her teeth, Maci wished she could just walk away from Evelyn. But she would follow. Telling her she shouldn't be here would just ensure she showed up again.

"Three hundred."

Maci sighed but was once again grateful she'd gotten her life together. Three hundred dollars was a lot, but Maci had made sure she had money in savings and enough in her checking to cover three months of bills if she needed.

There had been way too long when she had absolutely nothing.

"How's Pop?"

Evelyn waved one bony hand. "Same old, same old."

Hugo Ford's drug of choice was alcohol. The last time Maci had seen him had been the week after she turned eighteen. He'd thrown her out of the house in a booze-filled rage, and she'd never returned. Still, she'd never been able to put him out of her mind. It was exhausting constantly worrying about people who didn't care about themselves or her.

The rumbling sound of a familiar engine pushed Maci into action. She thrust her hand into her purse and pulled out her wallet, quickly counting out as much cash as she had. Maci held out the stack of bills, but didn't let go when Evelyn grabbed it. "This is all I have, Mom. You're wiping me out."

"Yeah, yeah. I know. This is the last time."

Maci didn't believe that even for a second. She let go of the money as Evelyn nodded then tucked the bills in her pocket and her hair behind her ear. Then without a word she was gone.

No hug, no thanks. It should hurt, but all Maci felt was relief that she was gone.

"Who was that?"

Everything in her body responded to the deep timbre of Chance Patterson's voice. She'd been helpless against it from the very first day.

She spun, just as affected by his appearance. All long legs and broad shoulders, as if he could easily carry the weight of the world—and Maci knew for a fact he tried regularly to do. His face was too rough to be traditionally handsome—jaw and cheekbones hard and unforgiving.

The only thing soft about him were his eyes. Brown, but not a traditional brown—a lighter color, more of a molten honey.

She knew full well how those eyes could pin someone. Make them feel like they were the only person in the world when Chance's attention was on them.

"Who was that?" he asked again.

"Good morning to you too," she said, straightening her purse strap on her shoulder. There was no way she was going to explain the situation with her mother to him.

Those honey eyes narrowed. "Was that lady bothering you?"

She shook her head and started walking toward the office door. "No. Just wanted to know where she could buy tampons."

Chance had three brothers and no sisters. Maci was betting on the fact that the word *tampon* would shut him up.

It worked. He let it go, walking with her toward the office.

"The Nicholas LeBlanc case might get messy," Chance said. "Let one of us know if anything is happening out of the norm."

She had no idea why he would think the LeBlanc case would affect her, but she nodded. She didn't want to start the morning with a fight.

Chance unlocked the door and held it open for her. She walked through, heading toward her desk in the lobby.

"Maci," he said and she stopped, turning to him.

Those eyes pinned her for a long moment. She wanted to be unaffected but knew that was the opposite from the truth.

"Yes?" she finally asked when he didn't say anything else.

He still kept looking at her.

I've been waiting for this all day.

This morning's dream came crashing back into her mind, as well as the heat that went along with it.

They were alone here in the office. Chance was always early. Nobody else would be here for at least another forty-five minutes.

She took a step toward him as if she was being pulled by a string.

"Chance?" she whispered.

He took a step toward her also.

She shouldn't do this—shouldn't let the moment build between them. But she was powerless to stop it. Powerless to resist those eyes. That jaw. Those cheekbones.

The man.

They both took another step, but then Chance blinked and stopped. He stiffened, backing away from her.

The moment was lost.

"Good morning," he said. Then without another word, he turned and walked to his office, closing the door behind him.

Chapter Three

In all her time of working for them, Maci had never seen the Patterson brothers as flustered as they were working the LeBlanc case.

After their meeting with Nicholas LeBlanc, they'd camped out at the conference room table with the case notes from the tycoon's head of security. Dorian Cane and his team had collected all the stalker's letters and gifts as evidence, storing them carefully since LeBlanc hadn't wanted to bring in law enforcement. That meant one wall of the San Antonio Security conference room was now piled high with boxes of letters, notes and printed photographs, plus the reports to go along with everything.

Three days and too many pots of coffee later, they were all frustrated, exhausted and no closer to having any leads on the stalker or any clue how to keep Stella LeBlanc safe. Every day that they didn't have a plan, Chance became more stressed, the furrow between his brows more pronounced.

It'd only gotten worse when another of the stalker's letters found its way into Stella's mail. Whatever the letter contained was bad enough that Maci thought Chance might put his fist through the wall.

She had no idea why he was taking this so personally—he hadn't seemed to do that for most of their other cases since she'd worked here. Maybe stalking was a sore subject for him.

And whether Chance was taking this personally or not didn't matter. All of them needed help, so she'd done what she could. She'd secretly ferried sustenance of all kinds to the brothers in between her own phone calls and office work. Nutritional snacks and meals, since none of them were eating well.

Despite her best efforts to keep them functioning, they all had bags under their eyes the size of Volvos, with attitudes to match. It would have been almost funny if she hadn't been so exhausted herself.

She'd somehow gotten some sort of stomach bug that wouldn't quit right when the guys needed her most. She couldn't take a sick day right now, so she hid it as best she could. She sprayed down everything with disinfectant and powered through.

"He could've killed her," Luke said, rubbing his eyes as he tossed down a stack of photos from the most recent stalker incident. Maci tidied them, then walked around the table, replacing the tray of sandwiches and bringing a fresh pot of coffee.

Chance hit play on the video images. "I don't think that was the intent. Stella and her driver were followed home from a local boutique she was doing a spotlight on for her YouTube channel." He paused the video as all the guys studied it. "See how the other car nicked the trunk? He could've done a lot more damage."

"See how the driver keeps his face averted?" Chance pointed to the image. "He knew we'd pull all photo and video footage we could get. It was a carefully constructed hit."

Chance resumed the footage, and Maci winced as the vehicle containing Stella and her driver went into a tailspin. Thankfully, the guardrail stopped it before there was any major damage.

"This is a break in the pattern," Chance said. "The first incident of actual violence."

They all watched the footage again. Then again, sandwiches and coffee ignored.

It was Weston who finally stopped it. "We need a break. Watching this on repeat isn't changing anything. Dorian has Stella on lockdown. Nothing is going to change tonight."

Luke stood up. "I concur. I'm heading home to see my wife and get some sleep. Let's meet back early and tackle this with fresh eyes."

Maci could tell Chance wanted to argue but knew they were probably right.

"I need to see my tiny terror." Brax stacked up some files in front of him. "He's running Tessa ragged."

It wasn't long before they were heading out of the conference room.

"You coming, Chance?" Weston asked.

"I'm just going to look this over one more time and then I'll leave." The brothers didn't respond to him with anything but eye rolls. If he had it his way, Chance would stay at the table until his body gave out or he found a solution. They knew better than to argue with him.

"You head out too, Maci. We'll help clean up this mess in the morning," Brax said with a mock glare and a wave.

Despite Brax's words, as soon as the door locked behind them, she started gathering up the cups from the conference room. If she cleaned it up, they'd be able to think clearer. Starting again fresh tomorrow was a good idea.

"You're exhausted. You should go home too," she said when Chance threw down the pictures Luke had been looking through.

It was the first time she caught a good glimpse of Stella LeBlanc, and she stopped in shock.

Holy hell, the woman could have been Maci's twin.

Stella had slightly longer hair in a more elaborate style, and her fashion and makeup were much more complex than what Maci wore, but they could easily have been sisters.

It was almost creepy how similar they looked.

"Yeah, I know I need to go home." Chance scrubbed a hand down his face. "But this car accident doesn't make sense. For so long, the stalker didn't change his tactics. When they stopped working, he just found new ways to get his messages to Stella. He could've gotten dangerous much sooner...so why now? What caused him to attack her like that? And in a way that's not terribly personal or inventive."

Maci forced herself to look away from the photos of Stella. "Could the stalker have been upset about something? Maybe it was a warning."

She stacked the cups and took them to the office's small kitchen sink. She was rinsing them out, startled when she found Chance just behind her. She hadn't heard him follow her—the man could be so damned silent when he wanted to be.

But he'd followed her into the kitchen to continue talking to her. That was something.

He sat down at the small table in the middle of the room. Her entire body was aware of how close he was.

"What the stalker did doesn't feel like an emotional response. It feels like something else."

She shut off the water and dried her hands. "Like what?" She gave in to her urges and stepped closer.

As if her hand was being powered by someone else's brain, she ran her fingers through his soft hair. Chance tensed, and for a moment she thought he'd pull away. Then he relaxed into her touch, letting his head fall back to rest against her stomach. She nearly groaned, having forgotten how good it felt to touch Chance casually. The soft sigh as she scratched his scalp was enough for her to keep going.

"I don't know. If the motive was profit, the stalker would've taken her and tried for a ransom. He—and I use that pronoun because statistically that's the case, not because we know for sure—seems to want to get close to Stella, but not too close."

"Could revenge on Nicholas LeBlanc be a motive?"

"Possibly, but if so, he's moved very slowly over the past few weeks. Maybe the stalker is just toying with her."

"That's not generally the case, right?" Maci didn't

know much about stalking, but she did know that stalkers who did it just to toy with their victims were the minority.

He let out a sigh and leaned more fully against her. "Yeah. Generally, stalkers crave the emotional response the invasions of privacy forces on their victims. Someone doing it just to mess with Stella or Nicholas would be much more unpredictable."

"Maybe it's jealousy. She's successful in her own right as an influencer, so maybe someone's coming after her for that. Or they could feel slighted that she doesn't see their support for her or something. A fan who has gone a little over the edge."

Chance didn't answer, but Maci could tell he was thinking, so she didn't push. She just let him think.

"Maybe." He pulled away, then turned to look at her. "How are you doing?"

She looked down at him, brows furrowed. "Me? You're the one who hasn't slept in days."

Chance stood and cupped her cheek, running a thumb under her eye. "That may be true, but you haven't been feeling well lately either. Are you okay?"

She knew she'd pay for it later but she let herself lean into Chance's touch. Even in the middle of the week's chaos, and with things so strained between them, he'd been watching. Checking on her. "Maybe we're both working too hard."

His eyes tracked over her, cataloging everything from her limp hair to her baggy clothes. She really hadn't been feeling great, and her look was definitely more casual than usual. She almost apologized, but he shook his head. "You should go home, Maci. Get some rest."

"I will if you will," she joked, poking him in the stomach. When he pulled her into his arms unexpectedly, she knew she should pull away, but couldn't force herself to do so. She couldn't remember the last time he'd held her, and even though her brain was screaming at her to take a step back, to walk away, she couldn't deny how well they fit together.

Of course, fitting together physically had never been their problem.

He trailed his nose across her cheek and down until it rested in the crook of her neck.

"Come home with me," he whispered. His lips were so close to her skin, but he didn't kiss her, and Maci wasn't sure if she wanted him to or not. "We can just sleep if you want, but I want you in my bed again, Maci. I never wanted you to leave."

There was no hiding the shiver that coursed through her body at his words, just like there was no hiding the gasp that came when he finally brushed his lips so softly against her skin.

Don't let your libido cloud your judgment. Think before you act, Maci Ford.

Especially since her impulsiveness was what had gotten them into their awkward situation in the first place.

But his proposal was so tempting. She wanted to go home with Chance. She really did. She wanted to crawl into his cool sheets and fall asleep wrapped in his arms. She wanted to wake up in the morning to find him staring at her again. She wanted his hands on her after the two-month hiatus she'd forced on them.

But nothing had changed. Her mother showing up here

in the parking lot a couple days ago was a reminder of that. Giving in, going home with him after so long, would make things even more muddied.

And honestly, she wasn't sure how many more times she had the strength to walk away from him. She wanted him so much.

He wanted her too. He wanted her to say yes.

She was so tempted.

But when he found out about her past—who she'd come from, the things she'd done—it would be *him* walking away.

Not just him.

Maci's breath froze in her lungs. Losing Chance would be terrible, but losing her job and the family she'd built here at San Antonio Security? That would be devastating.

She not only cared about Chance's brothers but all their significant others... Tessa, Claire, Kayleigh. Maci loved baby Walker and Sheila and Clinton Patterson too.

It was already difficult to have a working relationship when no one knew what had actually happened between her and Chance. If she wanted to keep her life and job intact, Maci had to do her best to stay away from him. Even when every part of her body was begging her to stay.

"It's better if I don't," Maci said, stepping out of his embrace even though it was agony.

He stiffened and let her go. "Okay. I'll walk you to your car."

He sounded so defeated that Maci almost took it back. She bit her tongue, holding back the words she wanted to say.

When he didn't speak either, the two silently grabbed

their things, locked the door and headed into the night together. Chance stuck close as they walked across the parking lot and checked the backseat after she unlocked the doors. Once he was sure the car was safe, he opened the door for her.

"Get home safe," he said before closing her into the car. He didn't move or look away until she was pulling out of the lot. Maci slowed, watching as he climbed into his truck and drove off.

Even after she'd rejected him, he'd still made sure she was safe. He was a protector in his very DNA. A good man.

And she was definitely the wrong woman for him.

Chapter Four

Maci stepped into the office the next morning with a cup of tea wrapped firmly in her shaking hand. She'd thrown up twice before she left the house thanks to her stomach bug, but there was no way she was going to take the day off.

Not when she had a plan that could work to help with the Stella LeBlanc situation.

Chance and his brothers were already in the office, huddled around the conference room table once again. "Good morning. Is everyone feeling better?"

The guys all grunted unintelligibly and threw up random waves in her direction. To her surprise, everyone looked like they'd actually gotten some sleep—even Chance.

Someone had already started a pot of coffee in the conference room, but it was nearly empty, so she dropped her purse at her desk and started a new pot. When she looked up, she found Chance studying her.

"Our coffee not good enough for you now?"

Maci grimaced at the cup she'd set down. "Tea, actually."

Tea was nowhere near as good as coffee, but she knew

there was no way her stomach could tolerate her normal brew.

Chance stood and walked over to her. "Still not feeling well?" he asked, low enough that his brothers wouldn't hear.

She shrugged. "It's a bug. It'll go away soon enough."

"If you need to take the day off—"

"I'm good," she interrupted, smiling to soften the blow. When he just stared at her, she sighed. "If I need to go home and rest, I will. I promise."

"Okay. We're meeting in ten to discuss new options on the case." Maci nodded and looked away, trying to settle the nerves in her stomach. She didn't normally offer many tactical suggestions. Between the four Patterson brothers, they pretty much had that market cornered.

She had no idea how they'd take her suggestion. But ten minutes gave her just enough time to do what she needed to build her case.

She stepped into the bathroom and pulled out her special occasion makeup. She'd watched a few online tutorials last night, one from Stella LeBlanc herself.

When she left the bathroom ten minutes later, she looked less like Maci and more like Stella.

Chance and Brax were in the same seats as yesterday, sleeves rolled up and eyes focused. Luke and Weston were poring over a tablet, pointing out things to each other. She walked to one of the conference room chairs and sat, firing up her laptop so she could take notes like she usually did. She wasn't sure when she should bring up her idea.

"Is everybody ready to officially start?" Chance asked.

"We're not leaving here today until we have a plan for catching Stella's stalker. Nicholas is demanding action."

"Can't blame him for that," Weston muttered. The rest of the brothers agreed.

Brax used a remote to turn on the large-screen television near the head of the table. "Should we start by looking at the wreck again with fresh eyes?"

Once they got into that it might be difficult to drag them back out. Now was the time to tell them her plan. "Actually, before you do, I have something to run by you."

All the eyes in the room zeroed in on her.

Luke shook his head in what looked like genuine fear. "Please don't tell us you're quitting. We'll never get unburied from the paperwork."

"No, not that." Maci laughed. "I have an idea for the Stella LeBlanc case."

Luke's relief was palpable as he slumped back into his chair and heaved a breath. His aversion to paperwork was near legendary.

"What kind of idea?" Brax crossed his arms and sat back in his chair.

"Why do you look like that?" Chance asked gruffly before she could answer Brax's question. "Your makeup. It's…"

She ignored him, knowing she had to get to her point before things derailed. "I think you should employ a decoy. Someone to take Stella's place publicly to draw out the danger and eliminate it."

"You want to be the decoy," Weston guessed. Maci nodded.

A heavy silence followed, but it only lasted for three

seconds before Chance exploded. "That's what the makeup is about, isn't it? Showing how much you look like Stella. There is absolutely no way we're using you."

Brax leaned forward, eyeing Maci critically. "It's not a bad plan, actually. And the makeup does make them look remarkably similar. Since Stella doesn't have a sister, that would make it even more likely to work."

"Did you hear me?" Chance glared at Brax. "I said no."

Maci took a breath to answer, but Luke shook his head across the table. She didn't argue because she could see the beginnings of a sibling "chat" brewing, and she was better off staying out of it.

"Last I looked, San Antonio Security was an equal partnership, Chance." Brax's nonchalant brush-off caused a vein in Chance's forehead to pulse. "Not a dictatorship."

Luke nodded. "We're in the business of protection. We would make sure Maci is safe. If we use her as a decoy, we'd plan it right so that no one gets hurt."

Chance scrubbed his hand down his face. "You're all out of your mind. We're not sending Maci out untrained so we can catch a stalker."

Maci had had enough. "You aren't sending me anywhere. I'm volunteering," she snapped.

Chance glared at her from his chair. "You don't know the first thing about being in the field."

"So, train her, Chance." Luke leaned forward across the table so that Chance's attention was forced onto him. "She's already more tactically aware than most civilians. She's smart and self-reliant. Give her some physical defense lessons—quick and dirty basics—and let's do this."

Chance turned to Weston, who, in normal form, hadn't

yet said anything. "Will you please help me get them to see reason?"

Weston studied Maci for a long moment, then looked back at Chance. The two of them were super close. "I get why you're worried. Maci is part of the family, and we don't like the thought of any family member in potential harm's way."

Hearing Weston say she was part of the family warmed something inside Maci. Chance turned to her, and for a moment she was afraid he was going to blow the whistle on her. To explain that, since she'd snuck out of his bed in the middle of the night two months ago, maybe *family* didn't apply to her.

But if anything, Chance's gaze was more protective. More possessive. More...*everything*.

The warmth she'd felt ratcheted up to a full heat.

"It's the best plan we've come up with yet," Brax said. "Let's at least keep it on the table while we continue looking at other options."

Chance finally looked away from her and nodded. "Okay. But if we send her out, we're going to damn well make sure she's safe."

All three brothers offered their agreement.

"Stella always has some sort of bodyguards around, right?" Luke asked.

Chance let out a small sigh, as if he knew he'd already lost this battle. "Yes. She has at least three nearby at all times."

"Great," Luke said. "So, we ship the original Stella off on an international vacation, so she's out of any danger."

Weston nodded. "And also so we can control the situation more. We can send our new Stella only to events that we can have a greater measure of control over."

Brax grinned. "Plus, Maci isn't spoiled like Stella. She's an asset, not a liability. Especially will be after some defense training and running potential scenarios so she knows what to look out for."

"Fine," Chance said finally. That one word was low and gritty, like it was painful for him to speak at all. Maci's stomach swooped deliciously at the sound, and she inwardly cursed her body for responding to it. "I'll agree to this plan if you take at least three days of self-defense training with me. I'll also be with you every step of the way when you're undercover."

Maci's eyes widened. Staying in close confines with Chance day after day? That wasn't going to be easy. "I'm sure I could learn the basics from anyone. You don't have to do it all yourself."

"They've all got people waiting for them at home. You and I are the single ones of the bunch. That makes us the best people for an undercover job like this. It's me, or we scrap the plan altogether."

Chance's smile was tight. He knew she was stuck. She would always agree to anything that let the others go home to their families, but she was also desperate for a reason for her and Chance not to be alone. She had to preserve the distance between them.

She knew how easily that distance could disappear.

"What do you say, Maci?" Chance finally said. "Are you ready to work together?"

Anyone could see that he was waiting for her to say no, but she wasn't going to do it. "I'm sure it'll be a blast."

"Oh, there will be a blast somewhere," Luke muttered. Brax and Weston laughed under their breaths while Chance watched and waited. He wanted a real answer, and she could tell he wasn't going to leave without it.

Maci was simultaneously ecstatic and panicked, but she shoved it all down. Nothing else mattered but finishing the job. She had to help Stella get her life back before something—or someone—wrecked it forever.

She stared into Chance's brown eyes. "I'm in."

Maci felt like she'd just signed her soul to the devil but had no idea why.

As Maci closed up the office later that afternoon, she still couldn't believe the guys had agreed to her plan. She hadn't seen any of them for most of the day. They'd been too busy going over the plan with LeBlanc's security team, working on the details of getting Stella out of the country and narrowing down the social events where Maci would take Stella's place.

Maci was really going to do it. She was going to take an active part in capturing a stalker and making a young woman safe again. Maybe it could even count as penance for some of her own past sins.

If only that was the way it worked.

Pushing those thoughts aside, she locked the door to the office and drove to the popular Thai restaurant down the street from her place to grab the order she'd put in. A big bowl of noodle soup and too many appetizers sounded like the perfect dinner to celebrate becoming an undercover super-agent.

At least her stomach could handle it. Thankfully it

had settled since this morning. Hopefully the bug was gone for good.

The last thing she needed was the flu plus three days of one-on-one with Chance. It was going to be hard enough to keep her wits about her at full strength.

Thai food would help.

She'd just put the bags on the floor of the passenger seat when her phone rang. It was Claire, Luke's fiancée.

"What's going on, woman?" Maci and Claire had become good friends when Claire had needed Luke's help a couple years ago. He and the other Patterson brothers had helped clear her name of murder.

"You have no idea how much money I would give to have seen you talk Chance Patterson into using you as bait for this stalker."

Maci winced as she put the phone on speaker so she could drive. "I'm not using myself as bait. Chance would've freaked out. I'm a decoy."

Claire chuckled. "You and Stella do look a lot alike. I still would've liked to have seen you talk him into it."

"Actually, I just suggested it and played up my makeup to look a little more similar to her. The other brothers were the ones being reasonable and listening."

"Chance is not known for his reasonableness when it comes to you."

Maci knew Claire suspected the truth. Her friend had never asked Maci outright if she and Chance had slept together, but she'd been closer than anyone else to putting the pieces together.

"Probably the most dangerous part of this entire operation will be the next few days with Chance attempting to train me. After that, a swarm of ninjas would probably be a breeze."

More laughter from Claire. "You be careful. And if it all starts to feel like too much, let someone know. Heck, you can let me know and I'll make sure Luke understands. You don't have to do anything you're uncomfortable with."

"I know. None of them would want that, even if using me is the best option. But I'm actually excited about it." She pulled up to her apartment and grabbed the bags from the passenger side.

"Good."

Maci heard some purring over the phone. "Is that my buddy Khan I hear?"

Claire's giant Maine coon acted more like a dog than a cat, and Claire loved him to pieces.

"Yeah, he's hanging here on the couch with me. I've got awful cramps and he's my emotional support animal for the day."

"He's a good one to have. Okay, I'm home. I'll talk to you later." She disconnected the call and headed inside, hoping her own period wasn't going to make the next few days even more difficult.

She froze in the process of setting her food on the counter.

Maci couldn't remember the last time she'd had cramps.

Dread bubbled up in her stomach. Her period had been regular since she was thirteen, and for the first time ever, it was off.

"No, no, no," she whispered, swiping to her period

tracking app only to groan again. She'd missed not one but *two* periods. One month she could chalk up to the stress of everything that had been going on, but two?

Two was unprecedented, and something in her gut said she was out of her depth.

Don't freak out when you aren't sure what's happening. The first step is to pee on a stick.

The next thing Maci knew, she was standing in the drugstore with no idea how she'd gotten there. She threw test after test into her basket. One test wasn't enough. It could be a false positive. That happened sometimes.

Checking out and the drive home were also blurs in her timeline. She shoved the Thai into the fridge—there was no way she was going to eat now—and dumped every test she'd bought onto the bathroom counter. She picked up a random one and opened it, shoving the rest into a very un-Maci-like pile to the side.

A quick pee and two minutes later, she was curled up with her back against the tub and the test clenched between her shaking hands.

Two lines.

"No. This cannot be happening," she told herself. "Take another one. You have to be…" Positive. The mental pun was just terrible enough to send Maci into near-crying laughter.

The next test was one of the smart tests, so when the timer went off, there were no lines, just a single word…

Pregnant.

Pregnancy had never been in her plans. She wasn't fit to be anyone's mother.

And Chance… Just the thought of him had her stomach lurching. She barely made it to her knees in time to throw up in the toilet.

He was going to think she'd trapped him. How could he not?

Now he was stuck in her life forever. After all the effort to keep him away from her, their lives were intertwined all because she was keeping this baby.

Amazing how no other option even boded consideration. Even if he didn't want anything to do with her and the baby, she still wasn't making any other choice.

You're going to be a terrible mother. You'll ruin your kid like you ruined your life.

She tried to fight back against the malicious thoughts, but she couldn't. She didn't know anything about motherhood. Her own mother used her as an ATM.

Maybe Chance might fight her for custody. Maci thought about what had happened to Brax's wife, Tessa, and how she'd briefly lost custody of her own child.

No, Chance wouldn't do what Tessa's ex had done. That had been lies and manipulation.

But maybe he would decide she wasn't worthy of his child.

There's nothing to do about it yet. Focus on the pregnancy and work—

Work. Of course, what should have been a great day had ended in such chaos. The plan for Stella's protection hinged on her and now she was pregnant. She didn't know whether to quit the plan already or...

"No. I'm doing this," she told herself, hunching over the sink to wash her face. "I'm going to decoy for Stella because she needs it, and I'm not going to worry about it. Chance will keep me safe just like he always has, and when everything's over, I'll tell him about the baby. It's going to be fine."

Maci stared at herself in the mirror and wished for the first time in ages that she had someone she could call. A real mother who could give her advice.

But she didn't have that.

She straightened, taking a deep breath. She may not have any parental figures in her life, but she didn't drink or do drugs. She was organized and clean and would do her damnedest to take care of this baby.

Feeling marginally better, she pulled out her phone and made an emergency appointment through her doctor's scheduling app for in the morning. She needed to get an official test done and check how far along she was. Then she needed to see if self-defense training was going to be a problem.

She walked into the kitchen and pulled out her food. She wasn't hungry, but not eating now wasn't an option. Then she grabbed a notebook from the junk drawer. Between bites she listed everything she needed to ask the doctor before she went to work in the morning.

She'd just follow the list, stick to her plan, and everything would be okay.

She hoped.

Chapter Five

The next morning, Chance was getting the plan ready for Maci's training when she texted about a last-minute doctor's appointment. Good. He hoped she could get some meds for that bug she had.

Or, even better, that bug would mean she couldn't take part in this plan at all.

Chance had always been logical and strategic in his thinking. That, combined with his protective instincts, had meant he'd spent a lot of time taking care of the younger kids at the group homes he'd lived in before being adopted by Sheila and Clinton.

He'd been the one to plan things out and make sure everyone had what they needed. He'd been the one able to anticipate unexpected events and pivot to plan B, C or Z.

Those logical and strategic parts of his brain knew that Maci's decoy plan was the most likely to be successful. Wasn't the fact that she and Stella looked so much alike the reason he'd been compelled to take the case in the first place? And despite the fact they fought all the time, he knew Maci was intelligent, competent and situationally aware, like his brothers had argued.

But the logical and strategic parts of his brain weren't what he wanted to listen to. He wanted Maci as far away from potential danger as possible.

And if the safest place was in his bed—*him with her*—was that really a bad thing?

But he'd agreed. He'd stand by his word and make sure she was as prepared as she could be.

Unused to the extra time, he picked up a cup of coffee for himself, adding a tea for Maci at the last minute. She could heat it up later if she wanted.

He'd rented a private room from his favorite local boxing gym. It was quiet and familiar, which was what he needed when it came to being around Maci. Being in the office with her was tough enough, but here there would be no brothers holding him back from saying things he should leave in the past.

There would be no offices to shut himself in to stop himself from demanding once again why she'd called their relationship off with no explanation.

It would just be the two of them and a few layers of cotton and Lycra separating skin from skin.

It was going to be torture.

When Maci walked through the doors, Chance could already tell she was distracted. Bloodshot eyes and bite-chapped lips were framed by messy hair, like she'd shoved her hands through it endlessly.

He caught her at the door and led her toward their training room. "How'd your appointment go? Find out anything interesting?"

Her blue eyes grew wide. "Wh-what?"

"Your doctor's appointment. Your sickness? Are you okay to move forward with this plan?"

"Oh." She forced a laugh. "I'm fine. Just a little… upset stomach. Doctor gave me a little nausea medicine, which should help."

She was lying or at least wasn't telling the full truth. He'd been studying that beautiful face and those cobalt eyes for way too long not to recognize it.

Maci was stubborn as hell and didn't like to talk about her feelings. She was blowing him off; nothing he said was going to get her to share what was really going on.

He should be used to her shutting him out by now, but he wasn't. The best he could do was ignore the burn of the slice. "Good. Then let's get you warmed up and ready to go. I got you some tea if you need it."

He led her through his favorite stretches, letting her modify them when they agitated her sensitive stomach and making a note to avoid touching that part of her body if at all possible. He wanted to train her, not make things worse.

The stretching should've helped her relax, but by the time he got her on the floor stretching her hips, she was nearly vibrating with stress.

"Maci, have you changed your mind? There's no problem if you have." There was nothing he'd like more.

"No, I haven't changed my mind." She shook her head, leaning forward to stretch her hamstrings, keeping her face averted.

He didn't like that she felt like she had to hide herself from him. A thought struck him and he had to swallow down the lump in his throat before he could verbalize it.

Finally, he pushed the words out. "Would you like someone else to train you? If you're uncomfortable with me being here, we can swap Luke or Weston out."

It would gut him to do it, but her safety was the most important thing. If she would be more comfortable with someone else, Chance needed to step aside.

"No. It's fine. I just... I've got a lot on my mind."

"If you're sure—"

"I am. I want you to train me, Chance. I trust you." Her blue eyes pinned him.

Something eased inside him. She trusted him. She had no idea how much that meant. Hell, he'd hardly understood how much that meant until the words had come out of her mouth.

He walked her through the final stretches and warm-ups before she stood there catching her breath and waiting for instructions.

"Before we get started, let's level your expectations. I'm not going to teach you to fight."

Her face screwed up in an adorable frown. "Why not?"

"We don't have the time to get you to a comfortable proficiency with fighting. That means your goal is always going to be getting to safety. Survival is always the most important thing. Say it."

"Survival is always the most important thing."

"So, to that end, we're going to utilize your size and stature to get out of some common scenarios."

Maci stared at him with a quirked eyebrow and her usual sassy grin. He was surprised at how much he liked seeing it. The last few days—hell, *weeks*—she always seemed to be stressed. He'd missed the sass.

"You realize I'm not exactly tall, right?"

Oh, he realized it. He gave her a grin of his own as he dragged his gaze down the length of her body, grinning wider when a hint of pink colored her cheeks.

Maci wasn't terribly short, but the fact that she fit under his chin was something he'd always enjoyed. "Exactly. Your height means that any attackers who are taller than you will have to contort their body to grab you. That gives us a small window of time to get you out and away."

She considered that and nodded. "Okay."

"We'll go through a few holds and how to break them today. Tomorrow, we'll work on escaping a few common restraints and reiterating what we learned today. The last day is basic self-defense moves that any person should know."

"It doesn't seem like a lot," she said doubtfully.

Chance agreed. "Like I said, the goal isn't for you to win a close-quarter fight. It's for you to get enough room between you and the danger to escape."

"Alright, Sensei. Teach me."

"The most important thing you have to do in any attack is keep your head. That sounds easier than it really is." And was a situation nearly impossible to replicate in training, but he wanted to mention it.

"Okay."

"You're smart and a quick thinker. Use that to your advantage."

She blushed. "Thanks."

He wasn't saying it to flatter her. "In a battle against someone stronger than you or with more fighting experience, you have to use your strengths. For you, that's going to have nothing to do with your physical muscles and everything to do with your brain."

She was listening and taking this seriously. That was good.

"Okay, let's start with a hold from behind. An attacker is likely going to wrap around you in an effort to either pick you up or hold your arms still. They won't want you to be able to fight back since this position is mostly about the element of surprise."

She nodded, taking it all in. "Okay."

He spun a finger to signal for her to turn. He then stepped behind her, forcing himself to keep focus on the task at hand and not the closeness of her body.

"If the bad guy's arms are around you, that leaves you with your legs. Go for the soft spots and try to unbalance him. Groin attacks, knee shots, anything. If you can twist your body around, you have the ability to claw at their eyes or headbutt them. Whatever you do, it's not going to look pretty, so don't worry about form. Just make sure it's effective."

He showed her the best places to kick the kneecap, and how high up on the inner thigh to aim for maximum pain if she couldn't hit the groin.

She seemed riveted as he taught her the weakest parts of the ankle and how to rotate herself so that she could slither out of his grasp. None of it was perfect, but she managed the basics well enough, and every time she succeeded, she got happier.

Making Maci Ford happy was a heady feeling. One he wished she'd let him try to do full-time.

"Alright," he finally said after they'd been at it for a

couple hours. "Break free one more time and we'll move on to other things."

Chance wrapped his arms around her, hands on either bicep, but for a moment Maci didn't move and he didn't want her to. He had his arms wrapped around her for the first time in months and he was in no hurry for her to escape them again.

He tried to commit the moment to memory. The softness of her shirt sleeves under his fingers, the sound of her breathing as he kept her close to his body. He even pressed his nose to the crown of her head and took in the smell of the shampoo she loved so much. When he was sure he'd remember it for good, he squeezed her arms lightly, a reminder to focus and escape.

Maci took a deep breath and dropped her bodyweight. It was unexpected enough that he nearly released her, and she used it to her advantage. She twisted, grabbed the back of his knee and shoved her shoulder into his stomach like a football star. As soon as he was on his way down, she let go of him and scuttled to the back wall of the room.

"Perfect. That's exactly what I wanted to see. Use whatever means necessary to surprise your attacker and put yourself in a position to escape. Let's take a break for a bit then get back at it."

Chance grabbed his water bottle and did everything in his power to focus on rehydrating rather than on Maci eating some granola bar and drinking her cooled tea on the other side of the room.

Even with dried sweat plastering her hair to her head and in shorts and a T-shirt she was damned beautiful.

How had things gone so wrong between them?

How could he make them right again?

How was he going to survive two and a half more days of being this close to her?

After the break she walked back over. She was looking a little tired, not that he could blame her. Maybe they'd take it easier this afternoon. They ran quickly through what they'd already worked on. The more it could become muscle memory for her, the better it would be.

Then it was time to move on to frontal attacks. "Alright, next up we'll go over what to do for a choke hold. In this case, you'll have eyes on your assailant and—"

He reached for her throat, but before he could connect, Maci flinched. Her whole body shifted away from him and her eyes closed. The furrow of her brow and the tight set of her mouth told him that it wasn't a voluntary response—it was some sort of unexpected reaction.

And he had no idea why she'd had it.

Instantly, he dropped his hands and stepped back. Maci had never flinched from him before. Not in the time when they'd been lovers and not when they sniped and snarled at one another.

He couldn't recall a single moment where she'd looked scared or fearful of her physical safety with him. Seeing this flinch, even though it wasn't an extreme reaction, shattered something inside him.

"Maci? Are you okay?"

Those blue eyes popped open, and she seemed to realize what had happened. "I—I'm sorry."

"Are you scared of me?"

He hated that he had to ask, but he needed to know.

"No."

"Are you sure?" Had he been misreading her all morning long, thinking she was doing okay when really she'd been hiding fear? "I don't want you trying to push through some mental block. If this training is triggering for you then—"

"It's not. I'm not scared of you."

Her voice was firm and it sent a wave of relief rushing through him, one that was almost immediately taken over by confusion. If she wasn't afraid of him, then why did she flinch? Had someone hurt her in the past?

And why the hell didn't he know the answer to that question? He barely knew anything about her past at all.

He wanted to ask. Wanted to demand to know what that flinch had been about, but knew it would lead to a fight. The real kind with them yelling at each other, not the self-defense training kind.

"I think we've done enough for today," he finally said. "Let's call it quits."

"No."

"Can you tell me what caused you to flinch like that?"

He expected her to shut him down or joke around the question. When she remained silent, he thought maybe she wouldn't answer at all.

"My parents would sometimes get violent with each other. Both ways. I guess choking was part of it, although I didn't actively remember that until you came at me."

Chance was stunned. He'd never heard her talk about her parents. Had no idea she'd had a less than ideal home life.

He didn't talk much about his parents either. Maci had

met Clinton and Sheila and knew what great people they were. But Chance had never really known his biological parents at all, so there wasn't much to say about them.

"Mace, I—"

She held out a hand to stop him. He wasn't sure what he was going to say anyway. "We're on the clock. A woman's life is at stake. I flinched but I'm fine now. Let's keep working."

"Are you sure?"

"There's a lot of things I'm not sure about, but this isn't one of them."

Chapter Six

Chance stared down at Maci in the sparring ring. Both of them were near snarling.

It was the end of the final day of training. Tomorrow she'd be heading undercover as Stella at some bigwig art gala. Whether she was ready or not.

Chance knew she was ready, or as ready as someone could get in just three days. There was so much they'd been trying to cram into the limited time. The hours of defense training may have been the most physically demanding, but all the other elements took their toll also.

Maci had spent hours studying footage of Stella's mannerisms and nonverbal communication in order to effectively impersonate her. Weston's fiancée, Kayleigh Delacruz, had come by the office to help Maci style her hair and makeup as close as possible to Stella's.

Maci, Chance and his brothers had spent an ungodly amount of time studying the people who would be at the gala, as well as friends and acquaintances of Stella's. There were a few friends—surprisingly few—who would recognize Maci wasn't Stella. Nicholas had helped make sure those friends wouldn't be in attendance—mostly by offering them a weekend trip to the French Alps.

Must be nice to have those sorts of resources.

Rich Carlisle, Stella's companion, had come in to coach Maci on how she would act with different groups of people. That entire process was distasteful. Not only was Stella basically a self-centered snob to most people, Rich was slick and handsy with Maci.

Chance had to stop himself from breaking the man's fingers every time he tucked a strand of Maci's hair behind her ear or touched her shoulder. Every time he gave her one of his charming smiles, Chance wanted to punch him in his perfect teeth.

Logically, he knew Rich was behaving the same way he did with Stella. He was trying to help the best he could. He would actually be the biggest part of selling this whole ruse—Stella rarely went anywhere without Rich.

But Chance still found his hands balling into fists way too often around the other man. Especially when Maci laughed at something charming he said.

To avoid bloodshed, his brothers had put him on layout duty—which honestly played to Chance's strengths anyway. He'd studied the layout of the gala building, determining potential places the stalker might make some sort of attempt to get near Maci. Dorian Cane had offered backup guards to place at any locations they were needed.

Chance had studied the exits and made sure Maci knew about them. And backup exits. Ignoring everyone's rolling eyes, he'd even pointed out a couple of large air shafts she could use to hide in if needed.

Long after everyone had gone home each night, he'd

run possible scenarios in his head. How he would react to different threat types. How he would get Maci to safety.

Over and over. As many situations as his mind could come up with. He wanted to be as prepared as possible. It was how his mind worked. Always had been.

But now, looking down into Maci's blue eyes, he was afraid they might kill each other before the stalker had the opportunity to do any damage.

It was a stressful situation and they both were exhausted, but that wasn't really the issue here.

She was hiding something from him.

Hell, not *something*...everything. The more he thought about that flinch on the first day and what it had revealed, the more he realized how little he actually knew about this woman.

He knew they were combustible in bed. Knew that everything about her stimulated him mentally and physically.

But she had very carefully kept the details of her past from him. And the more he thought about it, the more he was convinced that it had something to do with why she'd run from his bed two months ago.

She still wanted him. And he damned well wanted her. Training so closely together over the past few days had proven that on both sides. There'd been way too many times when they'd had to take a step back from each other—both of them breathing hard and not just from exertion—to settle down.

Multiple times he'd tried to get her to talk about anything—them, her past, why she was keeping so much from him. But she'd avoided his attempts every time.

"That's it," he said, dropping his hands from her and stepping back. He'd been teaching her how to break a wrist lock, and he'd spent the entire time feeling the racing of her heartbeat under his fingers.

"What's it?" Maci asked, stepping back herself. He hated the distance. "Did I mess up?"

"No, you're doing great, but I want to talk."

Immediately, the open expression she'd been wearing morphed and he felt her shutting him out. Again.

"Let's just get this lesson done with, okay?"

"We're going to finish it, but we're going to talk too. I can protect you more effectively if you stop trying to keep silent about every personal thing about yourself."

Her shoulders tightened, creeping up toward her ears. "Chance, we've been doing so well. Just don't."

"Think about that flinch when I came at you the first time in a choke hold. It totally caught me off guard."

She shrugged. "It caught me off guard too. But we worked through it and I don't flinch anymore."

"But what if something happens while you're undercover? Something else triggers you."

"We can't possibly work through every possible scenario that might trigger me. It's impossible for anyone."

She was right. There were always internal factors at play in undercover work that could momentarily cripple even the most seasoned agent. There was no way to prepare for them all.

But this was different. His very gut told him so. "I want you to answer me one question."

Her eyes narrowed as she planted her hands on her hips. "What?"

"You're deliberately hiding something from me, aren't you. Something important."

The blood drained from her face, and he knew he'd hit his mark. Maci Ford was hiding something.

"Let's just finish the lesson, Patterson. I'm tired and tomorrow is a big day."

She was exhausted—he could see it in the bags under her eyes and the tight set of her mouth. He knew she'd been sick at least once a day despite her medication.

He should let this go, but couldn't. He had to know.

"I'll make you a deal. You break out of my hold in under two minutes and I'll leave it all alone."

"And if I don't?"

"Then you tell me why you keep saying you don't want to be with me when we both know we can hardly stay away from each other."

He saw her throat working as she gulped. "I don't think—"

Chance stepped into her space and ran a fingertip down her cheek. "I should've pushed way before now. But I didn't want you to feel like you were pressured into being with me," he whispered. "That you had to sleep with me for job security."

She blinked in shock. "I never felt that way."

"Good." They were so close, it wouldn't take much to bend down and kiss her. He was so tempted. "I thought maybe you'd just lost interest in me, which was a blow to the ego, but acceptable. You've done a good job of hiding that you're still attracted to me, but the last couple days I could fairly taste it in the air between us. You still want me, Maci Ford."

She swallowed, drawing his eyes to her throat where he desperately wanted to press his lips, but didn't answer.

"So, if you can't break my hold in under two minutes, then you tell me why you're so damned determined to keep away from me."

"And if I don't take the bet?"

"Then I'll be knocking on your door every day until I find out the truth. Your call."

Either way he was going to get the truth.

"Fine." She took a step back, stretching her neck from side to side. "Let's do this."

Chance set a timer on his phone and gave her a three-second warning before he lunged. He kept them both on their feet, coming at her from the side to trap her arms with his own. It made it harder for her to reach him with a kick. As she struggled, Chance kept an eye on the timer.

One minute left. Maci was breathing hard and grunting with her every move. He could see the panic setting in, and he wasn't sure if it was his arms restraining her or that she knew she was going to lose. Either way, it pushed her to fight harder. Her nails dug into his stomach where they could reach and her teeth gnashed at his arms.

Good for her. It hurt, but she was using the tools they'd worked on.

Thirty seconds left. Her energy flagged, which he'd been counting on. In a real fight against someone bigger, she'd have to use bursts of speed and power.

They were down to the last twenty seconds when the gym door opened and Brax walked in with his phone in his hand.

"Hey, Maci. There's an issue at the office. We need to get you back."

They both looked over at him, and Chance's arms loosened just enough that she collapsed hard to the ground then wrenched herself away.

The alarm went off, but she'd already won.

They stared at each other for a long moment before she turned and rushed toward the locker room.

"Everything okay?" Brax asked, glancing between Chance and the door she'd disappeared behind. "You look like you need to actually spar rather than work on training basics."

There was no doubt about that. Chance's arms were nearly quivering with the need to hit something. "Let's go."

Within a few minutes they were geared up and circling each other in the sparring ring.

"What was the emergency at the office?" Chance asked, keeping a close eye on his brother. Bastard was fast.

"There wasn't one. You two were so involved in your conversation, you didn't hear me come in the first time."

Chance stopped. "How much did you hear?"

"Just the end. The bet if she couldn't break out in two minutes or less, she would tell you why she's been keeping away from you."

That wasn't as bad as it could've been, but it was bad enough. "Brax…"

"What's going on with Maci?" Brax jumped forward and threw out a cross and jab with his gloved fists.

Chance dodged the first, but took the second on his geared chin. "Nothing's going on."

Brax snorted. "Never pegged you for a liar. Are you sleeping with her?"

Chance's glove sailed toward Brax's nose, only to miss when his brother skipped out of the way. "Things between Maci and I are complicated, but no, we are not currently involved with each other."

"Currently." Brax threw another swing. "That implies that you were involved. Is that why you threw such a fit about her going undercover?"

"She doesn't know what she's doing." It wasn't a lie, but it wasn't a real answer either.

"Her risk is minimal, given the circumstances and us being glued to her every second."

"Still a risk. How would you feel if it was Tessa?"

At hearing his wife's name, Brax stopped messing around. His blows became quicker. So did Chance's. They both dodged what punches they could and took the ones they couldn't.

Eventually Chance began to withdraw. This could go on for a long time. He and Brax were too evenly matched and knew each other too well. Brax slowed down too.

"This isn't a good use of our time," Chance said. He dropped his hands. He knew his brother could get a dirty swing in if he wanted, but also knew Brax wouldn't do that.

"Agreed. We need to be firing on all cylinders tomorrow. I'm glad Maci went home. She looks like she needs some rest."

Chance just grunted as he used his teeth to loosen his

sparring gloves. He was well aware at how pale and tired she'd looked.

"You going to tell me what's going on between you two?"

"There's nothing—"

"Don't lie. We've all seen the way you look at her. I just wasn't aware that it had progressed."

Chance ripped off his sparring helmet and ran a hand through his hair. "Progressed then completely stalled."

Brax shot him a boyish grin. "Maybe you should look for a girl somewhere else, man. Maci doesn't seem interested."

"I can't," he eventually answered. It was the best he could do for his brother. There were too many things unsaid for him to walk away from Maci, even if she'd already done it to him. There was too much potential between them, and Chance had never been one to squander a good thing. "I'll try not to let it mess with work though."

Brax threw him a bottle of water and they both took a sip. "I think you and Maci would be good together."

Chance sputtered his water, coughing when it went down the wrong pipe. "But you just said to look for someone else."

"That was just a test to see if you were truly interested in her. Seems like you are."

"Are you telling me you wanted to check my intentions with her? I thought I was *your* brother."

Brax grinned. "You are, but Maci's family too, and she doesn't have anyone else to step in for her."

How the hell did Brax know more about Maci than Chance did?

Because Chance had been so caught up in the physical aspect of their relationship that he hadn't started talking to her about important stuff. He'd thought he'd have more time. That they would take it slow and get to know everything about each other.

It definitely hadn't been because he didn't want to know.

They both grabbed their gym bags and headed toward the door. Brax slapped him on the back. "I had to make sure you were ready for the long haul, because a woman like Maci Ford is a lifelong commitment."

"Don't I know it," Chance muttered. Brax laughed and changed the subject to details about tomorrow's operation. Chance barely heard him, consumed in his thoughts.

What was he going to do about Maci Ford and the secrets she clutched so tightly?

Chapter Seven

"Maci, breathe. You can do this."

She was glad for Chance's voice in her ear through the comm unit. It was the only thing keeping her even remotely grounded.

She didn't look like herself, didn't sound like herself. Didn't feel like herself.

And despite the fact that she should be focusing on this mission, her thoughts kept coming back to her pregnancy and her near-showdown with Chance yesterday.

The urge to cover her stomach made her fingers twitch, and it was all she could do to stop herself. Though she couldn't see them, all four of the Pattersons were close by. She couldn't give her secret away yet. It wasn't time.

But she knew she couldn't keep it from Chance forever. He was a pit bull when it came to solving mysteries, and she'd somehow made herself a mystery he was determined to solve.

She would tell him about the pregnancy after they caught this stalker. Right now, despite not looking or feeling like herself, she had to focus on what she was doing.

"I'm okay," she murmured into the hidden comm unit. "These are just not my normal type of people."

Chance chuckled. "I hear that."

He was in full support mode for this mission—leaving behind their personal conflicts—and she appreciated it. He'd been the one to show her how the comm unit worked and had been the voice in her ear all evening.

"Most of these people seem so fake," she murmured.

She'd known an art gallery was way out of her norm and had expected to feel out of place and generally clueless about the art. But it wasn't the art that made her uncomfortable, it was how the people were acting.

The gala was for a new contemporary artist, an in-your-face, Banksy-type multimedia creator. Maci would be the first to admit that she didn't understand any of it.

But it didn't seem to matter. The people here were less about the art and more about making sure they were seen and photographed from all different angles. Social media was the true artist here.

Rich was by Maci's side, constantly touching her—like he would Stella—but it grated on Maci's nerves. She ignored it, focusing on her smile and posing for pictures herself. They already had some pictures of the real Stella that would be superimposed over shots of the gala. Those were what would be posted online.

But right now, Maci had to be Stella enough to fool the stalker.

An hour later, despite her best attempts and Rich all but fawning over her, Maci was convinced she was failing. Hardly anyone was talking to her.

She gripped the glass of champagne she wasn't drinking tighter. This was a mistake. She'd never considered herself a good actress even when she wasn't distracted, so why had she thought she could do this? Mingling with the elite, with their designer clothing and bejeweled shoes. Even dressed to the nines in Stella's clothes, she felt separate from everyone else. It wasn't her world and it never would be.

The urge to run, to admit her mistake and leave the room—and the case—to the professionals had her looking for the nearest exit.

"Relax, Mace," Chance told her, his voice tinny through the comm in her ear. "You look like you're going to bolt."

"I almost think it would be preferable to all of this," she mumbled into her glass.

The huff of Chance's laughter was a balm to her nerves, as was the reminder that he and the others were close by. They wouldn't let her fail, and despite the potential danger being Stella attracted, Maci couldn't help but feel safe with Chance nearby.

"Who pays this much to get in then basically ignores the art?" she murmured as Rich turned to talk to someone a few feet away.

The price tag to get in the door had been over a thousand dollars per person. San Antonio Security hadn't had to pay that, of course, but still, the thought that everyone else here had done so and then were hardly paying attention to the art...

"People who are willing to spend thousands of dollars for a single social media post," Chance answered. "Or the opportunity to network. To be seen somewhere important."

She barely refrained from rolling her eyes. The money people paid to get in here tonight could've been used for much better causes.

An arm wrapped around her waist, and lips pressed against her hair. "There you are, Stella darling."

Even knowing it was Rich and that he was supposed to do this, she had to force herself not to stiffen.

She heard Chance growl and struggled not to smile. They may have all been on the same team in trying to catch the stalker, but Chance didn't like Rich at all.

Rich was on LeBlanc's payroll even though he didn't need the money, and even Chance had admitted the man made a great secret weapon. He'd grown up in the same elite society as Stella, so it wasn't an issue for him to show up to the same events as her best friend, making him the perfect incognito bodyguard.

Or at least Maci assumed he was. She'd never actually seen him in bodyguard action, only in flirt mode. He flirted with anything that moved, including Maci. With golden hair and a tall, lean-muscled body to match, it was no surprise that his charming behavior caused people to write him off as nothing more than a playboy.

Still, Maci wished he wouldn't touch her quite so much.

Rich dipped his head, letting his breath warm Maci's hair. "You look uncomfortable. Is everything okay?"

"Fine, just needed a second. It's all an adjustment," Maci said honestly, taking a half step back to give herself some breathing room.

"You're doing great." He stopped, his arm slipping around her waist as he plastered her body to his side.

"Incoming. Amy and Angelina Kendrick. Twin influencers on YouTube. They're a couple of Stella's biggest competitors. Definite frenemies."

Maci nodded, giving him a flash of Stella's signature smile, one that had taken her hours of practice in the mirror. It felt wrong on her face, but she knew she'd gotten it right when Rich winked. "You're sure they won't recognize me as not being Stella?"

"Nah. They'll want to move on quickly, get ahead of Stella in terms of photo ops and talking to important names. I can sell this."

Maci nodded.

"Ladies, so lovely to see you again," Rich said, kissing the sisters' hands and leading the conversation like he was born for it. He kept their focus on him and away from the Stella imposter at his side.

She kept her shoulders back, chin up and bored smile on her face. "Maybe you two would like to have lunch with us sometime," Angelina said. "We could talk shop."

"I'll have to check my schedule." Maci kept everything about herself loose, adopting the pretentious, distant air Stella perpetually seemed to have in public in all the footage Maci had studied.

The twins' eyes narrowed for a moment and nerves made Maci's stomach pitch and roil. Had she messed up? Said something wrong? She wanted to look to Rich, but knew it would be a giveaway. Stella didn't look to others when making decisions, she simply made them and left everyone else to deal with the consequences.

"I'm going to get a drink. I need something much stronger than this champagne." She turned without looking at the two women and left, praying it was the right thing to do.

Rich caught up with her at the bar. "That was great! I would've sworn you were Stella if I didn't know better."

"I agree, Maci," Chance said in her ear. "You handled that like a champ."

Too bad her stomach didn't think so. It twisted and ached as Rich turned to get her a drink.

"Whoa, you okay?" He slid a drink toward her. "You really did do great. That will help sell you as Stella."

Maci couldn't pay attention to his words or the drink. All she could focus on was the nausea clawing at her insides.

Oh, no. She hadn't taken any morning sickness medicine today, since she'd felt fine this morning for the first time in a couple weeks. Evidently morning sickness wasn't limited to just the early hours of the day.

"Excuse me." She walked away from Rich, her mind whirling as she desperately tried to remember where the bathrooms were. Chance had made sure she knew where seven different exits were out of this building, but nothing about bathrooms.

Her stomach gave another lurch, and she cursed under her breath.

"Maci, you okay?" Chance asked. "Why did you leave Rich? Did he do something?"

Maci didn't want to say anything, afraid that just opening her mouth would be enough to trigger her stomach, but she knew Chance would assume the worst if she didn't. "I'm going to be sick. I need a bathroom."

She could hear Chance and his brothers talking, trying to figure out where she was going, but she didn't pay attention once she saw a sign for the bathroom. All her focus was on getting to it before she made a scene.

The relief she felt when she found the door was almost enough to send her stumbling. She shoved through, thankful there was no one else inside, although not caring if there had been, and fell to her knees inside a stall just as her dinner came up.

They really shouldn't call it morning sickness when it could happen anytime.

Maci didn't know how long she knelt there before she felt cool hands brushing her temples as they gathered up her hair, helping to soothe her overheated skin. She couldn't even be startled, could only try to remain upright as her stomach tried to empty more, even though there was nothing left.

"You're going to be okay."

Chance.

He crouched behind her, whispering soft words as his big hand rubbed soothing circles across her back.

She had no idea how she was going to explain this.

Eventually, the urge to puke disappeared and all that was left was the weariness that came from it. With one hand on the wall, Maci got to her feet, grateful when Chance's hand on her elbow stabilized her.

The first thing she did when she got out of the stall was rinse her mouth out with water and wish she had a toothbrush. Or at least some mints in her purse.

"Thanks," she muttered. She felt much better—as she always did—just weak.

"Are you alright?" Chance hadn't moved far from the stall, his arms crossed over his chest as he studied her.

She didn't have it in her to turn around and face him head-on, so she lifted her exhausted eyes to his in the mirror. "I'm fine."

"You aren't. We need to call this off."

"No."

"There will be other events, Maci."

Her eyes flashed to his in warning as she looked under the stalls. No shoes, so they were most likely alone, but still, he shouldn't be mentioning the mission.

"I locked the door behind me when I came in. We're alone."

Of course he had. The grand strategist always had a plan.

"I'm fine to keep going. It was just nerves." There was truth to that, although she knew that wasn't truly what had just happened.

She turned back to her reflection and opened her clutch, grateful for the touch-up makeup kit she'd thrown in last minute. With her makeup fixed and all signs of her bathroom interlude wiped away, she looked and felt a million times better. "How do I look?"

He took a step closer. "Are you sure you still want to do this? We can try again another night."

"I'm fine," she said. "I feel much better now."

She moved for the door, but he stepped in front of her. She could feel his gaze on her face like it was a touch, and she had to fight the urge to flinch away. Or move closer.

Those brown eyes of his were trying to dig her secrets

out of their hiding spots. It was unnerving, especially when her biggest one involved him.

"The sooner we go out there, the sooner we can be done," she whispered. "The sooner Stella is safe."

He held her gaze for a moment, then another. Finally, he walked out the door, holding it open for her. "If this happens again, we're calling it."

She nodded and slipped back into the crowd.

For the rest of the night, Maci played it safe. She talked with all kinds of people, sticking close to Rich. It was Brax in her ear now rather than Chance. She thought he might be mad at her until she caught him moving around the gala with the other patrons—blending in perfectly in his black pants and shirt.

He was staying near her in case she needed him. The thought both warmed and terrified her.

By the time the gala was winding up—no sign of anything suspicious from anyone—Maci was exhausted.

"We're done for the night, Maci," Brax said through the comm. "If the stalker was going to try something he would've already done so. You and Rich head to the car, then we'll make the switch."

She was staying at Stella's penthouse apartment to further the ruse. The place was much fancier than her own, but right now that didn't matter. She just wanted a bed and to sleep for a hundred hours.

"Who has babysitting duty tonight?"

"You get me, the best Patterson brother," Brax said. "That okay?"

She forced a smile. "You know it."

Not Chance. Probably for the best. Being alone in an

apartment with him would just make everything more complicated and sleep probably impossible.

But still, she couldn't stop the disappointment pooling in her gut. She liked all the Patterson brothers, but Chance was always the one she would choose to have nearby.

Even when she knew that would spell disaster.

Chapter Eight

Nothing.

Three public events over the next four nights and they were no closer to catching the stalker than they had been when Maci first went undercover. It certainly wasn't Maci's fault. She was playing the role of Stella damn near perfectly.

And Chance hated it.

He disliked seeing her face made up to look like someone else—someone not nearly as spunky and *real* as Maci. He even disliked the clothing she wore. The outfits may have been much more expensive than her normal wear, but he preferred her in her jeans and blouses over these gowns and heels.

And Rich… If Chance had to watch that man touch the small of Maci's back—the very place Chance's fingers itched to be—much longer, he wasn't sure he could be responsible for his actions.

"Any sign?" Chance asked his brothers.

"None." Brax's frustrated voice matched his own. "Is this guy playing with us?"

"I don't know." Chance rubbed the back of his neck.

Tonight he was in the control room and Brax was out on the floor as immediate backup for Maci should she need it. He and his brothers had taken turns, so no one would remember seeing them at other events.

The pattern had been the same. They showed up, Maci played her role remarkably well, and they studied everyone around her. Anybody who talked to Maci got checked. Hell, anybody who'd looked in her general direction got checked.

Dorian Cane and his team had provided assistance—checking identities and running unknown people through facial recognition software. Dorian himself had sat in the control room with Weston yesterday in case he might recognize anything they were missing. As an experienced security professional who kept his ego out of the situation, his presence had been appreciated by all of the Pattersons.

But still nothing.

"I think maybe the stalker is on to us and knows Maci isn't really Stella. To continue to parade her around isn't going to change anything," Chance said.

They'd already had this talk with Dorian. He had upped the security on Stella in Europe, although there hadn't been any suspicious events there either.

"I agree," Weston said into the comm unit. He was positioned at the staff entrance near the back of the building. "There's something we're missing. Guy is ahead of us."

There'd been nothing at each event, nothing as they followed Rich each night as he drove Maci back to Stella's apartment, and nothing as she stayed there for a couple hours before sneaking out a private basement entrance to go home.

Even worse than the nothing was the strain the situation was putting on Maci. Each time, as the hours wound down, she was slower to move, her smile a little less bright. By the end, she was exhausted and nearly weaving on her feet despite being completely sober.

Chance had had enough. "Maci's done," he said into the private channel only his brothers could hear. "Let's call it."

"Roger that," Weston responded. "I'll go make sure the apartment is clear."

Chance could hear the exhaustion plain in his brother's voice too, so he made a decision for them all.

"No, you all head home and get some rest once we get Maci to the car. I'm going to let her go home rather than go to Stella's apartment. Luring him out isn't working, so tomorrow we need to figure out a new plan."

None of his brothers argued. They all knew this wasn't working the way they'd hoped.

"Call if you need anything," Luke said. "We won't be far."

Chance switched over to the channel Maci could hear. "Maci, we're calling it quits for tonight."

On the screen, he watched her turn discreetly so she could talk to him without anyone noticing. "We're heading back to the apartment?"

"No. For whatever reason, this method isn't working. I'm going to take you home. Everyone needs a good night's sleep."

He watched her rub her eyes. "I feel like I let you down."

"No, don't say that. You've been a stellar Stella."

He watched the corners of her mouth turn up at his horrible joke. "I wish it would've worked."

"Don't worry. We're going to get him. You and Rich start to move toward the car."

Brax agreed to stay and watch until the end of the event and oversee packing up all equipment. Chance met Rich and Maci in the parking garage. Maci was already inside the car.

"Giving up?" Rich asked.

Chance narrowed his eyes. "Maybe for tonight. No use beating a dead horse."

Rich's smile was full of charm. "I try not to get beat ever. Let me know what the next step in the plan is."

Chance watched Rich saunter away before getting in the driver's seat of the car. He looked over to ask Maci how she was doing.

She was fast asleep, cheek leaning heavily against the door. He stared at her for a long moment. They'd definitely made the right choice by ending early tonight. Enough was enough.

Chance didn't drive fast. Maci needed the sleep and at least here he got to be close to her. She was still keeping secrets he wanted to get to the root of. Maybe if she wasn't actively part of the investigation he could focus on that—something he'd been thinking about since that last day of training.

But maybe instead of trying to crash through her walls, he needed to try to *gentle* his way through them. Not his strong suit, but he would try. She was worth trying that for.

They were only a few minutes from the party when

Chance noticed a car that seemed to be following them. Not wanting to wake Maci without reason, he took a roundabout way that led them back toward Stella's apartment. If someone was following them, that's where they'd expect the car to be going.

At a red light, Chance made a last-minute turn, hoping the car would simply drive on.

It followed.

Nerves prickling at the back of his neck, he continued to drive around in a circle. Each turn he made, the car did too.

Definitely following.

"Maci. Maci, wake up."

"Are we there yet?" her sweet, sleepy voice asked.

As much as he hated to do it, she needed the truth. "We're being followed."

Her head jerked up. "What do we do?"

He dialed Weston on the car's speakerphone. "We're okay. Just stay low."

"What's wrong?" Weston answered his phone with the question.

Chance rattled off their location. "Black sedan is following us. As soon as I spotted them I headed toward Stella's place to keep them on us."

"On our way." Chance could hear the squeal of tires as Weston spun his car around. "Luke is with me."

"I need to get Maci into the apartment. I want to take this on the offensive."

Maybe it could all end tonight. There was nothing Chance wanted more.

"I'll just stay in the car with you," she said. "You don't have to drop me off."

"No." There was absolutely no damned way. If this turned into something ugly, he didn't want her anywhere around it.

He slowed down just slightly to buy them more time. A few lights later he turned again and the car followed.

"We're blocks behind you," Weston said. "Luke sees the sedan. They're definitely following you. We'll block them while you drop her off."

A few moments later, Weston smoothly cut around and in front of the sedan, blocking its view just as Stella's building came up on the right.

He looked over at Maci as he stopped the car. "Run inside. Don't stop for anyone. Get into the apartment and lock the door. We'll be back as soon as we can."

Thankfully, she didn't argue. "Be careful."

Chance watched until the doorman let her in the building, then pulled away fast. He got a glimpse of the black sedan as it sped past his brothers' car, and watched them lurch after it.

"I think they're on to us. They're speeding up." Weston told him. "We're heading south on Market."

"Stay with them. I'll be caught up to you in less than a minute."

"Damn it," Luke said. "They just turned south on Fourth, heading toward the interstate. They're trying to lose us."

Chance was less than three blocks away. He jerked the wheel in a sharp right into an alley, hoping it would allow him to gain speed and cut off the sedan. "I'm coming in hot from the east in a parallel alley."

"What's your plan?" Weston asked.

"Get in front of them and make them stop."

"That's a terrible plan," Luke and Weston said at the same time.

It was the only one he had.

He gunned the engine and pulled out of the alley. He'd done it—the sedan was speeding toward him.

"We see you!" Luke yelled.

They were now in the more industrial section of town, which worked to Chance's advantage—there was little other traffic at this time of night. He positioned his car in the middle of the street so there was no way to go around it, then got out.

He spared a moment to wonder if they'd try to ram his car, but the car slammed to a halt instead. Chance's brief flare of relief died when not one but two doors opened, the people inside the car bailing and running in opposite directions.

Luke and Weston squealed up behind them.

"I'll get the driver," Chance shouted, taking off in a sprint. "You get the other one."

The driver ran back through the alley Chance had just driven through, trying to get back to the main street. Chance had to stop him before he did that. He forced speed from his legs, gaining on the smaller man. Finally he leaped, hitting the man in a flying tackle, taking them both down.

They both hit the ground hard, but for the first time since he noticed the sedan, Chance felt like he could breathe.

Finally.

He dragged the man back through the dark alley to the cars, glad when he didn't put up much of a fight. Luke and Weston had gotten their perp too. From the light of the streetlamp Chance finally got a look at the pair.

Holy hell. They were *teenagers*.

He looked over at Weston and Luke and realized they were thinking the same thing.

It had been damned *teenagers* stalking Stella LeBlanc?

"How old are you?" Chance demanded.

"Seventeen." The driver tipped his chin up defiantly, and Chance could see the rosy edges of his eyes.

"What's your name?"

The kid rolled his eyes. "I'm Bert." He hooked his thumb toward his friend. "This is Ernie."

Chance's jaw tightened, but he let it go. They would get IDs later. He looked closer at the boys' red-rimmed eyes.

"Are you high?"

That didn't make sense. How had a stoned kid managed to slip past so many layers of security over the past few weeks?

"Who wants to know?" Ernie asked with a smirk.

Chance crouched down beside them, ignoring the question. "Why were you following us?"

Bert scoffed. "We're not telling you anything."

"Fine." Luke took a step closer. "We'll call some friends of ours with the San Antonio PD and get you transferred to lockup. Harassment, speeding, DWI. You broke enough laws that they could take your license permanently. And seventeen is old enough to go to real jail for a couple of nights. Maybe you can make a few friends. I hear they like fresh meat."

Both boys paled. "Look, we didn't want to hurt anyone."

"So why were you following Stella LeBlanc?" Weston asked.

"Who?" Bert asked. "We don't know who we were following."

Ernie shook his head, looking like he was about to pee his pants. "Yeah, someone paid us to follow your car and make sure you knew we were doing it. We didn't think you'd get all psycho!"

Chance met eyes with Weston. This didn't make sense. "Start over. What exactly did they pay you for?"

"Just to follow the car. They said you'd probably find us, so we should keep the chase going as long as we could."

"Who?" Luke took a step forward, scaring the kids even more.

"I don't know!" they both shouted.

Chance grabbed Bert by the collar. "Who hired you? A man? Woman? What did they look like?"

Bert started shaking. "A man. We were hanging out outside the convenience store, and he offered us five hundred dollars to mess with you guys when your car pulled out of the garage. He stayed in the dark. I didn't see him."

"Why would someone do that?" Weston asked. "He didn't pay you to hurt or chase a woman who would be in the car?"

The boys shook their heads. "No, not hurt anyone. Just follow and be sneaky."

Chance looked over at Weston, his stomach sinking. "They were a distraction. I sent Maci inside alone."

Alone in an apartment that the stalker had already proven he could get into.

Chance was moving before he'd even finished his sentence, sprinting to his car. He could hear his brothers talking to each other about who would stay with the kids, but didn't care.

He drove as fast as he could back toward Stella's apartment building, dialing Maci's number as he went.

No answer.

Not the first time he called. Not the second. Not the third.

A couple of miles had never seemed longer as he drove at reckless speeds. Finally, he pulled up to the building and left the car illegally parked at the front.

The doorman stared at him as he sprinted to the elevator and pressed the button for the penthouse. Anxious energy prickled across his body, his fingers twitching as the floors passed in no time.

Maci was okay. She had to be okay. She'd been so tired. She'd probably fallen back to sleep.

Why didn't he believe that?

The second the elevator doors opened, he knew he was too late. The door to Stella's apartment was cracked open. Lock the door, he'd said. He didn't know if Maci had even had a chance to try.

Please let her be alive. He pulled his gun from under his jacket and pushed through the door.

Please let her be alive.

The stillness of the apartment made the hair on Chance's neck stand up. He wanted to call out for Maci, but he didn't want to risk alerting anyone that he'd arrived before he was in place to take them out. He quickly and silently glanced around the living room, then headed down the hallway toward the bedrooms.

He heard a slight noise behind him and spun back with his weapon raised. He lowered it when he saw it was Weston.

Weston gave him a brief nod, his own gun in hand. Without a word they both moved silently down the hall. Chance cleared the guest bedroom; Weston cleared the office.

Where was Maci?

She wasn't in the master bedroom or any of the bathrooms. Had she been taken?

They made their way back out to the living area. When he caught sight of her foot lying limply on the floor of the kitchen in the doorway, he dropped all pretense of silence and ran to her.

If it wasn't for the cut on her forehead, he could've believed she was just sleeping right there in front of the dishwasher. Ignoring the blood, since head wounds always bled a lot, Chance dropped to his knees beside her. His fingers shook as he searched for a pulse.

Please. Please. Please.

"Is she—" Weston didn't finish.

A pulse. Thank God. "She's alive."

Chance pulled out his phone, and his voice cracked when the operator asked about his emergency. "We need an ambulance."

Chapter Nine

Maci woke slowly to the sound of steady beeping and the realization that she wasn't where she was supposed to be. Before she could figure out why, the incessant tone stole her attention again.

Had she left on an alarm?

"Make it stop," she croaked. Her mouth was dry and her voice sounded weird. She heard rustling nearby and forced her eyelids open, wincing at the bright light. Lights too bright for her apartment or Stella's. "Where am I?"

"You're in the hospital." Chance. Just the sound of his voice was enough to help calm her.

At least until she looked at him. Stubble lined his cheeks, and his eyes were bright red with exhaustion. His dark hair stood up on end as if he had been running his fingers through it for hours.

Then his words hit her. *Hospital.* Instinct had her hands flying to her stomach to protect the baby. Was something wrong? Had she lost it?

Did he know?

"Are you going to be sick?" He stepped closer, then paused at her side.

"No. How long have I been here? Am… I okay?"

"Two hours. You've been in and out the whole time." Nervous energy crackled around him, and Maci wasn't surprised when he started to pace. "You got hit on the head in Stella's apartment. Do you remember that?"

The apartment. Getting inside and deciding to make some tea.

The man.

"There was a man inside Stella's apartment," she whispered. "I didn't see him."

Her breath hitched. All that self-defense stuff she'd done with Chance and she'd never even had an opportunity to use it.

Chance reached for her hand, squeezing it. "It's okay. You're safe now."

A nurse walked in. "Awake for good this time, it looks like. How are you feeling?" She shined a small light in Maci's eyes and had Maci follow her fingers with her eyes.

"My head hurts, but otherwise I think I'm okay. Is everything okay?"

Maci had no idea how to ask about the baby with Chance in the room. She looked nervously over at him.

The nurse caught her look. "Do you want to be alone? We let Mr. Patterson in because he was listed as your emergency contact, but some people feel like they recover better on their own."

Maci shook her head, then stopped at the ache. "No, it's okay. I'd like Chance to stay." She didn't want to be alone right now.

The nurse smiled. "Your pupils are responding well

and you're quite coherent—both good signs. Dr. Ashburn will be in soon and will probably want a CT scan to see if we're dealing with a concussion."

"Have I had any bleeding or anything, um, not on my head?" Maci wasn't sure how to ask about her pregnancy outside of stating it outright. "Any other problems anywhere else in my body?"

The nurse smiled. "Everything else looks fine. You're young and healthy."

That didn't answer the question exactly but reassured her a little.

The nurse left and Chance sat down next to her.

"I'm so glad to see you fully awake and talking. When Weston and I found you in that kitchen…" He scrubbed his hand down his face.

"The guy was already there when I came in. He had to have been waiting for me."

"Are you okay to talk about it or do you want to just rest?"

She let out a sigh. "I'm okay to talk. I know that will help with the case."

His eyes met hers. "The case isn't as important as you and how you're feeling."

She couldn't look away from him if she tried. "I'm okay to talk about it. I promise."

"The guys are out in the waiting room. Do you mind if I bring them in or is that too much?"

"It's okay."

He stepped out and a few moments later came back with Brax, Weston and Luke. All four brothers looked pretty haggard.

"There she is." Brax rushed over and kissed her on the cheek. "Thank goodness. Luke was out sobbing over having to file paperwork himself."

Luke grunted with a smile. "That's not completely untrue. We're glad you're okay, Maci."

Weston, solemn as always, nodded. "You gave us quite a scare."

"She's feeling up to talking about what she remembers, before the doctor comes back in," Chance said.

He sat back down next to her and grabbed her hand. It gave her the strength she needed to tell what had happened.

"You dropped me off and I rushed upstairs. I was so nervous the whole way up, but I knew once I saw the door, I was okay. I got inside Stella's apartment and locked it, but he must've already been inside."

Chance squeezed her hand and she concentrated on that.

"I went into the kitchen to grab some tea and he came up behind me. Pushed me against the wall and told me he knew I wasn't Stella."

"Did he say anything else to you?" Chance asked.

"Yeah. But his voice was weird. A low whisper." She grit her teeth. She was never going to forget how his voice sounded, how terrified she was, the words he said. She dropped her voice in an imitation of his. "How stupid do you think I am? I know you aren't her. A pale imitation of the real thing. Then again, there's strength in you. You stayed to battle while she ran. There's honor in that."

She looked at each of the Pattersons. "Those maybe weren't the exact words, but it's pretty close."

"How did you get hurt?" Weston asked quietly.

"He shoved me into the cabinet and I hit the knob." Maci remembered the pain of hitting the sharp metal, the warmth of blood dripping down her face. The man had scoffed at it, and when she lost her balance, he let her fall. "When he saw me bleeding, he let me go. I don't even remember seeing him leave. I passed out. I don't know if he meant to take me or not."

"He might have but then once you were hurt it changed his plans. Harder to hide in plain sight with a bleeding woman." Brax's frown said he didn't like the idea.

"Maybe worried about a blood trail leading us to him?" Luke guessed.

"He may have gotten word from the driver that we'd caught up to them." Weston and Chance looked at each other, but neither looked convinced. "We'll take a look at surveillance around the apartment and see what we can find."

A knock interrupted and an older woman in a white coat stepped in. "Hello, Maci. I'm Dr. Ashburn. It's good to see you awake and alert."

She did the same routine as the nurse, shining a small light in Maci's eyes and having her follow the finger.

"We did an initial CT scan when you first came in and that showed very minor swelling—good news. Your tox screen and blood work came back normal."

"CT scan?" Maci could feel herself tensing. "Could that be…bad for me?"

The doctor seemed to understand what Maci was truly asking about and shook her head kindly. "CT scans pose very minimal risks."

"I had CT scans all the time when I played sports in high school." Brax knocked on his head. "I wasn't great about avoiding concussions, but a CT scan was never any issue."

"Everything about you is just as healthy as it was yesterday," Dr. Ashburn said. "Except for the bump on your head."

"Is there anything we need to look out for?" Chance's fingers tightened on Maci's briefly, but he kept his focus on the doctor.

"Other than signs of a worsening concussion, no. The cut is superficial. It won't even need stitches. The butterfly bandage will keep it closed so it heals on its own."

"Should we watch her overnight or something?"

As much as she liked how protective he was, Maci didn't need Chance focused on her. It would be so much harder to hide the baby. "Chance, I'm fine."

"But what happens if—"

"Chance." He looked at her, and Maci saw the fear that drove him to nearly smother her. She'd been hurt on his watch and he was suffering for it. She squeezed his hand softly. "I'm fine. Tell him, Doc."

"We'll send you home with instructions for the next few days, but all in all, Ms. Ford is fine. She's in great health." She turned to Maci. "You don't need to be concerned about anything but your head. Okay? Everything else is fine."

But Chance wasn't letting it go. "What about the fact that she's been throwing up multiple times over the past few weeks? She's exhausted all the time and is crazy sensitive to certain smells. Even the flu shouldn't last this long. Plus, sometimes she seems fine and then it just comes on her without warning."

She squeezed his hand. She'd had no idea he'd been paying such close attention. "Chance, it's okay. I'm okay. Let's just worry about the concussion and getting this case solved."

He brushed a strand of hair back from her forehead. "You're here at the hospital. You might as well let them run some tests or whatever. If something is wrong with you, let's find out now. Find out early. Whatever it is, I'm here."

"Dr. Ashburn said my bloodwork came back normal. I'm okay."

He leaned closer, his brown eyes pleading. "Mace, you and I both know something is wrong. Let them check you over while you're here. What if it's cancer or something like that?"

"I don't have cancer."

"How do you know?" he whispered. "I've been watching you suffer and I can't stand it anymore."

She had to tell him. It wasn't ever going to get easier. "I'm not sick, Chance. I'm pregnant. About ten weeks along."

Chance's eyes got big, but thankfully he didn't let go of her hand.

"And I can attest that the fetus is fine, even despite the bump to the head," Dr. Ashburn said. "Maci, let me know if you have further questions. We'll do one more CT scan, then release you if everything looks good."

The doctor said goodbye to everyone and headed out the door, but Maci couldn't focus on that. All she could focus on was the raw shock on Chance and his brothers' faces.

Her secret was out.

PREGNANT.

The word kicked around in Chance's brain. *Maci is pregnant.*

Had she known when she made the suggestion that she go undercover?

Was it his?

That question stuck around the longest. Was the baby she carried one they'd made together? They'd used protection, but it wasn't always perfect. Birth control failed and condoms broke. The how wasn't the issue, the *who* was.

Who was the baby's father and what would Chance do if it wasn't him? He and Maci had no commitments to each other—although that hadn't been by his choice.

"Give us the room, guys."

His brothers knew him well enough not to argue in any way.

"You owe me ten dollars," Luke muttered to Brax as they left. "I told you there was no way there wasn't something between them."

Weston was the last one out, laying a grounding hand on Chance's shoulder. "Be gentle, brother. She's been through a lot tonight."

He didn't say anything as Weston left and shut the door behind him. If there was any word that didn't fit the way Chance currently felt, it was *gentle.*

Off balance, amazed, fearful, angry... But not gentle.

Although he would find it. He knew right now that was what Maci needed, so he would find it.

Maci adjusted herself in the hospital bed, and it brought Chance's focus back.

"Is it mine?" For some reason, he couldn't look her in the face when he asked, so he stared at his lap instead. "You and I never had any commitments, so I don't want to assume…"

"Yes, it's yours. I haven't been sleeping around with a bunch of people."

Now his eyes flew to hers. "I didn't mean it that way at all. Truly. I didn't think you were involved with anyone else, but I thought it would be more rude just to assume the baby was mine."

She nodded, but he felt like an ass when a tear leaked out of her eye and she wiped it away quickly.

"I'm sorry," he whispered.

"It's okay."

Holy hell. Maci Ford was pregnant with his baby.

"Are you keeping it?" He tried to keep this as neutral as possible too. He refused to influence her decision, but he was flooded with relief when she nodded.

He was going to be a dad.

For minutes, neither of them said anything, Chance just trying to take it all in. Then his brain restarted and suddenly he had dozens of questions.

"How long have you known?"

Maci looked away, and his blunt fingernails dug into his palm. He wasn't going to like this answer. "A few days."

"A few?"

She turned back to him then, the fire that was normally so bright in her eyes nothing but embers. She looked tired, and Chance had the urge to wrap her in his arms while she slept, but he had to get some info first.

"I found out for sure the day before we started training."

The last-minute doctor's appointment. Fear and anger tightened Chance's throat, and he had to take a deep breath just to curb them. His voice was rougher than gravel when he spoke. "You did all that training and went undercover knowing you were pregnant."

He thought back to the moves he'd taught her. None of them should've affected her belly area at all, but he hadn't been taking extra care like he would've if he'd known.

And then the attack tonight…

There was guilt all over her expression and in the way her shoulders slumped. "The doctor said it was fine. I specifically asked about the self-defense training, and he said at this stage I was fine as long as I wasn't taking direct hits to the stomach. He said even then my body would work to protect the baby even at risk to myself."

That barely made him feel better. "You went undercover on a case where your doppelgänger was getting stalked by a newly-violent offender while you were pregnant with my child. Tell me you understand why I'm having an issue with this, Mace."

"I promise you, I was being careful. You guys were there to—"

"You were attacked!" The need to move pushed Chance out of his chair. "You're sitting in a hospital bed, hurt."

"That isn't fair. We both know this isn't my fault."

Chance's heart dropped to his stomach. She was right. It wasn't her fault, it was *his*. He'd left her to go upstairs alone, certain he was needed somewhere else.

He'd left her defenseless.

His whole life had been spent taking care of others, and then one mistake had nearly cost him Maci and their child. What would've happened if he hadn't gotten back in time, or if the stalker had decided to take Maci with him?

What if he'd decided to kill her right there in that kitchen when he found out she wasn't Stella?

For a moment there wasn't enough oxygen in the world.

"Chance, stop it," she snapped. She snatched his wrist, yanking him back into his chair. "This is not your fault. You didn't know that the stalker was waiting for me, and who knows if you being there would have actually helped. He might have killed you."

"You can't know that." He sat back, a bone-deep exhaustion pulling at him. So much more than from just a sleepless night.

"I'm okay. The baby is okay. That's all that matters."

That was true, but he still couldn't shake the terror wrapped around him. "No more undercover. You're done."

Maci's eyes widened at his tone, only to narrow into slits. "You don't get to command me, Chance Patterson. I'm not yours to control."

"Like hell am I allowing the mother of my child to work in a situation that's already proven to be out of control. It's not happening." Maci opened her mouth to respond, but he continued. "Besides, your cover is blown. You said it yourself…the guy knew you weren't Stella."

"Then you ask me. You don't demand."

Chance's jaw was tight. He drew on every bit of love and respect he'd ever seen between his mom and dad. Clinton and Sheila had some fights, but in the end, their respect and admiration for each other won out over any arguments.

He grabbed Maci's hand gently, grateful when she didn't snatch it away. "Maci, your cover is blown. If it was any of my brothers I would say the same thing. We need to regroup and come at this a different way. Please help us do that."

"What about Stella?"

"She's still out of the country. Between us and her other security team, we'll keep an eye on the situation and find the stalker before she comes back in the country. She's safe, we've got time, but you going undercover is no longer viable. Agreed?"

Maci sighed. "Agreed."

That took one problem off Chance's list. Now only a thousand more to go.

Chapter Ten

After another round of vital checks and a clear CT, Dr. Ashburn agreed to release Maci. While the rest of his family went home to grab some sleep, Chance stayed so he could take her home. The shock of learning about the baby hadn't worn off, but his trepidation had.

His brothers would spend the bulk of tomorrow following up on what happened tonight—finding out what they could about Bert and Ernie and checking all the footage from the apartment building. He trusted them to handle it thoroughly, because he wouldn't be there.

Maci was pregnant with his baby, and he was going to be there for them both. Whatever it took. He'd already sent Weston by to get a bag of his clothes and necessities, because he wasn't going to leave Maci alone. Not today. Not tomorrow. If he had his way, not *ever*.

The sun was starting to come up as they got her discharged and wheeled out to the car.

"What's with the bag?" She nodded to the duffel in the back seat.

"Clothes for me. I'm taking you home and I'm going to stay with you for a few days."

She let out a small sigh. "Chance, this isn't necessary. The stalker isn't after me, he's after Stella. I can take care of myself."

"That's all true, but I want to be there anyway." He sighed, running a hand over his face. "It's been a rough twenty-four hours, and I'd just feel better if I was close to you. You and the baby. Is that okay?"

She looked like she was going to fight him until she caught sight of his face. Something in his expression convinced her otherwise. "Okay."

"I thought you were going to fight more on this," he admitted with a laugh.

"I know Dr. Ashburn wants to make sure I'm monitored for a while. And you're right. We've all been through a lot the last few days."

It wasn't until Chance put the car in Drive that he realized he didn't know where she lived. They'd spent nights at his house and days together in the office, but he'd never gone to her place.

Not that he hadn't wanted to. It was just how things had always ended up. Was that part of the reason she hadn't wanted to immediately tell him she was pregnant? Part of the reason she stopped wanting to see him a couple months ago? She thought he wasn't interested in her life?

"Uh, I don't know where you live."

She nodded then gave him directions as he drove. The farther they went, the more Chance's frown grew. It wasn't the worst area of town, but it wasn't anywhere he wanted Maci and their child to be. When she directed him to pull into an older apartment's parking lot, he tried to refrain from making any comments. The window frames drooped with water damage, and the squat buildings themselves had definitely seen better days.

Maybe he could convince her to move in with him before the baby came. It would be a tough sell, but he would try. Even as uncertain as everything was, he wanted the three of them to be a family.

In the meantime, he'd stay with her wherever she was.

He found a spot close to the doors and helped her out of the car—despite her grumblings that she wasn't an invalid—giving her space once she was steady on her feet.

They made their way to her apartment silently, with Chance taking everything in and Maci watching him. She seemed to shrink the closer they got, like she was embarrassed.

"It's not pretty, but it's home."

He shrugged. "I've lived in worse places."

Hell, he'd spent most of his childhood in worse places.

"Yeah?" She glanced at him as they rounded the final bend in the stairs. Chance tried not to read into her expression too much.

"Yeah. I didn't always live with Clinton and Sheila. Some of my group homes left a lot to be desired. So yeah, I've lived in worse places than this."

"Me too," she said quietly, stepping into the hallway and leaving him to trail after her. For a moment, he couldn't.

Had Maci Ford grown up like he and his brothers had? Had she been forced to grow up too soon, to take care of herself when no one else would? Had her home situation been something no child should have to go through?

And why hadn't he ever asked?

She'd had him listed as her emergency contact, for God's sake. Didn't that state a lot about her relationship with her family?

He was so lost in his own thoughts he didn't realize Maci had stopped in the hallway not far from her door.

"What's wrong?" Out of instinct he wrapped an arm around her waist and pulled her behind him. But other than a middle-aged woman standing in front of one of the doors, he didn't see anything amiss.

"Going to introduce me to your friend, May May?" the woman asked, her eyes traveling over Chance's body. While he didn't like her ogling him, he could definitely see a resemblance between her and Maci.

"Mom." Maci stepped around and in front of Chance and moved to the door. Her knuckles were white as she gripped her keys. She definitely wasn't excited to see the woman standing at the door. "What are you doing here?"

"Can't a mama come to visit her only child every once in a while?" She looked at Chance again. "Aren't you going to introduce me to your friend?"

"No."

That was it. Just no. Maci's mom looked irritated but not surprised. It was easy to see in the way Maci kept her eyes angled toward her mother that she didn't trust the woman. Chance stepped closer to her on instinct.

Maci unlocked the door and shoved it open. She moved to step inside, but he grabbed her arm.

"Can I clear the apartment first?"

Maci nodded. Without another word, he stepped inside.

The one-bedroom apartment was just as small as he expected, but neatly furnished. Everything looked well used, but it was tidy and clean. Pops of vibrant colors bled through the white-on-white color scheme, reminding Chance of Weston's gardens. It was beautiful and homey, just like Maci.

He took his time clearing each room, even going so far as to check the window locks. There were a few things he'd do to up the security of the place if he couldn't convince Maci to move in with him.

Once he was satisfied that the apartment was clear, he went back out to Maci and her mother. The two were talking to each other in low, tense voices. They stopped when he approached.

"We're clear."

"I need to talk to my mom for a minute alone."

He had to fight the urge to push himself into their conversation. Maci looked tense and almost scared. This definitely wasn't a good relationship.

But pushing now wouldn't do him any favors. They had to learn to trust each other, and there was no better first step than giving her the space she needed. "Okay. Are you hungry?"

He almost slipped and mentioned the baby. That would've been a huge error, given the nonverbal interaction between the two women.

"I could eat. Grab whatever you want to eat or drink too," Maci said, nodding toward the kitchen with her chin as she gripped her mother's arm. Maci practically dragged the woman into the bedroom without a single glance back.

Chance tried to think of logical reasons that Maci would be so detached from her mother, but nothing good came to mind. The desperate need to do a background check on Maci's mom pressed against him until his skin felt tight, but he wouldn't. Not without Maci's permission first.

If she wanted him to know about her past, she would tell him.

Though it was a solid reason, it still chafed—especially knowing the woman was his child's biological grandmother. The reminder that they'd eventually have to tell his own mother filtered through his brain, and he actually smiled. Sheila Patterson loved children, and she had been not so subtly hounding his brothers for more of them since Brax's son, Walker, entered the picture.

She was going to lose it when she found out Maci was pregnant. The two of them had met quite a few times since Maci started working for San Antonio Security.

Finally, the ladies came back. Maci looked even more tense, but her mother was smiling.

"See you soon, May May!"

Maci didn't respond and she definitely wasn't smiling. The second the door closed on her mother, Maci collapsed onto the threadbare couch in the living room. As suddenly as she dropped, she was on her feet pacing again.

He cleared his throat, gathering her attention. He pushed the sandwich he'd made toward her over the counter, but she shook her head, obviously too wound up to eat.

He wanted to push. This was part of the secrets she was keeping and he wanted to know. But when he looked at her, Chance could see the exhaustion setting in. It had already been a traumatic night, and the strained relationship Maci had with her mother was taking a further toll.

He pushed the sandwich toward her again. "I'm not going to pry, but I'm sorry having your mother here made things more stressful."

Maci rubbed at her eyes. "Mom has a gift of making everything more stressful."

"Does she show up a lot?"

"More than I'd like."

That didn't tell him much, but it gave him an idea. "Would you like to come home with me instead of us staying here? It'll be a lot calmer there, plus no unexpected visitors."

He held his breath, fully expecting her to say no. And if she did, he'd honor it. But at least at his house he felt like he could better protect her.

Even from foes he didn't even know she had.

"Yes, please."

No arguments. No complaints. Nothing. Chance couldn't help the grin that spread over his face, one that got bigger when she let him hold her hand. "Let's pack a bag and take you home then."

Chapter Eleven

Maci woke up the next morning in Chance's guest room feeling much better. Her head still hurt, but not as bad as it had. Plus, she didn't have to worry about going undercover as Stella anymore.

Most importantly, she didn't have to pretend like she wasn't pregnant. It was okay if she got sick, okay if she needed to sit down, okay to be completely overwhelmed. She didn't have to hide it.

Chance had taken the news much better than she'd thought he would. She definitely hadn't expected him to want to stay with her. If she could've thought of a reason to tell him why she shouldn't go back to her apartment, she would've done it.

She wasn't embarrassed by it, per se. But compared to his place, hers was pretty run-down. Everything was clean, but secondhand. The place fairly screamed that Maci was barely on her feet financially.

And then Evelyn being there... Maci rubbed her eyes. It could've gone much worse than it had. Once she'd gotten her mom back to the bedroom, she'd offered her all the cash she had on hand to leave.

Long-term, it wasn't the best way to deal with Evelyn. But Maci hadn't been thinking long-term. She'd just wanted Evelyn out before she revealed all Maci's sordid secrets—or the few she was sober enough to remember.

At least Evelyn wouldn't be showing up here. That was the most immediate reason why Maci had agreed to stay at Chance's house when he offered.

She'd slept most of the day, so there hadn't been much chance for them to talk. She knew he must have questions. She was less sure whether she had answers for any of them.

When they ate dinner across from each other, it was mostly silent. Chance's life had changed practically overnight, and she wanted to give him time to digest everything. He deserved a second to breathe. Truthfully, she wanted the time too.

She wouldn't avoid the big conversations forever. She just needed a second to get her bearings.

When Chance sat down on the same couch she'd curled up on after dinner, Maci knew her time was up.

"We should talk—" he started, only to be interrupted by a knock on the door. Frowning, he turned to her. "Were you expecting anyone?"

"Nope." Especially not here.

She stayed where she was as Chance headed toward the door, grabbing his weapon from the gun safe as he did. She heard him let out a sigh.

"Open the door, Chance! We want to see your baby mama." Claire's voice was muffled through the front door, but Maci could still hear her friend's cheerful pep.

"Incoming," Chance muttered, then opened the door.

It wasn't just Claire, Luke's wife. It was also Brax's wife, Tessa, and Weston's fiancée, Kayleigh.

"We wanted to come over and see how Maci was doing," Kayleigh said. "You know, have some girl time."

"Right." Chance met eyes with Maci from behind the women, eyebrow raised. He was making sure she was okay with company. She knew without a doubt that if she said she wasn't ready, he'd kick the girls out, even if it meant taking flak from his brothers for it.

His protectiveness did something to Maci. She'd never had someone care about her like that. She gave him a nod, letting him know it was okay. She knew her friends had questions, and she owed them a face-to-face talk.

He followed the women as they gathered around Maci. "Can I get you all something to drink?"

Maci hid her smile behind the blanket. Despite not having them their whole lives, Sheila Patterson had raised her boys right. The impeccable, gentlemanly manners proved it.

"No, no. We're fine." Tessa pointed at Maci. "We just want to talk to this one."

He nodded. "I'll go back to the other room and call the office. I'll get an update on what's been happening."

Maci knew he'd already done that today, but appreciated him giving them time alone. "Thank you."

As the others got comfortable, Chance disappeared into the kitchen again. When he came back, he dropped a sleeve of crackers, some ginger ale and a trashcan in arm's reach of Maci. When she arched an eyebrow, he grimaced. "In case you start feeling sick. Need anything else?"

Well, swoon.

Aware of everyone watching them, Maci shook her head and thanked him. Chance looked her over again and leaned down to press a kiss to her forehead. "Yell if these three get out of hand."

As soon as the home office door shut behind him, all three friends started talking at the same time.

Claire let out a sigh. "I hope Luke acts like that when I eventually get pregnant."

"That was the most romantic thing I've ever seen." Kayleigh fanned herself.

Tessa crossed her arms over her chest. "So, you and Chance? You're a sneaky one, I'll give you that."

Claire nodded. "We all knew you two needed to get together, but we had no idea you already *had*."

Maci let out a sigh. "We were casually seeing each other a while ago."

It wasn't quite the truth, but it wasn't a lie either. They had been casual, but their time had mostly been spent wrapped up in one another.

"And you aren't anymore?" Kayleigh asked.

"I broke it off." Even that made her cringe. She hadn't broken it off, she'd ghosted him as much as she could with them working together. Suddenly, the half-truth didn't feel right in her mouth. "It was just sex."

"Not anymore," Claire quipped, grunting when Tessa nudged her in the shin. "So, why'd you break up?"

"I'm not the type of person someone like Chance should settle down with."

Kayleigh frowned. "Why not?"

Maci's past rushed through her mind, fragments of

moments she barely remembered. Ratty mattresses and worn-down people. Broken bottles and dark, desolate places. Bad decisions that haunted her. Most days she used them as fuel to make a better life for herself, but sometimes they served as reminders of how far she could fall.

But her friends didn't know about her past either. "Let's just say that my history doesn't make me a good candidate for someone like Chance for a serious and long-term relationship."

"Who cares about your history?" Tessa frowned. "We've all got a past. All that matters is right now. You're a good person, Maci Ford. You're hardworking and kind and loyal to a fault. Anyone would be lucky to have you, especially Chance."

She knew Tessa was just being a good friend, but every part of Maci disagreed. Chance needed someone better at his side. Someone stronger and with far less baggage. Maci could fill an entire closet with hers.

"Did Chance demand long-term and serious?" Claire asked.

"No, but…" Maci couldn't finish. She'd cut Chance out of her personal life before he could even get close to that point.

"No, but you were afraid he'd go there," Kayleigh guessed.

Maci nodded. She'd intentionally tried not to dream of a future with him, but every time they gave in to their off-the-charts chemistry it became harder. She knew if he'd started talking about commitments, she'd never have the strength to deny them both.

Claire shook her head. "So, it's not that you're not with him because you don't have feelings for him. And I already know he has feelings for you."

Maci definitely had feelings for Chance Patterson. "It's complicated, you guys."

"It always is." All three women said it at the same time, then laughed.

"Can't be any more complicated than Brax and I," Tessa said. "He thought I was Walker's nanny, not his mother."

Claire shrugged. "Luke wasn't sure if I was a murderer at first."

Kayleigh grinned. "I thought Weston was the groundskeeper, not my bodyguard."

Maci couldn't help but smile herself. "I guess it is always complicated."

"So, what are you going to do?" Tessa asked.

"About what?"

Claire squeezed her hand. "About the baby, about Chance, about everything. You have the opportunity to point things in the direction you want them to go."

"Chance and I are going to be coparents and maybe friends. That's it." Even if she was the one who had to draw the line between them. Chance was always protecting her, and this was her chance to protect him for once.

"Uh-huh," Tessa said. "Do you still want to be with him?"

Yes. It wasn't even a question. Maci wanted everything with him, she just wasn't sure that she could have it. So, once again, she took the coward's way out. "I don't know."

Kayleigh called her on it, eyebrow raised. "Yes, you do. You just don't want to admit it."

"I already said—"

"We know." Kayleigh rolled her eyes. "You're not a good fit. You'll drag him down. Blah, blah, blah. Have you ever asked Chance what he wants?"

Tessa moved to sit on the coffee table directly in front of Maci, grabbing her hands tightly. "Instead of trying to protect him, why don't you let him make his own choices? It's what you would want if the roles were reversed."

She winced. "But he doesn't know—"

"Then tell him." Kayleigh squished onto the table with Tessa, setting a hand on Maci's knee.

Claire slipped an arm through Maci's and suddenly they were all connected. "Chance is a big boy who knows how to weigh risk and rewards. He's capable of choosing whether he stays or goes and in what capacity he wants to be in your life, but it's unfair of you to take that choice from him."

"I'm scared. I don't want to hurt him."

"You already have," Claire said softly, grimacing when Maci flinched. "I don't say it to make you feel bad, but you have to know. Pushing him away when anyone can see that he wants to be closer is hurting him. Especially when he has no idea what he's done wrong."

"He hasn't done anything wrong."

"So, tell him that. Talk to him. It's okay to be scared, but you two are going to have to find a way to coexist for the rest of your lives. Wouldn't it be better to do it with a clean slate?"

Maci didn't even have to think about it. The girls were

right. Chance deserved to make his own decisions, but how could she tell him everything he needed to know? How could she give him the reason he needed to walk away from her?

And how would she survive once he did?

"You don't have to do it right now, but just think about it. Okay?" Tessa pulled Maci off the couch and into a hug. "We're here for you."

"Anytime, anywhere," Claire added, snuggling into Maci's back.

"Whatever you need." Kayleigh slid an arm around her waist.

Wrapped in her friends' arms, she heaved a deep breath for the first time since she found out she was pregnant. Tessa, Claire and Kayleigh—because of their connection to the Patterson brothers—had become pillars of her life and the best friends she'd ever had.

They were just pulling away when Chance came out of his office. "I can come back if you need more time."

"Actually, we're heading out." Tessa pulled Maci back into a hug, whispering, "Let him make his own choices."

After the others said goodbye too, she ushered them out the door.

Chance closed the door behind them, but didn't move. He stood by the entryway and stared at Maci. Something in the way he watched her made Maci feel almost vulnerable, and she wrapped an arm around herself as if the added barrier would help.

"What are you doing?" she finally asked.

"Looking at you."

Uncomfortable under his gaze, she fell back to her default snark. "Obviously. Why are you doing it?"

"Because you're beautiful."

Maci opened her mouth, but nothing came out. What was she supposed to say to that? The air thickened around them as the silence grew, and suddenly it was too much.

"I'm sorry," she blurted.

Chance's brows lowered, shadowing his eyes. "For what?"

"I should have told you about the baby. I should have told you—" She cut herself off. It wasn't the time to invite her demons into the conversation. Not yet. They'd have to talk about them eventually, but that was a problem for future Maci.

"Why didn't you tell me?" His tone held no malice.

She walked back into the living room and plopped back onto the couch and looked down at her lap, twisting her fingers over and over. Finally, she decided that if they were going to have a chance at coparenting—*or more*— she had to be honest with him. They'd never be able to be anything if she kept hiding the truth. Baby steps.

"I was scared."

"Oh, honey." Just like that, he was kneeling at her feet, big hands cradling her face. "What were you scared of?"

Nothing. Everything.

She wanted to tell him, but she knew she couldn't. He didn't need to see how big of a mess she was. Eventually it would be clear, but for now, she wanted him to never stop looking at her the way he did. Like he cherished her. Like he understood her. Like he wanted to know every thought she ever had.

As if he could read her mind, he leaned in so close that their breath mingled. "You don't have to tell me right now. There's no rush." He pressed a soft kiss to her lips, the barely-there touch making them tingle. "Keep your secrets for now, Maci Ford. I'm not going anywhere."

Maci's chest ached at the tenderness in his voice and the way he held her. As she reached for him, pulling his face to hers, she knew that she was already gone. There was no avoiding the path back to each other that faith had put them on.

She wasn't optimistic enough to believe they'd have forever, but for now, she'd enjoy having Chance at her side again.

They kissed slowly, eventually moving to Chance's room where they relearned each other's bodies. Every kiss, every touch, stoked the need that months of distance had created. Maci's skin burned, aching for more with every sweep of his hands, and when they came together again, the look on Chance's face was like nothing else.

His eyes spoke his truth in waves of reverence and awe. The way he touched her, the way they moved together, felt a little like worship.

When they were spent, Chance curled his body around hers with his hand resting protectively on her stomach, his lips pressed softly to the nape of her neck. The steady counts of his breathing lulled her to sleep, and though she told herself not to fall for the dream, for the first time since she'd run from him, Maci felt at peace again.

Chapter Twelve

For the first time since he and his brothers had opened San Antonio Security nearly five years ago, Chance didn't really want to be here in the office.

He'd left Maci curled up in bed and hadn't wanted to leave this morning. She hadn't wanted to let him go either, but he was pretty sure it was more because she wanted to get back to work than because she would miss him.

Promising to bring home dinner from her favorite Italian restaurant if she took the day off to rest had finally worked. She'd agreed, though she'd glared when he suggested spending the day in bed napping.

He chuckled. Maci wasn't someone who enjoyed a lot of idle time. The food bribe had worked today, but he had no doubt it wouldn't work for long. Especially since she felt guilty that he was going out of his way to get it.

He didn't mind. He liked taking care of her. *Wanted* to take care of her. Wanted to make up for lost time when he hadn't taken care of her.

Chance had spent the morning holed up in his office, mostly because he needed to catch up on the intel his brothers had been gathering while he'd been gone. He read about Bert and Ernie—real names Daniel Neweth and Miles Dary—although official questioning of them hadn't led to much more info than what they'd said the first night. Someone had paid them; they didn't know who nor had they seen a face.

Dead end.

He also spent time writing up the report for Maci's attack and the car chase. He forced himself to tamp down the terror that still wanted to overwhelm him just at the thought of finding her lying so still on the floor. And that was before he'd known she was pregnant. He got the report done and sent it out.

But the real reason he was hiding in his office was because he knew his brothers were waiting to pounce. They wanted the details about Maci and the baby.

He couldn't avoid *the talk* forever, but he could avoid it for now. They were scheduled to meet Nicholas LeBlanc today for an update.

By the time Chance came out of his office, it was past lunch and time to leave for the meeting.

"He lives!" Luke joked, but slid him a travel mug of coffee and a deli sandwich. "Thought we were going to have to smoke you out to get you in the car."

"Just trying to get caught up on everything. Especially paperwork."

Luke's pronounced shudder at the word made Chance laugh into his cup. Coffee in hand, the pair found their way to the SUV out front where Brax and Weston were already sitting.

"So, Maci…" Brax said as he drove. "She feeling better?"

Chance hoped this wasn't the start of the inquisition. "No residual issues from the attack. She's feeling tired and sick, but said it's just normal pregnancy stuff."

He took a sip of his coffee and made a note on his phone to pick up a pregnancy book or two. "I promised to grab food on the way home if she'd just stay home and rest."

Home. He'd let himself drift off to the idea of walking through his door after a long day and finding her in his house more than once. It was almost too much for Chance, especially when he'd woken up that morning with her hair on his pillow and the utter certainty that she belonged there. With him and their baby. Always.

"Good. Let's get this meeting over with quickly," Weston said. "The sooner we finish this, the sooner you can get home. No one wants to make a pregnant woman wait."

His brothers let it go with that—no further questions. Chance shouldn't have been surprised. They wouldn't push if he wasn't ready to talk. Especially when they needed to be focused on the case at hand.

They parked at VanPoint Tower and headed up to Nicholas LeBlanc's office, finding him with both Dorian Cane and Rich Carlisle.

Chance tried to hide his distaste for Rich as best as he could, but all he could see was the other man's hands on his Maci. It left a sour taste in his mouth.

LeBlanc shook everyone's hands, despite the obvious tension surrounding him. "Dorian let me know about your teammate's injury. The woman who was impersonating Stella. Will she be alright?"

"She's recovering, but we won't be using that style mission anymore." There was no way in hell Chance was allowing that. "Her cover was blown anyway, so it's a moot point."

"That's a shame." Rich's charming smirk covered his face, as always. "I enjoyed spending time with her. She's feisty."

Chance's hands clenched into fists at his side. It was only Weston's hand squeezing his shoulder that helped him remain focused rather than leap across the room and knock the smirk off Rich's face.

Dorian stepped forward. "Did the teenagers who were paid to get you to chase them provide any usable intel?"

The idea that teenagers had been paid to send grown men on a car chase throughout the city didn't sit well with any of them. What if they'd crashed? What if they'd hurt someone?

"Nothing." Luke shook his head. "No phone number or contact information for the person who paid them. They never saw his face."

"We have contacts with the San Antonio PD so we called it in with them," Weston continued. "Kids were brought to the station, but they ultimately were only held for driving under the influence."

While his brothers talked, Chance kept his eye on Rich. Chance's dislike was definitely personal, but it was also more than that. Something about the man was beeping all over Chance's threat radar.

Rich's background check had come back clear when they'd run it, but something still felt off.

"How much did the guy pay them?" Dorian asked.

Weston shrugged. "Enough to get high a few times. That's all they cared about."

"So, you have an injured employee, we have two teenagers who are useless for providing info, and we are still no closer to finding Stella's stalker," Nicholas said.

Chance grit his teeth. The other man was correct in his summary of the situation. "Yes. Using a decoy isn't going to work anymore. Before knocking Maci unconscious, he told her he knew she wasn't Stella. We don't know when or how he figured it out."

"We know he knew where all the security cameras were in your daughter's apartment," Brax said. "He took out the one in the elevator completely and was able to avoid the hall and lobby cameras."

"Even the ones we set up in secret?" Dorian asked.

Chance nodded. "Guy kept his head tucked down and face averted for everything. Avoided the cameras but didn't seem to know where they were specifically beyond the elevator. Doorman didn't see anyone, so he came in through the service door."

Dorian looked as frustrated as all of them felt. It was like the stalker was always one step ahead of them.

And even worse, he was starting to escalate. No more letters and two violent instances in a row. When stalkers changed their MOs so abruptly, it could spell disaster for the object of their obsession.

"Stella isn't happy about keeping out of the limelight this long," LeBlanc said.

Brax quickly shook his head. "Coming back now could be the worst thing she could do. The stalker obviously doesn't know where she really is because there's been no attempts on her in Europe."

The rest of them, including Dorian, were quick to agree.

"Mr. LeBlanc, we're still committed to solving this case," Chance said. "Doubly so, now that the stalker hurt one of our own."

LeBlanc rubbed the back of his neck. "What's the next step then?"

"We'd like to look through the footage for the last few months of events to see if there are any guests or patterns that we can discern. We'll need a full accounting of Stella's schedule to match up the times she got the stalker's letters we've already got at the office."

"Full staff list too," Weston said.

Rich shifted slightly in his seat. He looked uncomfortable. Was he nervous? Bored? Hungover from going out last night? All were possibilities.

"We've got all the security footage already. I'll get that for you," Dorian said. "I'll make sure to include who was guarding Stella and her apartment as well."

Chance nodded, glad the other man wasn't offended by them wanting to double-check his work. "If we continue to work together, we'll catch this guy. Everybody makes a mistake at some point. We'll figure out a way to hurry that along."

Not long after, with the meeting over and a plan in place, the Patterson brothers headed home. No one spoke until they were pulling away from the building.

"Rich didn't like that we're investigating the past," Weston said.

Chance tapped his fingers on the seat next to him. "No, he didn't. He especially didn't like that we're going to have full access to the staff list."

"Could he be the perp?" Luke asked.

Chance shrugged. "It wouldn't make much sense. He's had unfettered access to Stella for years. Why start being a pseudo stalker at this point?"

His brothers all murmured their agreement.

"Who wants to bet money we're going to find him doing something shady on the footage?" Luke asked.

No one was dumb enough to take that bet.

"For now, let's just focus on the plan," Chance said. "We look through the footage and dig through employees and people closest to Stella. We look again at the people who message her or follow her obsessively on social media. I think whoever it is has to be someone close."

"Why do you say that?" Weston asked.

"They know too much to just be watching. This feels like intimate knowledge."

"They could have a mole in the staff," Luke suggested, writing the idea down on his phone's notepad for later.

They all let out a groan.

"Don't say that," Brax muttered. "That'll make our lives indefinitely harder."

Chance scrubbed a hand down his face. "We have to consider the possibility."

A mole would have enough knowledge to evade them for a long time, and all he wanted to do was clear this case up and concentrate on Maci. He didn't have time for chaotic stalkers when he had a baby on the way.

They made it back to the office and everyone started

to pack up for the day. Funny how Chance wasn't even tempted to try to talk his brothers into staying late and working.

Having someone at home waiting made all the difference.

"I'll see you guys tomorrow."

Brax stopped him with a hand at his chest, pushing him back toward the office kitchen. "We've cut you some slack with the questions of what exactly is going on between you and our beloved office manager."

Luke smiled. "But there's no way in hell we're leaving here without a toast to our new niece or nephew."

Weston wagged his dark eyebrows. "And to you becoming a father, ready or not."

Luke pulled out a bottle of whiskey—the expensive one they used very rarely. "This is usually for celebrating big wins. I think Chance becoming a daddy is the biggest win of all."

With a grin at Chance, he poured them each a drink, and all four of them lifted the glasses in a toast.

"Chance," Brax started, "fatherhood is the wildest ride with the most amazing reward." He was the only one of them able to speak of fatherhood with intimate knowledge. "I know you're going to ace it."

Weston clapped him on the back. "You've been fathering everyone around you since we all became Pattersons. Probably did it before that too. That's how we know you're going to be so good at it. You've got a lifetime of practice."

Luke held his glass up and they all joined. "Congratulations on becoming a dad and making us all uncles again. To fatherhood!"

"To fatherhood!" They clinked their glasses and sipped.

Once again it hit him. *He was going to be a dad.* Maci was having his baby.

"So, Maci, huh?" Luke waggled his eyebrows, making Chance laugh.

"Yeah. It was…unexpected."

That really made his brothers laugh.

"Only to you," Brax said, shaking his head. "It was plain as day to anyone else with working eyeballs, despite the hostility you both threw. Tessa and I had a bet on when you'd get together."

Though he was curious, Chance decided he didn't need to know who won in the end.

Brax nodded. "You and Maci aren't a surprise. It was inevitable."

"Maybe," Chance conceded.

"So, are you two together now?" Luke asked. "Should we add another place for family dinner this week?"

"We'll see about dinner. Depends on how she's feeling." He finished the last of his whiskey. "And no, to us being together. At least, I don't think so."

Luke's eyes sharpened on Chance's face. "You can still be part of the child's life without being romantically involved with Maci. Do you want to be together?"

"I do." The answer was immediate. Chance knew months ago he wanted her as more than whatever they were. She'd just run before he could admit it. "Maci is… Well, you know her. She's great. She's funny and smart as a whip. I love how she keeps me—keeps all of us—on our toes. I like how easy it is to rile her up and that she can throw back whatever I dish up. We just fit."

"Have you told her that?" Weston asked.

He let out a sigh. "No. She's skittish. It feels like she's two seconds away from bolting at any given moment." Like she'd done the first time.

"I'm no expert on relationships or women, but why don't you start by telling her that? Maybe it'll help, let her put down some roots. It's hard to be real with someone when they aren't sure where you stand."

Chance knew Luke was right, he just didn't know how to tell her.

There was something fragile about Maci, despite her prickly exterior. She could argue and fight with him all day, but something still made him want to protect her even from herself.

"You're probably right," Chance admitted. "But for now, I've got dinner to pick up."

He headed out of the office, already looking forward to getting home to his girl, whether she knew she was his or not.

Chapter Thirteen

Maci lasted three days cooped up in Chance's house.

And while she loved the closeness the two of them had shared, she was ready to get back to work.

"Be reasonable," Chance said, snatching the sweater out of her hand and throwing it back onto the bed. "You just got out of the hospital."

She picked up another sweater and pulled it on, only to realize it was Chance's. She debated taking it off, but it was too comfortable. Dressed, she faced him again. "Three days ago. I'm fine, Chance. I'm not an invalid."

"You need more rest. So does the baby." He crossed his arms over his way-too-sexy chest.

But if he thought bringing up the baby—or crossing his arms over his chest like some supermodel—would help his case, he was wrong.

"The baby needs a mother who isn't bored out of her skull, especially since I'm not planning on being home-bound for the entirety of my pregnancy. Besides, I have things to do at the office."

"One more day. Relax here for just one more day."

Maci had done nothing but relax for days. She was

done. She looked him over with narrowed eyes. His casual work clothes weren't the suits he wore when bodyguarding, so she knew he was likely doing desk work. "Are you doing anything dangerous in the field today?"

He frowned. "No."

"You guys scoping out another hostage situation?"

"No." His jaw clenched and she smiled. He already knew he was on the losing side of this argument.

"So, why can't I go into the office?"

Petulant silence. It was almost enough to make Maci laugh.

"That's what I thought. I heard you talking to your brothers about going over the party footage today. That's desk work. I can help with that."

"Maci..."

"I'm not made to sit around and eat bonbons. I need something to occupy my time or I'm going to go nuts and start redecorating this house to look like a ninety-year-old cat lady threw up everywhere. I'm talking doilies and lace on every possible surface. Pink walls. The works."

He stared at her and Maci could tell he wanted to argue, so she went for broke.

"Please, Chance. I don't want to fight. I just need to get out of the house. Plus, I was there at those parties. My insight might be useful."

He sighed, running a hand through his hair. "Fine, but only for a few hours, and if I see even a single wince, you're leaving and you'll stay home tomorrow."

Maci didn't bother to hide her giddy smile. She hopped across the room and popped a kiss to his cheek. "Deal!"

STEPPING INTO THE office after so long away was like coming home for Maci. She'd missed the soft gray walls and warm wood. Even the sticky note reminders everywhere put her at ease.

Seeing the mess the brothers had left in the kitchen was far less enjoyable.

"Did we get rid of the dishwasher while I was gone?" She raised an eyebrow at Luke, who was in the process of leaving his dirty cup in the almost-full sink. He froze, eyes wide when he saw her hovering in the doorway.

"I forgot?"

"I'll just bet you did," Maci grumbled. Luke wisely loaded the dishwasher before turning back to her.

"Didn't know you were coming in today, Maci."

"That's because she should still be home resting," Chance said from directly behind her. He'd barely given her an inch to breathe since they walked in the door.

Maci waved his words away. "Ignore him. He's annoyed because he lost the argument."

"I didn't lose the argument. I chose to stop fighting because you asked me to."

That took the wind out of her sails. He was trying. Chance was overprotective of everyone on his best of days. Her pregnancy certainly hadn't quelled that behavior in any way.

He didn't like her being here, but he was *trying*.

She made herself some tea and found her way to her desk. It wasn't until she pulled out her chair to sit that he spoke again. "What are you doing?"

"I have hundreds of emails and dozens of invoices to get through. Thought I would get started doing the job you guys pay me for." Maci turned on her laptop and waited for it to boot up.

When she glanced up, Chance was back to scowling. It wasn't fair that he was so handsome when he brooded. "We're all working in the conference room."

"It's easier for me to work out here."

"I want you in there."

She wasn't about to delude herself that it was because he wanted to be near her. Nurse Chance just wanted to micromanage her choices.

"I've only got a few hours in the office, at your request, so I'll work here where I can actually get things done."

She moved to log in and Chance pulled her chair back, spinning it so she faced him. "It's not a request, Maci. You wanted to come back to work and I'm respecting that—"

"I hardly consider badgering me at every opportunity respecting anything."

"—but I'm going to keep an eye on you while you're here. I know you won't tell me if you're hurting, so consider me your shadow until it's time to go."

Now it was Maci's turn to glare. "You going to follow me to the bathroom too?"

"If I have to." He didn't look a bit like he was bluffing.

Maci debated arguing more. That's what they did, argue. Chance didn't have any right to tell her what to do with her time or her body, she knew that. But she could see the furrow in his brow and the tenseness in his shoulders.

He was *worried* about her.

The attack had scared him, and now that he knew

about their baby, he was doubly afraid. What was the harm in letting him coddle her a bit longer? Especially since she had every intention of moving back into her own place soon.

"Fine. I'll stay in eyesight, but so help me, if you really follow me into the bathroom, I'll be using those defense moves you taught me to take *you* down."

He kissed the top of her head, then moved her things into the conference room, greeting the others. She pretended not to notice as he brought in extra water and snacks for the table as well, knowing they were actually for her.

And definitely didn't let her heart get all gooey at it.

While the brothers talked about the case, Maci put in her headphones, falling into her spreadsheets and files with easy bliss. She'd missed her desk job. Missed answering emails and doing paperwork. It suited her much more than her single attempt at undercover work did, that was for sure.

She dug through the backlogged emails, sending invoices to clients and vendors, and getting caught up on everything the guys had let slide the last few days. By the time the scent of takeout filled her nose, she was feeling pretty tired and hungry, but the sense of accomplishment she'd been missing filled her with joy.

Chance rapped his knuckles softly on the table at her side. She pulled out her headphones, and he nodded to the white foam boxes everywhere. "Time to eat. You've been in the zone for hours."

"Perfect timing. I'm almost done." With a few more keystrokes, she finished her last email and sent it off.

Shutting her laptop, she moved everything to the side and grabbed the container Chance set in front of her. Chow mein with extra sauce and egg rolls. Perfect.

"This is so good." Chance smiled at her as he and the others pulled their usual orders out of the bag. It didn't escape Maci's notice that he'd gotten her food out first.

The guys were mostly quiet as they ate. "Anything with Stella's case?" she asked.

Chance stabbed a piece of meat with his fork. "We've been going through party footage from the last two months trying to find any repeats or patterns that we didn't notice before."

Luke ate a big bite of ramen. "So far, we've got nothing. No leads, no patterns, no suspicious faces. And the boys we chased were a dead end—they didn't know anything. Nothing on Stella's apartment security feed either."

She pushed her food away from her, not feeling as hungry. "I guess I was pretty useless too."

Chance pushed the food back toward her. "No. You survived and are healthy and whole. That is definitely not useless."

"Would you mind if we ask you a few questions about the voice you heard?" Weston asked.

Chance turned and glared at him. Obviously, Chance had told them not to ask her about it.

Enough was enough. "Yes, please do. I want to help if I can."

"You don't have to," Chance muttered.

She rolled her eyes. "What harm exactly do you think is going to come to me by trying to remember how the stalker sounded?"

"I don't want it to upset you."

She folder her arms over her chest. "You know what upsets me? Possibly being able to help stop a stalker but someone deciding for me that it's too much, rather than allowing me to make my own decisions."

There were snickers around the table but she kept her eyes on Chance.

He gave in with ill grace. "Fine."

Now she turned to Weston. "What do you want to know?"

"Did you recognize the voice at all? Or maybe there was some sort of accent or noticeable trait?"

"It was a weird, spooky whisper. Like he was trying to be menacing." As if him breaking into the apartment hadn't been menacing enough.

"Do you think it could've been anyone you talked to at one of the events?" Brax asked.

She shook her head. "Not that comes to mind."

"What about Rich?" Chance asked.

"Rich?" Maci turned to Chance. "Do you think it was him?"

"We aren't sure. We're trying to eliminate all possibilities."

Maci thought back to the attack, to the voice echoing in her ears. "I don't think so. Rich's voice is warm all the time. The man who spoke was cold. Empty."

Lifeless. The man who grabbed her had sounded lifeless.

"But then again, it was a sick whisper," she continued. "I've only ever heard Rich's regular voice. But still, I don't think it was him."

The brothers glanced at each other. Chance frowned again. "Alright, so not Rich. Could you pick the voice out if you heard it again?"

"Yes." Maci knew that for certain. "It's not something I'll ever forget."

"I know you didn't get a look at his face, but what about smells or strange sounds?" Brax asked. "Anything you can remember will be helpful."

She tried to think back, but other than the voice, everything else was a blur. "I'm sorry."

"Would you mind if we try something, since he was behind you?" Weston asked.

"Sure."

"Stand up for a second." Weston offered her his hand to help get her to her feet. "Okay, so think of the voice, when the guy was behind you."

She nodded.

Weston looked over at Chance. "You go stand behind her."

Even knowing it was Chance, that she was completely safe, she was already tensing.

"Where did you hear the voice when he was behind you?" Chance asked. "Think about it. Was it high above your head, like where I am now? Or maybe a little lower."

She closed her eyes and forced herself to really think about it. "Lower. Closer to my ear."

She opened her eyes, not wanting to relive that any longer.

"So could be someone around five foot ten," Weston said. "Someone as tall as Chance would've been higher."

That made sense.

"But the guy also could've been leaning in toward her," Brax pointed out.

Maci sat back down in her chair but didn't reach for her food. She'd definitely lost her appetite.

"I'm sorry I'm not more help."

"It's fine. You're doing your best." Chance rubbed his thumb across her knuckles. "Why don't you help us look through some footage for a bit? Your half day is almost up anyway."

He was giving her an out and she was beyond grateful for it. "I'm going to come back tomorrow. Do you even know how many emails came in while I was gone?"

"We're supposed to check emails?" Luke joked, wincing.

They got out the footage and she pulled the screen closer. Maybe she'd be more useful this way. But as minute after minute scrolled by, she didn't hear or see anything that reminded her of the man in the apartment.

It was mind-numbing to sit there and watch it all. She had no idea how the guys did it.

She was only an hour or two in before her back was a tangle of knots and everything hurt. She leaned back in her chair and grimaced at the sharp ache in her muscles. Of course, her nursemaid saw and immediately swooped in.

"Alright, you're done," Chance said, ushering her out of the building and into his SUV, barely giving her time to grab her things and say goodbye.

She didn't even argue. She was exhausted.

And even worse, she hadn't been useful at all.

Chapter Fourteen

Chance arrived at the San Antonio Security office the next morning, coffee in hand, glad he'd been able to talk Maci into sleeping late and working a half day in the afternoon. She could talk tough all she wanted about how she wasn't an invalid. But the truth was her body had been through a trauma with the attack and was already exhausted from the pregnancy.

His phone pinged with a reminder as he stepped inside the building and he smiled. Maci had an ultrasound the next day and he was going.

The thought that they'd be able to actually see their baby—at least the heartbeat—had Chance shaking his head.

He was going to be a dad.

"You are a godsend." Brax snatched a cup of coffee from Chance's tray, gulping half the drink down in one go. "Walker is in the middle of sleep regressions. I was up most of the night."

Brax's two-year-old son was technically his biological nephew, but his son in every way that mattered—getting him to sleep included. Brax had officially adopted him once he married Tessa, Walker's mom.

"Maci and I are going to the ob-gyn tomorrow. Check on everything." Chance handed out the other two coffees to Luke and Weston.

Brax grinned. "Exciting, terrifying stuff, isn't it?"

"You better believe it."

Weston wasn't paying attention to any of the baby talk. He was zoned in on the footage in front of him. "The stalker has been inactive for too long. Something's not right. He's going to strike soon."

Chance met eyes with Brax, then Luke, behind Weston's back. Weston was definitely the quietest of the four of them, but his intuition was generally spot-on.

If Weston was saying the stalker was going to make another move soon, all of them were willing to believe him.

"I'll get on the phone with LeBlanc and Dorian. Make sure the security around Stella is tight." Luke was already walking out of the conference room, phone in hand.

"She's still in Europe, right?" Brax asked, all traces of tiredness gone.

Chance nodded. "Switzerland, unless they've moved her again." It was possible. Stella didn't like staying too long in one place.

Chance looked over at Weston, who was still studying the footage. "Is there something in particular that has your spidey senses tingling?"

He shook his head without turning from the screen. "No. It's less this footage and more talking to Maci about the guy in the apartment. Do you remember what she told us he said at the apartment?"

"That he knew she wasn't Stella?"

"Actually, the part about battle and honor. That there was honor in staying when Stella had run and hid. It tells us something about his mindset."

Chance rubbed the back of his neck. "That he sees this as some sort of war or competition."

Now Weston turned to look at him. "Yes. All this time we've been searching for the stalker as someone who's obsessed with Stella. And honestly, he may be. But I also think he's obsessed with the *process* of stalking."

Luke came back in the room. "LeBlanc has Stella on lockdown. Guards have eyes on her and will be preparing for a possible attack."

"Did you talk to Dorian?" He had enough experience to understand that sometimes a gut feeling was actionable intel.

"Not directly. He's handling some other business for right now. But I did talk to his second-in-command, and we should be getting a call from Dorian soon to provide any info we can."

"We have reason to believe the stalker might be former military or even law enforcement. Let's run guests at Stella's past events based on that filter and see if we can come up with anything useable."

For the first time they didn't feel like they were looking for a needle in a haystack.

They were maybe thirty minutes in when Chance's phone buzzed. He looked down, expecting a text from Maci or maybe Dorian. But it was from an unknown number.

Are you particularly attached to your office's front window?

"What the—"

"I just got some sort of weird text about the front window," Brax said. Luke and Weston had gotten it too.

"Sales promotion?" Luke asked.

"From an unknown number?" Brax responded. "Not going to get much business that way."

This wasn't right. All of them knew it. They moved into the office lobby, but the only things there were Maci's empty desk and a few other pieces of furniture.

The window shattered in front of them as a bullet struck it, a sea of glass flying everywhere.

All four of them dove to the ground—Chance behind Maci's desk, Luke and Brax behind a couch, Weston at the corner of the room.

They paused, waiting for another shot to come, but there was nothing but the sound of tinkling glass.

"I have a feeling the stalker just brought the war to us," Luke said.

"Yeah, Weston, why do you have to be so damned right all the time?" Brax backed away from the couch. "How about next time your intuition tells you I'm going to win a million dollars rather than someone shooting at us."

Chance was staring at the chair Maci normally would've been sitting in. It was covered in glass. Rage was bubbling in his gut. "If Maci had been here…"

"There aren't too many places that someone could have made that shot from," Weston said. "It had to have been from the building across the street."

Chance nodded. "The roof. Let's go. If we move now, maybe we can catch him."

It was an office building with three stories. The shooter would've had a clear range.

Luke was already running toward the weapons room. He yanked out bulletproof vests, throwing them to each of his brothers. They all grabbed their weapons from their desks.

In under a minute they were running out the back door. They all knew this could be a trap, but they weren't going to let that stop them. Not when they had a chance to get the upper hand.

As they rounded the corner from the back alley and had the building across from their office in sight, Chance barked out the plan. "Weston and Brax will clear the top two floors, while Luke and I do the roof. Good?"

His brothers called out their affirmations. They kept their weapons holstered as they ran for the building. It was already pandemonium on the street.

"You think they heard the shot and are panicking?" Luke asked.

As they got closer, the problem became evident. Someone had set off the fire alarm.

He and his brothers looked at each other. "He's giving himself an easy way to escape."

"Split up and look around. Let's see if we can catch anyone acting strange." Weston pulled out his phone and started recording as he walked inside. "I'll try to get as much footage as I can, see if we can match someone to one of Stella's events."

Brax grabbed Chance's arm as someone rushed by, sobbing and yelling about smoke. Maybe the stalker had started an actual fire to make sure there was real panic. "We need to get up on that roof."

Chance shook his head. "There's no way, not with so many people pouring downstairs. Plus, he's already gone. You know he's around here somewhere. Let's record like Weston said."

They spread out, Chance checking every face he passed. He didn't bother looking for a gun bag. The shooter wasn't stupid. He'd either stored the weapon to come back for it later or got out of Dodge immediately after taking the shot.

Chance tried to ignore the most panicked people and the ones who didn't fit the profile. He looked for those who were more calm despite the chaos, and concentrated on recording those.

When the fire engine parked in front of the building and the firefighters began crowd control, Chance knew there was nothing else they could do. They'd talk to local police about the shooting and hopefully get the footage from any security cameras around, but they were limited in what they could do until then. He walked outside as the firefighters demanded it.

Annoyed at the situation, Chance yanked out his cell with a growl when it rang. Weston. "Please tell me you have good news."

"Unfortunately, nobody walking around with a shirt saying I Just Shot Out a Window. I didn't see anything or anyone who seemed too suspicious," Weston said. "You?"

"A few people who were too relaxed, but nothing concrete."

"Let's get back to the office. We can compare footage

and start calling in favors to get the local security feeds. Maybe we caught something."

"I'll meet you there."

A flash of something in his peripheral had him turning, eyes locked with the back of a plain black hoodie. Besides standing slightly taller than the crowd, the man blended in with everyone around him.

Except he was walking away rather than watching what was going on around them.

Chance knew from experience it was human nature to stay at the scene of an emergency. Curiosity and the desire for drama had people sticking around.

Using one hand, he called his brother back.

"I may have something. Man in a black hoodie leaving the scene just to the west of the front door. I'm following."

"We're right behind you."

Chance sped through the crowd, having to jostle to the side as he tried to keep his eyes on the man in the hoodie. At the end of the block the crowd cleared out, and Chance could finally put on some speed. When he was close enough to touch, he reached out and clamped his hand down on the man's shoulder, whirling him around.

Not a man. Another damned teenager. The kid ripped one of his headphones out of his ear with a frown. "Can I help you?"

"Were you in the building back there?" Chance asked.

"No. I stopped by because I heard the sirens, but it doesn't look like there's an actual fire. So I've got better things to do."

Chance still had him by the shoulder of his hoodie. "How do you know there's no fire? People were talking about smoke. Seemed pretty panicked."

The kid shrugged. "Whatever, man. There's no fire."

Chance wanted to push, but knew there was no way in hell this was the stalker. He let the kid go. "You see anything suspicious?"

The kid raised an eyebrow. "You mean besides a random dude grabbing teenagers? No."

Chance fished out a card from his pocket, telling the kid to call if he thought of anything strange. He snapped a picture of the kid's face while he was looking at the card.

They would run him and make sure he didn't have any ties to Stella they should know about. But besides that there wasn't much Chance could do.

He turned and walked back to the office, calling to tell his brothers the hoodie kid was another dead end.

When he got back to the office, he found his brothers hovering around Maci's desk.

"What's going on?"

Luke held up a piece of paper in a gloved hand. "The stalker left us a note."

You made me better, but I want to be the best. First one to the prize wins.

Chance didn't know what to make of that. "Is the prize Stella?"

Brax dropped his phone to the counter. "I just talked to Dorian, and Stella is safe. No attempts on her."

Chance rubbed his eyes. There were so many things he didn't like about this situation. The stalker actively communicating with them, and coming into their personal space. Him making it into some sort of game he wanted them to play.

But most of all he didn't like the fact that if Maci had been at work today she might have been at that desk when that bastard shot the window out. Might have been covered in glass.

"I need to make a call." He needed to hear Maci's voice.

Chance stepped into his office, dialing before the door was shut.

"Chance? Is everything okay? I was just about to leave so I can work the half day."

Just the sound of Maci's voice—relaxed and calm—soothed his frayed nerves. She was okay. That was all that mattered.

"You're not going to believe this, but we're going to need you to not come in today."

"Damn it, Chance. I am not going to let you—"

"I promise this is not me trying to get you to rest. The front window of the office…broke, and we're going to have to close everything early today and get it fixed."

"Oh, my gosh. Did you throw someone through it?"

He chuckled. "You're not here. So, no."

She laughed at that. "Ha-ha. I've thought about throwing you through that glass once or twice too. What happened?"

"I'll tell you everything when I get home. Do me a favor and make sure the doors are locked."

She didn't respond for a second. "Something happened, didn't it?"

He'd never lied to her and wasn't going to start now. "Yeah. But nobody was hurt."

"Okay," she finally said. He knew she wanted to demand details and appreciated that she didn't. "You all be careful. Come home safe."

Home. To her. "I will. See you in a while."

He walked back out to the main room. Although he hadn't touched it, Luke had found the bullet where it had wedged into the wall. Definitely a downward trajectory. The shooter had been in the building across the street.

"I called some friends on the force," Weston said. "They're going to come pick up the bullet and run it. Brax is on the phone with the window replacement company."

"Maybe we should put in bulletproof glass." Chance meant it as a joke, but Weston's bunched eyebrows said he was really considering it.

Luke stood from where he was studying the bullet. "Good news is that Weston did his voodoo, and because of the special circumstances of our ongoing case, the police have kindly offered to share the security footage from the high-rise to see if we spot anyone we recognize from our own research."

Chance looked over at Weston. He was the one who'd served on the San Antonio PD for a few years. He nodded. "Although, they're more interested in catching the guy who caused the fire panic in the office across the street than they are our window."

Chance shrugged one shoulder. "Since we're almost positive it's the same person, I'll take it."

Luke rubbed his eyes. "Means going through more footage."

It wasn't what any of them wanted to do.

But this bastard had brought the fight to their front door. Chance and his brothers were going to take him down.

Chapter Fifteen

If this was how Chance had felt when he'd found her unconscious in the apartment, then Maci probably needed to cut him some slack.

She was staring at the gaping hole at the front of the office where the wall of glass used to be. Chance had explained what happened last night, but until she saw it with her own eyes this morning, she hadn't truly been able to process it.

It was hard to believe that one bullet had done that much damage. The guys had explained that it had been a rifle bullet, so a big one, but still...*one bullet*.

What if one of the guys had been walking through the lobby, as they did a thousand times a day, when that bullet had hit? Only a little bit of glass had sprayed back far enough to hit her desk—well, hit where her desk *used* to be; the guys had moved it into the conference room where there were no windows—but if Chance had been standing there talking to her when the glass broke, it would have cut him to ribbons.

Now she understood his need to constantly keep her

behind him so he was between her and any unknown threats. Because she felt like doing the same thing to him.

She knew if she stayed out watching the workers replacing the window for too long she'd get a lecture from one of the Patterson brothers. As it was, she was only allowed to peek her head around the corner—definitely was *not* allowed to stand in the open room.

But she wasn't going to argue. As long as Chance and his brothers didn't stand in the open room either. Protectiveness went both ways.

The guys were back poring over the new security footage from yesterday. Maci had work she could do at her now-conference-room desk, but could hardly focus. Between the shock of the window and her ob-gyn appointment later that afternoon, she was frazzled.

Her phone buzzed in her pocket and she took it out. Evelyn. Definitely not what she needed today. Maci hadn't answered any of the other five texts since they last saw each other, and planned to ignore this one too.

Maci knew better than to fall for the I miss yous or Let's catch up, babys.

Meet me at your apartment or I'm coming to you.

Maci grit her teeth as she typed back. Today really isn't a good day.

I can either come to that office or your boyfriend's house. Either one. Amazing how quick her mother could be when she wanted to.

Maci rubbed her eyes. She doubted Evelyn had Chance's address, but it wouldn't be impossible. Maci didn't want her showing up at either place.

Especially not today when she and Chance were going together to the doctor. Maci didn't want to produce proof in living color of the poor genes their child would be getting from Maci's side of the family.

Not to mention the questions it might lead to about Maci's mothering ability. *Legitimate* questions.

Ones she'd asked herself every single day since she found out she was pregnant.

Fine. I'll be at my place in twenty.

She headed into the conference room. The guys were so closely watching the footage, none of them even realized she was there. She walked over to Chance.

"I'm going to go and rest for a little while before the doctor's appointment."

Chance was on his feet immediately. "Are you okay? Do you feel sick? I can drive you home."

They'd ridden in together. She'd forgotten about that. "No, no. You have important and time-sensitive work to be done. I'm okay to drive myself."

He was torn, she could tell. She hated that she was deceiving him, but what choice did she have?

She reached out and touched his arm. "No smothering, remember? You can walk me out to the car, and I'll text you when I...get there."

That was vague enough not to be a complete lie.

He still didn't like it, but agreed. "Okay, I'll walk you out." He wrapped an arm around her shoulder and led her to the back alley, where they'd all parked today to avoid the front door.

He pulled her in for a hug at the car. She hugged him back. She needed his closeness.

"Be careful," he said into her hair. "And let me know you're okay. I'll see you at home."

Guilt ate at Maci. Chance wanted her to be safe and she was running off to meet with an unstable woman, but if she could spare him another run-in with her mother, she would. With a wave to Chance, she got in the car and headed back to the past.

MACI'S MOTHER WAS pacing in front of the door when she arrived.

"Took you long enough."

Maci ignored her, quickly texting Chance that she was okay, before ushering them both inside. The sooner she took care of this, the sooner she could get back to the better parts of her life.

"What do you want, Mom?"

As if she didn't know. As if calling Evelyn *Mom* wasn't practically a joke.

"You could at least pretend to be happy to see me." Evelyn walked around looking at things in the apartment like she'd never seen them before and was fascinated by how Maci had decorated. "I don't even know what's going on with you. You rushed me out of here so fast last time."

Maci grit her teeth. She knew how this game was played. Evelyn was going to do whatever was the exact opposite of what Maci wanted.

If Maci wanted to spend time and try to connect, Evelyn would want to leave. If Maci was on a tight schedule, Evelyn would be clingy and refuse to leave.

It was a childish game, and they'd been playing it for as long as Maci could remember—even when she lived at home.

"I need cash."

Of course, she did. "What happened to what I just gave you the other day? You can't have run through it all already."

"You didn't give me that much."

"Because I don't have much to spare. Any, actually."

Evelyn spun around to stare at her, crossing her thin arms over her chest. "We both know that's not true. I saw the car your boyfriend was driving when he took you out of here. I know he owns his own company with those so-called brothers of his. I don't believe they all aren't loaded."

Maci hated hearing her even mentioning Chance or his brothers. The Pattersons were all good. Chance deserved better than to be dragged into Maci's toxic family drama.

"First of all, he's not my boyfriend. And yes, I may work for the Pattersons, who own their own business, but that doesn't mean they're loaded and it especially doesn't mean I have extra money."

Evelyn started walking around again. "But you could get it if you wanted to. Especially to help out family."

Maci sat down in the kitchen chair by the small table. This pattern with her mother was never going to end. Not if Maci continued to let it go on like this.

"Mom, I don't have money to give you. I need it for myself."

Her mother turned to scrutinize her. "I thought you were done with drugs."

"I am." She took in a deep breath, hoping she wasn't about to make a huge mistake. "I need the money because I'm going to have a baby."

Maci's pregnancy was too new for her to have thought much about how she would break the news to Evelyn. But sitting here, she realized that she hoped the news would bring about some sort of positive change.

Evelyn had never been able to clean up for Maci, but maybe she would for her grandchild. Maybe they could have a relationship after all.

Her mother stopped and stared at her. "You idiot. You let him get you pregnant? You've ruined your life."

Knots formed in Maci's stomach. Definitely not the reaction she'd been hoping for.

"Thanks for the vote of confidence. Regardless of my *poor decisions* I don't have the money, so go find someone else to extort."

Evelyn was silent, turning back and walking around the room, peeking at all of Maci's things. Every time she picked something up, Maci ached to reach out and slap her hands away. This was her space, her sanctuary, and she wanted Evelyn out of it.

"You think I'm stupid?" Evelyn picked up a book and tossed it on the couch. "I know you have a rainy-day fund. I'll take that. You can ask your baby daddy for more money for raising some thankless brat."

"You should leave, Evelyn. I've made my decision."

Evelyn's eyes were flinty. She didn't like when Maci called her by her name instead of Mom. As if Evelyn hadn't just described her as a thankless brat.

"You've made your decision?" She picked up another

book, flipping through the pages before tossing it to the side. "Do you think you're better than me?"

"This isn't about better or worse. This is about priorities."

"Oh, yeah?" She put her hands on her hips. "How do you think your little boyfriend would react if he knew what you used to do to get high? Don't you think someone should explain that to him so he knows what he's getting into?"

Dread pooled in Maci's stomach as she steeled herself against the memories. She refused to go back to that time, even in her mind. "I made mistakes. He would accept them, especially since I won't make them again."

Maybe if she said the words forcefully enough she could believe they were true.

Her mother laughed, a harsh bark of a sound. "I doubt that. He seems like an upstanding guy. A professional and respectable businessman."

"He is."

Evelyn's lip curled up in a snarl. "Men like that have one thought when it comes to drugs—once addicted, always addicted."

No. Maci wasn't addicted anymore. She was in recovery. She'd done everything she could to get better. She *was* better.

"I'm not like you. I'm not going to keep doing drugs when I've finally made a life for myself. I'm not going to spend forever chasing a high I'll never be able to keep. I'm happy sober."

It was the wrong thing to say and it threw Evelyn into a rage. Maci stood there in horror as Evelyn swept out the rest of Maci's books off the bookshelf and onto the floor, then knocked the bookshelf over. The coffee table ended up on its side, with the empty glass that had been sitting on it shattering on the floor. Evelyn tore pillows and ripped the paintings and pictures from the walls.

It was impossible to believe someone as petite as Evelyn could do this much damage—the drugs in her system gave her the boost of strength. Maci knew not to get near. Evelyn didn't have these rages often, but her violence wasn't just targeted on inanimate objects. Maci kept far out of reach.

By the time Evelyn was done, the apartment that Maci had fought and scrounged for was nothing but scraps and trash.

"You ungrateful little bitch." Maci watched her mother's chest heave with every angry breath. "You either get me my money or we'll see what your boyfriend says when he finds out his baby mama was a drug dealer and a whore."

There it was, Evelyn's trump card. There was nothing else to do. Maci knew it and so did Evelyn. Her smarmy grin was enough to prove it.

"Fine. Let's go find an ATM."

Twenty minutes later, Maci's bank account was empty—including the five hundred dollars she'd saved for emergencies.

And so was her heart. She felt hollowed out as she watched her mother slip away laughing, leaving her alone with her thoughts.

Now that Evelyn had a button to push, Maci would never be free. She'd lose everything she'd worked so hard for and Chance... Chance would eventually find out what Maci had done. The first time she tried to refuse Evelyn, she'd tell him everything and he'd hate Maci for it. It was only a matter of time.

Maci didn't know what to do with herself but she couldn't move yet, so she curled up on her couch and cried, as the future she'd been so desperate for slipped from her fingers for good.

Chapter Sixteen

Something wasn't right.

Chance told himself not to read into Maci's stiffness and slightly weird pauses as he walked her out to the car, but he couldn't help it.

Certainly, there were a lot of things for her to be stressed over…the window, the doctor's appointment, her head wound, the stalker in general. But something hadn't been right about how she'd left.

He'd still let her go and still forced himself to come back into the office once she was gone. He'd felt slightly better when he'd received her text—Made it okay—but something still didn't sit right in his gut.

He made it another hour before he decided to stop fighting it. "I'm going to go. Maci and I have that doctor's appointment this afternoon and… I don't know."

"You alright?" Weston looked up from his screen.

"Yeah. I just want to make sure she's okay."

None of them argued. Luke just tossed Chance his keys since Maci had taken Chance's car.

But when he got home neither his car nor Maci was there. Normally stepping inside the house—especially since Maci had been staying there—made him relax, but not this time. Everything was silent.

Hoping there was some reason she was here despite the car not being in the garage, he called for her. "Maci?"

Pulling out his phone, he dialed her number and was immediately sent to voice mail. He sent texts, but got no response and no indication they'd been received.

He checked everywhere. The bedrooms were empty, the living room was clear and so was the backyard. There was no sign of trouble or forced entry. Every window was closed, every door locked.

Everything was exactly how it should have been, just without Maci.

Chance tried to focus. There hadn't been any other signs of attack. Nothing was out of place, no blood anywhere. Plus, no one except his family knew that Maci had been living with him.

So, she probably hadn't been kidnapped. Had there been a car accident?

No, because she'd texted him that she'd arrived safely.

He froze in the process of looking around again. Maybe she'd left? Like the night she'd snuck out of his bed and never returned. Maybe she'd decided she didn't want to be here with him anymore.

Maybe she'd decided to cut him out of her and the baby's life completely.

He rushed to the closet, heaving a sigh of relief when her clothes were still there.

He was about to dial his brothers to start a search party when he heard the garage door open. Relief warred with frustration so acute he had to take deep breaths to keep from losing his cool.

How he acted now was important. Because ultimately Maci was a grown woman and she didn't have to report any of her actions to him. He needed to show her that he was concerned but not smothering.

She walked in the door and his eyes combed over her—no injuries; that was good.

"Where the hell were you?" he barked.

Great, Patterson. Nice and calm.

She stilled on her way past, eyes narrowing. "I was driving around."

She looked tired, pale. Why?

"You were supposed to come straight home. Do you have any idea how—"

"I needed some time to think, Chance. Give me a break."

He could feel frustration bubbling up inside him. "You promised you'd come straight home and let me know you were okay. When I got your text, I assumed that's what it meant."

She flinched. "I had something to do first."

"Which was?"

Maci's hands clenched at her sides. "Nothing that concerns you."

"Everything about you concerns me."

"Well, it shouldn't! I'm a grown woman, Chance. I can take care of myself for a few hours."

Chance deflated. He was messing up...again. Letting fear drive him. If he wasn't careful, he knew he'd drive them apart.

He took a deep breath and tried again. "I know you can take care of yourself. I was worried. I came home and you weren't here and I couldn't get ahold of you. We have an active stalker who's targeting San Antonio Security, so now is a bad time to go AWOL without anyone knowing where. That's true for all of us."

Maci's eyes closed and she sighed. Chance watched the defensiveness in her posture slowly disappear. For a long moment they stood there in silence, then she came over and slid her arms around him.

The knot in his chest finally loosened as he clutched her tight. She was okay. She wasn't hurt and she hadn't left him.

When she spoke it was hushed. Apologetic. "I'm sorry. I wasn't even thinking about all that. I thought I would make it home before you. I didn't mean to make you worry."

He stroked her hair, brushing it off her face so he could see it better where it rested on his chest. "I'm sorry that I snapped at you. Are you okay? You look pretty stressed. Is it office stuff? The window?"

He couldn't blame her if she didn't feel safe there anymore.

"No. I can't stand the thought of you guys getting hurt, but that isn't it. I was at my place with my mother."

He wanted to ask why being with her mom made her look so defeated and bone weary. But he wanted her to tell him because she wanted to tell him, not because he was prying. "Can I do anything for you?"

"This is good. I think I needed it."

He wrapped her up tighter, nuzzling his cheek against her hair. "So did I."

"It's almost time to get ready for the doctor's appointment," she murmured. "They're going to tell us the gender. Are you nervous?"

"No, not nervous. Are you hoping for a boy or a girl?"

"Maybe a handsome little boy like his father."

He grinned. "I think I'd like to have a little hellion of a daughter. She'd be the spitting image of her mama."

Maci stiffened against him for a moment, then relaxed. "Two Maci Fords in the world is probably one too many."

Chance wasn't sure what that meant, so he let it go. It sounded like a cliché, but boy or girl didn't matter to him. He just wanted both mother and child healthy.

MACI AND CHANCE sat in silence a few hours later in the ob-gyn's waiting room. She was feeling more nervous every minute.

When her name was finally called, Chance stuck by her side. He helped her into the gown and moved one of the chairs right next to the exam table. Although she didn't like to be fussed over, Maci couldn't help but admit it was nice to not be alone.

A nurse came in and did some medical basics, then the ultrasound tech entered, all smiles. For some reason that made Maci even more nervous.

"Have you seen the baby yet?" the tech asked. Both Maci and Chance shook their heads and she smiled. "You're in for a treat."

With a squirt of cool gel and a wiggle of the ultrasound wand, a whooshing sound filled Maci's ears.

"That hummingbird-like sound is the heartbeat," the tech explained.

Maci felt the pinprick of tears at the back of her lids. That was her baby's heartbeat. Chance's baby. As if she'd called to him, he reached for her hand, squeezing her fingers lightly. She looked up and saw the faintest sheen of moisture in his eyes too.

They watched the wiggling bean on the screen until it was over, and the tech handed them page after page of sonograms. The tech explained that the doctor would answer all their questions, including the gender if they wanted to know, and then left with as big a smile as she'd had when she came in.

"Alright, Ms. Ford. It seems like you're doing great!" Dr. Harris was also full of smiles when he entered. "You and baby both look healthy."

"So, the all-day puking she has sometimes is normal?" Chance asked.

Dr. Harris laughed and kept his eyes on Maci. "Yep. Morning sickness is a terrible name considering it has no internal clock, but it's completely normal. You haven't lost a lot of weight, so I'm not worried about it. Just keep doing what you can to take care of yourself. That part should be over soon."

"Thank goodness." Maci grinned. "I won't miss it at all."

Dr. Harris continued to go over test results from both today and ones that had been run at the hospital. He reassured Maci and Chance that the baby was fine. No damage had come from the attack, and there didn't seem to be any genetic issues either.

"You elected to get an early gender test. We have the results if you still want to know."

Maci looked at Chance. He shrugged. "Your choice. I'm good either way."

She looked back at the doctor. She wanted to know. "Tell us."

Dr. Harris smiled. "Congratulations. You're having a girl."

A girl. They were having a daughter. Maci couldn't pull her focus from that thought.

She was bringing a new Ford woman into the world.

The rest of the appointment felt like it moved at lightning speed, with Maci only partially aware of it. Dr. Harris provided suggestions concerning exercise and foods that might help settle her stomach. He answered all the questions Chance had while Maci sat there feeling numb. By the time she refocused on the world around her, Chance was bundling her into the car.

He slid into his seat and just sat there, keys in hand while he stared out the windshield. "We're having a baby. A girl. *Our* girl."

There was awe and adoration in Chance's voice. When she glanced over, his eyes practically twinkled with joy. His smile was about to split his face.

So why did Maci feel the heavy weight of despair in her stomach?

A *girl*. She felt stuck on the knowledge that she and Chance were having a daughter. What did Maci know about raising a daughter when Evelyn was supposed to be her example?

Evelyn had been so deep in her own drug addiction, in and out of court-required rehab, that she didn't have the ability to protect Maci from anything. Then Maci had followed in her footsteps without a care. She'd found peace at the bottom of a pill bottle or heavier drugs.

It didn't matter that Maci had cleaned herself up, that she'd been sober for years. She was still always only one bad choice away from being back in that pit.

What kind of person brought a baby into the world to have a mother with addiction?

She put her hands on her stomach. Her baby was just one more cog in the chain of messed up Ford women. Maci didn't know how to break the cycle. She didn't know how to raise her daughter right. She didn't know anything about boundaries or parenting. She didn't know how she'd keep her child safe.

Her daughter was going to pay the price for Maci's stupidity. The thought made Maci sick.

She'd ruined her baby's life before she'd even got a chance to live it.

As they neared Chance's house, panic forced her breaths to come faster. The second he parked, she shot out of the car—she was going to be sick and it had nothing to do with morning sickness.

She couldn't be near him, couldn't speak to him. She'd ruined it all.

"Maci?" Chance grabbed her arm to reel her into his body, but she yanked it away.

"I'm going to go to bed."

"What about dinner? You need to eat."

The idea of sitting down and facing Chance made Maci's stomach clench even worse. "I'm not hungry."

She could feel Chance's eyes on her the whole way into the house, but she didn't turn back. She couldn't. Not when she'd ruined his life and he didn't even know it.

Chapter Seventeen

Chance barely slept a wink. All night long, his thoughts drifted to Maci. He couldn't stop picturing her after the appointment. The hunch of her shoulders as she bolted into the house, the stiff set of her lip as she tried not to cry.

Was it the baby? Did she not want a girl? Even if that was the case, he couldn't see Maci getting that upset over something like gender. It was something else, he knew it, but he had no idea how to find out. Maci had locked herself in the guest bedroom, refusing to come out for dinner, even when he'd asked as gently as possible. He'd almost decided to break down the door and demand to know what was going on.

Then he heard Maci crying.

Even through the door, Chance could tell that her tears were agonized. It wasn't just the typical fear of being a bad parent, she was terrified about something else, and that took the wind out of his sails. As frustrated as he was, Chance refused to badger her when she was obviously going through something difficult.

Worst of all, it was a reminder that, as much as he

cared for her, he didn't know a lot about Maci. So, as much as he wanted to demand answers, he stepped away and let her be.

It was the hardest thing he'd ever done.

By the time he'd gotten up this morning, the kitchen showed signs of Maci having made herself tea and breakfast. That was good. He wanted her to talk to him, but if she wouldn't, at least she was taking care of herself.

He'd barely made his own coffee and breakfast when his phone rang.

"We got another message from the stalker," Brax said.

A sliver of unease dug into Chance. He didn't like the way Brax's voice sounded—too careful and controlled for his free-spirited jokester of a brother.

"What did it say?"

"I think you should come in and see for yourself."

Chance didn't even have to think about it. "I can't. I need to stay here with Maci."

That got Brax's attention. He cursed under his breath. "I forgot about the appointment yesterday. Is everything okay with the baby?"

"The baby's good." Chance was careful not to let the gender slip. He wasn't sure if Maci wanted people to know yet. "Maci's just having a…tough time."

Brax was quiet for too long, and the foreboding got stronger.

"What's going on, Brax?"

"The message was a threat."

"Did you guys already let Dorian know? Is Stella secure?"

"It wasn't a threat against Stella."

Chance let out a curse. "Against us again?"

Brax didn't answer.

"What the hell is going on?" Brax was never this quiet.

A second later he heard a click. "Bro, it's Weston. Luke's on too. You and Maci both okay?"

This definitely wasn't good. "Yeah, we're fine. You guys need to tell me what's going on right damned now."

"The new threat is against Maci," Weston said quietly.

The world stopped. "What kind of threat?"

"I sent a picture to your email."

Chance reached for the computer, fingers slamming down on the keys as he found the picture of the letter Weston had sent. Curses flew out of his mouth as he read, fury burning through him with every word.

It's a pity when the innocent get caught in the cross fire of battle, don't you think?

But war is what this is and I'm determined to win.

With your queen as a prize, I'll do whatever it takes to defeat you. I'm looking forward to it.

You make me good, but she will make me better.

Included with the letter was a picture of Maci coming out of the office. It was impossible to tell how long ago it had been taken.

Every nerve in Chance's body demanded action. He wanted to move.

He wanted to *kill*.

Whoever this bastard was who wanted to drag Maci into his sick games… Chance wanted to erase him from the planet.

"Hang on," he said into the phone, before tossing it onto the kitchen table. He was tempted to throw his laptop across the room in rage, but knew in the long run that would only hinder his ability to protect Maci.

Right now he needed to see with his own eyes that she was alright. Especially after last night's disappearing act.

He knocked on the guest bedroom door. "Maci? I just need to know that you're in there and you're okay."

To his surprise, she opened the door. She looked pale and a little fragile, but otherwise fine.

Before he could stop himself, he yanked her into his arms.

"Chance?" she whispered.

"We've got trouble," he said, not letting her go. He wasn't going to keep this from her. He respected her too much not to tell her if she was in danger. "A threat from the stalker directed at you. I'm on the phone with the guys."

Her face got paler, but she nodded. He led her back out to the kitchen and grabbed his phone as she sat down in one of the chairs, pulling her knees up and wrapping her arms around them.

She looked so young and vulnerable. Her personality was so big, it was easy to forget that Maci was only in her early twenties.

He put his phone on speaker mode. "I'm back. Maci's here with me."

"Hi, sweetheart," Brax said. "We're so sorry about this."

"I'm okay," she said. "Let's treat this like it was any other case. Try to keep our emotions out of it."

The hell he could. But Chance just nodded. He spun the laptop in her direction so she could see the note.

"Where was the letter sent?"

"The office," Luke said. "It might have been there a day or more, honestly. Mail hasn't been a priority."

"Guy is talking about war and battle," Weston said. "I think we were on the right track when we were narrowing the list to people who are former military or law enforcement."

"I don't understand what's made him change from Stella to me." Maci's voice was small.

Chance reached over and grabbed her hand, rubbing his thumb along her soft skin. "We think this has never necessarily been about Stella. Stalking is a game for this guy."

"Probably closer is that he considers it to be an exercise or a military mission," Weston interjected. "He's trying to improve his skills and feels like going up against us will help do that."

"So, targeting one of our own makes sure we're willing to engage with him," Luke said. "If he stuck with Stella, he has no guarantee we won't quit or get fired."

She shook her head. "Did I do something to make him come after me?"

Chance squeezed her hand. "No, honey. He thrives on a challenge. That's what all of us are to him."

But Chance damn well wished they'd never put Maci undercover to begin with. Then this bastard would've never known she existed.

"You and Maci need to get somewhere safe until we can figure this out," Brax said. "Definitely can't bring her to the office or let her be at her apartment alone. Hell, I wouldn't even stay at your house."

"I'll take her to Mom and Dad's."

Luke snorted. "Finally, it's your turn."

Chance's mouth twitched into a small smile. It did seem like Sheila and Clinton's home had turned into an unofficial safe house over the past couple of years. All three of Chance's brothers had brought their women there at one point or another.

"I'll get Maci settled, then be back."

The brothers went over a few more details before Chance got off the phone. A quick call to his mother and everything was ready to go.

Maci was still sitting with her arms wrapped around her legs.

He brushed a strand of hair back from her face. "You okay? We should pack and get ready to go."

"I don't want your parents to get hurt. I know they watch Walker too."

"We'll leave if anything gets dicey for them, I promise." It was an easy promise for Chance to make. He didn't want his family getting hurt either.

"Does..." She trailed off and started again. "Do your parents know about the baby?"

"I doubt it. I know the guys know, but they wouldn't tell, and I didn't want to just drop it on them via text or something."

"Oh. Okay."

"We can keep it hushed for now if you want."

She nodded. "That would probably be best."

He wasn't sure exactly what that meant. He still wasn't sure why she'd been so upset last night.

Had she changed her mind about keeping the baby? The thought crushed something inside him, but now wasn't the time to get into it.

They packed up and twenty minutes later were on the road. Neither of them spoke much and the silence strained between them. He wanted to say something to make things easier for her but had no idea what to say.

The last thing he wanted to do was share Maci with anyone, even his parents. He wanted to sit her down and talk, to get everything out in the open—especially after yesterday's appointment and breakdown. But her safety had to come first. They'd have plenty of chances to talk about her past when the time was right.

Right now, Maci's past didn't matter. What mattered was keeping her safe from this stalker.

Chapter Eighteen

Maci felt like her life was falling apart on every possible level.

She was still reeling from yesterday's panic attack, then discovered she was the target of a stalker, and now had to stay with her not-boyfriend's parents who didn't know she was having his baby.

She wasn't sure which terrified her most.

Sheila and Clinton Patterson had always been kind to her. They'd often invited her over for holiday dinners and brought coffee for her on the rare occasion that they stopped into the office to visit their sons. They were good people.

But being nice to Maci as one of San Antonio Security's employees was much different than accepting her as the mother of Chance's child.

This was definitely something she'd need to keep hidden.

"You planning to stay in the car until you blend into the seats?"

Maci startled at Chance's voice. She'd been so stuck in

her thoughts that she hadn't noticed him park. He stood next to her open door, waiting.

He held out his hand to help her out. "You ready?"

Not even remotely. But she nodded and got out of the car. At the door, Sheila Patterson stood with a smile on her face and her arms open wide. Even from feet away, Maci could see how much love she had for Chance.

She had that much love for all of her family.

"Chance, honey, good to have you home. Maci, welcome. You're looking well." Sheila wrapped them each in quick hugs before grinning. "There's someone here to see you both."

Chance smiled at his mom and took off for the living room, scooping the young boy from the carpet. Walker, Brax and Tessa's son, was babbling his uncle's ear off in unintelligible toddler language, but Chance didn't seem to mind. He gave the boy his full attention, nodding and adding to the conversation as much as he could.

Maci's heart turned to mush. What an amazing father Chance was going to be. She wished she could say the same about being a mother.

Walker continued to coo as Chance handed him over to Clinton. "Thank you for letting us stay for a while. We just need to get off-grid."

Sheila smiled. "At this point we're used to it. And you boys know this is your home too. You're always welcome. You can stay in your room, and I've made up the guest room for Maci."

"I have to get back to the office. There are some things that need to be handled immediately, but I'll be back later." He kissed his mother's cheek and waved at his dad, who was getting an earful from Walker.

Then to Maci's surprise, he wrapped her in a hug, pressing a kiss to her temple. "Get some rest."

Well, it was obvious she wasn't just an employee anymore.

The tension felt thick, despite baby Walker's jabbering and giggling as Maci stood there with Sheila and Clinton.

"Why don't I show you up to the room where you'll be staying?"

Maci grabbed her small bag and followed Sheila. She showed Maci to a simple guest room, and Maci dropped off her stuff. The bed wasn't very big, but it looked inviting. She wished she could crawl into it and pull the covers over her head.

"Bathroom is just down the hall." Sheila turned and smiled as she opened a door to another bedroom. "And lest you think I'm completely old-fashioned or disapprove of you in any way, this is Chance's room."

Maci had to smile as she saw the twin bed and small desk. Sports posters all over the wall. There definitely wasn't room for a second person. "Oh."

"I know, I should redecorate. But I haven't touched any of the boys' rooms. They came in and made the space their own. For all of them it was the first bedroom that was truly only theirs."

"That's wonderful."

Sheila shrugged and led her back downstairs. "I guess these rooms are a reminder that sometimes families are formed in nontraditional ways, but that doesn't make them any less of a family."

Families definitely weren't Maci's area of expertise.

Sheila walked back downstairs, blowing kisses at Clinton and Walker still playing in the living room before leading Maci into the kitchen. "It's been a stressful day for you. How about some coffee? The boys got me one of the fancy espresso machines for Christmas last year. You like cappuccinos, right?"

"I, uh, I switched over to tea recently."

Shelia spun to look at her. "You're pregnant."

Maci wasn't sure what to say. "You got that from tea?"

"More that I knew the boys weren't telling us something. I thought maybe it had to do with a case. But Chance's protective hug clarified it all for me." She smiled gently. "Although it was the tea that clinched it. You love cappuccinos."

"I do miss cappuccinos." Maci chose a tea bag from the tin Sheila held out. "Are you mad?"

"Why would I be mad?"

Maci shrugged. "I don't think anyone in the family even knew Chance and I were…together. Maybe you think I'm trying to trap him or something."

It's what Evelyn had done to Maci's father… Gotten pregnant to force him to marry her.

Sheila gave a little laugh. "Honey, have you met Chance? Nobody forces him to do anything he doesn't want to do."

She relaxed and let out a little laugh herself. "Yeah. That's pretty true."

"We already considered you part of this family. You and that baby are Pattersons, and we'll have your back no matter what. Even if it doesn't work out between you and Chance."

"That means a lot to me."

They fell into a comfortable silence as Maci sipped her tea and they listened to Walker and Clinton play. She thought of Chance's interaction with his nephew.

"Chance will be such a good dad," Maci whispered.

"You'll both be great parents."

"I'm not so sure about me."

"I am." Sheila reached over and patted her hand. "Parenthood is more about instincts than anything else. I've seen you with Walker and you're great with him. I'm not worried one bit."

Sheila thought she knew Maci, but she really didn't. Maci frowned into her cup until a hand on her shoulder lifted her gaze again.

"I know my son. He's been enamored with you since the day you met. All the fighting? Everybody knew that was you and Chance's way of flirting with each other. Like kids on a playground."

Maci gave a half smile. "Yeah, we definitely have a tug-on-the-pigtails vibe."

"There for a bit a few months ago, Chance was happier. Smiling more and laughing. Then it was gone."

Because Maci had come to her senses and left him sleeping in his own bed. She didn't want to explain any of this to Sheila.

When Maci didn't say anything, Sheila eventually nodded and leaned back. "Regardless of what happened, I think you two can make it work."

"I don't," Maci blurted. She was not in line to be the

next Mrs. Patterson. Chance needed someone better. "I wish we could, but regardless of everything that's happened, there's a lot he doesn't know about me. I'm not who he needs."

"I'm not so sure that's your choice, but if there are things he needs to know, tell him."

"You say it like it's easy."

"I don't mean to," Sheila admitted. "Baring your soul to someone you care about is the hardest thing you can do, but I will say that it's usually worth the pain. My son isn't a weak man. He's not going to run at the first sign of trouble with you. He hasn't yet, has he?"

No, he hadn't. Chance had been right there at Maci's side every day. He'd given her space when she needed it, yet still pushed her to talk to him whenever he could. He wanted answers, but he hadn't been cruel or malicious.

He'd been gentle. Not a word anyone would normally associate with Chance.

As if she heard Maci's thoughts running wild, Sheila grabbed her hand and smiled. "Chance is a born caretaker. It's how he shows his love. Trust him to take care of you and the baby. He's always going to do right by his family, and you can be the heart of that if you just tell him what you need and what scares you most."

Maci bit her lip, processing the words.

"Trust that what's in his heart for you is enough to keep him at your side," Sheila continued. "It may not be easy to fight your natural skepticism, but the battle will be worth it. I promise."

Maci had nothing to say to that, but Sheila didn't seem

to need her words. This woman seemed to understand more about Maci than her own mother ever had.

Emotion urged Maci forward and she drew Sheila into a hug. "Thank you."

"There's nothing to thank me for." She ran a hand down Maci's hair, and for a moment, she knew exactly what a mother's love felt like. It was beautiful.

"Now, give me your cup and go take a nap," Sheila said with a playful smile and nudge toward the stairs. "Growing my grandbaby is hard—but very important—work."

Feeling lighter than she had in ages, Maci went upstairs to rest.

Chapter Nineteen

Chance could feel exhaustion weighing him down by the time he got back to his parents' house. It was well after midnight, so everyone was already in bed. Dad had kept him updated via text throughout the day just to reassure him everything was okay on the home front.

He was glad stuff was okay somewhere, because it surely hadn't been in the office.

Weston had called in every favor he had left with the San Antonio PD to get a rushed lab report on the stalker's letter, only for the report to come back with nothing. The letter was completely clean—not a single fingerprint or hair, nothing that could give them a clue. Even the stamp hadn't been licked.

It was a complete dead end.

They'd pored over more footage. Ran faces and names through every program they had available to them. Dorian and his team had shown up to help too. Just because the stalker seemed to have moved on to Maci didn't necessarily mean Stella was safe.

They all wanted to catch this bastard.

But he was still one step ahead of them, because once again, all their work had amounted to nothing.

Everyone had finally decided to call it a night. His brothers went home to the women who loved them. Chance went home to the woman who seemed only a half breath away from taking off in a dead sprint.

Chance scrubbed a hand over his face as he sat down in the kitchen. He didn't know how to help Maci with whatever was going on in her mind any more than he knew how to stop this stalker.

Uselessness wasn't a feeling he was accustomed to or liked.

Chance sat on a stool in the dark kitchen and thought about the past twenty-four hours. The doctor's appointment, Maci's silence, the note—he wasn't sure the best way to handle any of it. He wanted to wrap Maci in bubble wrap, to insulate her and their daughter from the world, but that wasn't his call.

Their *daughter*.

When they heard her heartbeat for the first time, he'd been overwhelmed by emotion. He could already see a little girl with Maci's nose and his eyes. He was ecstatic.

The baby and Maci were every dream he'd never let himself have. He had no recollection of his own biological parents. And while he would lay the world at the feet of Sheila and Clinton, this baby would be the only biological relation Chance had ever really known.

But where he was full of joy, Maci was shutting down and shutting him out. Running. *Again.*

Why did she always run?

Even after all the passion between them. Even when

they could hardly be in the same room with each other without touching one another—magnets drawn together in a way they couldn't resist.

But still Maci refused to truly get close to him.

Chance wasn't surprised when he heard his mother's soft footsteps come down the stairs. Had he ever sat in this kitchen having a crisis without Mom somehow knowing and making her way here?

"Hey, Mom." He stood to put some water on for tea. Maybe something warm with no caffeine would help him settle down.

"Hey, baby. You just getting home? Long hours for you."

"I've been home for a little while, but yeah, long hours."

"You've got a lot on your mind. And not just what's going on with this case. I had a talk with Maci today."

"You know about the baby." He gave her a shrug and a smile. "I'm surprised she told you. But I shouldn't be, I guess."

"It was more that I put the pieces together than she actually told me, but yeah. Congratulations."

She wrapped her arms around him and he let himself sink into his mother's hug. Sheila Patterson had always been his safe space. From the moment he'd finally stopped fighting them, his parents had become his rocks, grounding and centering him when nothing else could. They'd earned his trust over and over again.

It was what he wanted to be for Maci, if she'd let him.

They finally broke apart when the kettle whistled. Sheila moved to put tea bags in the mugs.

"We found out we're having a girl yesterday."

"You excited about that?"

"I didn't care either way, but yeah. To think about a little Maci running around, that makes my heart happy."

He thought of Maci's reaction and his smile faded.

"But?" Sheila prompted.

"Maci seemed fine and then she just shut down. I'm talking practically catatonic. She hid in the bedroom as soon as we got home."

He stood, pacing the length of the kitchen as he tried to work out his thoughts. "I always seem to mess up with her, Mom. She runs away, and I don't know how to make her understand I would do anything for her and the baby."

His mom was silent as she watched him move, sipping her drink with that calmness that made it so easy to share his feelings. Finally, she set the cup down and folded her hands.

"You've been taking care of others since before you could take care of yourself. It's your first instinct with the people who are important to you."

Chance frowned. "Yeah."

"I know you've been taking care of Maci, that's what you do. But when's the last time you listened to her or even asked what she wanted? Do you even know if she wants to be a mother?"

Panic seared through Chance. He wanted his baby, but he wanted her with Maci. He wanted them to be a family. The idea that Maci might not want it too was almost too much to take.

His mom reached out and grabbed his hand. "Do you want to know what I see when I look at Maci? I see someone who's scared."

Chance shook his head. "Maci's the strongest person I know. She's not scared of anything."

But there was something in the back of his mind that was screaming at him, that maybe his mother was right.

Sheila shrugged. "That could be exactly what she wants people to think. I think maybe her past is haunting her, and with a baby representing such an important future, it's scary for her."

He rubbed his eyes. "Why doesn't she just tell me this?"

"I think our Maci's been alone for a long time. She might not know how to."

She didn't know how to say what she needed to say, so she ran instead. Put walls up.

"There's nothing she could tell me about her past that's going to change how I feel about her."

His mother smiled gently. "In this house, we've always believed in second chances. We've always believed that the past didn't dictate the future. I think you're going to have to introduce her to those concepts."

"Yeah, I think you're right."

"I'm going back to bed. I hope you'll get some sleep too." She stood up. "And, Chance, when you talk to Maci, really listen to her. Take off your I'll-fix-everything hat, and just really listen. I think that's what she needs most of all."

JUST AFTER DAWN, Chance woke, rubbing grit out of his eyes as he stumbled into the kitchen. He'd gone to bed right after his talk with his mother and gotten a few hours of sleep, but what she'd said still kept playing in his mind.

He needed to listen to Maci. Not do. Not fix. *Listen.*
He found a note from his mother on the counter.

Dad and I are out for the day. Be home by dinner.
Make your girl some breakfast and talk. Love, Mom

Chance hunted down the pots, pans and food he'd need
to make a great pancake breakfast, something he knew
how to do, since he and his brothers had been in charge
of breakfast on the weekends. Maci shuffled into the
kitchen just as he was finishing.

"Perfect timing," he said with a smile.

She stopped in the doorway. "I thought you would be
Sheila."

"Mom and Dad went out for the day, but I was in-
structed to make you breakfast. I made pancakes, home
fries, toast and even some eggs if your stomach is up for
them. There's some cut fruit in the fridge too."

"Wow. That's quite the spread. What's the occasion?"

Chance shrugged. "You need to eat and we need to
talk. Might as well kill two birds."

"Talk?"

"Talk," Chance said firmly. "Well, you need to talk
and I need to listen."

She sat down at the kitchen island, and he pushed some
food toward her to get her to eat. She took each bite
slowly, as if each mouthful brought her closer to a firing squad.

He sat down next to her with his own plate. "Before
we start, I wanted to say I'm sorry."

She looked over at him, still chewing. "What do you have to be sorry for?"

"This whole time, I've been more concerned about myself and my feelings than yours. I didn't even ask the most basic question."

"Which is?"

"Do you want to be a mom?"

"You did ask me. You asked me in the hospital if I was keeping the baby."

He nodded. "I know. But that's not the same thing. What I'm asking you now is if you *want* to be a mom."

She swallowed, setting her fork down. "I do, but..." She trailed off to silence.

"But what? Whatever it is, speak it."

"My mom is pretty unstable. She was addicted—*is* addicted—to drugs." Maci stared down at her plate, moving a piece of pancake around in circles. "When I was younger it was mostly booze like my dad, but by the time I was a teenager she'd moved on to harder stuff. The type of drugs you don't get away from without professional help. Not that she's ever wanted help."

His heart ached for Maci already. "That's really hard. I had no idea."

"Studies show that addiction can be genetic." She stared down at her plate. "That was true in my case."

Chance's stomach dropped, but he forced himself not to say anything. He needed to *listen*.

"I started dabbling in middle school. Pot first, then harder stuff as I got older. By the time I was seventeen, I dropped out of school to be my dealer's live-in girlfriend.

If I wanted a fix, all I had to do was ask. And do whatever he wanted, of course."

The implications of what she was saying made Chance want to throw up.

She looked up at him. "Whatever you're thinking to put that expression on your face, you're right. I did it all. Prostituted myself for drugs. I'm not the type of person who should be raising a child. Especially not yours."

He frowned. "Especially not mine? What does that mean?"

"It means, look at your life!" She waved her hand around. "You have this great, tight-knit family who would do anything for you. You're the best person I've ever met, and you'll be an even better father. Why do you deserve to be saddled with my baggage forever?"

"Stop." He'd promised his mother he'd listen, but he wasn't going to let Maci tear herself apart like this. "The past only defines us as much as we let it."

She rolled her eyes. "Tell that to a greeting card company, Chance. This is real life. Our choices always come back to haunt us."

"Maybe they do, maybe they don't, but that doesn't matter. You're clean now, right? Been sober for at least as long as I've known you."

There was no way she could've run the office with such efficiency if she had a drug problem. She was never late, rarely called in sick and was way too sharp to be intoxicated. They would've noticed.

"Yes, I finally got sober a little after my twentieth birthday. My boyfriend got violent one night and I ended up in the hospital. A nurse helped get me into a program and I got clean."

"You got your life together."

She shrugged. "The program helped me. Helped me get clean, helped me get my GED, helped me get some work-training classes under my belt."

For the first time, she'd had a support network, and look at what she'd done once she had it—dragged herself completely out of the pit. "You accepted the help that was offered and changed your life. Everybody would call that admirable."

"Did you not hear the part where I spent years basically selling myself so I could get high? It's amazing I didn't end up dead or with some disease."

He reached over and grabbed her hand. "Yes, I hate to think of you living like that. It absolutely guts me."

"And yet that's what the mother of your child is. A person with addiction who did sex work for drugs."

"The mother of my child is *recovering* from addiction, who survived and got out of a situation that would've destroyed many others. The mother of my child is strong and courageous and capable."

She shook her head, so sadly it broke his heart. "My mother has promised to get sober and fallen off the wagon so many times. What if I'm the same? Addiction runs in my family and I'm passing it along to our daughter. How could you want to be involved with someone like that?"

He had to make her understand something he'd thought about for years. "What about my family and what's passed down?"

Her brows pulled together. "What do you mean?"

"I don't know who either of my biological parents are. There's no info on them. The only thing we know for sure is that they both abandoned me, so they're obviously not the most upstanding of people. Who knows what sort of genetic mess I might be passing down."

"I—"

He put a finger gently over her lips. "Neither of us can stop what we pass down genetically to our children. But both of us can be there to show that any deficiencies we start with don't have to be what defines us. To help them navigate the rough waters."

"I'm afraid I'll be a horrible mom," she whispered.

"There may be patterns from our childhood that both of us have to undo. But, sweetheart, you did so much already with just a little help from the program. Think of all you can do with the full support of all the Pattersons behind you."

She gave him the tiniest smile. "That's a pretty great support network."

For the first time, he had a ray of hope. "You think Tessa or Claire or Kayleigh are going to let you be anything less than the best mother possible? You would do anything for them. They'll do anything for you too."

"I know," she whispered. "I love them. I love your whole family."

"And they love you too. We don't have to tell them all the details, but if you open up to them, you know they'll support you in whatever way they can. I will too."

"Really?"

He pulled her into his arms and rested his forehead against hers. "Yes. And not just because of the baby.

You mean the world to me, Maci Ford. We can't change the past and it doesn't matter anyway. I didn't know that Maci, and although I wish I could've helped her, she's gone."

He kissed her gently. "But I know this Maci and she's amazing. All that matters is the future. Our future. Do you understand?"

"No."

He chuckled, pressing his face into her neck so his next words were spoken into her skin. He wanted to imprint them there so she'd never forget. "It means, I'm all in with you, Maci. You and our daughter are my family and I choose the both of you."

He wanted to tell her he loved her, but that could wait. Baby steps.

She sighed and burrowed into his chest. Chance wished he could spend the whole day holding her like this.

"I'm glad you told me everything," he whispered into her hair. "No more running. If you start to feel overwhelmed, we work through it together. Deal?"

"Deal."

Now all he had to do was stop the stalker after her.

Chapter Twenty

Maci was still wrapping her head around the conversation with Chance as they finished eating and did the dishes.

He was still here. Hadn't told her to leave. Hadn't told her he wanted nothing to do with her or the baby. He wasn't acting weird or awkward.

It was more than she could've hoped for. Honestly, more than she could even understand. But he was touching her more, not less. Smiling at her gently in a way she could hardly resist.

And the thing was…she didn't have to resist anymore. He knew all the ugly parts of her past and was still here talking about baby names and something he'd read about pacifiers.

For the first time she had hope for a future that included Chance—which was more than she'd ever let herself dream of.

But a reminder that she had other very real problems came way too soon. Chance's phone chimed and he frowned as he looked down at the message.

"We've got incoming."

"Your parents?" she asked.

"My brothers. They're here."

Chance went and unlocked the door and let them in. All three men looked grim.

"We need to talk," Weston said. Chance nodded.

Luke took a seat at the dining room table. Brax grabbed a cup of coffee and did the same. Weston stood on his side of the table, his body tight with tension. Whatever he was going to tell them, Maci knew it wouldn't be good.

"Should I stay?" she asked.

Luke nodded. "This concerns you most of all."

Chance grabbed her hand and led her to the table, taking the seat next to her.

"First—" Weston rubbed his eyes "—when I got to the office, there was another note from the stalker. Hand delivered this time. It had been slid under the door."

He handed them a note inside a sealed plastic bag. There was also a picture of her and Chance leaving the ob-gyn yesterday.

It looks like congratulations are in order and the ante has been upped. I am up for the battle and will defeat you despite your attempts to stop me.

"He knows about the baby," she whispered. "He was there. He saw us."

"Actually, that image is from the medical complex's security camera," Luke explained. "He probably wasn't there, he just grabbed it later."

That didn't make Maci feel much better. She glanced over at Chance. Fury was burning in his eyes.

Weston held out a hand toward him. "I know you want

to lose it right now, but you can't. Believe it or not, it gets worse, and you're going to need to focus."

She could see Chance fight to release the rage enough to focus. Finally, he nodded.

"Even before this delivery this morning, something has been bugging me about the wording of the stalker's notes," Weston continued. "I decided to cast a wide net to see if anything came back. It did. This is—*was*—Brianna Puglisi."

He slid over a printed newspaper article from three years prior in Dallas. Maci frowned as she read about a local hairstylist found dead in her apartment—strangled. She'd barely been twenty-five, but was a favorite of the wealthy ladies in town. More than one of them had lamented over her loss in the article.

"What's this got to do with us?" Chance asked.

"There was a note found with the body. It wasn't published in the paper, of course. I found out about it through some police connections." Weston laid down a printed police report. "I highlighted the relevant part."

Battles require sacrifices. War demands it. I must be the best.

Chance looked up at Weston. "Battle. Wars."

Brax nodded, hands around his coffee mug. "Exactly. Same language as our guy."

Chance muttered a curse. "And he killed her. Not just a stalker."

Weston nodded. "Report states that Brianna had mentioned some weird notes she'd gotten, but she didn't show them to anyone and police didn't find any at her home or work."

"This escalates things," Chance said.

"You have no idea." Luke slid a file across the table. "Once we started looking we found three more. All women in Texas or connecting states. Some stalkings that turned into murders. Some with no proof of stalking, but still a dead woman. But all with the *war, battle, cross fire, be the best* sort of language in notes that were found."

Chance flipped through the police files of the other murders. "So we know there's four dead women."

Brax nodded. "At least. That's what we found in just a few hours this morning by looking for cases with this sort of language involved. There may be more."

Chance didn't look up from the file. "We're dealing with a serial killer."

"A smart one," Weston said. "Killed in different ways so that law enforcement didn't put together what they were dealing with. Even the notes weren't always associated with the killings. Sometimes they were left in a way that made them look like they belonged to the victim."

Maci couldn't stop the whimper that fell from her throat.

Chance pushed the file away and grabbed her hand. He entwined their fingers, stroking his thumb alongside hers in soft, soothing motions, as if he could feel the absolute panic rushing through her.

There was a serial killer on the loose. One who'd announced he was after *her*.

Luke attempted a comforting smile. "As scary as it

sounds, it makes sense. We were confused why the stalker was getting violent with little to no provocation when it's not typical for this type of fixation. But if he was a serial killer all along, violence was always the end goal."

She could understand the logic of what he was saying, but it didn't change the fact that a serial killer had set his sights on her.

Chance leaned back in his chair but didn't let go of her hand. "Let's work our way backward. He targeted Maci and us because of our connection to Stella. But I don't recall notes to Stella containing the same war/battle language."

Weston nodded. "You're right. There's nothing in Stella's notes with those words."

"Are we sure we're dealing with the same guy?" Luke asked.

"Definitely the same as those dead women." Brax took the last sip of his coffee, then pushed the mug away. "That language is too specific and similar for it not to be him."

"It's Stella who's the anomaly," Weston said.

Chance's eyes narrowed. "Or…"

He faded off and Maci could almost see his mind spinning, working through various scenarios. Chance was a master at strategy and seeing patterns.

His brothers knew him well enough to give him silence while he worked it out. Maci squeezed his hand, then let it go as he stood up to pace.

"The other victims besides Brianna Puglisi, what did they do for a living?" he asked after a few seconds.

Luke grabbed the file. "Waitress in Houston. Photographer in Albuquerque. Clothing store salesperson in Austin. No evidence that they knew each other at all."

Chance continued pacing. "They didn't have to know each other to be connected. See if they have any connection with Stella."

Weston caught on to his line of thinking first. "We have online access to Stella's calendar. We can look at back dates."

Chance nodded. "Start with the salon Brianna worked at. It catered to the upper echelon. Stella would've been willing to travel to Dallas to get her hair done by the stylist everyone was raving about."

Weston sat down and got out his computer. "Okay, this is going to take a few minutes. Most of Stella's appointments from over a year ago have been archived."

Maci grabbed her phone. There was another, easier way to get this information. It may not have as many details as what Weston would pull up on the calendar, but...

"I've got it," she said. "Stella was at the salon roughly eight months before Brianna was killed."

All four men turned to face her. "How do you know?" Chance asked.

She spun her phone around so they could see. "It was on her social media. She said she liked Brianna and the style, but didn't know that it would be worth coming to Dallas for every time, so she'd stick with her local stylist in San Antonio."

Maci grabbed the file and flipped to the clothing store salesperson who'd been killed. It was a high-end boutique in Austin. She turned to her phone again and within just a minute had social media proof Stella had been there too.

"Stella has shopped at that clothing boutique in Austin multiple times. No direct proof that she knew the woman who was killed…"

"But the fact that she was there at all ties those two women together." Chance looked around at his brothers. "Stella is the link."

"You think she's the killer?" Maci asked.

Chance shook his head. "No. But somebody close to her probably is."

Weston began typing frantically on his computer.

"But what about all the notes Stella got that aren't the same MO as the war/battle guy?" Brax asked. "Inconsistency doesn't seem to fit for him."

Chance shrugged. "Maybe after the first note he changed his plan or realized his normal language might get him caught. We don't know that he ever planned to harm Stella. Maybe he was just trying to up the ante."

Luke nodded. "This guy wants to be the best. But the best what? Killer? When he talks about winning, what is he referring to?"

With your queen as a prize, I'll do whatever it takes to defeat you.

Maci shuddered as the words he'd written in the note about her came to mind.

Chance rubbed his eyes. "I think we were on the right track when we said this is some sort of professional challenge to him. A matter of pride. He wants to be the best at…whatever it is. Killing, stalking, keeping ahead of law enforcement. Who knows? Stella and her level of security and exposure just upped the challenge for him."

Weston finally looked up from his computer. "I concur

and want to take it a step further. I think we were right when we said this guy was former military."

Chance nodded. "We need to check the full security team. Get Dorian in on it. He'd be the best one to say if there's anyone on the team who fits the profile and maybe has been acting strange."

"Before we do that, there's someone else we need to look into. I think your instincts were right all along, Chance." Weston spun the laptop around so everyone could see it. It was a picture of Rich.

"Rich?" Maci asked. "He's not military."

Weston hit a button that brought up a picture of a young Rich in a military uniform. "Nope, but he was Junior ROTC in high school. And his father, who died five years ago, was a decorated marine. Definite military ties we didn't look closely enough into."

"You really think Rich could be a killer?" Maci whispered. She thought of how much time she'd spent with him so close to her and felt sick.

Chance's eyes were already filled with rage. "That smug bastard has been toying with us from the beginning. It damn well is going to end now."

Chapter Twenty-One

Maci went upstairs soon after their discovery, claiming to need a nap, but Chance knew better. She was terrified and he didn't blame her.

If Rich was the stalker—now killer—then she'd been in his grasp more than once. He could have taken her at any time, especially knowing all the security measures in place.

He hadn't done it because it would've made it too obvious they were up against an inside man. Instead he'd bided his time, set the game up for extended play.

Bringing Maci into it as his target had been a mistake. There was no way in hell Chance was going to let anything happen to her.

"We need to figure out a plan of action," he told his brothers.

"We have to be careful who we bring in on this. If Rich is definitely our guy, we don't know what sort of internal measures he has in place to get info."

Chance had no doubt Rich was their guy. "He could have phones tapped. Hell, he could have someone else working with him."

Brax got up to get himself another cup of coffee. "Nobody in the LeBlanc organization would think twice about giving Rich intel. He was handpicked by LeBlanc himself."

Chance rubbed the back of his neck. "The last thing we need is for him to go to ground because he figures out we're on to him." Maci would never be safe.

"I say we go see LeBlanc in person and let him know what we suspect," Luke said. "He needs to make sure Stella is in a safe place where Rich can't get to her."

"Agreed. Then we can check the dates of the murders with Rich's known whereabouts." Chance was ready to move. "Let's get Mom and Dad back here. Someone needs to stay here too, just in case."

Weston pointed at his computer. "I'll stay here and see if there are any more cases I can tie this to. And we're going to have to come up with more than a couple years in ROTC in order for the police to take this seriously. Rich isn't just going to roll over and confess."

Chance nodded. "You're right. Let's make sure everyone is safe, then we'll figure out a further plan. Start pressing your PD contacts. Let's see what we would need for them to make an arrest."

"Once I show all this to my colleagues on the force and they see it's a serial killer, believe me, they'll want to make an arrest. You guys be safe and keep me posted."

Chance ran up to say goodbye to Maci, but she was sleeping. Good, she needed the rest.

He reached over and kissed the top of her head. "I'm not going to let anyone hurt you." He was talking to both mother and baby.

And he meant every word.

LESS THAN FORTY-FIVE minutes later they were back in LeBlanc's office.

"Gentlemen, should I call in Dorian and his team?" LeBlanc asked. "I'm hoping you actually have something useful for us this time."

The man was frustrated. Chance couldn't blame him.

"We'd actually prefer to speak to you alone, if that's okay," Chance explained. "We've had a breakthrough in the case, and we have reason to believe the stalker may be working inside your organization."

LeBlanc's eyes got wide. "What?"

Chance didn't want the man to panic, so he chose his words carefully. "We've found some similar cases from the past few years that we believe were committed by the same person."

Brax gave the man his most comforting smile. "We have some questions we think will help us nail down who the perp is. But first—do you have confirmation Stella is still safe?"

Once they started making their case against Rich, it was going to tip him off. They needed to have everyone secure before that.

"Yes, I spoke to her not long before you arrived. She's safe, but we're not going to be able to keep her out of the limelight much longer. She's doing a photo shoot at castle ruins in Scotland. That will hold her off a few more days."

Chance glanced over at his brothers. "And Rich? He didn't go over there, did he?"

"No, he stayed here in case he was needed."

"That's good. We might need him. What can you tell us about Rich?"

"He's worked for me for five years. Stella responds well to him so I've kept him around. My one rule was that he wasn't allowed to sleep with her and he's not broken that. Why do you ask?"

Brax shot Chance a look. Chance understood what his brother was communicating: this needed to be handled delicately.

"Before we get into specifics, we need to run a few dates by you and see what you, Stella, Rich, Jason Rogers and your office manager were doing on those days."

LeBlanc was confused. "Marguerite?"

Chance nodded. He'd tossed Jason, one of the main security guards, and Marguerite Frot into the mix for subterfuge. If Rich was listening or had means of accessing what they were talking about, maybe it would throw him off the scent.

LeBlanc sat down at his desk. "Okay, fine. What are the dates? My system will allow us to pull up schedules. It should list what security teams were working also."

Chance wasn't a huge computer person, but he was thankful for this program that was about to make their lives much easier.

Luke read off the dates. They waited as patiently as they could as LeBlanc started with himself and listed what he'd been doing on each day. Then moved to Stella.

Chance grit his teeth when he next listed what Marguerite then Jason had been doing the dates of the murders. Since both of them were red herrings, they didn't matter.

Finally, he got to Rich.

"On the first date, Rich wasn't working. He generally

takes Mondays and Tuesdays off since Stella's calendar doesn't tend to be full for those days."

Chance glanced at Luke and Brax. Rich not working meant he'd been free to commit the murder.

"Date two, it looks like Rich had a doctor's appointment. I vaguely remember that. A few weeks later he had a spot taken off on his shoulder that he was concerned might be cancer. Stella was distraught and did a six-week segment on different sunscreens."

"Okay," Chance said. They would have to follow up on that. He may not have gone to the doctor's appointment at all or it could've been very short. It was inconclusive at this point.

"Third date, Rich was not working again."

Chance grabbed his phone, ready to contact Weston. They were three for three with Rich, and Chance was sure LeBlanc was about to say the same for the date of the fourth murder they'd found.

They needed to be ready to move. Brax and Luke had the same tense body language Chance did.

"Okay, date four." LeBlanc clacked on his keyboard. "Oh, I could've given this to you earlier. Rich was with me the whole day that day in Los Angeles."

Chance's brow furrowed. "Are you sure?"

LeBlanc nodded as he looked up from his screen. "Yes, I remember it now. Half the office and Stella had that stupid virus. Rich was one of the few who tested negative, so he came with me to the opening of a new LeBlanc office branch there. He was acting as part personal assistant, part pretty boy for the press and part security."

Chance spun to face Luke. "What was the time on the fourth case?"

"Midafternoon, Texas time."

Chance looked back at LeBlanc. "You're absolutely sure Rich was with you that whole day? He didn't take a later flight or something?"

"I'm positive. I remember because we were almost late. Flying at that time during the height of the pandemic was problematic, even on a private plane."

Brax handed Chance his phone. Pulled up on it was the press report of the office opening. It had been a bold move on LeBlanc's part, considering most people were working from home, with no indication of returning any time soon.

There was Rich, smiling beside LeBlanc. The footage was time-stamped in a way that meant it was impossible that Rich had killed the fourth woman. When they looked further into the first three, they'd likely find the same thing.

Chance's jaw ached at how hard he was clenching it. Rich was a smug bastard, but he wasn't the killer.

"So, does all this information help you with your theory?" LeBlanc asked.

Brax and Luke looked as frustrated as Chance felt.

"Yes," he finally managed to say. Eliminating suspects was an important step to solving anything. But that didn't make Chance feel any better.

"Then can I ask exactly what this is about? What these *other cases* you're referring to are?"

Luke recovered quickest. "We've come across some disturbing facts, and we need to gather more information before we give you details. For now, let's keep this conversation between us, please."

Chance was trying to wrap his head around the fact that they would have to start back at square one when Dorian entered LeBlanc's office.

"I saw you guys on the door roster. Has there been a breakthrough in the case?"

Nobody answered. Neither Chance nor his brothers wanted to mention the words *serial killer* in front of LeBlanc.

It was LeBlanc who finally took charge. "Evidently, there is some sort of breakthrough but nobody wants to tell me what it is."

Brax tried his charming smile. "Only because we want to make certain of a few things first."

They were about to get fired, Chance could feel it. That was the last thing they needed. Access to information surrounding Stella was going to be critical.

Dorian came to their rescue. "Nicholas, sometimes security teams have to work in ways that don't make sense to the client. You and I had to learn that about each other early on. Let them do the job you hired them for."

"Fine." LeBlanc threw up a hand. "Take them to the conference room and help them with whatever they need. I have a business to run."

Once they were in the conference room, they explained the situation. They were going to need Dorian's help to catch this bastard.

Dorian sat down hard in one of the plush leather chairs as he took it all in. "Holy hell. We're dealing with a serial killer, not just a stalker?"

They gave him a little time to process it. They'd all felt the same way.

Dorian ran a hand over his jaw. "I need to double Stella's security now. Even though the guy's focus seems to have moved on to someone else."

Maci. Chance would be taking her to ground until this was over. He wasn't taking a chance with her. If he had to move her to a different country too, he'd do it.

"So, what's the killer's motive? How'd you put together that we're dealing with more than a stalker?"

They explained the similarity of terms used in the notes at the murder scenes and the ones the stalker had sent to their office.

"The guy wants a challenge," Dorian said after hearing them out. "Has the need to be the best."

Chance nodded. "That's what we concluded too. We've been looking at people who fit that profile—former military or even law enforcement."

"Agreed." Dorian was studying the reports Luke had brought with him. "I'd also widen the search to look at martial arts or MMA fighters. They use that kind of language also."

"Hell, gamers use it too," Brax muttered. "Maybe we tried to narrow it down too much."

"Honestly, we thought it was Rich," Chance explained. "He had some ROTC experience and his father was military, but it can't be because LeBlanc just provided an alibi for one of the murders."

Everybody grumbled about that.

"And this whole thing with Stella felt like the stalker

always had the inside scoop on what we were doing," Chance continued.

"It definitely feels personal. Like he's taunting everyone. And that the choice of victim feels less important than the actual challenge. First Stella, now Maci."

Chance agreed with Dorian's deduction, but the choice of victim was *very* important to him. "This still feels like an inside job to me. Or at least that the stalker/killer is getting inside info from someone."

"We'll run a complete security diagnostic. If there's info being leaked inadvertently from someone on my team, we'll find it."

"And if it's someone leaking it on purpose?" Luke asked.

"We'll find that too. It may take a little longer, but I promise you it will happen."

Chance walked over and shook Dorian's hand. "We're going to keep at it. See if there are any more murders we can link to this. We're bringing in some law enforcement contacts."

Dorian nodded. "That's one of the reasons Nicholas wanted to bring you guys in in the first place—your local contacts and influence here. I'll admit I was skeptical when he first mentioned it. But you've done nothing but prove me wrong."

"Let's just catch this guy," Chance said. "He made it way too personal when he targeted Maci."

Dorian gave him a tight smile. "I completely understand. He's messed with the mother of your unborn child. I'd stomp him into the ground."

"That's exactly what I plan to do."

Chapter Twenty-Two

When Maci woke up from her nap, she wandered downstairs. Weston was sitting at the kitchen table with his computer. His face was grim. Sheila and Clinton were back. Their faces were grim too.

"Chance, Brax and Luke went to meet with LeBlanc, see if we could get details about Rich. I have law enforcement waiting to move once we do," Weston said once he saw her.

"Okay." She was still having a hard time wrapping her head around the fact that she'd been so close to a possible killer. How many times he'd touched her.

"Do you want something to eat, honey?" Sheila asked.

"No." The word came out as a croak. "Chance made me a really big breakfast."

"Did you two talk?"

Maci nodded. It had only been a few hours ago, but seemed like forever. "Yes. It was good. You were right. Chance could handle my past."

Sheila pulled her in for a hug. "My boy can handle anything. He's going to handle this other thing too. Just you wait."

Maci hoped so. She felt like she couldn't breathe. "I think I might go take a shower, then lay back down."

The older woman smiled gently. "Absolutely. Hopefully you'll be more hungry at dinnertime."

Maci looked back over at Weston. "Did you find anything else?"

His face was almost haggard. "At least one more. I'm still searching."

Five murders.

She couldn't think about it too much right now or she was going to panic. She showered, then got back into bed, pulling the blankets up to her head, trying to shut out the world.

When she awoke the second time, things were actually worse. Her phone was buzzing with a call from her mother.

"What do you want, Evelyn?" Maci kept her voice barely above a whisper so none of the Pattersons would hear her.

"Maci, baby, I'm in trouble."

Maci really didn't have the time or mental energy to deal with her right now. "You're always in trouble."

"Baby." Her mother's voice was small, shaky. "I'm really sorry for how I treated you a couple days ago. That was wrong."

Maci rolled her eyes. "You can't blackmail me for more money. I've already told Chance everything."

"It was wrong for me to say what I did. So wrong. I thought about you being pregnant, and I knew you would need your money for the baby."

"Yes, that's true."

"My dealer has been trying to get me to sell for him for a while, so I told him I would. That way I wouldn't need money from you."

"Timothy?" He was low-level and not organized. Barely more than a thug.

"Yes."

Maci rubbed her eyes. This wasn't what she wanted. "Mom, that's dangerous."

"I know. I—I..." Evelyn let out a sob. "I was robbed last night. They took all the product."

Maci sat up straight in the bed. "Are you hurt?"

"No, but Timothy has given me twenty-four hours to come up with the money or he will hurt me. You know, he has to set an example." She listed the amount she needed.

"Mom, I don't have that much! Especially not since you just cleaned me out."

"I know. I know." Evelyn began to cry in earnest. "I don't know what to do. And it gets worse."

Oh, no. "What did you do?"

"Timothy was threatening to break my wrist when I told him I didn't think I could get the money. So I mentioned where you work." Her voice got smaller. "I think he's planning to jump your boyfriend or his brothers to get the money if I don't pay him back."

Maci thought through finances. If she pooled everything from every account and maxed out the cash withdrawal on her one credit card, then she might just have enough.

At least enough to keep Timothy and his buddies from attacking the Pattersons unawares while they were in the middle of a crisis. Maci could handle this for them. They would never even need to know.

And she could admit that, even though Chance already knew about her past, she'd prefer not to dump this on him in life-size Technicolor.

"Where are you, Mom?"

Her mom spit out an address on the south side of town near the warehouse district. Not the safest place, but not where Rich Carlisle would be hanging out, so at least she didn't have to worry about a serial killer.

Just run-of-the-mill family drug drama. No problem.

She disconnected the call and got dressed. There was no way Weston was going to let her go handle this, so she wasn't going to tell him. He had more important things to do. So did Chance.

She left a brief note on the pillow explaining she was going to see her mother in case someone wandered up to check on her. She didn't want them to think she'd been kidnapped.

She could hear Weston talking to his parents in the kitchen as she crept downstairs and out the back door. Luke had brought her car over a couple nights ago and left it parked on the street, so she slipped around the house and inside it.

She winced as the car started, hoping Weston wouldn't hear. Chance would kill her if he found out what she was doing. She pulled away from the curb.

So, she'd make sure he wouldn't find out.

"WESTON HAS FOUND one more murder tied to this guy and is checking further into another," Luke said as they walked back into the San Antonio Security office. "He's shown everything to his PD contacts, so it's more than just us looking into it now."

"Good. We need as many eyes on this as possible." Chance didn't care who figured out the identity of the killer. He just wanted Maci safe. "I'm going to take Maci out of town. Get us into a safe house nobody knows about. Mom and Dad's place is too easily connected to us."

Weston had been providing all clear updates since they'd left, but Chance didn't want to leave Maci there any longer than necessary.

"Agreed," Brax said. "Maybe we can get Stella to impersonate Maci to catch this guy."

Chance managed a grim smile at his brother's joke.

"You decide on a place to hide out with Maci. I'm going to start looking harder at the ob-gyn angle. How did he know you guys were going there?"

Brax froze. "We were talking about it here at the office before you went."

Luke and Chance froze too. If the killer had heard their plans, that meant he was either using a parabolic mic or had planted a bug in the office.

His brothers had realized the same thing. They all started searching for hidden recording devices in the office.

They found three.

Chance tilted his head toward the back door, and they went out into the alley so they could talk without being heard.

"Planted bugs means the person was in our office,"

Chance said. "He would know about Mom and Dad's house. I've got to get Maci out of there right away."

"Okay, we'll look into moving the office to a secondary location until we can make sure it's clean," Luke said.

"Good news is, this narrows down our pool of suspects quite a bit," Brax said. "There's only been a half a dozen of Dorian's team members here over the past few weeks. It's got to be one of them. I'll call him."

Chance was about to nod when Dorian's parting words when they left LeBlanc's building came back to him.

He's messed with the mother of your unborn child.

The curse that fell from Chance's mouth was vile. Both brothers turned to stare at him.

"Did you guys tell anybody at LeBlanc's office that Maci is pregnant?" he asked.

"Hell no," Luke said. "We didn't even tell Mom and Dad."

"It's Dorian," Chance whispered. "He's the killer. He knew Maci was pregnant today when he shouldn't have."

All three men sprinted back inside to cut to the front door and get to their vehicles. Chance had his phone in his hand and was dialing Nicholas LeBlanc.

"Patterson," LeBlanc answered. "Unless you have some sort of—"

"Lock down your building," Chance cut him off. "Do it right now."

Locking down the building would keep Dorian trapped inside.

"What? Why would—"

"Do it!" Chance yelled.

He heard LeBlanc initiate the lockdown.

"Okay, it's done. In fifteen seconds no one will be able to get in or out."

"It's Dorian Cane. He's the stalker. He's not only a stalker, he's a killer—that's what we found out with the other cases."

"That's impossible." LeBlanc's tone was heavy with shock.

"I'll prove it later. Right now, keep your office door locked until the police get there. Don't let Dorian in there with you for any reason." The last thing they needed was a hostage situation.

He could hear LeBlanc clicking at his keyboard. "I don't have to worry about that. Dorian left just a couple of minutes after you did."

Chapter Twenty-Three

It was depressing how little time it took Maci to liquidate nearly every cent she had available to her name. Twenty minutes after leaving Clinton and Sheila's house, she had the cash in hand and was on her way to meet Evelyn.

She parked outside the warehouse address, surprised her mother wasn't there to snatch the money out of Maci's hand like she'd done in the past.

Maci got out of the car and began walking toward the warehouse. This was it. This was the last time she was helping Evelyn in this way. The only thing Maci would be willing to help pay for from now on would be some sort of rehab.

"Evelyn?" Maci didn't know where her mom was, but she needed to get back to the Pattersons' house before they discovered she was gone. "Come on, Mom. I don't have time for this."

She called Evelyn's phone but got no answer. She got all the way to the warehouse before deciding to turn back. There was no way she was going into an abandoned warehouse by herself, and for whatever reason Evelyn wasn't here.

She turned and shrieked when she found a man behind her. Fortunately, she recognized him quickly.

"Dorian Cane, right? Oh, my gosh, you scared me."

He smiled. "Sorry, wasn't my intent."

"Oh, no. Did Chance send you to get me?" Damn it, had he already figured out she was gone? She was in so much trouble.

"Um, yes. Chance sent me. Wanted me to escort you somewhere safe. Things have escalated."

She nodded. "Rich, right? Ends up he's a killer, not just a stalker."

"Yes, Rich. Fooled us all. Chance really didn't want you out here alone and… I was close by, so I offered to come get you."

"I was supposed to meet my mother. You haven't seen an older lady around, have you?"

"No, I haven't. We should go."

"Yeah, I'm sure Chance wants to yell at me as soon as possible too."

Dorian smiled. "Only because he cares. I understand that."

They began walking back toward the cars.

"Yeah, you two are probably cut from the same cloth. It's what makes you good at your jobs."

"Yes, this job is a battle. Getting to know Chance and the other Patterson brothers has certainly made me a better me. I've always strived to be the best."

Maci tensed at his words. They were way too similar to the notes that had been left. She stopped.

"You know what? I should probably make one more

sweep to be certain my mom's not here. Do you mind waiting just a second?"

There was no way she was getting into a vehicle with Dorian until she talked to Chance. Maybe she was being paranoid, but under the circumstances, that could be forgiven.

She forced a smile at Dorian. "Just hang out here for two minutes. I'll be right back." She turned back toward the warehouse. "Mom? You here?"

She walked, calling for Evelyn as she pulled her phone out. She was just hitting Chance's number when a soft voice spoke behind her.

"You're not a pale imitation at all, are you?"

Maci tried to breathe through the terror. This was the voice from that night at the apartment when she'd been knocked unconscious.

Dorian was definitely the killer.

She turned to face him again. "You. Why?"

"Someone has to be the best. Learning how to stalk, learning how to kill... It made me the best security expert available."

"But you're Stella's stalker. How can you be the best at protecting someone when you're the one putting her in danger?"

"I never planned to hurt Stella—she's not worth the time or effort. I wasn't even her real stalker at first. I eliminated him early on and took over. Especially once Nicholas brought in the Pattersons. I quickly realized how much I could learn by going up against them. And knew I could up the ante when I targeted someone they cared so much about... *You*."

Maci took a few steps backward, trying to figure out what to say. "I'm just their employee."

He tsked and shook his head. "You're the mother of Chance Patterson's child. He would burn the world to the ground to get you back. His brothers would hold the matches for him."

"I'm not going with you."

Dorian smiled and slowly pulled up his pants leg at the calf, showing some sort of knife holder. "I don't think you're going to have a choice."

Without another word, Maci spun and ran. She didn't make it far before Dorian's arms wrapped around her from behind, stopping her progress. At least he didn't have the knife out yet.

She remembered what Chance had taught her in their training. She used her legs to kick back, aiming for his knees, groin, whatever. Dorian let out a curse as her foot connected to a sensitive spot and let her go.

She dropped her phone in the skirmish but didn't stop to pick it up. She sprinted as hard as she could for the warehouse.

She knew if Dorian got her into his car, she and her baby would be his next victims.

"What do you mean she's not there?"

Chance was ready to put his fist through a wall. He'd called Maci's phone half a dozen times, and each time it had gone directly to voice mail.

"We all thought she was taking a nap," Weston said. "She left a note on the pillow saying she needed to meet her mom and would be right back."

He'd already explained that Dorian was a killer and law enforcement had an APB out for his arrest.

That wouldn't help if he already had Maci.

The door to the office opened and Chance turned to bark that they were closed. "I'll call you back," he said to Weston when he saw who it was.

Evelyn Ford. And she had seen better days.

He rushed to her and helped her sit down. She had blood seeping from a head wound. "Mrs. Ford, where's Maci? What happened?"

His brothers rushed in to see what was going on, but remained silent.

"I needed money. She was supposed to meet me about a half hour ago."

"She didn't show up?"

"I don't know. Some man saw me, said he worked with you. Offered to give me the money I needed to pay back my dealer."

Chance grabbed a file and showed her a picture of Dorian. "This man?"

"Yes, that's him. I thought I was doing Maci a favor, not taking her money. You know, so she could save it for the baby. But then the guy knocked me on the head and dragged me into an alley."

"Evelyn, where's Maci? Her phone is offline, so we can't track it. I've got to find her."

"Guy left me with the money. I paid someone a hundred of it to get me here. I needed to tell you that my dealer may be coming after you."

He didn't understand what she was talking about and didn't have time to get her to explain.

"Evelyn, listen to me. My brothers and I can handle any drug dealer. We'll get you someplace safe so he can't hurt you either. But if you know where Maci is, you need to tell me right now."

Every second they wasted gave Dorian more time to hurt Maci.

"I was supposed to meet her at the warehouse district. I needed the money to pay back Timothy, my dealer. I promise I didn't mean any of those things I said to Maci." Evelyn started to cry.

He and Maci were going to have a talk—*again*—about the things she was keeping from him. But he needed to find her first.

"Where, Evelyn? Focus."

She got out the address.

"I'll stay with her and make sure no drug dealers do whatever she was talking about," Brax said. "I'll get PD there immediately too."

"Give us five minutes. Sirens may spook him into hurting her."

Brax nodded and Chance sprinted for his car, Luke on his heels.

MOST OF THE warehouses in this section of town had been abandoned years ago after a storm had caused massive flood damage. Maci could scream, but there probably wouldn't be anyone around to hear her.

And screaming at this point would tell Dorian exactly where she was.

She found an open door and rushed into a building. Hiding was her best option. It was dark in here, the only light from an emergency exit sign near another door at the side.

She ran for the far corner, zigzagging around various piles of crates and abandoned machinery. The door behind her opened and closed, and there was silence.

Maci struggled to hear anything over the pounding of her own heart.

The most important thing is to keep your head. Use your strengths.

She could hear Chance's voice in her mind. He was right. If she panicked, this was over.

"Now, now, Maci," Dorian taunted. "I love a good game of hide-and-seek, but this isn't your style, is it? You're more of a confronting things head-on type of gal, aren't you?"

She wasn't about to answer and give away her position. She needed to make her way around to the other door and try to get out.

He flipped on a phone flashlight, and she jerked her head back behind the crate she hid behind. The light would give Dorian more of an advantage.

"Do you understand the need to be the best at something, Maci? I was the best in my platoon until a stray bullet ended that part of my life. Do you know what it is to have the thing that is most important to you snatched away?"

Like a murderer trying to end you and your unborn child's lives? Yeah, I do, asswipe.

How she longed to say the words out loud.

"Then I had to find a new career pathway on which to be the best. Private security fit the bill."

He got quiet after that and the light switched off. She crept farther away from where she'd last heard his voice, keeping her body low and small.

"I've killed nine women."

Maci struggled to keep her surprised gasp silent. He was trying to get a reaction from her—any indication of her location.

"But listen, Maci, before you think bad of me... I did it for a purpose. Do you understand? With every woman I killed I became better at personal security. I learned more about how killers thought and what could be done to protect someone from a killer. Those women's deaths had *meaning*."

He was a complete psychopath. Could see no wrong in what he'd done.

The flashlight switched back on, aimed for where she'd been just a few moments ago. Damn it, he was expecting her to stay low to the ground. She needed to get higher, climb on some of the machinery all over this place. Dorian hadn't shone any light up there at all.

You're smart. A quick thinker. Use that to your advantage.

She found some debris on the ground—a piece of metal that had broken off something—and grabbed it. She threw it with all her might in the opposite direction of where she planned to go.

Then she scurried up onto what seemed to be some sort of bottling equipment piece, careful not to make any noise. That allowed her to move onto a conveyer belt a few feet higher that held her weight easily.

Dorian's light switched off once again when he heard

the noise. When it came back on, it wasn't pointed in the direction she'd hoped. It was right where she'd been five seconds ago.

If he pointed his light up now, she would be caught.

She swallowed her whimper.

The light switched off again. "Your death will have meaning too, Maci. So will the Patterson brothers'. I can't leave them alive. Leaving your enemy alive means you always have to be looking over your shoulder."

She held still. He was waiting for her to make a mistake. The slightest one and she'd be dead.

"Your mother too, probably, if she doesn't take care of that herself. She's got a pretty severe drug habit, you know. Was more than happy to take the money I gave her, although was probably less happy when I knocked her unconscious. I traced her phone. That's how I found you."

Maci had to push thoughts of her mother aside. She had to push everything aside but this moment.

Survival is always the most important thing.

She was going to survive. She had too much to live for not to.

The light came back on, once again looking in hidden corners and in low places to hide. It wouldn't take much longer for him to figure out she wasn't down there.

But in the silence, she heard the most beautiful sound: sirens.

The light switched off again. "Looks like the game has changed, Maci, and we won't be able to finish today. What a shame. But don't worry, I'll be back for you. For all of you. I'm the best, so you can count on that."

In that moment Maci knew she couldn't let Dorian

leave. He was telling the truth: he would be back. And one by one the people she loved would fall to his madness. Including her daughter. Maci had no doubt Dorian would hunt her too, even if it took years.

Maci could stop this right now. She *had* to stop it right now. Even if it cost her everything.

She stretched out her hand and found a small metal pipe. It wouldn't be much against that knife he'd taunted her with earlier, but she just needed to stop him long enough for the police to get here. The sirens were getting louder.

She shut everything out and listened for Dorian. As he passed under her she grit her teeth and let herself fall off the side of the conveyor belt on top of him.

Light flashed inside the warehouse from the far door as she fell, but she ignored it. She would only get one chance at this.

She landed hard on Dorian, swinging her pipe and yelling as loud as she could to let the police know where they were. She got two hits in before a blow to her face threw her backward.

She tried to get back to her feet but he was already over her, knife in hand. He grabbed the pipe out of her hand and threw it to the side, then pulled her up by her shirt.

"I am the best," he said simply.

He slashed the knife toward her chest, and she knew this was the end. She closed her eyes, waiting for the pain, distraught that she'd failed. Devastated she'd never told Chance she loved him.

But the pain never came.

She heard multiple cracks of thunder over the roaring around her but didn't open her eyes.

"Maci! Maci, open your eyes, baby. Come on."

Chance? She could barely hear him.

"Stop screaming, sweetheart. It's okay. I've got you. Dorian is dead."

All that noise was coming from *her*. She hadn't even realized it. She closed her mouth and silence surrounded them.

"Are you okay? Did he hurt you?" Chance was frantically pressing his hands all over her body, searching for wounds.

Luke was standing over Dorian, weapon raised. Dorian wasn't moving.

"I'm okay," she managed to get out. "I'm okay. I had to stop him. He was going to hurt you. Hurt everyone. I couldn't let him—"

Chance's lips pressed hard against hers and he pulled her against his chest.

"You did it. Dorian Cane will never hurt anybody ever again."

Chapter Twenty-Four

Three weeks later

"No, don't you dare touch me, Chance Patterson! If we are late to family dinner everyone will know what we've been doing."

Chance grinned from where he was stalking Maci in the kitchen of his house, loving the way she laughed as she threw her arms out in front of herself to keep him away.

As if she could keep him away.

As if anything was ever going to keep him away from her again.

He grabbed one wrist and used it to yank her closer. "We both took a full week off work and locked ourselves in this house without talking to anyone. I'm pretty sure everyone knows what we've been doing."

But they'd needed it. They'd needed a chance to decompress after what had happened with Dorian. Needed a chance to rest and be with each other.

Chance had definitely needed the opportunity to hold Maci close to him and reassure himself that she and the baby were really okay.

That could've so easily not have been the case.

Getting to Maci at that warehouse had been the longest twenty minutes of his life. Kicking open that door and watching her drop down onto a serial killer? Watching Dorian lift that knife to end her life?

Even knowing he and Luke had each plugged three bullets into Dorian, he would have nightmares about the image until the day he died.

Nicholas and Stella LeBlanc had been traumatized too by the thought that someone they'd trusted had been so evil. Stella had then figured out how to use it to become even more popular on social media.

Maci pressed her lips against his. "We can't be late. Mom is going to be there."

It was a first step for Evelyn, one they were delighted she was taking. She was a long way from kicking her drug habit, but joining them for dinner was at least a step in the right direction. Hopefully they would be able to show her some rehab options and she'd agree to treatment.

Maci had made it clear to Evelyn that if she wanted to be a part of the baby's life, she was going to need to be clean. They would help her as much as they could, but ultimately the choice had to be Evelyn's.

He kissed Maci tenderly. He'd kissed her so often over the past few weeks that they both should've been tired of it by now, but neither of them could get enough.

"I love you," she whispered. He would never get tired of hearing her say it.

"I love you too." And he would never get tired of saying it back.

He planned to do it every day for the rest of their lives.

Epilogue

One year later

Sheila Patterson's favorite place to be had always been the kitchen. As a child, it had been the heart of her parents' home, and she'd been determined to make it the heart of her own as well.

Though their usual Sunday dinner was still hours away, the house was already overrun with family.

Weston and Kayleigh had arrived first, their arms loaded down with drinks and snack packs for the kids. Instead of offering to cook, which wasn't always her strong suit, Kayleigh had kept Sheila company, talking all about her newest photography series and how Weston had transformed yet another elderly neighbor's garden into a little piece of paradise.

Sheila listened as Kayleigh spoke about her husband with pride, peeking up from food prep occasionally to see her son glancing at his wife, their eyes equally full of love and devotion. It soothed something in her to see her quietest child find the love of his life.

Halfway through an anecdote that involved a rampaging Weston and a mole he couldn't catch, Brax, Tessa and Walker arrived. The moment Walker saw his favorite auntie, Kayleigh's attention had been stolen, but Sheila didn't mind. She'd sat Tessa on a stool in the kitchen and talked baby names while sneaking her treats before dinner.

Tessa and Brax were pregnant with another boy, and the way Brax looked at her...it was like no one else existed when she was in the room. Like she was the light his life had always needed. And Walker? He was overjoyed at the idea of a baby brother to play with.

Luke and Claire's arrival was followed by much shrieking from Walker once he saw they'd brought their Maine coon cat, Kahn. Claire, once shy and quiet around them all, immediately began telling a story of a second cat they were adopting. Luke kept a firm arm around her waist, his eyes brimming with love too.

Sheila was putting the final touches on everyone's favorite potpie when the sound of cheers told her the last of her family had arrived. First through the door, Maci was glowing, even though little Autumn was five months old and had barely slept since she'd arrived earth side.

Still, there was a calmness that motherhood—and Chance—had brought Sheila's final daughter-in-law. A peace that had allowed her to settle into the family and really open herself up to the rest of the Patterson clan.

Evelyn had joined too. It hadn't been an easy road, and there had been more than one setback, but the woman was trying. For her daughter, for her granddaughter.

But most importantly, for herself.

Sheila looked around the chaos and couldn't help but

smile. Her family was here, made up of every skin tone and bound together by love.

Clinton wrapped his arm around her waist and pressed a kiss to her neck. "Remember how distraught we were when they told us we would never have children? Did you ever imagine we'd have this?"

Sheila took a look around at the sounds of yelling and laughter, the mess of toys already spilling out from the living room, the crush of bodies crowded into the kitchen.

Not only did she have four sons, but she'd gained four daughters.

She had a family that was happy, healthy and so full of love you could see it the second you walked into the room.

"No," she told Clinton, burrowing farther into the comfort of his embrace. "I would've never imagined this. But the reality is so much better."

* * * * *

CHASING A
COLTON KILLER

DEBORAH FLETCHER MELLO

To Carly Silver,
thank you for trusting me, encouraging me,
and pushing me out of my comfort zone.
I miss working with you.

Chapter One

The noise in the newsroom of the *New York Wire* rose to stadium-grade level, sounding like the last touchdown cheers of a winning football game. Reporters, editors and photographers were all shouting over one another, each desperate to make a point or get dibs in on a perspective story. It was chaos. Organized chaos but chaos nonetheless.

Stella Maxwell stepped into the space dubbed the "war room," having just left an early morning meeting with the editorial team. It wasn't even eleven o'clock in the morning, and she'd already put in five hours of work. Now her head hurt.

She stared at the computer on her desk. The screen saver was a quote by Joseph Pulitzer that read, "The power to mold the future of the republic will be in the hands of the journalists of future generations."

There was a time she believed that, but with each passing day, she was starting to think that the future lay in the hands of rogue teenagers who trolled the internet, spurned authority and put all their trust in the almighty dollar. She hated teenagers. In fact, she had a strong dislike for most children in general. Most especially since being assigned a story on dangerous TikTok challenges happening in New York City public schools. If the little demons weren't blowing up each other, they were blowing up someone's property.

Stella thought the future looked bleak if left in the hands of younger iGens, who had no boundaries and believed the entire world owed them a pass for simply breathing. Yes, she said it. To herself, of course. Now to figure out how to convey that message in a quarter page piece with her byline and not insult those people who actually liked the little monsters.

Working for the *New York Wire* was not Stella's job du jour. It paid the bills, but truth be told, it left her less than satisfied. Although she loved journalism and put every ounce of herself into all of her assignments, she would have preferred to be writing for the *New York Times* or the *Washington Post*, newspapers with better visibility and more credibility. Publications that were worthy of the substantial talent she brought to the table. She considered her current job a stepping stone to bigger and better, her career of choice eventually netting her Pulitzer gold. She suddenly laughed aloud, drawing looks from the men sitting in the cubicles beside her.

"What's so funny?" Garrett Hoffman asked. He was the pop culture editor, and they often lunched together while bouncing stories off one another.

Stella shook her head. "If I don't laugh, I'm going to cry. It's starting to be that kind of week."

"Can I help?" the young man asked, eyeing her with bright baby blue eyes and thick lashes the color of corn silk.

Shrugging her shoulders, Stella blew a soft sigh. "Just pray for me. I'm headed to PS 41 down in Greenwich Village later today to interview a gang of middle schoolers."

"Have you brushed up on your cool kid jargon so you don't come off old?"

"I am old. I'm about to be thirty, and in their eyes, that's ancient!"

"Exactly, which is why you need to know how to talk their lingo. Otherwise, those little monsters will eat you alive!"

The duo laughed.

"What are you working on?" Stella questioned. She leaned back in her chair, rocking slowly back and forth.

"Waiting for confirmation on a Kim and Kanye reconciliation."

"That will never happen!"

"Says you!"

"And Kim! She's had her rebound fling with Pete What's-his-name, and now she's ready to move on to something more serious. She's not going back to babysit her past mistakes."

"And if she does?"

"You'll be writing another breakup story in six months."

"And people say I need to get my life together." He sighed heavily.

Stella laughed again. The phone on her desk rang, the unexpected chime startling her ever so slightly.

Garrett laughed at her again. "It looks like duty is calling you!"

"With my luck, it'll be a wrong number," Stella said

as she reached for the receiver and pulled it to her ear. "Thank you for calling the *Wire*. This is Stella Maxwell."

"There's a man being murdered in the alley behind your building."

Stella bristled. "Excuse me? Who is this?"

"He'll be dead if you don't come now," the caller said. "Can you save him, Stella?"

Stella didn't recognize the voice and found it difficult to distinguish whether it was male or female. There was the faintest hint of digitization, and she knew, whoever the caller was, they were masking their sound with a voice modifier. With the many free apps that could be downloaded and used during gaming or phone calls, they had the ability to make a person sound deeper, higher or even like the opposite sex. For all Stella knew, the caller could have been anyone.

She asked again, the barest hint of anxiety in her own tone. "Who the hell is this? And why are you calling me?"

"I guess you don't want the story," the caller said, and then they disconnected the line.

Stella stared at the phone receiver for a brief second before dropping it back down on the cradle.

"What's up?" Garrett questioned.

"I'm not sure if I'm being pranked or tossed a story I can scoop," she said as she rose swiftly from her seat, grabbing her purse and her cell phone.

"Where are you going?"

"To check out a tip," she said, hurrying to the elevator. She shouted over her shoulder. "I'll call you later!"

As she rode the elevator down to the first floor, the

phone chimed, signaling an incoming text message. The message reiterated what the caller had just told her.

There's a man being murdered in the alley beside your building. Can you save him? Come now or he'll die on your watch, Stella!

Stepping out of the elevator, Stella paused, forwarding the message to a dispatcher friend at the 911 call center. She added the Forty-Seventh Street address and asked her to send a patrol car. Just in case it wasn't a prank.

Dropping her phone back into her handbag, she exited the building, turning toward the corner and the back side of the high-rise office building. People pushed past her, unconcerned as they made their way to their own destinations. It was the city and everyone was in a rush. They ignored her as she ignored them, a single thought on her mind. *Please, God, let this be a prank.*

Rounding the backside of the building, she entered the alley, her eyes skating swiftly back and forth. Her stomach suddenly pitched, her gaze widening as she caught sight of a man lying on the ground, blood beginning to pool beneath his torso. Stella looked around a second time as she inched closer to the body, and then she recognized him, his blue eyes meeting hers. It was Rockwell Henley, the boyfriend who'd dumped her via text message just days earlier.

Stella screamed Rockwell's name as she dropped down beside his body, noting the large butcher knife stuck in his chest. She pulled his head into her lap and cried out for help.

FBI AGENT BRENNAN COLTON had always loved New York City's theater district. The Midtown Manhattan neighborhood between 40th and 54th Streets and 6th and 8th Avenues had always represented the best times and great artistic expression. Just weeks ago, he'd been there with friends to see the musical *& Juliet.* Dinner had followed, the group heading to Nobu Downtown for sashimi and his favorite Wagyu beef served with their warm mushroom salad.

Now, he and patrolmen from the 130th Precinct were walking from theater to theater searching for the next potential victim of a high-profile serial killer. Weeks ago, a man named Mark Welden had been found shot to death in the area of Central Park known as the Ramble. There had been a typed note stuffed in his pocket. That note had announced the murderer's intent to kill in the name of serial killer Maeve O'Leary, a woman known as the Black Widow. O'Leary had recently been captured and charged with killing multiple husbands for financial gain. The murderer declared the objective to kill persons whose initials literally spelled out Maeve's name.

Soon after, a second body was found on the observation deck of the Empire State Building. His name was Andrew Capowski, and he also had a note in his pocket. Edward Pendleton had been murdered at the Met shortly after. With his last note, the killer had teased that he was jumping to the letter L to confuse them. It made no sense, but it was all they had to work with.

FBI profilers had determined the killer was male, deeply troubled and obsessed with a woman he couldn't have. His victims had all been blond, blue-eyed and in their thirties, another detail pointing them toward the killer. Because of the significant sites where the bodies had been found, the media had dubbed him the Landmark Killer.

The last note had been sent to Brennan's cousin Sinead Colton just days earlier. Sinead was also an agent with the FBI, and that note had pointed them toward Broadway as being the sight of the next murder. Brennan had been singularly focused on the forty Broadway theaters that were located on those streets that intersected Broadway in the Times Square area. They'd been searching for employees whose names began with the letter L and fit the physical profile of the previous victims.

Finding the Landmark Killer had become personal, and Brennan was willing to dedicate all his energy to searching out the murderer who'd also added harassing and provoking Colton family members to his list of crimes.

An officer, whose name Brennan had forgotten, suddenly tapped him on the shoulder. He jumped, the touch unexpected, as he'd fallen into deep thought.

"Sorry, Agent Colton, but we just got a call. There's been a murder near here. The sergeant thought you might want to follow us to the crime scene."

"Do they think it's our guy?"

The officer shook his head. "Not sure, sir."

Brennan nodded. He took a deep breath, and as the officer turned an about-face, heading in the opposite direction, he followed after him.

TEARS STREAMED DOWN Stella's face. Sirens sounded in the distance, their harsh ring drawing closer and closer.

The sirens were soon followed by the heavy patter of footsteps rushing in her direction.

"Put your hands up," someone shouted.

"Move away from the body," someone else hollered.

It was only when she heard the familiar click of guns being chambered that she turned to look over her shoulder. At least a dozen of New York's finest were pointing their weapons in her direction. She felt herself bristle, a flood of grief and fear washing over her.

"I didn't do anything," she shouted back. "He needs an ambulance. Please! Someone help him!"

"Move away from the body and put your hands up!" an officer shouted at her a second time.

Stella gently eased Rockwell's head back to the ground. She pushed herself up and onto her feet. As she took a step back, slowly raising her hands up and over her head, Rockwell gasped. She hesitated, wanting to move back to him, and then he uttered her name, the heavy rasp of his voice vibrating through the air.

"Stella… I'm s…s…s… Oh, Stella…"

Her name was a loud whisper blowing past his thin lips. Then he closed his eyes and blew out his last breath.

Stella was suddenly aware of the many guns pointed in her direction. The police were screaming instructions, and fear hit her like a tidal wave. She was a black woman, alone with the dead body of her ex-boyfriend. His blood stained the front of her blue-and-white striped blouse and covered her hands. Things looked differently from how they actually were, and she knew enough to trust that it would only take one nervous cop with a shaky finger on the trigger of his weapon to change the entire trajectory of all their lives.

"I'm not resisting," she cried out, her arms pushed skyward, her hands open and fingers spread. "I didn't do anything. I found him like this. I called for help," she shouted.

An officer eased behind her. He reached for her right arm and pulled it behind her back. He reached for the other, and then secured her wrists with handcuffs. A second uniformed patrolman grabbed her roughly, pushing her far from the body as EMS personnel hurried to Rockwell's side. The cop manhandling her pushed her to the ground, instructing her to take a seat. Someone else started firing questions at her, wanting to know what she knew. The moment was surreal, and Stella felt like she was lost in another dimension, her world suddenly turned on its head and spinning out of control.

"You have the right to remain silent. Anything you say can and will be used against you in a court of law. You have the right to an attorney. If you cannot afford an attorney, one will be appointed for you."

Stella suddenly balked as an officer began to Mirandize her. "Why am I being arrested? I didn't do anything. I found him like that! I'm a reporter with the *New York Wire*!"

BRENNAN TOOK IN his surroundings as he turned into the alley and moved closer to the crime scene. A forensics team and numerous detectives were already surveilling the area, and he turned to stare in Stella's direction as one of the detectives pointed her out as a potential suspect.

Brennan recognized Stella Maxwell from the professional photograph that always accompanied her byline at the newspaper she worked for. That photo didn't do her justice, because the young woman was breathtaking, in spite of her frazzled expression and the blood splatter on her clothes. He felt something pitch hard in his midsection as he stared, and a loud gasp blew past his thin lips. He ignored the fact that Stella Maxwell had been trying to reach him for weeks now, wanting a comment or interview about his progress with finding the Landmark Killer. He had sent her calls to voice mail and her emails to his trash bin. He had neither needed nor wanted any media attention on the serial killer who was proving to be so elusive.

Now, sitting there, she looked dazed, her teary expression pulling at his heartstrings. He found himself wanting to pull her close, to ease his arms around her torso and comfort her. The rush of emotion was unsettling and totally out of his character. Most especially since he had no idea how she was connected to the dead man now lying under a green tarp.

Stella suddenly called his name, screaming for his attention. "Agent Brennan Colton? Excuse me! Agent Colton, it's me, Stella Maxwell! Stella Maxwell with the *New York Wire*! We've been playing phone tag!"

Brennan took a deep breath as he turned in her direction. He sauntered slowly to where she was sitting. Her expression lifted, an air of anticipation washing over her face. There was something like hope that misted her large brown eyes. Something that punched him hard in the gut and took his breath away.

"Agent Colton, would you tell them who I am, please," Stella pleaded, those damn eyes of hers imploring him to step in and save her.

Brennan took a deep breath. He exhaled slowly, staring at her intently. "I'm sorry, Ms. Maxwell. I'm sure things will get sorted out down at the station." He turned abruptly, moving toward the detectives who were evaluating the case that had landed in their laps. As he walked away, he found himself feeling like a complete schmuck and not the decent guy his parents had raised.

Minutes later, Stella was settled in the back seat of a patrol car. The muscles in her face had tightened, and she looked as if she might explode. She glared in his direction, and he was suddenly unsettled. His instincts told him she had nothing to do with the murder, but he had no jurisdiction over this investigation. He needed to take a step back while the NYPD did their job. He couldn't afford to make waves with the department. Not as long as he needed their help to find the killer he was after.

Chapter Two

Daggers of ice shot from Stella's eyes as the patrol car pulled out of the alleyway and into midday traffic. Brennan Colton was staring as they took her away, and if she could have told him exactly what she thought about him, it would not have been pretty.

The elusive federal agent had been dodging her efforts to reach him for over a month. She had done everything short of showing up at his front door wearing a clown suit and pretending to be a singing telegram to get his attention. And all she wanted were answers to a few questions that could potentially lead to an award-winning article. Him eluding her was one thing, but for the man to blatantly disregard her cries for help when he could have easily vouched for her was another.

She sat back in the patrol car, fighting not to cry. A tidal wave of emotion was consuming her. It was an imbalance of feelings that had left her completely offsides. She was frightened and sad and angry, and she wasn't sure where to put it all. Someone had killed Rockwell Henley, and although the two had no longer been in a relationship, she had still cared about the man. Even worse, there were those who now assumed because she'd been there, then she must have done it. Such was so far south from the truth that she couldn't imagine anyone thinking she could be guilty.

She and Rockwell had dated for over a year. They'd been good together, until they hadn't been. Rockwell had come from a prominent New York family. His father had been a top political analyst before retiring, and his mother was a world-renowned visual artist. The couple traveled in elite circles, and they'd had grand plans for their only son. His parents had never really liked her, believing that Rockwell could do better, considering their position in high society. They hadn't been shy about showing their disdain for her, tolerating her presence in their son's life because he'd given them no choice.

Rockwell had attended all the right schools. Phillips Exeter Academy for high school, Columbia University for his undergraduate studies and Harvard Law School for his juris doctorate. He'd built a thriving legal firm and had been a rising political star. When he'd announced his candidacy for Governor, Stella had stood dutifully by his side, despite his mother's wish for her to find a hole and fall into it.

Things went left after that. One too many missed fundraisers, and Rockwell had suddenly felt she was too obsessed with her own job to be the woman he needed by his side. Stella hadn't been willing to play the role of a dutiful political wife and partner. Rockwell's eventual quest for the White House was supposed to take priority over her dreams of winning a Pulitzer Prize.

Sadly, letting the relationship go and saying good-bye

to Rockwell hadn't been as hard as she'd expected. The moment had been heartbreaking, but then she'd been over it just as quickly as it had taken him to write the text message calling an end to their relationship.

There had been no animosity between them. He'd gone his way and she'd gone hers. Although she hadn't anticipated running into him, since he ran in circles that didn't necessarily include her, she knew they could be cordial with each other if they ever did. They'd made good memories during their time together, and she had truly wished him well. Now her heart hurt for the loss, never imagining when she woke that morning that she would have to mourn his passing.

Stella looked up to find one of the officers staring at her. She stared back, snapping in his direction. "What?" she questioned, her eyes wide and seeping with rage.

The man shrugged but didn't bother to respond. He shot his partner a look, the two men cackling as if she'd said something funny. The driver's gaze shifted to his side mirrors, and then he refocused his attention back to the road and the steady flow of traffic.

Stella turned to stare out the window. She couldn't believe this was happening to her. How could anyone believe that she, Stella Maxwell, was capable of killing anyone? She was always kind and gracious to people. Rarely did she not get along with anyone. Stella made friends with everyone she met. Singularly focused on her career, Stella had worked too hard to get to where she was in the industry to just throw it all away over a relationship that had soured. Someone was setting her up. Someone wanted it to look like she had murdered Rock-

well. Someone who knew about the two of them. Someone determined to put Stella through hell.

Although she had bumped heads with people on multiple occasions to get a story, she couldn't begin to fathom
who would go to such extremes to do this to her. Who had
she pissed off, and why were they seeking retribution?

The patrol car pulled into the side parking garage of
the 130th precinct. They were in Midtown Manhattan,
on Forty-Second Street, near Lexington Avenue and the
Grand Central Station. The entrance led them to an un-
derground space where prisoners were routinely filtered
into and out of the building, either headed to court or inside to booking.

The cop who'd been staring at her opened the rear door
and gestured for her to get out. He was a slim man, his
blue uniform pristine. His dark military haircut framed
a round face riddled with acne scars. His cheeks were
chipmunk round, as if they were stuffed with acorns.
His head was almost bulbous, in comparison to his body
frame, seeming too large for his neck, and his dark eyes
were a degree from being ice cold.

"I want to speak with your superior," Stella quipped
as he grabbed her arm and escorted her toward a large
metal door. "And I need to make a telephone call."

The man laughed again, tossing a look around the
room. "You'll get your chance," he said finally.

Inside, she was pushed into a chair and told to wait
her turn. The room was overcrowded and loud. The dank
smell of unwashed bodies saturated her nostrils. For a
brief moment, she thought she might vomit, and then she

didn't. She muttered under her breath, "Why is this happening? I didn't do anything!"

The woman beside her laughed. "Honey, we are all innocent. I didn't do anything either." She paused. "Except shoot that bitch for messing with my Harry. No one messes with my Harry. Not on my watch."

"You shot her? Dead?"

"No! In the foot!" The woman laughed, her brunette curls shaking like jelly rolls atop her head. "It was just a flesh wound. I don't know why they're making such a big deal out of it."

"Maybe because you shot her," Stella said sarcastically.

The woman bristled. "Aren't you all high and mighty? I heard them whispering about you offing your boyfriend."

"I didn't *off* my boyfriend!"

"Well, since we're both headed to Rikers, I imagine whatever you did is just as bad as me shooting Harry's whore in the foot."

Stella's eyes widened. "Rikers? I'm not going to Rikers!" she said, shaking her head vehemently.

The woman laughed at her again. "We all go to Rikers," she said nonchalantly.

Stella jumped from her seat, moving toward the counter at the front of the room.

An officer held out his arm, his other hand resting on the weapon at his waistband. "Sit down!" he shouted.

Tears pressed hot against Stella's lids. "I really need to make a call," she said. "There's been a horrible mistake."

"I said...sit...down!" The man snapped at her, taking a step in her direction.

"It's okay," a voice said, the firm tone vibrating

through the room. "Escort Miss Maxwell to an interrogation room, please."

Stella turned to see a woman in the doorway staring at her, her vibrant green eyes serious and intense. She was petite in stature but clearly had a large presence at the station. Her dark hair was cut in a cute pixie style, and she wore a white blouse, khaki slacks and a shiny silver badge clipped to her belt. She gestured with her head and the other officer nodded.

"Yes, ma'am, Detective Colton."

Stella's brow raised. "Colton? Are you..." she started to say, curiosity perched on the tip of her tongue.

The officer grabbed her arm, stalling the question she was trying to formulate and ask. He pulled Stella forward and led her away in the opposite direction.

THEY WERE BEING too nice to her, Stella thought, feeling like the last hour was only the calm before the storm to come. A uniformed officer had allowed her to use the restroom and had brought her a glass of ice water. They'd offered her a cup of coffee and a sandwich and had finally removed the handcuffs that had begun to cut off her circulation. She rubbed at her wrists, her gaze moving to the large two-way mirror that made up one wall.

Stella wondered who was on the other side and why they were waiting to speak with her. She was past ready to be done with all of this so she could head home. Home was calling her. Loudly. Home was where she found peace and tranquility and could shut the world away without feeling guilty. She needed to be home if she was going to survive the day without really killing someone. She blew a heavy sigh and pushed herself from the table, beginning to pace the room.

Another hour passed before the door swung open and two plainclothes detectives entered the room. One reminded her of Pat Sajak from the game show *Wheel of Fortune*. The other was a dead ringer for Peter Griffin from the adult cartoon *Family Guy*. He had the same exaggerated chin, a bulging neckline, a beer belly and chocolate brown hair cut into a low beanie. Stella eyed them both with reservation, her gaze sweeping from one to the other.

"Ms. Maxwell, please, have a seat," the Peter Griffin doppelganger said. He nodded his head toward the chair she'd occupied minutes before. "Sorry to keep you waiting. My name is Detective Voorhies, and this is Detective Palmer."

The man named Palmer tossed her a slight wave of his hand. "We were hoping you'd be ready to make a statement so we can get you out of here."

Stella's gaze narrowed. "I was ready to get out of here hours ago, which is why I made a statement before I was dragged in here." Her voice rose an octave. "I have nothing to hide, Detective! I've shown you my phone and the text message that came in saying a man was being murdered. You can trace the telephone call that came into my office right before that. I've told you everything I know! At this point, all I can do is repeat myself. Again."

Detective Palmer forced a smile on his face. "Although we can appreciate your enthusiasm, we hope that you understand that under the circumstances, we do have protocols we need to follow." He scribbled something across the top of a sheet of paper. "Can you confirm your address for me?"

There was a moment's hesitation as Stella considered his request. Stella knew the routine. She knew they'd process her background information first, insuring she was who she said she was. She knew they would need to confirm her pedigree before they processed her arrest. She was also fully aware that anything she said, either orally or in writing, would go straight to the prosecutor, and its admissibility could derail any defense if they were ever to go to trial. She had no doubt that promising her she could go home was a ploy to get a confession out of her.

"Do you have a suspect?" she asked instead. "Any idea who might have done this?"

Detective Voorhies leaned back in his chair, crossing his arms over his belly. "We're interested in knowing what you think. I understand from Mr. Henley's mother that you and he recently ended a relationship. She says he broke up with you. I imagine that might have made you mad."

"You imagine wrong," she said, a hint of snark in her tone. "We had both agreed that it was for the best."

"You sure about that? I understand there were some heated text messages between you and the victim."

Stella felt her cheeks redden. Knowing that the last conversation between her and Rockwell was now being leveraged against her was embarrassing. And infuriating. She had no doubt that his mother couldn't wait to tell them it had all been her fault.

Palmer chimed in with his two cents. "Look at it from our perspective, Ms. Maxwell. You had motive, opportunity and means. You were the only one in that alley with the victim, and your fingerprints were on the murder weapon. So let's not play this game. Just tell us what happened. Was it a moment of passion? Were you two arguing? We'd understand if things went left when you were just trying to have a conversation with Mr. Henley."

Stella felt her entire body tense. She'd flinched, and she was certain it hadn't gone unnoticed. She shook her head vehemently. "There's no way my fingerprints are on the murder weapon," she snapped. "I never touched that knife!"

"Really, Ms. Maxwell. Let's not do this. You're going to have to tell us something. We will find out the truth."

Stella met the smug look the man was giving her. "I'd like an attorney," she said, sitting back in her own chair.

Detective Voorhies shot his partner a look. "That's fine, but all we want to know is—"

Stella pushed her palm toward his face, interrupting him. "I don't give a rat's ass what you want to know. I want my attorney," she said harshly.

Voorhies suddenly looked like a fish out of water, his mouth opening and then closing as if he needed to suck in air. He stood and Palmer followed his lead. "That's fine. We were willing to work with you, but if you—"

"Why are you still talking?" Stella snapped. "I said I want my attorney. That's the end of our conversation, or are you purposely planning to violate my rights?"

The man's expression was somber as the duo turned from her and made their way out the door. As it closed behind them, Stella turned her attention toward the two-way mirror, staring as if she could see who was standing on the other side. She suddenly grabbed the Styrofoam cup filled with water and flung it at the glass with every ounce of energy she could muster.

"Is that your best?" she raged. "You're going to need to do better than those two bozos!"

She paused, seeming to wait for something, or someone, to respond. Finally, she shook her head. "I didn't kill him," she said, her voice dropping to a loud whisper. "I didn't do it!"

Chapter Three

Rory Colton tossed her cousin Brennan a look. "Don't you dare laugh," she quipped. "If you laugh, I will hurt you."

Brennan held up his hands as if he were surrendering. "Did they really think they could break her?" he asked.

His cousin shook her head. "Who the hell knows what those two were thinking?"

The duo stood on the other side of that two-way mirror eyeing Stella. After her outburst, she'd paced the room for a good ten minutes before dropping back into the chair. Her arms were folded over her chest defiantly. Her expression was cold.

"What's your gut tell you?" Rory asked, turning to study her cousin's expression.

"She didn't do it."

"Her fingerprints are on the weapon. How do you explain that?"

Brennan shrugged. "I can't. But then I'm not investigating this case. Not officially."

"Like I need one more thing on my plate," Rory muttered.

"I know the feeling," Brennan said. He thought about

his own case and his need to get the Landmark Killer off the streets. The muscles in his face pulled into a deep frown.

Rory gave him a nod. "Well, you know we'll do everything we can here to help you out."

"I appreciate that. I really do."

There was suddenly a knock on the door. The two looked up as the entrance opened and one of the station's secretaries gestured for Rory's attention.

"I'll be back," Rory said, excusing herself from the room. "Try to stay out of trouble while I'm gone, please."

Brennan chuckled softly. "When do I ever get in trouble?"

As the door closed after Rory, Brennan turned his attention back to the woman in the other room. The smile that had been on his face fell into another sober frown. She was still sitting, staring out into space as she waited patiently for the NYPD to decide what they planned to do with her. If he could have carried the weight she was shouldering, he would have done so gladly. He would have done almost anything to put a smile on her face. He suddenly felt as if he'd fallen down and hit his head, every ounce of sanity gone from him.

Even in her sadness, she was still stunning. She drew her fingers through the length of her hair, the dark black strands falling past her shoulders. Her crystal complexion was a warm pecan, and she wore the barest hint of makeup. Her features were sculpted, complementing dark brown eyes, full pouty lips and a near-perfect button nose.

She stood and began to pace the room one more time. She was tall and willowy, definitely more leg than torso, he thought. She moved with the grace of a professional ballet dancer, and there was something almost ethereal about her presence. Standing there watching her, he was slightly mesmerized, unable to shift his gaze from her. But his thoughts were elsewhere, unable to focus on anything other than what he'd been sent there to investigate.

Although he wasn't privy to all the details about the murder Stella had been accused of, Brennan knew enough to say the death of political candidate Rockwell Henley was in no way connected to those of the Landmark Killer. He didn't fit the profile, and that killer had been meticulous about staying on script. This was something else, and now it too was consuming his thoughts.

Rory returned minutes later. "We need to cut her loose," she said, gesturing for him to follow after her.

"What's up?" Brennan questioned.

"We have an eyewitness to the murder. And video tape that clears Ms. Maxwell of any wrongdoing."

"I may need to see that video tape," Brennan said as he headed toward the door behind her.

Rory shook her head. "How did I know you were going to say that?" she said.

STELLA WAS READY to blow a gasket when the door swung open and the Colton woman from earlier moved inside. She carried a laptop computer in her hands. Brennan Colton followed on her heels. His sheepish expression only infuriated Stella even more. She tossed up her hands in frustration.

"Either get me my attorney and charge me, or I'm leaving!" Stella snapped.

There was a moment's pause as all three took a deep breath, blowing stale air out slowly.

"Ms. Maxwell, I'm Detective Rory Colton. If we can please talk for a moment."

"No! I'm done talking. I'm leaving!"

"I understand your frustration. I also have no doubt that you know we can hold you for seventy-two hours."

"Seventy-two hours! For what? I didn't do anything!"

"And we now know that. I'm hoping that you might be able to help us identify who did kill Mr. Henley." The woman's voice was calming, her tone even.

Rory's green eyes stared at her, and Stella found her gaze like an easy balm. She took another breath, then moved back to the table and sat down. Rory moved to the seat opposite her. Brennan was still standing, leaning back against the wall, his hands pushed deep into his pockets.

"We have video of the murder. I'm hoping you might recognize the killer," Rory said.

"Video?"

Rory nodded. "A tourist caught the murder on film. He was doing a panoramic video of the street and wasn't paying attention to everything he was filming. He didn't realize what he had until he went back to his hotel room and played the footage. When he saw he'd captured the murder, he brought it right to the police department."

Stella leaned forward as Rory opened the laptop and pushed the Play button on the device. The video on the screen was clear but devoid of sound. Rockwell stood in the alley wringing his hands together. Clearly, he was waiting for someone, and Stella couldn't help but wonder who or what had made him come. Why had Rockwell been there?

She watched as a figure in a black hoodie and mask, hands in the front pouch, moved to Rockwell's side. There was a heated exchange between the two, the duo arguing like they were familiar with each other, and then gloved hands pulled a large butcher knife from inside that hoodie.

The assault was unexpected, Rockwell caught off guard with the first jab. He was stabbed repeatedly until he fell to the ground. The killer hovered above him just briefly, then pushed their hands back into the pockets of that hoodie and hurried toward the street, disappearing into the crowd. Just moments later, Stella is seen arriving, finding Rockwell injured.

Tears sprang to her eyes as the video replayed her trepidation as she approached the body, the shock of recognition, the inhalation of her breath catching in her throat, her screams for help and the tears that had rained over her cheeks. It also captured the guns pointed toward her, more officers surrounding her than she had initially realized.

She sat back, her head shaking slowly from side to side. It was enough to have her crying again, but she pushed the emotion down, refusing to let one tear spill. Most especially with Brennan Colton in the room.

Rory pushed the pause button on the laptop to stop the video. "Was there anything familiar about our suspect? Anything you recognize that might help us identify them?"

"No," Stella said, her voice a loud whisper. "Sorry,

but no." She inhaled, a deep breath filling her lungs. "I think they knew each other though. The way they were arguing. Rockwell knew his killer."

Rory nodded. "We were thinking the same thing."

"The other detective said my fingerprints were on the murder weapon. Was that true?" Stella questioned.

"Yes, it is. Do you have any idea how that could be?"

She shook her head. "No. But someone's gone to a lot of trouble to frame me."

"Any idea who has that kind of grudge against you?"

Stella's gaze dropped to the table as she fell into thought. Over the years she'd probably made more enemies than friends if she was honest with herself. In her line of work, it had always been about the story, no matter the casualties left from her pushing for facts and truth. But she couldn't think of anyone who would have gone to such lengths to get even with her for doing her job and doing her job well.

She shook her head again. "No," she answered. "I don't have a clue who could have done this." She didn't bother to say that not knowing had her unsettled. Her eyes shifted toward Brennan, who was eyeing her intently.

She found his stare unsettling, his baby blue eyes igniting a wave of heat through her body that was neither expected nor wanted. He was lean and wiry, the suit he wore meticulously cut to his slim frame. He pushed the short length of his pale, blond hair off his forehead, and she gasped at the sheer beauty of him. Why did he have to be so good-looking, she pondered?

Her gaze narrowed substantially, her ire rising once again. She folded her hands over her chest. "Why didn't you vouch for me?" she suddenly asked, her gaze locked on his face. "Why would you let them drag me in here like I was a common criminal? And they put me in a jail cell!" she snarled, her voice rising.

Brennan took a step forward. "Sorry about that. But I had to follow protocols, and this isn't my jurisdiction. Besides, I knew *who* you were, but we really don't *know* each other."

"Maybe if you had answered just one of my calls over the last few weeks, we would have known each other. I think you're just a jerk. You could have helped me," Stella snapped.

"I've been called worse," Brennan said.

"He has," Rory interjected. "But in his defense, I don't think my cousin was trying to intentionally dismiss you. He's not that kind of guy."

Stella looked from one to the other. "He's still an ass!" she quipped, not an ounce of forgiveness in sight.

"I'll take that," Brennan said, a wide smile pulling across his face. "Now let me take you to dinner to apologize and make up for my mishap."

"You have fallen and cracked your skull if you think for one second I want to have anything to do with you now," Stella responded. She turned her attention back to Rory. "Am I free to leave?"

The detective nodded. "You are. I may have more questions for you later."

"Yeah, yeah!" Stella said snidely as she moved back onto her feet and headed toward the door. "I'll try not to leave town!"

"Can I give you a ride home?" Brennan asked. He took a step toward her.

"You can stay the hell away from me," Stella retorted. "I would rather crawl across Manhattan on my hands and knees before I ever ask you for anything again."

"Even a one-on-one interview?"

Stella's glare could have frozen hell. She heard Brennan chuckle softly as she swept past him, not bothering to respond to his comment.

"I THINK THAT went well," Brennan said as he stole a quick glance toward his cousin.

Rory laughed. "If you were trying to crash and burn, I think it went very well."

"How long do you think she'll stay mad at me?"

"You might not ever recover from this. Sorry."

"Why are you apologizing?"

"Because I think you might actually like the woman. And given a chance, she might have actually liked you back."

He shrugged his shoulders, not certain he would agree with her. He had never known any woman who had ever gotten past being that angry with him. That kind of anger usually ended his relationships, so any effort to potentially start one didn't stand much of a chance, he mused.

Stella had made a pit stop at the women's restroom before returning to the front desk to retrieve her personal possessions. Brennan debated whether or not to wait for her and try again. He genuinely felt bad about everything that had happened, but his feelings were bruised by her flagrant rejection. He figured there was no point in letting her scorch what was left of his emotions.

From where he stood, he could see her standing off in a corner on her cell phone. He imagined she needed to let family and friends know that she was well. He wondered if there was a new boyfriend or lover in her life, someone who would hear the details of her day and be there to console her feelings. The thought suddenly had him feeling slightly anxious, something like jealousy coursing through his bloodstream. He shook away the sensation and watched as she finally ended her call and headed toward the building's front entrance.

STELLA WAS STILL angry enough to kick rocks. She'd missed her meeting at the middle school and a meeting with the marketing department. One of her sources had left six messages for her and now wasn't answering her return call. The senior editor had left a message also, spewing words that shouldn't be spoken in proper company. And Rockwell's murder had made the breaking news, his parents vowing to ensure the killer would be found and justice would be served. Although they hadn't mentioned her name, a quick profile image of her in the police car had made the news loop, calling her a person of interest who was being questioned. Anyone who knew her wouldn't have much of a problem recognizing her, and now she was even angrier.

As she moved toward the front door of the police station, she thought about calling for a ride but reasoned she shouldn't have too much trouble waving down a yellow cab. Before stepping out into the afternoon air, Stella turned, looking around the room in search of Brennan. She hoped to see him one last time, to glare in his direction so that he was reminded once more that she wasn't happy with him. To catch one more glimpse of the man whose dazzling smile and boy-next-door good looks had taken her breath away. To remind herself, and him, that he was a complete and total idiot and that had he played his cards right, things could have been so good between them. Not that she really believed that, but she was feeling petty, which necessitated a unique level of bitchiness that Stella had mastered by the time she'd been twelve years old.

Her gaze skated around the space, and then there he was. His back was to her as he moved through a door on the other side of the room. As he disappeared from her sight, Stella turned and stormed out the entrance.

Chapter Four

Brennan was still thinking about his case, the other murder and Stella Maxwell. It had been close to an hour since the beautiful woman had been released. He had hoped to see her before she'd made her exit, but Rory had commanded his attention, wanting an update on the Landmark Killer case and the FBI's thoughts on the killer's next steps. Despite wanting to make sure Stella was well, he still had a job to do, and business came before all else.

Exiting the police station to head to his own office, he was surprised to find Stella standing on the sidewalk, her cell phone still attached to her ear. She was deep in conversation with someone, and frustration still furrowed her brow. At the sight of her, a wave of excitement began to build in his midsection, and he felt his face pull into a wide grin.

As he began to inch his way closer, he realized she too had shifted into business mode, the conversation sounding as if it were centered around an article she'd either written or needed to write. She wasn't happy and had no problems letting the other party know how she felt.

There was something about Stella that Brennan found

engaging. She spoke her mind, not bothering to hold her tongue under any circumstances. He had no doubt that she could hold a grudge for longer than most, and did just to be contrary. While he'd hoped she'd had some time to cool off, it was likely she hadn't and would still be angry with him. He braced himself, taking a deep inhale of breath as he took another step closer.

He noticed the white paneled delivery van before she did. It was the third time the vehicle had circled the block. He'd dismissed it the first two times, thinking the driver was likely having difficulty finding a parking space to make a delivery. New York traffic and the ability to park had its own reputation and wasn't talked about kindly. This time the van slowed down substantially as it eased into a no-parking zone near where Stella was standing. Intuition told Brennan something was amiss, but he wasn't certain what suddenly had his antennae on edge.

A uniformed police officer standing on the steps near him gestured toward the driver, yelling for him to move. There was a moment of hesitation, and with the tinted windows, Brennan wasn't able to see the driver's face or expression. He imagined the man or woman wasn't happy about being shooed away.

The van eased back into traffic and turned at the corner. Stella had tossed the officer and then the van a look. When she turned back, she noticed Brennan standing there staring at her. She turned toward him, still talking on her phone as people pushed dismissively past her. The look she gave him still held a lot of hostility, he thought. Brennan tossed up his hand in an awkward wave. Stella's gaze narrowed, and then she turned her back to him, stepping closer to the street as she reached out a hand to wave down a taxi. Clearly, Brennan thought, Stella was still angry with him.

Thinking it might be better if he gave her some more time, Brennan turned to head in the opposite direction. As he spun an about-face, he saw the van from earlier round the corner once again. This time the driver didn't slow down. Instead, they moved swiftly toward the empty space beside Stella, coming to an abrupt stop in front of her. The side door slid open and two masked men wearing all black jumped from inside. Just seconds later, Stella's screams were piercing through the late afternoon air.

STELLA WAS STILL SEETHING, and seeing Brennan standing at the door of the police station watching her had further fueled her rage. Contending with the fallout from her arrest had started with those missed calls and looked like it was about to end with her being suspended from her job. She and her boss had been going back and forth over the phone, him insisting that she take a personal leave of absence until things blew over. She didn't need, or want, a compulsory vacation. She needed to work, and the senior editor wasn't interested in hearing that. To add insult to injury, he'd had the audacity to ask her for an exclusive statement about her arrest and the murder of Rockwell Henley. She'd told him in no uncertain terms what he could do with that request, albeit politely worded and in a calm tone. Heaven forbid she risk being labeled an angry black woman, no matter how angry she might have been about her situation.

Stepping off the curb, she waved at a passing taxi,

hopeful that it would stop and pick her up. She knew she was just a few short blocks from a tunnel entrance, and she could have taken the subway back to Harlem, but she didn't have the patience. Not right then.

After the third taxi passed her by, she was starting to feel broken, her rage having morphed into something she couldn't describe. It had taken on a life of its own, and she struggled not to burst into an ugly cry. She tossed a quick glance over her shoulder to see if Brennan was still watching her. She wished him away, and as if her prayers were being answered, he turned an about-face and headed in the opposite direction. She turned back to the task at hand but was surprised when a large white van suddenly pulled up before her, blocking her view.

As she heaved a deep sigh to quell her emotions, the van's door slid open, and two men jumped from inside. At first, Stella didn't think anything of the masks they wore, their all-black attire giving them the appearance of cat burglars. It was New York, and people were known to wear a variety of attire to suit their moods. For all she knew, they could have been making a fashion statement. Masks had become a daily staple for many, the entire city once guarding themselves from the ravages of the COVID pandemic. Even she wore a mask when riding the subway.

As she moved to step aside, one man grabbed her arm roughly. The other began to push her toward the vehicle's door, and Stella began to scream like her life depended on it.

Everything was a blur. Stella's handbag and phone fell to the ground as she kicked and screamed. She was a banshee on high heels as she drew as much attention to her attackers as she could. It was a take-no-prisoner's moment as Stella clawed and punched and tried to inflict as much harm as she could muster.

Rushing to her side, Brennan threw his own punch, sending one of the men backward against the vehicle. He grabbed Stella around the waist and swung her away from the other, putting himself between her and them. As he reached for the gun holstered at his waist, both men jumped back into the van. It careened into traffic and headed swiftly down the street. As quickly as they had appeared, they had disappeared. The moment was surreal, no more than three minutes passing from start to finish. Stella was suddenly surrounded by police officers for the second time that day.

"Anyone get the license plate?" Brennan shouted. He slowly eased his gun back into its holster.

"Running it now," someone shouted back. "And we have a car on its tail."

Brennan turned his attention back to Stella. He gripped her gently by the shoulders. "Are you okay? Did you get hurt?" he questioned.

She shook her head. "I'm fine," she snapped. She shook herself from his grip, unsettled by his touch. "Really, I'm okay."

"Did you recognize anyone?"

She shook her head, those tears finally falling past the length of her dark lashes. "No!" she said, her voice a loud whisper. "Why would someone—" she started to say.

Rory interrupted, rushing to their side. "What happened?" she questioned. "One of my officers said there was a kidnapping in progress?"

Brennan nodded. "Stella was attacked. Two men tried to pull her into their van," he said.

Rory's eyes widened. "In broad daylight?"

"Criminals have no qualms about committing their crimes when it's inconvenient for the rest of us," Brennan said snidely.

Rory rolled her eyes at her cousin. She turned her attention to Stella. "We should get you inside," she said. "We can review the surveillance tape. Maybe you'll recognize something."

Stella had knelt down to pick up her personal possessions from the ground. She dropped her phone, a tube of lip gloss and her change purse back inside. She shook her head vehemently once she was standing upright, her purse strap back on her shoulder. "No. I'm going home. I am done with you people."

"It might not be safe—" Rory began to say.

"Obviously, I'm not safe standing here in front of the damn police station," Stella snapped. "I'm going home!"

Rory looked to her cousin for assistance. Brennan shrugged his shoulders.

"I'll take you," Brennan said, shifting his gaze back to Stella.

She started to argue, but he interrupted her. "I insist."

Before Stella could give him a hard time, he cupped his hand beneath her elbow and gently guided her in the direction of his car. He called out to his cousin over his shoulder. "I've got her. Give her some time. I'll get the answers you need."

Stella shot him a look, her head shaking from side to side at his arrogance. He didn't have a clue what he did or did not have. And despite what he might have been hoping, what he did not have was unfettered access to her.

BRENNAN TOOK EAST DRIVE to Madison Avenue, following it north out of lower Manhattan into West Harlem. Stella didn't bother to give him directions, and Brennan didn't ask the way to her home. Under different circumstances, she might have been disturbed by him knowing where she lived. These circumstances were unique, and it barely moved the dial on her personal radar.

She reasoned he'd probably researched her as much as she'd researched him. Her being in police custody had also given him access to her personal information had he been interested in knowing it. Clearly, he'd been interested, as he headed in the right direction.

She stared out the passenger window, not bothering to acknowledge him. He hadn't said much himself, not bothering with casual small talk. He seemed to understand that she needed time and space, and he was still far from being her favorite person. When he took the turn onto West 136th Street, she shifted in her seat, taking a deep inhale of air into her lungs.

"You can drop me off—"

"I'm not leaving you. Not until we can figure out who tried to set you up for killing your boyfriend. And who just tried to grab you."

"My ex-boyfriend," Stella said, as if the correction to disassociate herself from Rockwell would somehow make things better. "And I have been racking my head trying to figure out who could be doing all this. I mean... why would someone try to grab me in front of the police station, of all places? How did they know I'd be there? I mean…is it possible it had nothing to do with Rock's murder, and I just happened to be in the wrong place at the wrong time?"

"Anything's possible, but I don't believe in coincidences," Brennan said.

Stella took another breath. "Neither do I," she said. "I was just hoping something might make sense."

"Well, I suggest we pool our collective resources and work together. Two heads being better than one and all that." He gave her a smile before turning his attention back to the roadway and the traffic that had slowed their progress.

"I don't need your help, and I don't need a babysitter."

"Well, I'm not a very good babysitter," he said. "Just ask my family. I've lost a few of them, bumped one's head against a door, and if I remember correctly, picked up the wrong kid from day care trying to help out my boss. It wasn't pretty!"

Stella laughed, amusement painting her expression. She appreciated his attempts at humor, although he clearly wasn't going to win any awards for his comedic efforts.

She suddenly changed the subject. "Why didn't you return my calls?"

Brennan gave her a quick glance. He answered her matter-of-factly. "Because you were a royal pain in my ass. Obviously, if I didn't answer, you should have taken that as a hint I wasn't interested in talking to you. Clearly, I didn't have any answers for you or anything to say for your story."

"You could have said just that. I had only hoped to

keep people informed about the investigation so they would know you were actually out there doing something. You would not be the first person to tell me no. I could have accepted your rejection. But you were just out and out rude."

Brennan shrugged. "I don't agree."

Stella shrugged her own shoulders. "I didn't expect that you would, Agent Colton."

BRENNAN DIDN'T BOTHER to hide his surprise at Stella's Harlem address. Although it had been some time since he was last in that end of the Manhattan borough, it was an area and neighborhood he was familiar with. Brennan had family who'd once lived in the area. It was also not far from the property the former president Bill Clinton had moved his offices. Although it had been some twenty-plus years since he'd moved in, much had been said about the rapid gentrification of an area that had once been predominantly African American. Harlem had been home to thousands of African American families and had been the cultural apex for the community. Businesses were owned and operated by Blacks, and houses were affordable for working class families. As Harlem started seeing gentrification, both businesses and houses became a place where African Americans could no longer afford to live in. Residents who had spent their entire lives in Harlem were forced to move elsewhere. The dynamics of the entire area changed.

Stella's home was in close proximity to parks, public transportation and landmarks like Strivers Row, the Apollo Theater, Columbia University, City University of

New York, Barnard College and less than a mile from five major subway stops. It was situated close to the Henry Hudson Parkway so that she could get downtown, uptown or out of town easily. It was prime New York real estate.

Stella led the way to the front door of a beautifully remodeled townhouse in Central Harlem's St. Nicholas Historic District. It was an elegant three-story structure with a professionally landscaped backyard. The classic facade had been impeccably restored, harkening to the days of the Harlem Renaissance.

Spanning three floors, the stunning home welcomed Brennan with an open layout on the parlor floor, exposed brick walls, high ceilings and exquisite hardwood floors. The sun-filled living area spilled over to the dining area and an open chef's kitchen. The eat-in dining space featured plenty of storage room, all new stainless-steel appliances, including a wine cooler and a large open island. Brennan could only begin to imagine what visual delights the other levels held.

He followed on Stella's heels as she led him into the living room and gestured for him to take a seat. His eyes followed after her as she dropped her purse onto an end table and moved to a corner bar, where she pulled two lead-bottomed tumblers from the shelf. She reached for a bottle of bourbon and filled both glasses. She moved back to his side, passed him a glass then dropped down onto the sofa beside him as she rested the bottle on the coffee table.

"This is very nice," Brennan said as he took a sip of the beverage. "If you don't mind my asking, what's the square footage?"

Stella shrugged. "It's just a little over four thousand square feet."

"It's a big house for one person. It's not at all what I expected. I might need to reconsider my own career choices. The rent here has to be…what…close to four, maybe five thousand per month?"

Stella rolled her eyes skyward. Her impatient look was like an arrow of ice thrown in his direction. "I wouldn't know," she responded, her tone equally as chilly. "I own it and I don't have a mortgage. Anything else you want to know, Agent Colton?"

Brennan swiped at his brow, his cheeks reddening with embarrassment. "Sorry! I didn't mean to get into your personal business."

"Yes, you did!"

Brennan grinned as he nodded his head. "Yes, I did. I was being nosy. But I really didn't mean to be rude about it." A hint of contrition creased his brow.

She shook her head. "Next time just ask me what you want to know. Be direct. Don't beat around the bush. I hate when men do that."

He nodded again, still unsure how to question what was still clearly on his mind. Stella answered as if she could read the thoughts spinning through his head.

"The house was built back in 1910. My great-grandparents were the first family to own it, and they passed it down to my grandfather. I was raised in this house, and I inherited it debt-free from my parents. That's how I can afford to live in a multi-million-dollar home on a journalist's salary," she said sarcastically. "Does that answer your question?"

Brennan's eyes widened. He felt embarrassed that she had read him so well and was saddened about her loss. "Your parents... They've both passed?"

Stella nodded. "My mother when I was twelve, and my father died six years ago."

"I'm so sorry. I know how that feels. I was young when we lost my father too."

"Your mom is still alive?"

Brennan nodded. "She lives in Florida, now. I was lucky to have a big family to lean on. My siblings understood what I was feeling, so we had each other to commiserate with. I hate that you had to endure that kind of hurt alone."

Stella shrugged. "We do what we have to do. How many of you Coltons are there?" she asked, realizing she knew very little of his personal life.

Brennan smiled. "Well, there's my twin brother, Cashel. Cash for short, but when you meet him, call him Cashel. He hates it!"

Stella chuckled. "Not fond of St. Patrick's Rock of Cashel, huh?"

"I'm impressed you know it."

"Don't be. I visited Ireland for my twenty-fifth birthday."

"Even more impressed," Brennan said. "I've never been to Ireland. Or out of the country, for that matter."

"We'll need to work on that. I love to travel. Morocco's next on my bucket list."

Brennan smiled, noting her use of the word *we* in her comment.

She shook her head. "So, is it just you and Cashel?"

"No, there's my brother Patrick, who would technically be the middle kid, and our baby sister Ashlyn. Then of course, if you start counting cousins..." His voice trailed off.

"Wow! That is a large family, especially if you're an only child with no cousins. Are you all close?"

"I wouldn't say that," Brennan quipped. "We have our issues. There's some dysfunction, but I like to think that the love we have for each other makes up for the rest."

Stella pondered the comment, but she didn't respond. She reached for the bourbon bottle and filled her glass a second time. She changed the subject. "I need a shower. Make yourself comfortable," she said, rising from her seat and heading toward the door. "We can talk more when I'm done."

As she reached the bottom of the stairwell, Brennan called her name, meeting her stare evenly as she turned to give him a curious look.

"Yes?"

"I'm really not the jerk you think I am."

Stella hesitated as she considered the comment. She chuckled softly. "That's yet to be determined, Agent Colton."

He smiled. "I look forward to proving it to you."

Chapter Five

Brennan sat with his own thoughts for a few minutes. He could only imagine what Stella was doing up on the floor above, and those things he was thinking had him offsides. For a brief moment he pondered what might happen if he were to venture up those stairs into that shower with her. Heat rippled through his southern quadrant at the perverted thoughts, and he bit down on his bottom lip. And then he considered the pain he knew she would inflict upon his person if he were to even try. They were still establishing boundaries, and although he reasoned it would be nice to know her better, he also sensed that she wasn't interested in being his friend and definitely not his lover. He pondered how he might change her opinion of him, considering her rage had waned substantially since he'd driven her home. Despite his best efforts, another wave of salacious thoughts crossed his mind. Maybe he was a jerk, he mused. Brennan needed to do better, he thought. But he was still very much a man, and she was very much the most desirable woman he'd met in quite some time. But he was getting way ahead of himself, and for the life of him, he couldn't begin to explain why.

STEAM BILLOWED THROUGH the master bathroom in soft swells. Stella stood beneath a flow of hot water, allowing it to beat gently against her narrow shoulders and over her back. Tears rained from her eyes, falling past the round of her dimpled cheeks. Stella didn't cry often, but the day had left her emotionally depleted, and crying was all she could manage to do. She cried as if she'd lost her best friend, and in some ways, she had. She sobbed as if her cat was gone. If she liked cats. In that moment, there was little that Stella liked or even imagined herself being fond of. All she wanted was to turn back time and get a do-over for the entire day. Maybe even the week, she thought.

Instead, she had to figure out who had murdered Rockwell and why they were trying to pin the offense on her. She had more questions than she had answers. Who had lured Rockwell to that alley, and what reason had they used to bait him there? Had he gone expecting her to make an appearance? Had he been ambushed, hopeful for one thing and surprised by another? Who would brazenly stick a butcher knife in his chest in broad daylight and not expect to get caught? Or was getting caught their objective once they were done toying with her emotions?

She blew a soft sigh as she lifted her face to the spray of water, allowing the droplets to wash away her tears. Her thoughts wandered to the man downstairs in her living room. Brennan was too cute for his own good. And likeable. She found it difficult to stay angry at him, and staying angry would have kept a large enough wall between them that she wouldn't be thinking about his hands trailing down her torso, allowed to play with her girl parts. He left her heated in the most pleasurable way, and Stella knew she had no business thinking of him like that. Nothing could happen between them. Not one damn thing that could leave her vulnerable with a broken heart. But for the life of her, she couldn't get him off her mind. With a shake of her head, Stella reached for the water faucet and turned it to cool.

WHEN STELLA BOUNDED back down the stairs and sauntered into the kitchen, Brennan was pulling a baking dish out of her oven. She took a deep inhale of breath, savoring the decadent aroma wafting through the room.

"What's that?" she asked. "It smells really good."

Brennan smiled as he placed the dish on the stove and lay kitchen mitts onto the counter. "It's chicken and rice in a rich cream sauce. One of my many specialties."

"A man who cooks. I'm impressed."

"You will soon discover that I'm a man of many talents." The grin that spread across his face was canyon wide. "Why don't you set the table," he said, the comment more command than request.

Stella's brow rose ever so slightly as she considered the order. Any man making demands of her in her home would pinch her the wrong way. But Brennan doing it wasn't nearly as disconcerting as she would have expected. She took a deep breath and let the facts of that wash over her. When those thoughts starting heading toward things more decadent, she shook away the reverie she'd fallen into and nodded. She reasoned that she had more important things that needed to be done so that he could go home and get out of her personal space and her head.

Moving to the cupboards, she pulled plates and glasses from inside and then gathered silverware from a drawer near the fridge. Right off the kitchen was a massive wood deck that overlooked her private backyard. It was still hot outside, and Stella thought that they could dine alfresco. She added two place settings on the wrought iron table and then headed back inside to select a bottle of wine from the wine chiller.

"Sauvignon blanc or chardonnay?" she asked, tossing Brennan a quick look.

He hesitated, then shrugged his shoulders. "You choose. I'm good with either."

"Moscato it is, then," Stella said with the softest chuckle.

Brennan laughed. "If that's what we're doing, then I'd prefer a beer," he said.

Minutes later they were seated on the patio. The sun was still shining, but there was a sweet breeze blowing gently through the warm evening air. The end of the day for both was proving to be far better than how things had started.

Stella took a sip of her wine and rested the glass on the table. "You never did say how you showed up to the crime scene as quickly as you did."

Brennan set his own bottle of beer down. "We were working on the Landmark Killer case down in the theater district. When the call came in, they thought it might be related to that case."

Stella nodded. "Interesting..." she muttered.

"Not really."

"How's that case going?"

Brennan gave her a narrowed gaze. He hesitated for a brief moment. "I'd love to tell you, but I can't risk you sharing the information with your readers."

Stella laughed, her head bobbing up and down. "That's fair. Since our current situation is a little strange, I'm willing to agree to keep anything shared within these walls *off* the record."

"*Off* the record?" Brennan echoed.

Stella held up her right hand before pressing it to her chest. "Cross my heart," she said, a bright smile on her face. She motioned for him to continue. As she did, she crossed the fingers on her other hand and made a grand gesture of pulling her arm behind her back.

Brennan laughed, his head shaking from side to side. "Nope," he said. "I can't with you!"

"Seriously," Stella said. She looked him in the eye, her stare even with his. "I won't do that to you. I'm a woman of my word. If you want to share, then share. I promise it will stay between the two of us, and it won't go on the record."

Brennan took a deep breath. There was something in the look she gave him. He felt a level of trust and understanding that he hadn't expected. He trusted her, and that spoke volumes since he knew so little about her.

He began to speak, seeming to unburden himself from the thoughts running through his head. "We're pretty certain we know *where* he'll hit next. We were hoping to find *who* he might target based on the clues from the previous murders."

"And you're certain the killer is male?" Stella questioned.

"We are very sure. And he's taunting us. He sent my

cousin Sinead, who's also with the FBI, a text message that indicated his next murder would happen on Broadway."

"That's like looking for a needle in a haystack. With all the theaters, the number of employees is astronomical. You've got ushers, actors, concession stand workers..." Her voice trailed as she fathomed the number of potential victims.

"Exactly. Countless blond, blue-eyed men fit the profile, and we were trying to find one whose first name starts with an L."

"Could you search employee records?"

"All the theaters we visited no longer have access to their employee files. The online records have vanished as if someone purposely deleted them."

"And this has happened at more than one theater?"

Brennan nodded. "Multiple. I spoke with the managers, and they are just as baffled. Whoever our killer is, his ability to hack those records tells us he's technically proficient with serious computer skills. He's also making it very hard for us to get ahead of him."

"Wow!" Stella said. "Just wow!"

There was a moment of silence that descended over them. Stella savored a bite of her meal, the decadent seasoning of the sautéed chicken and rice bathed in the creamiest garlic sauce. The meat melted like butter in her mouth, teasing her taste buds.

She hummed her appreciation. "Mmmm! This is delicious!" she said.

Brennan grinned. "Thank you! And I have to tell you,

I'm very impressed with your pantry. I thought my own was well stocked, but yours puts mine to shame."

"I like to cook." Stella smiled back.

"Something we have in common."

Silence blanketed their conversation once again as they both ate with gusto, realizing how hungry they were. The day had been long in many ways, and their missed meals hadn't been an issue until good food had been put in front of them.

Stella was swiping a wedge of Italian bread across her plate to catch the last remnants of sauce when Brennan turned the conversation back to business.

"Who needed Rockwell dead and wanted you to go down for the crime?"

She swallowed the last bite of her food and sat back against her seat. "I've been racking my brain to answer that question, and I don't have an answer that makes an ounce of sense."

"How long were you and Rockwell together?"

"We had celebrated our one-year anniversary in the Bahamas a few months ago. He had surprised me with a weekend getaway." The light in Stella's eyes diminished slightly as she began to reflect back on her relationship. "Rockwell and I met when I was doing an article on the proclivity of candidates using fraudulent campaign finances. We had an instant connection. He was sweet and I liked him."

"Sounds like your trip was a good time."

"Not really," Stella said, her eyes shifting across Brennan's face. "That's when Rockwell announced I needed to start being a better partner if I planned to go the distance with him. Those were his exact words. 'If I planned to go the distance with him.'"

She shook her head ever so slightly. "It really was the beginning of the end. I found out that he was letting people think that I was some poor girl from the projects, who'd lived in low-income housing and put herself through school. I know his mother and Tobias had a lot to do with that, but he never did anything to correct the narrative. It infuriated me!"

"He sounds like a jerk!"

Stella shrugged her narrow shoulders. "He was never overly affectionate and was very pedestrian in his approach to life, but when he decided to run for the governor's office, everything revolved around the campaign. Suddenly, I wasn't the woman he loved but the woman who could help him pull in the African American vote with my rags-to-riches story. Everything I said or did needed to be construed so that it made him look good. I was told how to dress, who I should associate with and how I should behave in public. We began to fight from sunup till sundown, and neither of us were happy. Him telling some donor that I had once worked as a waitress to support myself was the final straw. Had it been true, it wouldn't have been a problem, but it was a blatant lie, and I refused to support his lying to people. I retreated to my corner and cut off contact. I needed space to think things through."

She blew a soft sigh before continuing. "Then last week, he sent me a text message after I refused to show up to an NRA fundraiser, saying that it wasn't working for him anymore. He blocked my number, refused to take my calls and the rest is history."

"Definitely a jerk!"

"He had his moments."

"Did you still love him?"

The quiet between them was suddenly thunderous as she pondered the question. It had been something she'd thought a lot about even before she and Rockwell had gone their separate ways. Their relationship had been a timeline of super highs and super lows. The good times had been some of the best moments she'd ever had. When things went left, she had questioned more than once if they would be able to come back from the fallout. Over the last few months, she had often questioned if the feelings between them had anything at all to do with love.

She sighed again before she answered. "I really cared about Rockwell. When he wasn't trying to live up to other people's expectations, he was really a good guy. Those were our greatest times together, when I was able to see the best of him. Once he took that nosedive into politics, those times became fewer and farther between. Love became an unnecessary commodity for his goals. He just needed me to stand quietly by his side and to smile pretty."

"Would you have married him?"

"I never had any illusions about us having a future together. I think we both always knew that what we shared was only supposed to be momentary," she said. "Does that answer your question?"

"I think I get it," Brennan said softly. He swallowed the last of his beer, depositing the bottle back onto the table. "Rockwell Henley was an even bigger jerk than I gave him credit for, because you clearly are not the trophy wife type."

Stella laughed. "No, I definitely am not."

"Who in Rockwell's inner circle might have had it out for you?"

"I'm fairly certain his parents are on the top of that list. They didn't think I was good enough for their precious son. In fact, when we first got together, his father offered me cash to go away and never see Rockwell again. His mother was just blatantly nasty toward me. To hear her tell it, I am too outspoken, and me working for a *tabloid* newspaper made Rockwell and the family look bad."

"So, we have Ma and Pa Henley. But do you think either of them actually harbored ill will toward their son to want to see him dead and blame you for it?"

"Not at all. His mother doted on him, and Rockwell idolized his father, fawning over the man every chance he could. His father ate that crap up like expensive caviar."

"Who else? Did Rockwell have any siblings?"

"No. He was an only child. But you can add Tobias Humphrey, his campaign manager, to that list. Tobias is definitely not a member of my fan club."

"What problem did he have with you?"

"To hear him tell it, I added 'negative value' to the campaign. After running a background check on me and trying to dig up whatever dirt he could find, he actually had the audacity to tell Rockwell that dating me was not a good look for a man of his stature. We butted heads every time we ran into each other."

Negative value. Brennan winced. Clearly, Tobias Humphrey had not bothered to know the woman before him. "Do you think he said that because you're black?" he suddenly questioned, unable to shake the thought.

"What do you think?" Stella answered. Her brow lifted as she gave him a look that spoke volumes. She suddenly rose from the table, reaching for the dirty dishes. She moved back into the kitchen to the sink. Brennan's eyes followed as she began to clean up what remained of the mess he'd made.

Brennan felt his body tense, a hint of ire rising in his midsection. His gaze dropped to the table as he contemplated the challenges Stella had been made to endure. The thought that someone had given the woman a hard time for no good reason wasn't sitting right with him. He glanced up as she continued, her voice raised slightly so as to carry the sound through the open door.

"Oh, and let's not forget Miss Rebecca Farrington! Rebecca Farrington of the *South Hampton* Farringtons!" Stella exclaimed sarcastically.

"Who's she?" he questioned as he moved into the kitchen with her. He leaned his elbows on the counter, then rested his head against his closed fists.

"Rockwell's ex-girlfriend. She was livid when he broke up with her, and she had been harboring a lot of animosity toward him. When he and I started dating, she suddenly wanted to reconcile. She has tried everything short of hog-tying him in the basement to get him to come back to her, and nothing had worked. She blamed me for that. To hear her tell it, I had him bewitched."

"Do you think she may have wanted him dead?"

"It was only a few weeks ago that she threatened to kill him."

"Was she serious?"

Stella rolled her eyes skyward. "She said it, that's all I know. And there was enough concern about it that Tobias requested the police go pay her a visit. I'll admit I may have thought it a time or two, but I never said it out loud."

"Please, don't admit that to the prosecutor or any of the detectives working this case!"

Brennan gave her the slightest smile and Stella smiled back. There was a shift of energy that swept between them, something easy and light. It felt like an old slipper that fit perfectly. It was comfortable, like home.

For a second, he thought about wrapping his arms around her and pulling her close against him. It was an urge he was finding difficult to ignore, desire pulling at him with the force of a freight train. It unnerved him as he felt his entire body quiver with emotion. He took a deep breath, needing to exorcise the thoughts running through his head. "Do you have a computer I can use?" he asked, hopeful for a distraction. He tried to sound calm and collected, but his voice cracked ever so slightly.

Stella's smiled widened even more. She gestured with her head. "Upstairs in my office. It's off the master bedroom. Make yourself at home."

She swiped her hands across a blue plaid dish cloth. Taking a moment to uncork a second bottle of wine, Stella reached for her glass, carrying both as she headed toward the patio and back outside.

As she settled down, lifting her feet onto an ottoman, Brennan didn't take his eyes off her. Wisps of hair had fallen over her eyes. The tension that had been in her face earlier that day was gone, a relaxing glow washing over her. She was breathtaking beneath the setting sun, the last radiant beams spotlighting her delicate features.

"I could get use to this," Brennan muttered to himself as he finally turned and headed up to the second floor of her home.

Chapter Six

Make yourself at home. Clearly, I have lost my mind,
Stella thought as she refilled her glass. She sat the bottle
of wine on the ground beside her chair. She needed a few
minutes to simply unwind, and although she felt relaxed
for the first time that day, she was still unsettled by everything that had happened, and Brennan's presence in
her home wasn't helping.

She liked him. He wasn't the asshole she'd first figured him for. Although there was still much she didn't
know about him, she sensed he was really one of the
good guys. And she liked him more than she had ever
anticipated.

She had never imagined herself sharing so much about
her previous relationship with anyone. But there was a
level of comfort with Brennan that was unexpected. He
was easy to talk to, and she found herself chattering away
like they'd known each other for years. The fact that she
had subconsciously given him free rein in her home also
spoke volumes. But she was secure about him being in
her space, and that had never happened with any man
before. Not even with Rockwell Henley.

BRENNAN FOLLOWED THE exposed brick walls and hardwood floors that carried through to the upper level. On the second story, he found the bright master suite complete with a large walk-in closet and marble-covered bathroom. The decor was minimalistic, with Stella favoring a subtle sage green and light tan. He peeked into the second bedroom, which also had a private bathroom and gorgeous large arched windows. Curious, he ascended the skylit staircase to discover two additional bedrooms with a shared bathroom and walk-in closets. He was duly impressed.

Back on the second floor, he entered the master suite and moved to the office area connected by a sliding barn door. The desk inside hosted a Mac computer and a picture of Stella and her parents. She'd been young, wearing bell-bottom jeans, large framed glasses and an oversized afro. Her distinguished parents were dressed in their Sunday best. They looked happy, and he imagined it was a memory that was near and dear to Stella's heart.

If she actually worked in that office, he would never have known it. Like the rest of her home, the space was immaculate. If he'd been trying to discover what she was working on, he would have been challenged. There was no evidence of anything but her having hired a really great cleaning company.

Brennan liked Stella. He liked her a lot. He was enjoying himself so much that for the briefest moment, he forgot that he was there to solve a crime. His time with her wasn't meant to be personal. It needed to be all business. But she was making that harder than it needed to be. She was proving herself to be quite the distraction. And he was putting the blame on her because…well…why not? Admitting she had him completely smitten didn't fit his image. And it wasn't going to help them find the bad guys. Blaming her helped him rationalize his own shortcomings. Putting the onus on Stella helped him not feel bad about being distracted if she were to blame.

He closed his eyes as he waited for her computer to turn on. There was no password, and he bypassed the screen saver picture with the push of the Enter button. That she had given him permission to use the device and access that didn't require her looking over his shoulder said much about her level of comfort with him in her space. He respected that and knew he'd do nothing to lose her trust. They were becoming fast friends and because he didn't have many people that he himself trusted, he didn't want to mess things up between them.

After weeding through his email, Brennan called his cousin to check in. Rory answered on the second ring.

"Where are you?" she questioned, not even bothering to say hello.

"At Stella Maxwell's home."

"Is she okay?"

"I think so. Did you get anything on that van?"

"It was stolen a few hours earlier. They ditched it a few miles from the station, leaving it in a parking garage. It had been wiped clean."

Brennan heaved a deep sigh. "That's not a lot of help."

"No, it isn't," Rory replied. "Have you been able to come up with anything?"

"Nothing. But something about this case isn't sitting right with me," Brennan said. "Why would someone try to set Stella up and then try to snatch her? Assuming both were connected."

"Do you think they're not?"

"I'm not sure what I think. We have more questions than we do answers. Starting with how someone knew she'd be released in order to be outside waiting for her?"

"What are you thinking?"

"How well do you know everyone on your team?" Brennan questioned.

There was a moment of hesitation before Rory responded. "How well do you know everyone on yours? Even if you are related to most of them."

"My point precisely. It's possible our perp is working with someone in the department. Someone privy to Stella's case. Someone able to pass along information about her comings and goings. Someone neither of us would suspect, because we think we know them, and we really don't know them all as well as we think we do."

"You seem pretty certain that this is all about Stella and not Rockwell Henley, the victim."

"I think setting her up and then going after her puts a spotlight on Stella. Think about it. If I wanted Henley dead, I would have just killed him. Why go through the trouble of setting Stella up to take the fall, unless my grudge was against her, and Henley was just a means to an end. I think he was collateral damage. And I think whoever did it isn't finished. Them trying to grab her this afternoon says that."

"Unfortunately, if your theory is true, we don't have the man power to give her twenty-four-hour protection. Hell, we barely have enough men to investigate the murder. Between budget cuts and staff shortages, we are stretched thin."

"Don't worry about it. I'm not going anywhere."

"What about the Landmark Killer case? You certain Sergeant Blackthorn won't have an issue with you shifting your focus? He already had issues with the FBI team working the case anyway."

Brennan thought about Sergeant Wells Blackthorn. He was the lead on the Landmark Killer case, reporting to the precinct captain, Colleen Reeves, who had called in Brennan's team to help with the case. They were a specialized unit of the Manhattan FBI and brought a unique perspective to their work.

Wells didn't like that the FBI was involved, although the team was full of experts who specialized in serial killers. It included Brennan; his cousin, Special Agent Sinead Colton; his twin brother, Special Agent Cash Colton; his sister, Agent Ashlyn Colton, who was their technical expert and his brother Patrick Colton, an FBI CSI expert.

Brennan's cousin Sinead and Sergeant Blackthorn had bumped heads hard in the beginning, both wanting to go it alone. Despite the tension between them, the duo had grown close, soon bumping other body parts that Brennan chose not to think about. He was happy for Sinead and grateful she'd been able to find love and a modicum of happiness in the midst of so much darkness.

"I'll talk to him," Brennan said. "I can work both cases. It'll be okay."

Brennan could just imagine his cousin's expression.

He hadn't sounded so convincing, and he had no doubts she too had reservations. He shifted the conversation.

"I'll keep my eyes on Ms. Maxwell."

"Well, the NYPD appreciates your assistance. As long as you don't get in our way."

"What have your guys done thus far?" Brennan queried.

"My men have talked to Henley's friends and his family. We've also spoken to his political opponent. Most of those interviews pointed back to Stella and their relationship ending on bad terms. She's been described as a woman scorned. To hear them tell it, everyone else loved him. He was a great guy and Stella was the problem."

Brennan shook his head. He blew a soft sigh, realizing he was faced with another case that would prove to be an uphill battle.

"If you turn up anything, let me know," he said.

"You do the same," Rory responded. "And be safe, please."

Brennan smiled into the receiver as if she could see him. "Yeah, yeah," he answered.

STELLA WOKE WITH a start. She hadn't planned to doze off sitting out in the garden, but the warm late-night air had pulled her into the sweetest slumber. Gathering her bearings, she sat upright and shifted her body forward in the seat. Filling her lungs with a deep inhale of air, her eyes darted back and forth across the landscape. It only took a quick minute for her to remember the hard day that she'd had. Her heart was still reeling over the murder of Rockwell, and remembering that someone had tried to cause her harm cramped her stomach with fear. Then she remembered that her hard day had ended with an air of hope and a man making himself comfortable in her home. A man who'd seemingly disappeared since climbing the stairs to her second floor.

She rose from her seat and headed inside, securing the door behind her. The stereo was still playing, the softest jazz billowing out of the built-in speakers throughout the house. She dropped her wine glass and the empty bottle of Moscato into the kitchen sink, then headed upstairs to her bedroom.

She saw Brennan from the top of the stairwell. She paused to stare into her bedroom. He too had given in to the exhaustion that had hit like a tidal wave. He'd sat down at the foot of her bed and had fallen asleep. His feet were still planted firmly on the floor, but he'd fallen over on his side, his torso lying awkwardly atop the mattress. He snored loudly, and Stella sensed it had been some time since he'd slept so soundly. The sight of him made her smile.

Easing her way back down the staircase, she checked the locks on her front door one last time, peering out the sidelights to the street. All was quiet, nothing seeming amiss. She stared out into the darkness for a good few minutes, rehashing everything that happened one more time. Despite being hopeful that things might go back to normal after a good night's sleep, she instinctively knew normal wouldn't be visiting her anytime soon. With a deep sigh, she settled herself down against the sofa. Pulling a light cotton blanket over her legs, she drifted back to sleep with thoughts of Brennan Colton still spinning in her mind.

THE SMELL OF freshly brewed coffee pulled Stella from a deep slumber. The sound of pots rattling was startling, and her heart was suddenly racing. She sat upright, unaccustomed to the sounds and aromas wakening her from her sleep. She started to reach for the baseball bat she kept hidden beneath the sofa when a booming voice called her name.

"Good morning! I was starting to wonder if you were going to get up or if I was going to have to wake you." Brennan Colton grinned broadly.

Stella found his cheerful expression off-putting, considering her side and back ached from sleeping on the sofa. She needed time to stretch and loosen those muscles and a moment to whisper a quiet prayer skyward before having to face the world. She winced as he called her name a second time.

"Are you okay, Stella?" Brennan questioned.

"I'm fine. Why are you so damn chipper?" she asked. She tossed off the blanket wrapped around her and slid her feet to the floor. With a wide yawn, she stretched her arms skyward, then twisted her head from side to side.

"It's going to be a good day," he responded. "I can feel it!"

"Well, I can't," Stella snapped.

"Coffee will help. How do you take yours?"

"Black," she said.

Brennan nodded and disappeared back into her kitchen. He returned minutes later with an oversized mug filled with a rich blend of Columbian coffee beans. At the first sip, Stella felt her mood shift. She closed her eyes and settled into the comfort of the hot brew.

"Mmmm," she purred. "Okay, this is good." She hummed her appreciation a second time. "So why are you up so early?" she asked. "And where'd you get the suit?"

It had taken her a moment to notice that Brennan was wearing a clean change of clothes, his outfit from the previous day replaced by a navy silk suit, white dress shirt and red paisley necktie. He'd shaved, no hint of morning stubble on his face. The waves in his blond hair lay pristinely atop his head, and his blue eyes shimmered with excitement.

Brennan chuckled. "One, it's not early. It's almost one o'clock in the afternoon. And two, while you were asleep, I went home to shower and change. I borrowed your keys to let myself back in. You were sleeping so soundly that I didn't want to wake you. You looked like you needed the rest."

Eyes wide, Stella stole a quick glance at the watch on her wrist. She was suddenly feeling out of sorts again knowing he'd gone and come back, and she hadn't heard a thing. That most of the day had already passed her by without her accomplishing a thing felt wrong on many levels. She jumped from seat still holding tight to her coffee mug.

"I need to change," she muttered. "I need to…"

Brennan interrupted her. "You need to come and get something to eat. Then you need to just rest. I don't want you leaving the house. We still don't know who came after you, and I don't know that it's safe. I need you to be safe."

"Did they get anything on that van?"

Brennan shook his head. "They hit a dead end. Which

is why you need to stay low until we have more. All of this feels very personal, and I think there's someone coming after you. Maybe because of Henley, or maybe he was just a casualty of the war being waged against you. I don't know which, but I do know I don't want anything to happen to you."

Brennan's eyes were piercing as he stared at her. Stella felt her face flush, a wave of heat flooding her from her head down to her toes. She wasn't sure how to respond, having nothing to say that would have made sense. She shook her head, her eyes darting around the room so to not meet his.

"What are you cooking?" she finally questioned.

Brennan smiled. "Breakfast casserole. I'm warming up a slice for you. There's also some fresh fruit: grapes, mandarin oranges, watermelon, cherries and some blueberries. I stopped by the grocery store on my way back."

Stella's eyes widened again, and her stomach rumbled at the thought of food. She moved in his direction, following him into the kitchen. He pointed her to the counter.

"Did anyone tell you that you're bossy?" Stella said as she moved onto one of the bar stools.

Brennan shrugged. "I've been called a few things over the years, but I don't know if *bossy* was one of them."

He gave her a smile as he set a plate of food down in front of her. Stella hesitated before starting to eat, watching him as he put everything away. She wasn't sure how she felt about him being so in control in her space. What irked her most is that he didn't bother her as much as she would have imagined just days earlier.

"I need to run," Brennan said. "I have an appointment

with Rockwell's family, and I want to catch up with his campaign manager. I'll be back later this evening."

"I should go with you."

Brennan pointed his index finger in her direction. "Do not leave this house, Stella. I mean that. I can't be certain it's safe for you out there alone."

"I won't be alone if I'm with you," she snapped back.

He shook his head. "That's not possible. And I need you to work with me on this. Please."

Stella narrowed her eyes significantly, like thin slits of hostility and anger. Her face reddened beneath the warm brown of her complexion, her cheeks heated and bulging as she clenched her teeth tightly together. Words were lost to her, a lengthy list of profanity flying from her thoughts. She wanted to curse him, but the energy wasn't there either. Instead, she blew a soft sigh and shoved a spoonful of baked eggs, cheese, mushrooms, onions and bacon into her mouth.

As Brennan moved past her, he rested a large hand on her shoulder and squeezed it gently. "I'll be back a few hours," he said.

"You plan on staying another night?" she questioned.

"I'm here every night until we find who's after you. Is that going to be a problem?"

Stella shrugged. "Just stay in the guest room. I like my own bed."

He grinned. "I liked your bed too. It's very comfortable! I appreciate you not throwing me out of it, because I slept very well last night."

There was a hint of amusement in his tone. And innuendo, as if he wanted to say the only thing that would have been better was if she had been in that bed with him. Or maybe, Stella thought, she was imagining that part, and those thoughts were her own.

Brennan squeezed her shoulder a second time and then headed out the door. As he disappeared through the entrance, that lengthy list of profanity came back to her, and Stella cursed out loud.

Chapter Seven

Brennan was early for his appointment with Dayn and Silvia Henley, the parents of the late Rockwell Henley. He was met at the door of their West 57th Street apartment by a doorman who was all brawn and minimal brain. His gray uniform looked two sizes too small, his muscles bulging through the cotton fabric. His voice was nasally, sounding like he needed a tissue to clear his sinuses. He was intimidating, until he talked, his voice giving playful helium balloon vibes.

He looked Brennan up and then down before informing him that the Henleys were not ready to see him, and he would have to wait in the lobby for their okay to send him up to the penthouse.

Brennan gave his watch a quick glance. "Can you let them know this won't take long? I understand they have someplace to be and so do I."

The doorman simply stared. Clearly, he was not going to be moved. With nowhere for Brennan to sit, he moved to the other side of the room and leaned against the marbled wall. The doorman cleared his throat as though he wanted to say something, but he bit back the comment; instead, pausing to sign for a package for another tenant.

Time dragged ever so slowly. Ten minutes passed before the doorman gestured for Brennan's attention. He pointed him toward the elevator. "The Henleys will see you now," he said.

Brennan sighed as he stepped into the conveyor, the doors closing after him. The elevator moved swiftly, the ride so smooth that it barely felt as if he'd left the first floor. When the doors opened, he was standing in the Henleys' living room, the couple meeting him at the entrance.

Dayn Henley stepped forward, his hand extended. He looked like old money, Brennan thought. He was nicely tanned, his complexion boosting weekly skin care treatments done by a professional. His gray hair had been neatly combed, a slight wave to the thick strands. He wore a short-sleeve, polo-style shirt with his initials embroidered on the pocket and tailored black slacks. He exuded confidence, an aura of conviction and determination wafting off him. Under different circumstances, he and Brennan would probably have liked each other.

His wife held court behind him, not budging from where she stood. Her hands were folded politely in front of the short, plaid skirt she wore. She stood on stiletto heels that complemented toned legs that said strip club, not country club. Her blonde hair was thick and lush with just the barest hint of a curl, and she wore enough makeup for three women. Brennan instinctively knew she would never like him, and he didn't see himself caring much about her.

"We'll need to make this quick, Agent Colton," Dayn Kenley said. "My son's law firm is holding a small community vigil later today to honor him."

"Do you have any new leads?" Mrs. Kenley interjected. "Do you know who helped that woman kill our son?"

"We have our best men investigating your son's murder. I just have a few questions for you."

Mrs. Kenley rolled her eyes skyward, annoyance furrowing her brow. "We've answered more than enough questions. It's time we got some answers. Have you spoken with that woman?"

"And what woman might that be?" Brennan asked, already knowing the answer.

"Stella Maxwell!" the older woman spat. "Our son was associated with her briefly. He recently ended the relationship, and she didn't take it well. I wouldn't be surprised if you discover that she is somehow responsible."

"It's my understanding that Rockwell and Stella dated for over a year. That would be a little more than a brief association, wouldn't you say?"

Silvia Kenley rolled her eyes again. "Their relationship was done and finished, that's all that matters."

Dayn shot his wife a look before shifting his gaze back toward Brennan. "They were very good friends, Stella and Rockwell. He cared for her very much, but they had very different life goals."

"Do you think she was involved in your son's murder?"

"I think their relationship ended on bad terms and we never know what we'll do if we're pushed too far."

"So, you think Rockwell pushed Stella to her breaking point?"

"Stella could be difficult," Silvia interjected. "And mean-spirited. People like her can be dangerous."

"People like her?"

"Do you have any more questions, Agent Colton?" Dayn asked. He stepped in front of his wife, quietly silencing anything else she might have had to say. She turned abruptly, scurrying from the room in a huff.

"Do you know of anyone else who might have had a grudge against your son?" Brennan asked.

Dayn shook his head. "If you've spoken with anyone from his law firm, you know he was very well-respected."

"He practiced corporate law, is that correct?"

"Yes, and he was well-liked by the companies he represented. Since he never practiced criminal law, he never made any enemies that we know of. Rockwell was very much a people person. Everyone liked him. It's what made him a great political candidate."

"Do you think Stella Maxwell was involved in your son's death, Mr. Henley?"

The patriarch shook his head. "No, I don't. Stella made my son happy. She cared about Rockwell. But his political ambitions and his mother's influence didn't serve their relationship well."

"Thank you," Brennan said. "I appreciate you taking time to speak with me."

"Find my son's killer, Agent."

"I'm doing everything we can, sir."

"Well, do more!" Silvia snapped from the doorway.

Both men turned toward her, noting the look of disgust

on her face. She was not a happy woman and Brennan imagined her unhappiness had made her son, and Stella, miserable. With one last nod of his head, he stepped back into the elevator, the two men still eyeing each other before the doors closed and the conveyor returned to the first floor.

THE CAMPAIGN OFFICE of Rockwell Henley for Governor was deserted. When Brennan stepped through the doors, he hadn't known what he'd find. But he didn't expect it to be quite so desolate. Any evidence of a campaign being waged no longer existed, everything packed up or tossed away. Something about the space felt out of sorts, feeling as if all traces of Rockwell Henley had been erased in the twenty-four hours since he had died.

"Hello?" He called out, noise coming from someplace in the rear of the building. "Is anyone here?"

The noise stopped but no one appeared. The quiet was slightly disconcerting. Brennan called out a second time, his hand moving to the gun holstered beneath his arm. "Hello? Is anyone here?"

"Yes, hello!" A young woman suddenly rushed forward. A wide, gummy smile pulled across her face. Her thin lips showcased a mouth full of picture-perfect teeth resulting from years of orthodontic and periodontal work. Mousy brown hair framed nondescript facial features and hazel eyes that were flecked with gold. She had beautiful eyes, with lengthy lashes that she batted easily when necessary. Brennan found himself staring at her eyes, those flecks of gold shimmering in the light.

She was slim, but not overly thin, nor did she have a

figure that garnered second looks. She wasn't homely, nor was she outrageously beautiful. She was plain, and average in appearance with the bubbliest of personalities to make up for whatever she thought her physical short-comings might be.

Her arms were wrapped tightly around her torso as she moved toward him. "May I help you?"

"Yes, hello." Brennan flashed his badge at her. "I'm with the FBI and I was hoping to speak with Tobias Humphrey. My name is Colton. Special agent Brennan Colton."

"Is this about Rockwell?"

"I just need to ask Mr. Humphrey a few questions," he said with a slight nod.

The young woman sighed, her hand brushing the length of her hair from her face. "It's just so horrible!" She suddenly started crying, tears raining over her cheeks. "We loved him so much!"

Brennan nodded, caught off guard by her waterworks. "And you are?"

She swiped at her eyes with the back of her hand. "Pamela. Pamela Littlefield. I'm Mr. Humphrey's personal assistant." The tears stopped as quickly as they'd started.

"Is Mr. Humphrey available or do you know how I might reach him?"

The woman named Pamela shook her head. "He's not here. He may be with the Henley family. They were all very close."

Brennan nodded. "I imagine you knew Mr. Henley well. Have you been with the campaign since the beginning?"

"Yes. I've worked for Mr. Humphrey for years. And I

knew Rockwell from school. It turned out to be a great partnership. Until…well…" The tears started again.

"Is there anything you can tell me about Mr. Henley? Anything that might explain someone wanting to kill him?"

Pamela shook her head. "No, not really. Everyone loved Rockwell." She pulled a hand to her chest, manicured fingers tapping lightly at that dip between her sterna. "He was such a generous man and so kind. People were drawn to him. I didn't know anyone who didn't love everything about him. Everyone except, maybe, Stella Maxwell." There was a sudden edge to her voice as she mentioned Stella's name.

"Stella Maxwell? You know Stella?"

She nodded. "Stella and Rockwell dated, but it didn't work out. His mother didn't care for her. Stella wasn't overly supportive of Rockwell's political aspirations. It was a huge problem between them. They fought all the time. It started to affect the campaign, so he broke it off with her. Tobias felt that was for the best. I heard she didn't take it well."

"And where did you hear that?" Brennan questioned.

"His mother. I heard Mrs. Henley tell Tobias that Stella really went after Rockwell. She said she sent him some hateful messages. Threatening him and such. Apparently, it was bad."

Brennan listened as she regaled him with a lengthy list of Stella's wrongdoings. Things that had irritated his mother or annoyed the campaign manager. It was apparent that short of walking on water, there was nothing Stella could have done that would have impressed any of them. From all the woman shared, the only individual who didn't complain about Stella had been Rockwell. Rockwell, who'd neither defended her nor castigated her, but seemed hopeful that if he ignored the peanut gallery tossing their two cents in on his relationship, it would work itself out. When it hadn't, he'd given in to the pressure.

Pamela shook her head from side to side. "That's what I heard, but I don't know how true it is, of course."

"Do you think Ms. Maxwell had something to do with Mr. Henley's murder?"

There was a lengthy pause before the woman answered. "Rockwell's mother thought she was problematic. Tobias didn't have good things to say about her either. But I honestly don't know her well enough to say if she was capable of murder or not. She was always very nice to me. I liked her. Had she been around longer, I think we would have been good friends."

"One last question," Brennan said. "Where were you yesterday morning between nine and eleven o'clock?"

"Me?" Her voice cracked as if the question surprised her. "I was here, closing down the office," she said as she gestured behind her with an open palm.

"Can anyone confirm that?" Brennan asked.

Pamela shrugged her narrow shoulders. "I'm sure Mr. Humphrey can verify my whereabouts. He was here too. On the phone mostly."

Brennan pulled a business card from the inner pocket of his suit jacket. "Would you please have Mr. Humphrey give me a call when he has an opportunity? It's important that I speak with him."

Pamela took the card from his hand. "I will. And if I think of anything that might be important, I'll make sure to contact you."

"Thank you for your time, Ms. Littlefield."

"It was my pleasure," Pamela said, tossing in one last sniffle before that wide smile returned.

OUT ON THE SIDEWALK, Brennan could feel Pamela Littlefield still staring at him. When he turned around to look, she was closing the thin white blinds that covered the windows, disappearing from view. She was what his mother would call an odd bird, he thought, although he found her friendly enough. She was one of those people who seemed almost too eager to be helpful and that never boded well with Brennan. People like that always made him wary. He made a mental note to ask Stella about the woman. He was curious to know her opinion of the personal assistant who would have been besties with her in another life.

Thus far, the general consensus from those he'd spoken with, was that Stella was evil incarnate. They presumed she could projectile vomit, eat small children and castrate the male species on a whim. Most wanted her to be guilty of Rockwell Henley's murder. He imagined that once they learned she had an alibi and was innocent, they would still choose to believe that she was somehow involved.

Brennan checked the time, adjusting the watch on his wrist. He planned to show up at Rockwell's memorial, standing in the back to watch the crowd. He also hoped to have a conversation with the ex-girlfriend who Stella claimed wanted to reconcile with Rockwell. Before then though he needed to see where the local police were with the Landmark Killer case. He hadn't heard anything, which told him they hadn't been successful in their search for the next potential victim. He was starting to feel like that case was going nowhere fast. He didn't want to admit that they might not be able to stop the killer from dropping another body into their laps.

STELLA FOUND EVERYTHING she needed to know on her computer. She had never unsubscribed from Rockwell's campaign newsletter and news of his death had come just hours after his body had been found. Shortly after there was an announcement about a vigil being hosted by his law firm, campaign team and his parents. It included the date, time and address, and only gave her a few short hours to get ready and get there. They planned a private funeral for family only, later in the week.

She thought about Brennan's admonishments for her to stay put, but following directions had never been her strong suit. Not even as a child. Stella had always done things her own way no matter the consequences. She needed to be at this memorial. If for no other reason to show the naysayers that she hadn't killed Rockwell and she wasn't afraid of whoever might be coming after her. That was, of course, a lie. She was scared to death, but she refused to let it get the best of her. She also knew that not going made her look guilty. She'd be damned before she allowed them to whisper behind her back about killing the man. She'd done no such thing and she intended to say so. And not even the likes of Brennan Colton, was going to stop her.

Hours later, Stella was showered and primped, her hair pulled up into a neat bun, and her makeup meticulous. She'd chosen a black silk tank dress with a matching duster coat. The dress material was form-fitting and the long-sleeved duster lightweight enough for the warm weather. With just the hint of a black heel, she looked polished and professional, like the grieving ex-girlfriend of a New York politician.

Staring at her reflection in the mirror, Stella suddenly kicked off the black heels. She searched the bottom of her closet until she found the perfect pair of shoes; a pair of vintage, Dolce & Gabbana, lime green alligator pumps that Rockwell had gifted to her for her birthday the previous year. With one final glance in the mirror, she felt more like herself, still polished and professional but not nearly as stifling and cold as Rockwell's family and friends would have liked. Lime green had been Rockwell's favorite color.

Hours later, Stella was traveling to the Upper East Side, taking the subway from 125th Street to 86th Street. From there, she walked to Pratt Mansions on Fifth Avenue. She took her time, moving casually to her destination, refusing to be overheated and sweaty when she arrived.

As she turned the corner onto Fifth Avenue, Pratt was on one side facing the grandeur of the Metropolitan Museum on the other. She smiled at the sight of the stonework that decorated the outside of the building. She'd attended a wedding or two at that location and always marveled at the beautifully detailed marble and woodwork inside. Rockwell had announced his candidacy there months earlier, so it was fitting that his parents had chosen the space to bid him farewell.

Stella paused on the sidewalk watching as mourners trickled into the building. It was a cornucopia of the city's elite making an appearance. News crews were posted around the building, snapping photos of those who were coming and going. Everyone who wanted to be seen paused long enough at the entrance to have their picture taken. Many of the sad faces and tears were disingenuous, most not even knowing Rockwell personally. Stella had no doubts his mother was duly pleased with the turnout and the displays of emotion for her son. Minutes passed as she gathered her nerves. When she had sufficiently collected her thoughts, Stella took a deep breath, crossed the street and headed inside.

BRENNAN HAD BEEN one of the first to arrive to pay their respects to the Henley family for their loss. Mr. Henley had given him the barest of smiles and quick nod of his head, before turning back to the conversation he was having. Mrs. Henley had bristled, clearly displeased with his presence. She whispered hurriedly to the man standing before her, then gave him and Brennan her back. That man came rushing in his direction, his hand extended in greeting.

"Special Agent Colton! Tobias Humphrey," he said, as he grasped Brennan's hand and shook it quickly.

"Mr. Humphrey, it's a pleasure. Thank you for a moment of your time."

Tobias stole a quick glance toward his watch. "And I only have a quick moment. I'm sure you understand."

"I do and I won't intrude any longer than necessary."

Tobias nodded again. He was a small man with even smaller features. He was balding and had taken to combing the last strands of hair holding on across the top of his head from one ear to the other. He wore an expensive silk suit that had been tailored to his stature and leather shoes that would have been a year's salary for Brennan.

"When was the last time you spoke with Rockwell?" Brennan asked.

Tobias sighed. "We were talking the morning he died. He said he had an appointment to keep and that he would meet me at campaign headquarters when he was finished. I asked him what the appointment was for, and he said he was meeting Stella Maxwell at her office to talk. I expressed that I didn't think that was a good idea. They had recently broken up and she hadn't taken it well. Obviously, I was concerned about the optics if she'd intended to publicly embarrass him. He wasn't at all concerned. Clearly, we both should have been."

Tobias pressed a hand to his chest and shook his head vehemently. He continued. "I feel very guilty. I should have insisted he not go, or that I go with him. He might still be here with us if I had."

"Or you might be dead too," Brennan said matter-of-factly.

The man's eyes widened. He suddenly fanned his hand in front of his face as if he could wave that thought away. "Well," he said, "we're grateful that the NYPD were able to make a quick arrest. Them catching her in the act means justice can be served swiftly and without prejudice."

"If she were guilty," Brennan said nonchalantly.

"They caught her in the act!" Tobias repeated. His voice rose slightly, and he took a quick glance around the room to see if anyone had heard. He steadied himself, taking a deep breath, and brushing his hand down the front of his suit jacket.

Brennan didn't bother to tell him that Stella had been proven innocent and released. "Is there anyone else that may have wanted Rockwell dead?" he questioned.

"Not at all. He was well-respected. And very affable. He didn't have any enemies that we were aware of."

"And the party didn't find anything concerning before giving him their support?"

"Nothing, and he had been fully vetted."

"It's my understanding that you recently reported some concerns with a young woman named Rebecca Farrington. I understand she and Rockwell had dated before he and Ms. Maxwell were together?"

"It's campaign policy to report any threats made against our candidates. Rebecca was brokenhearted and said some heated things in a moment of passion. She was very apologetic, and the police found nothing credible to be concerned about. In fact," he said, gesturing toward the Henley family who stood at the front of the room by an oversized, framed photo of their son. "Rebecca has been by the family's side supporting them since the news broke."

Brennan looked to where he pointed. The young woman standing beside Rockwell's mother was quite a beauty. Long and lean, she flipped the length of her brunette hair with severe blond highlights over her shoulder. She wore a tailored, pale blue pant suit. There was a single button holding it closed and with the hint of cleavage showing, Brennan fathomed there wasn't much beneath it. She looked quite comfortable with her hand holding tightly onto Mrs. Henley's elbow.

He turned his attention back to Tobias. "Did Stella Maxwell ever make any threats that campaign policy dictated you report? Any threats against Mr. Henley's life that were concerning enough for the police to become involved?"

Brennan felt the man bristle, a hint of indignation washing over his expression. He pulled at the collar of his shirt, adjusting his necktie. "No, not that I was ever made aware of," he finally muttered.

"Can anyone verify your whereabouts yesterday morning, Mr. Humphrey?"

The man paused as if he needed to think about it. "I was at campaign headquarters until I came here to meet with the caterer and the venue manager. My assistant saw me there and multiple people saw me here."

Brennan stared at the man before finally extending his hand. "Thank you again for your time, Mr. Humphrey. I plan to stay a while longer. I promise not to get in the way."

The two men shook hands one last time before Tobias turned and scurried to the other side of the room.

Moving to the rear of the spacious event hall, Brennan positioned himself against the back wall. His arms were crossed over his chest as his eyes darted back and forth, taking it all in. People were steadily filing in and soon, most of the chairs were filled, everyone waiting for the speech to begin.

He kept his eye on Rebecca, who continued to stand with the family. She'd made hair flipping an art form. Every other comment or gesture included a toss of her lengthy strands. There was a brief exchange between her and Tobias, the two seeming unhappy with each other. She displayed classic, mean girl attitude, dismissive of those she considered beneath her.

Brennan had also done the requisite Google search on Miss Farrington. She too had come from money; the oldest daughter born to a plastic surgeon father and orthodontist mother. She and Rockwell had gone to school together. They'd been college sweethearts betrothed to each other on graduation day. The engagement had ended when she'd left Rockwell for a New York Giants football player with a five-year, multi-million-dollar contract. That relationship ended when the football player injured his back, his career cut short.

Rebecca was also a former Miss New York contestant, placing in the top twenty-five the first year she competed, and the top ten her second year. The verdict was still out on whether she'd compete a third time. She relied heavily on her looks and only because they often took her far. She was very much a younger version of Rockwell's mother in demeanor, the two women cut from the same angry burlap cloth. Brennan had dated many women like her. More than his fair share if he were honest. Pretty packages with questionable content. Without exchanging one word with the woman, he understood why Rockwell had shown no interest in a reconciliation and why his parents had considered her perfect trophy wife material.

Eyeing the who's who of New York as they pandered

to one another was proving to be both boring and entertaining, on the same level as bird-watching, Brennan thought to himself. There was no one who stood out, looking like they may have killed the man everyone was there to honor.

Pamela Littlejohn flitted about anxiously, trying to make herself useful. She followed after Tobias, ready to fulfill any order before he even needed to make a request of her. She wore the same bright smile she'd greeted Brennan with earlier, peppered with the same glassy tears that occasionally damped her lashes. She'd changed into a less stylish black dress that stopped just below her knees. The youthful Peter Pan collar was fitting and would have been almost infantile on any other woman. She'd waved at Brennan excitedly, her exuberance as if they were old friends. He waved back, thinking that building a rapport with the young woman might be to his advantage. Her eagerness might be useful as he continued to search out information.

Brennan's brow lifted ever so slightly when his cousin Rory entered the room. She'd come dressed for the occasion, attired in her requisite dark suit, white blouse, brass badge on her hip and her government-issued weapon secured in the holster beneath her arm. He and his cousin exchanged a look, their gazes meeting at the same times.

Rory eased her way to his side and greeted him warmly. "What the hell are you doing here?" she asked. "I thought you were keeping your eye on Ms. Maxwell?"

Brennan shrugged. "She's safe at home. I thought I'd

do just a little reconnaissance work. I figured this would be a good place to check out potential suspects."

His cousin shook her head. "Did you come up with anything?"

"Not really," he replied. "Everyone here loved Rockwell. He was the golden boy, well-liked, respected, with nary an enemy."

"Except the person who stabbed him," Rory countered. "Anyone have any thoughts on that?"

"All fingers point to Stella. I don't think she has a single friend in this room. The general consensus is she did it."

"Were you expecting different?"

"Not really. I was just hoping something, or someone, would have surprised me."

There was a moment's pause. Then Rory chuckled. "Humph!" she muttered. "It looks like your prayers have been answered." She pointed him toward the door.

Looking over, a wave of shock crossed Brennan's face. His stomach suddenly felt like it was doing a gymnastic floor routine; a back handspring, somersault, two cartwheels, a scissor leap and then a roundoff. His breath caught deep in his chest and his mouth was dry. Because Stella stood in the entrance, her gaze locked on the front of the room. She was stunning, looking regal, poised and ready to take on the world.

Chapter Eight

Stella had no idea what she expected when she made the decision to show up for Rockwell's memorial service. What she hadn't expected when she moved to the front of the room to offer her condolences to Rockwell's parents was the bloodcurdling scream from Rockwell's mother. It was loud and guttural, pulled from somewhere deep in the matriarch's midsection, and it brought the entire room to a standstill.

"Murderer!" Mrs. Henley cried out, spitting the word in Stella's face. "How dare you show up here! Murderer!"

The chaos that ensued was something straight off the WorldStar video blog. Cameras were flashing, people were shouting, and all Stella could hear was Silvia screeching and Dayn trying to calm her down. She was suddenly aware of Tobias grabbing her arm and shouting in her ear that she needed to leave, and then Rebecca pushed her way forward, her arm raised high as if to slap Stella's face. Stella braced herself, her fists clenched as she readied herself to strike the woman back and then Brennan stepped between them, wrapping both his arms around her as he gently pushed her back toward the door.

They were blocks away, having crossed over and dipped into Central Park when Brennan finally came to a halt, satisfied that no one had followed them. It was only then, his arms still wrapped protectively around her, that Stella realized she was crying. She turned, leaning into his chest as she sobbed. Brennan continued to hold her, allowing her to release the hurt and pain she'd been holding on to with an iron grip, refusing to allow herself a moment of weakness that anyone could see. He hated to see her this way, wishing that he could do something, anything, to ease the pain she was going through. And then, as if she read his mind, she pulled herself from him, digging into her purse for a tissue.

He shook his head. "I thought I told you to stay put. What were you trying to accomplish?"

"I wanted to pay my respects to the family."

His head was still waving from side to side. "We should have discussed that first."

Stella bristled. "Why haven't you told them that it wasn't me? That I didn't kill their son?"

"We were hoping the real killer would get comfortable. If you looked good for the crime, then they might let their guard down and get sloppy. But I'm sure they know by now," Brennan answered. "I have no doubts Detective Colton told them after that display. But it doesn't mean they're going to welcome you back with open arms, Stella."

"I don't need them to welcome me back. I need them to not look at me like I'm the Antichrist!"

"You don't need them to validate you!"

"No, I don't, but I deserve to have them respect me.

That's all. I have not earned the level of disrespect that they continue to show me."

"And what happens if you never change their opinion? If they still dislike you?"

"Nothing happens. I just go on with my life."

Brennan nodded. His voice dropped to a loud whisper. "Baby, it's time for you to move on," he said softly. He reached for her again, pulling her against him.

Stella settled into the warmth, his words washing over her ears in a heated wave. He'd only said what she'd been feeling for months. What she'd resigned herself to when the Henleys had first voiced their displeasure with their son's relationship. What she had always known deep in her heart but had still hoped to change.

She stared down to the green shoes on her feet. A dark stain blemished the left toe, the smudge trailing along the outer edge toward the heel. She blew a heavy sigh as she grabbed Brennan's arm for support. She stepped out of the high-heeled pumps, retrieving a pair of foldable walking shoes from her purse. She pushed her foot into the lightweight slip-on, then bent down to retrieve her designer shoes. She eased over to a wooden bench and rested the shoes on top.

Brennan eyed her curiously. "Those look like a nice pair of shoes. You're just going to leave them?"

Stella nodded. She couldn't begin to explain to Brennan, but she was past ready to kick them and the memories of Rockwell Henley to the curb. "I'm ready to go home," she said softly.

With a nod, Brennan turned, guiding them back in the direction they'd just run from. Neither spoke, and it was just as they exited the park that Stella realized he'd called her baby with all the affection and commitment of a man who genuinely cared about her.

BABY. HE'D CALLED her baby. *Baby!* And it had come as naturally to him as breathing. Clearly, Brennan thought, he had officially lost his mind. He'd had no business calling the primary witness in a murder case that he was investigating *baby*. If any of his team found out, he'd be snatched off the case so fast his head would spin. He needed to apologize to Stella. He couldn't blame her if she filed a complaint with his superiors. He had overstepped the professional boundaries of his position, something he had never done in his entire career.

He threw his body back against the mattress of the king-sized bed. When they'd gotten back, Stella had disappeared up the stairs, not bothering to return. As the sun had set, the evening air cooling comfortably, he'd climbed up to the second floor hoping they might have a conversation. He found her bedroom door closed, so he'd stood in the hallway, respecting her desire to be alone. It killed him not to check that she was okay, but he heard her moving about, so he let her be until she was ready to talk to him.

Moving into her spare bedroom, he found that she had put fresh sheets on the mattress and had left him clean towels on the dresser. Now he lay there wondering what he'd gotten himself into and how he was going to get himself out of it.

Reflecting back on the day, something didn't feel right. Something was off, and he couldn't quite put his finger on it. Brennan lifted his arms above his head and clasped his hands together. He thought back to his conversations with Mr. and Mrs. Henley. And then he reflected on his questioning of Tobias Humphrey and his assistant Pamela. He thought back to everything he'd heard at the memorial service, the hushed whispers and choice words people didn't think anyone would hear or remember. He replayed each conversation over in his head. And it was on the third replay that what was bothering him clicked, the pieces falling into place.

Pamela had said that Rockwell's mother claimed Stella had made threats against her son. Mrs. Henley had told him the same thing. From what he'd been made to understand, Mrs. Henley had relayed her concerns to Tobias. But Tobias had clearly stated there had been no threats from Stella that he'd been aware of. None that had required his attention or police intervention. Now Brennan had to consider what had been the truth and who had been less than honest with him.

WHEN STELLA OPENED her eyes, the clock on her nightstand read 2:15 a.m. She lay curled in a fetal position in her bed, still in the dress she'd worn to the memorial service. It had been a long day and she was still feeling out of sorts. Thinking about what had happened at Pratt Mansion left her shaking and sent her into a fit of tears. She felt emotionally battered, slightly lost and monumentally embarrassed.

She appreciated Brennan's kindness. He had made her feel safe and protected and not at all as foolish as she felt over everything that had happened. She should have stayed at home like he'd insisted. If she had, then she wouldn't be feeling as vulnerable as she was.

Hiding out in her bedroom had been necessary for her to regroup and get herself together. She'd needed time to herself. Time that hadn't required her to explain herself or share her feelings. Time to actually mourn the loss of someone she had cared about. Time to process the wealth of emotion that felt all-consuming. Time to revel in her own pity party until she felt normal again.

She'd left Brennan to his own devices. She had heard him puttering around in her kitchen, then he had turned on the television, an episode of the old television series *The Unit* playing loudly from her family room. Just before she'd dozed off to sleep, she'd heard him climb the steps, pausing in the hallway. She'd stood on her side of the entrance listening as she pondered whether or not to open the door and invite him inside. The moment passed when she heard the guest room door close shut.

She'd questioned what she'd been thinking, then had laid back down, drawing her knees to her chest and wrapping her arms tightly around her body. Sleep had come on the tail end of one last good cry, the tears dampening her pillow. As slumber eased into her space, the sweetest inhale of air pulling at her gently, she heard Brennan's voice in her head, and Brennan was calling her *baby*.

It was a sweet memory, Stella thought as she rolled across the mattress. She threw her legs off the side and sat upright. Rising, she stripped out of her clothes and headed toward the shower. Hot water would feel good, she thought. The rest would fix itself in the morning. Be-

cause in the morning, Brennan would still be there trying to help her make sense of it all.

BRENNAN'S PHONE RANG, pulling him from a deep sleep.
He didn't bother to open his eyes to check the caller ID before pulling it to his ear and depressing the answer button.

"Hello?"

"You alone?" Rory asked, her voice ringing loudly
in his ear.

"And you're asking me that, why?"

"Because I saw how you were looking at Ms. Maxwell yesterday."

"Don't bust my balls, Rory. I'm not in the mood."

His cousin laughed. "How is she doing?"

"I don't know. She locked herself in her room when
we got back to her house, and I haven't seen her since."

"At least she's keeping her head down. That should
make your job a whole lot easier."

"You think?"

Rory laughed. "Wishful thinking! I know how much
you could use a break."

"What's up? You don't usually call so early in the
morning."

"Just wanted to give you a heads-up. Wells needs you
to give him an update on the Landmark Killer case."

"Something happen I need to know about?"

"He's got the mayor breathing down his neck. I informed the Henley family that we do not have a suspect
in their son's murder, and now they're on a rampage. The
mayor wants to make sure we don't give either case more
priority than the other. Both are equally important for us
to solve. But he needs both of them closed yesterday."

Brennan cursed. Logistically, it could take months for them to solve a murder case. Most especially when there was little to no evidence to point them in the right direction. The mayor's office poking around would only prove to be problematic. And unnecessary problems made for mistakes. "So, was that the bad news or the good news?" he asked.

"Who said anything about good news?" she countered.

"A man can hope, can't he?"

Rory laughed again. "Well, since I'm piling it on. There's a press conference this afternoon. The mayor wants Captain Reeves to give the public an update. It's supposed to calm nerves and ensure we stay transparent."

"So, tossing the bottom feeders a bone is supposed to keep them happy?"

"Calling the news media *bottom feeders* isn't cool. It's actually an insult to bottom feeders. Besides, I don't think your new friend will take kindly to you insulting her profession."

"You're right. I should be more creative with my choice of words. Do I need to be at this press conference?" Brennan asked.

"He'd like the whole team there, but we understand that you can't make it. We've got you covered."

"I owe you one," Brennan responded.

"Yes, you do."

Brennan sat upright, shifting his body to the side of the bed. "Things good otherwise?"

"Of course not, but that's a conversation for another day."

Brennan chuckled softly. "You know I've got your back, right, Rory?"

"Ditto. And please, keep that woman safe."

"Yes, ma'am, Detective Colton. I promise to return her just like you gave her to me."

As Rory disconnected the phone line, Brennan smiled, knowing his cousin was shaking her head at him.

THE PHONE RANG twice before Garrett Hoffman answered Stella's call.

"What's going on with you?" her friend questioned. His voice was low and slightly muffled. Stella knew his hand was cupped over the receiver to keep nosy ears from hearing his conversation. "Girl, you made today's cover!"

"You're kidding me, right?"

"Of course! The boss shut that down, but there's a great shot of you going toe to toe with a Miss New York wannabe that's making the rounds here in the office. Did that heifer hit you?"

Stella rolled her eyes skyward. "You know good and well if that woman had put her hands on me, I would have made the front page mopping the floor with her."

"I know that's right. But really, what's going on?"

"First, why is Taylor calling me? She's left a dozen messages in my mailbox."

"She's trying to scoop an exclusive with you about the Henley killing. Your boss was ready to roll the story about you being arrested until they released you. Once your name was cleared, Taylor pitched doing a story on what happened and how journalists are falsely accused and weaponized when it's convenient for the status quo. Or some crap like that."

"I'm not giving her an exclusive. I'd write my own damn story if I thought it was newsworthy."

"Don't shoot me! I'm just sharing what I heard."

"What have they said about me taking a leave of absence?"

"Just that you needed some personal time until this all blows over. But someone from Human Resources came up to look through your desk yesterday."

"Damn vultures! My body's not even cold yet, and they're ready to give my desk away!"

"All I know is that there's some concern about your negative press reflecting badly on the newspaper. They just want it to die down before you come back."

"Yeah, right."

"It's what I heard."

Stella blew a soft sigh. "I need to get back to work, or I'm going to go crazy."

"Just take some time. You'll get past this. Stay in touch, and if I hear anything new, I promise I'll call you."

"Thank you, Garrett!"

"You're welcome, Stella! Keep the faith, girl!"

"I love you too, dude! I love you too!"

WHEN BRENNAN FINALLY made his way to the lower level of Stella's home, she was at the kitchen counter consuming a bowl of Frosted Flakes cereal. She looked like she had conquered the world and could have taken on another. Something like joy shone from her eyes and her complexion was crystal, not a single frown line to be found. He had worried what their first encounter might be like, but the sight of her eased every ounce of anxiety from his spirit.

"Good morning," he said, a wide smile filling his face.

Stella tossed up a hand. "Good morning! Did you sleep well?"

"Like a baby."

She pointed toward the Keurig machine on her counter. "There's coffee and cereal if you're hungry. I'd cook, but I'm not in the mood."

"No problem. I would have gladly cooked for you."

"You've done that twice now. And I appreciate it. I'm sorry I missed last night's dinner."

"It'll be great for lunch. I put the leftovers in the refrigerator for you."

"Aren't you considerate?" she said.

Their conversation felt slightly awkward, almost mechanical, as if the ease they had previously felt had suddenly disappeared. Brennan sensed that Stella felt it as well.

"Look," he started to say, "I need to apologize…"

"I'm really sorry about yesterday…" Stella said at the same time.

They both paused and then laughed, and just like that, an air of comfort settled back over them.

Brennan took a seat on the stool beside her. "If I did anything yesterday to upset you or make you uncomfortable, I want to apologize. I would never want to overstep my boundaries with you."

"Not at all," Stella answered. "I'm the one who owes you an apology. I should have listened and kept my happy ass right here at home. I would never have purposely caused that kind of drama."

"I was concerned about your safety. I haven't forgotten

that someone tried to come after you. For all we know, that someone was in the room yesterday."

Stella shook her head. "I wasn't thinking. What I did was reckless."

Brennan gave her another smile and nodded in agreement. "It was reckless, but I understand it. You were grieving somebody you had loved once. You should have been allowed to do that without being harassed."

There was a moment of pause as the two considered each other. Brennan leaned across her countertop with a large mug of hot coffee pressed between his palms. Stella pulled a spoonful of cereal into her mouth.

"I think it's going to be eggs and bacon for me," Brennan said. "Can I interest you in a plate?"

Stella laughed, "What, you don't like cereal?"

He laughed with her. "I need a hearty meal. There is nothing hearty about cereal. Most especially sugar-coated corn flakes."

"What about all the athletes on the Wheaties boxes?"

"You're not eating Wheaties!"

Stella winced. "They're not my favorite, but if you need a heartier brand of cereal, I'll make sure there's always a box on hand just for you."

"Have I earned special privileges?" Brennan questioned, his brow raised.

Stella's gaze narrowed ever so slightly. "Don't get ahead of yourself, Special Agent Colton. *Special* is not that kind of special!"

The duo laughed heartily.

STELLA SAT AND watched as Brennan prepared himself two eggs over easy with two slices of bacon and a single slice of buttered toast. She liked having him in her space, enjoying the camaraderie between them. She appreciated that he didn't take himself too seriously and that he made her laugh. With everything that had happened, she needed to laugh.

When he sat down to enjoy his morning meal, she rose from her seat to wash away the few dirty dishes that had piled up in her sink. She was growing comfortable with his presence, and although she didn't say anything, she wasn't sure how she felt about that. Most especially since Brennan Colton seemed very content to be sharing space and time with her.

"So, what's on your agenda today?" she asked.

"I'm going to have to leave you for a bit," Brennan said. "The mayor is planning a press conference this afternoon about the Landmark Killer case, and I need to meet with the team before that happens. I also want to follow up with Rockwell's business colleagues to see if any of them know anything."

"Did you find out anything yesterday?"

"Just what you already know. Everyone loved Rockwell, he was God's gift to us all and you should be our one and only suspect."

Stella winced. "Rockwell wasn't the prize people thought he was. Just ask Pamela."

Brennan's eyes widened. "Pamela? What about her?"

"Rockwell and Pamela were friends in school. Someone had set them up on a blind date. He showed up, ate his meal and then ducked out when the check came. She papered the entire campus with Photoshopped flyers of him in a dress or something crazy like that. He begged her for a second chance, made reservations at some five-star restaurant, then wined and dined her the entire weekend to make amends. They used to laugh about it, but I could tell that him being mean to her had hurt her feelings. She got even though, and obviously, they got past it. In fact, she was the one who recommended him to Tobias. I don't know if he would have even considered politics if she hadn't pushed him to run for office."

Brennan nodded. "Was Pamela close to Rockwell's mother?"

"Define close," Stella responded. "Silvia isn't your typical warm and fuzzy, cookie-baking PTA mom."

"Did they get along? Were they friends?"

"Actually, they seemed to be quite close. But then, Pamela is friendly with everyone. She likes to be helpful, and Mrs. Henley enjoys bossing people around. She had that poor girl running all kinds of errands for her and Pamela never complained."

"Interesting..." Brennan muttered, reflecting back on what he'd been thinking earlier.

"Not really," Stella said. "That whole little clique of theirs, including Tobias, made me itch!"

"What do you mean?"

"It was like some unholy alliance. They were always plotting together and covering for each other. It drove Rockwell crazy because he thought his mother was behind it."

"Did you agree?"

"No, I put my money on Tobias. He loved having Mrs. Henley's attention."

"Enough to be jealous of Rockwell?"

Stella paused, wiping her damp hands against a dish towel. "I never really thought about it," she said finally. "He and Rockwell got along well. I never got jealousy vibes from Tobias."

"And nothing sketchy from Pamela?"

"I once thought she might have had a crush on Rockwell, but the way she chases after Tobias, I think she might be in love with him."

"And Tobias?"

"Tobias loves Tobias, like Silvia loves Silvia!"

"Do you think it's possible one of them killed Rockwell?"

Stella took her dear sweet time before she answered, giving the suggestion some serious thought. She finally shook her head. "No. I wouldn't think so. They were head of his fan club. They wanted him to do well. Obviously, anything is possible, but I don't see that."

Brennan nodded, moving to the sink to wash his plate and silverware.

"Why all the questions?" Stella asked. "What do you know?"

"Nothing. I'm just trying to cover all my bases."

"Want to know what's on my agenda today?"

"Does it involve showing up someplace you don't need to be?"

"Ha ha!" Stella said sarcastically. "It doesn't. In fact, I have no plans to leave the house. I plan to park myself on that sofa and binge-watch episodes of *Housewives of New York* while I stuff myself with chocolate chip cookies."

"You don't mean that bag of mini cookies that were in the cupboard, do you?"

Stella cut an eye in his direction, her tone suddenly changing. "Did you eat my cookies?"

"I might have had one or two or the entire bag last night."

She tossed up her hands, feigning frustration as she glared in his direction. "You don't want me to leave the house, but you eat all my snacks."

"I didn't eat them all."

"But you ate the best ones."

"I'll bring some cookies when I come back."

"You better." Stella pushed her bottom lip out in a pretend pout.

Brennan laughed. "There will be a patrol car outside keeping an eye on things while I'm gone. Courtesy of my cousin Rory. Please stay out of trouble while I'm gone, Stella."

The look Stella gave him was priceless. There were daggers shooting from her eyes, and she was biting back a retort that probably would have cut him deep. With a nod of his head, Brennan hurried to the front door. He waved good-bye as he made his exit.

"I won't be long," he called over his shoulder.

As the door closed and locked behind him, Stella grinned, thinking she couldn't wait for him to return.

Chapter Nine

The internet is forever. Stella remembered the first time she'd heard the statement, thinking *forever* was only as long as the systems that held it in place. Eventually, all things came to an end. Now, scrolling through the numerous photos, stories and opinions of her encounter with the Henley family and the conspiracy theories on how she was connected to Rockwell's murder, *forever* felt like an unending attack that she would never be able to recover from. She should have kept watching the *Housewives*, she thought. Even that absurdity didn't feel quite so painful. She heaved a deep sigh, closing the lid to her laptop.

For a split second, she wanted to cry. Then she didn't. Raging would have made her feel better. But she didn't have the energy for that either. She stole a look at her cell phone. She thought about calling Brennan but figured that wouldn't be a great idea. They weren't friends like that, and there was nothing wrong that she needed to report. But they were friends like that, she thought, suddenly questioning her relationship with the handsome man. *Weren't they?*

She decided to text him a message instead. She sat in

thought as she pondered what to say. With a quick push of the buttons, she typed, deleted, typed then typed some more until she was happy with the message. She paused one last time and then she hit Send.

A noise at her front door suddenly pulled at her attention. She moved to the window to peek out. A postal delivery truck had pulled up out front, and the delivery person was standing in conversation with the police officer. The two men were chatting easily.

Moving to the front door, Stella pulled it open, looking from one to the other. She lifted her hand in greeting. "Hi, Pete!"

"Hi, Stella! I have a package for you. Online shopping again?"

Stella laughed. Most of her shopping was online, so she and the delivery persons for the neighborhood had become well acquainted. So much so that they were on a first name basis with each other, shared stories about work and family, and every Christmas, she gave the regulars a gift card.

The police officer chimed in. "My wife is just as bad. She's taken to hiding the boxes before I get home, hoping I don't see them!"

"That's why I don't need a husband." Stella laughed, the two men joining her.

"It's from someplace called the Rose Wheel?" the officer questioned. "Something you're expecting?"

Stella shrugged. "I buy from them regularly. I don't remember ordering anything recently, but that doesn't mean it isn't mine."

The officer laughed again as he took the midsize box from the man named Pete.

What came next would always be a blur in Stella's mind. She would remember the police officer starting up the short length of brick steps, that box extended out in front of him. She had taken a single step down, intent on meeting him halfway. Before she could take that second step, the entire world exploded before her eyes. Neither Pete nor the police officer were standing in front of her, and what remained of that box was nothing but dust blowing off into the distance. The sound of the explosion resonated from one corner of the block to the other. The force of it was so intense that Stella felt her entire body being lifted off her feet as she was thrown backward, slamming hard against her front door. As she fell to the concrete landing of her front steps, she heard herself cry out. Her voice sounded muffled with pain and confusion. Tears ran over her checks, and her head felt heavy against her thin neck. There was a ringing in her ears and a sharp pain vibrating through her head.

She lay perfectly still for as long as she could. Her eyes were closed, and time seemed to spin in slow motion. At the sound of sirens, Stella forced herself to open her eyes, wanting to see the cavalry when they arrived. She imagined that they would ride in like soldiers on white horses, determined to save the day. The sun was still shining brightly, but dark wisps of smoke trailed upward, marring the beauty of a crisp blue sky.

Stella heard voices, a cacophony of noise that didn't make any sense. She felt cold and her body began to shake. She wanted to lift her hand and wipe her eyes, but her arm was too heavy, and she was too tired. She closed her eyes again and waited. Brennan would be home soon, she thought. Brennan would wipe away her tears. Brennan would bring home those cookies.

BRENNAN HADN'T PLANNED to be in his office for as long as he had. He'd been trying to leave for the past hour, but the phone wouldn't stop ringing and agents wouldn't stop asking him questions. He finally pushed himself from his desk, hanging up the phone with the intention of leaving when Xander Washer poked his head through the door.

"Sorry to be a bother, but do you have a minute?" Xander questioned. Xander was the assistant to the FBI director, Roberta Chang. He knew Brennan would give him however many minutes he needed.

"How's it going, Xander?" Brennan responded. "What can I do for you?"

"Director Chang is stuck at an agency meeting in Washington. I have to send her an update on everyone's case load, and I hear you pulled a side job with the local police department investigating a murder?"

Brennan nodded. "The 130th precinct caught the murder of a local political candidate. We initially thought it might be related to the Landmark Killer case, but thus far, I haven't found any connection."

"Can you get me something in writing by tomorrow morning? I spoke with Detective Colton, and she said her office requested you. That you had ties to the case that they thought would be useful. She says you knew the suspect, who's now a potential victim?"

Brennan struggled not to laugh out loud. He'd have to

thank Rory later, he thought. He nodded. "Yes," he said. "It's a complicated case. But I did clear it with Sergeant Blackthorn of the NYPD. I didn't want there to be any conflicts with our two offices."

"I'm sure Director Chang will appreciate that!" Xander said. "Just get me a brief update on everything you're working on. It'll be a big help."

"No problem," Brennan responded. "How's everything going with you?"

"No complaints. The job is keeping me busy. In a good way."

"Well, if there is anything I can give you a hand with, don't hesitate to ask."

Xander smiled and gave him a slight salute. "Let's grab a beer sometime. I don't get out much."

Brennan chuckled. "Say no more. I know what that's like. Just let me know when. I'll be there."

The young man nodded and disappeared down the hallway. Although he'd been with the agency for some time, Brennan hadn't had an opportunity to get to know him well. He was quiet, staying to himself most of the time. But he was popular with the women in the agency, his GQ looks garnering him much attention. Director Chang often remarked how fortunate she'd been to hire him.

Brennan made a mental note to document his cases as requested. He was ready to make his exit when his cell phone chimed for his attention. He paused to read the message on the screen, realizing he'd missed an incoming text message. He smiled as he read it quickly.

I'm missing my chocolate chip cookies.

The device chimed a second time, signaling an incoming call. He eyed the caller ID and answered it on the third ring. "Rory! I was just about to call you!" he said, his good mood vibrating through the telephone line.

"There's been an incident," Rory said, her tone tempered. "They've taken Stella to Mount Sinai Hospital. I need you to meet me there."

"What's happened?" Brennan said, hurrying out the door as they spoke.

"There was a bomb," Rory replied, and then she disconnected the call.

Brennan's good mood was suddenly shattered.

STELLA HADN'T SPOKEN much since waking up in the hospital. Between local police, agents from Homeland Security and the FBI, she had answered more than her fair share of questions. She didn't have much else to share with anyone.

This time she'd made the front page of every major newspaper in the city. Peter Vincente, an employee of Federal Parcel Service and Officer Alfonzo Barrett, a ten-year veteran of the New York Police Department were both memorialized in the columns beside the story of the bombing. Both were survived by wives and children, and every time Stella thought about it, she withdrew into herself, nothing at all to say to anyone.

Online, photos of her home and the ensuing damage from the bomb blast scrolled in rotation with those earlier images from Rockwell's memorial. Someone had even gotten pictures of her sprawled out at the top of her steps and of her being taken away on a stretcher. But none of that mattered anymore. All Stella could think about was that someone had tried to kill her and took two innocent persons instead.

It had been a whole week since her world had been up-ended yet again, and all Stella wanted was to go home.

She looked up as Brennan gathered her belongings. There was an overnight bag with a change of clothing that he had packed for her and a multitude of floral arrangements sent to wish her well. One even included a cellophane balloon that read, Get Well Soon.

"I'm going to take these to the car," Brennan said softly. "The nurse should be here soon with the wheelchair to bring you down. I'll be right out front waiting for you. Okay?"

Stella nodded as he reached for her hand and squeezed her fingers. She wanted to smile, but every muscle in her body still hurt. She was badly bruised, looking like she'd gone ten rounds with a heavy-weight boxer. She also had stitches, twenty-three total, that closed gashes across her shoulder and the back of her head. She'd had a concussion, and it only when they were certain the head injury would not be permanent did the doctors agree to let her convalesce in her own bed.

Brennan hadn't left her side since he'd arrived at the hospital. He proclaimed himself her next of kin, ensuring that she'd had the best care. She had no idea when he'd found time to sleep or work, because every time she opened her eyes, he was there watching over her. He had been the only one who hadn't asked her any questions.

The drive back to her home was a quiet ride. Brennan's radio played oldies from the seventies and eighties.

Simon and Garfunkel's "Bridge over Troubled Water" played softly out of the speakers. Stella was surprised that she remembered the words, and she hummed along with the tune as Brennan made the trek across the borough.

As he turned onto her block, she braced herself, certain the emotion that would come might be overwhelming. She was not prepared for the new railing and replacement bricks and concrete that had returned the front of her home to almost new. No hint of the blast remained. Her head snapped in Brennan's direction.

"You did this?"

He shook his head. "No. I didn't. The Henleys made all of this happen. Mr. Henley said they felt bad about everything that had occurred and were concerned knowing whoever killed their son might be trying to kill you too. He said he and his wife were also grateful that someone who cared about their son was there when he took his last breath."

"Wow!" Stella said. "Just wow!"

Minutes later, she was settled comfortably on her living room sofa. Brennan wanted her in bed, but she refused. She'd had enough of lying around. She was ready for a semblance of normalcy, if such a thing were possible.

Brennan had made himself comfortable in her kitchen, promising a meal that would rival everything she had ever eaten in the past. He was trying to take her mind off the memories, wanting her to find a level of comfort in the space that had been violated by someone else's obsession with her. She followed him into the room and took a seat at the counter.

"You're supposed to be resting," he said. He shook a metal spatula in her direction.

"I thought I'd pour myself a glass of wine."

"You know you can't mix alcohol with the pain meds you're on. Not going to happen on my watch."

"Who deemed you my keeper?"

"You did. You were whispering my name when they took you to the hospital. I was called and I came. Now you're going to have a hard time getting rid of me."

Stella smiled. "Well, it's a good thing I like having you around," she said. "Good friends are hard to come by."

She gave him a quick glance, waiting for a reaction, but there was none. At least, not what she'd expected. He glanced back and amusement danced in his eyes.

"Dinner's going to be a minute," he said. "Do you want a snack?"

"I'm going to need something! The hospital food was horrible. I'll probably have nightmares over it."

Brennan moved to her pantry and swung open the door. "I think I have something for that," he said. He pointed inside and Stella shifted her gaze to see what he found so amusing. Inside, an entire shelf had been dedicated to her favorite bag of chocolate chip cookies.

"I would only do this for my friends," he said, his tone smug.

Stella laughed. The first good laugh she'd had in a long while.

BRENNAN POKED HIS head into Stella's bedroom to check on how she was doing. She'd fallen asleep shortly after dinner and was still snoring softly beneath the large down comforter that adorned her bed. It had been a few rough days for her, and she had been desperate for those things that were familiar to her.

Much had happened while she'd been in the hospital. Brennan had interviewed more people, followed up on other leads and was still no closer to solving her case or finding the Landmark Killer. With the bombing, additional manpower was now helping with the investigation, and they still hadn't gotten anywhere.

He had been worried that she wouldn't want to return to her family's home. What happened would be hard for anyone to overcome, but Stella had been adamant that the Harlem brownstone would be the best medicine she would ever need.

He left her bedroom door ajar in case she wakened and called for him. He eased back down the stairs and settled himself against the living room sofa. He debated whether or not to turn on the television but decided against it. He needed to think, and for the first time since Rory had called with the bad news, his head was clear enough for him to focus.

He revisited the details of Rockwell's murder and the conversations he'd had with everyone he'd spoken with. Nothing made sense, and he was starting to feel as if he were spinning his wheels and going nowhere fast. He needed help and he didn't have a problem asking for it. Reaching for his cell phone on the table, he sent a text message to his cousin Sinead. Minutes later, her response vibrated on the telephone screen. She promised to meet him the next day.

With a deep sigh, Brennan sent one last text message

to the patrolmen watching the home outside. He stood and moved to the window, lifting the blinds so that they could see him. He checked the door lock and shut off the lights. Sitting back down, he leaned his head back and blew another deep breath out of his lungs. He was exhausted, and ready to close his eyes. Stella was home and safe. He looked forward to a good night's sleep. He had a long day ahead of him, and he needed to be ready for whatever might come his way.

Chapter Ten

Brennan had grabbed a table in the Starbucks on Madison Avenue. His cousin Sinead had chosen the location. Arriving before she did, he ordered a hot coffee for himself and her favorite chai tea latte with steamed soy milk. When she came through the doors, he lifted the familiar green-and-white cup and waved it at her.

Sinead waved back, greeted him with a nod and one of the brightest smiles he'd seen in a very long time. She moved to the table and took the seat beside him, leaning to kiss his cheek as she sat down. In line with most agents in the FBI, she rarely took a seat with her back to the door.

Sinead exuded confidence and strength and the attitude that she was ready to fight tooth and nail for everything she believed in. She was one of the best FBI profilers in the field and rarely missed the small details that helped them solve their cases.

"What's up, cousin!" she chimed, grabbing the coffee cup from him and taking a sip.

"You tell me," he answered. "I need help!"

Sinead nodded. "I heard things have been rough."

"I'm spinning my wheels and getting absolutely no-where."

"How's Ms. Maxwell?"

Brennan's brow lifted and he shrugged. "She's strug-gling. She doesn't want anyone to know, but I can see it. Someone tried to kill her. They almost did, and two people died in the process. That's a tough pill for any-one to swallow."

Sinead took another sip of her morning brew.

"Did you get a chance to review the materials I sent you?"

She nodded. "I did. I also saw the video of the mur-der." She sat back in her seat. "Everyone's assumed the murder was all about the victim. But so far, you haven't been able to find a motive that makes any sense. You do know someone went to a lot of trouble to make sure Stella showed up when the victim died. So, let's consider this has everything to do with Stella and Stella, alone. Some-one wanted her in that alley, and they made certain to get her there for whatever reason. Right after, someone tries to grab her and that fails. Then, a day later, a bomb is mailed to her home. Everything thus far says this is all about Stella Maxwell."

"That had already crossed my mind, but I hit a wall there as well. Stella hasn't allowed too many people into her personal space."

"Well, whoever it is, you can bet they're going to come for her again. You and she both need to be ready. You also need to consider that maybe, your perp is female, with a grudge. Because in all honesty, this feels like jealousy energy. Is there someone who didn't want her to be in a relationship with the boyfriend? Or someone she pissed off in her line of work? You may need to dig a little deeper into her past to find the answers."

"Really? You really think the perp is female?"

"Statistically, although the percentage of women who offend is low, women are more inclined to be emotionally invested in the persons they kill."

"But the victim was Rockwell, not Stella!"

"Is it possible Stella was the intended victim, and Rockwell was supposed to find her body? That whoever called her did so knowing she would show up if for no other reason than to get a story? Maybe Rockwell arrived early and threw off their plans? Which is why they keep coming for her. Trying to finish the job."

Brennan's eyes danced from side to side as he pondered his cousin's comment. Everything she'd said made sense, but then it didn't, opening a whole other can of worms that had him baffled. Because if Stella had been the intended victim, then who was gunning for her and why?

"What about the video?" Brennan questioned. "Nothing stood out?"

"Nothing that hinted at the identity of your perp. The body frame was slight, which could definitely indicate the killer was female, but it could also be a man with a small body frame. The victim wasn't an overly big guy either."

Thoughts of Tobias shot through Brennan's mind. Tobias fit the physical description, but he lacked motive. He had nothing to gain from Rockwell's death. And nothing against Stella that Brennan was aware of.

For the next hour, the two tossed possible scenarios back and forth at each other. Brennan realized he would need to revisit the women he had previously interviewed. And any other woman connected to Rockwell and Stella that he might not have considered. Maybe Silvia Henley wasn't the doting mother and had more involvement than Brennan gave her credit for. He hadn't met any of Stella's friends, but maybe it was time he did so. Maybe someone calling themselves her friend really wasn't.

"I can't afford for this case to go cold," Brennan said.

Sinead nodded her understanding. "I get it, so start thinking outside of the box."

Brennan shifted the conversation. "Anything new on the Landmark Killer case? No new messages?"

"Not a thing," Sinead responded. "He's gone quiet. The team is still beating the pavement down in the theater district, but no one's coming up with anything."

"I hate my job," Brennan muttered, pulling both hands over his face.

Sinead laughed. "And that would be a lie."

"Yeah, maybe, but there are days."

"So, what's going on with you and this woman? I hear you two have gotten very friendly and that you're still staying at her home?"

"Where'd you hear that?"

Sinead grinned as she shrugged her shoulders. "A little birdie told me."

"You must be talking to Rory."

"You know better than anyone that my sister and I don't share like that."

"I thought things had gotten better with you two?"

"They have, but we still have issues."

"So, who said something?" Brennan leaned forward, folding his hands together atop the table. "I need to know who's talking before they get me in trouble with my director, your boyfriend, and lose me my job."

"*Your* twin likes to talk!" Sinead finally said. "And I don't think you'll have a problem with the bosses. Wells and I are a thing now, after all. Unless Stella really is guilty and you try to cover for her."

Brennan laughed. "I'm going to kill Cash!"

"If you do, I'll try to make sure you and Ms. Maxwell get side-by-side jail cells," Sinead said with a hearty laugh.

AFTER WAVING GOOD-BYE to Sinead, Brennan debated where to go next. He was still mulling over the prospect of the perpetrator being female. Not that he didn't know women could kill, but he was having a hard time pinpointing a potential suspect who was laser-focused on taking down Stella. Who despised her that much and why?

Two telephone calls later, and he was headed back to the former campaign offices for Rockwell Henley. Tobias had agreed to meet him there. Brennan had no doubt the man was more than curious to learn what Brennan knew, not that Brennan would be eyeing him sideways for the crime. Pamela and Tobias had alibied each other, both claiming to have been at campaign headquarters when Rockwell had been murdered. Brennan couldn't help but wonder if the two could possibly be covering for each other. He might be wrong, he thought, but he couldn't afford to not question every single lead in front of him.

When Brennan reached campaign headquarters, he was surprised to discover Henley had been replaced. The office was open, staffed and promoting a brand-new candidate. A man named Marshall Tucker. Posters with Marshall Tucker's image had been hung in the windows and all around the space.

As Brennan stood looking around, actually surprised by the swift transition, Tobias came rushing from the back, seeming eager to have Brennan there. The two men shook hands.

"I appreciate you taking time to talk to me," Brennan said casually.

"Not a problem. The team is stuffing envelopes today and cold-calling perspective campaign donors. I've just been catching up on some paperwork, so I appreciate being able to take a break." He turned and gestured for Brennan to follow.

They headed toward the back of the building, Tobias leading him down a short hallway to an office in the rear. The space was quiet, and when Tobias closed the door, any noise coming from the front was nonexistent. He pointed Brennan to a cushioned chair as he eased behind the desk.

"Marshall Tucker?" Brennan said, pointing at the poster behind Tobias's head.

The other man shrugged. "He was the party's second choice. Since the deadline to run hadn't passed, they decided to throw him into the ring." He leaned forward across the desk, the gesture feeling conspiratorial. "Between me and you, Rockwell was a better choice, but we have to work with what we have. Unfortunately, Marshall's penchant for too much wine and too many women will eventually be his downfall."

"So, why support him?"

"We need that seat. As long as he sticks to script and does what he's told, we're willing to help him get the crown."

"And that's why politics and politicians get a bad rap," Brennan said.

Tobias laughed. "Since I know you didn't come here to debate the political climate with me, tell me how I can help you."

"I want to talk about Stella," Brennan said.

"I thought she'd been cleared of any wrongdoing?"

"She has. But Rockwell's killer is still targeting her, and I need to figure out why."

"I don't know that I can help you with that."

"Knowing how deeply the party vets everyone associated with your candidates, I know that if there was something to find out about Ms. Maxwell, you've found it."

"I wish I could hand you a file that's six inches thick. But in all honesty, working for that rag newspaper was her biggest crime."

"I'm told you weren't a fan of Stella's."

"I wouldn't say that. My job, Agent Colton, is to get the party's candidate elected to office. Part of that process is building an image that voters want to get behind and support. Stella didn't fit into the image we wanted for Mr. Henley."

"And what image was that?"

"Their relationship was too...well..." Tobias hesitated, seeming to strain his mind for the right words. Or not to say the wrong thing. Finally, he said, "In a nutshell, it was just too liberal. The party wanted to showcase his conservative edge. They wanted him to emulate the family values his parents projected."

"And their relationship didn't fit that image?"

"Stella wouldn't play her part. She refused to be dutiful and obedient."

"Was Rockwell seeing anyone else?"

"Define seeing?"

"Did he have other women, or another woman he was involved with?" Brennan chuckled.

It was at that moment that Pamela poked her head into the room. "Tobias, we need—" she suddenly paused, seeing Brennan for the first time "—Agent Colton! What a surprise!" she gushed.

"Miss Littlefield..."

"Can it wait, Pamela?" Tobias interjected.

"Of course," she responded, that bright smile filling her face. "It's good to see you again, Agent," she said as she stepped back out of the room and closed the door.

As Brennan turned his attention back to Tobias, the man was rolling his eyes skyward. Realizing that Brennan had caught him, he tried to explain himself.

"Pamela is a wonderful employee, but she can be a little too helpful sometimes. Now, to go back to your question—no, Rockwell had great integrity. He was totally committed to whoever he was dating. He truly had feelings for Stella, but she wasn't a great fit."

"Because...?"

"Because she was too strong-willed and refused to stay in her place. Stella's aspirations went against the grain of the image we had for Rockwell. He agreed."

He was a bigger jerk than I initially thought he was, Brennan thought. He didn't say so out loud, but he had no doubt that Tobias could read the emotion on his face.

"Did he and Pamela ever date?" Brennan asked.

"Pamela? Oh, no! They were just friends. Pamela has a boyfriend she's been with since elementary school. His name's Tyson something or other. He's a little challenged from what I understand. Social situations bother him, so he rarely leaves their home. She's totally dedicated to him."

Tobias's phone rang, and he reached for the device on his desk. "I need to get back to work, so if you don't have any other questions, Agent Colton…"

"Thanks for your time," Brennan answered as he turned toward the door.

Tobias's voice rang out as Brennan made his exit. "Marshall Tucker for Governor! How may I help you?"

BRENNAN WAS THREE blocks away when he stopped to place a call. It rang twice in his ear before it was answered, the voice on the other end surprising him.

"Agent Colton's office. This is Xander, how may I help you?"

"Xander, hey, it's Brennan. I was trying to reach Cash. I'm surprised to hear your voice."

"Brennan, hello! I was just leaving some files on your brother's desk when the phone rang. I knew it might be important, so I answered it. We try to be efficient around here."

Brennan chuckled. "No problem, dude. We all appreciate what you do. Is he around?"

"He's out in the field. Is there anything I can help you with?"

"Just leave a message for him, please. I need him to run a full background check for me. The party's name is Pamela Littlefield."

"Is this related to the Landmark Killer case?" Xander asked.

"No, she's a potential suspect in the Rockwell Henley murder and the assault on Stella Maxwell."

Brennan could hear the man scribbling notes on paper. "Got it," Xander said.

"Thank you. I appreciate your help. And just tell Cash to call me when he has a chance."

"Will do. Be safe out there, Agent," Xander said before disconnecting the call.

Appreciating the sentiment, Brennan nodded into the receiver as if Xander could see him. Minutes later, he was headed back to Harlem.

WHEN BRENNAN FINALLY arrived back at the Maxwell home, Stella was out in the backyard. She was sitting on the patio sunning herself. A copy of the most recent *New Yorker* magazine lay across her lap. She'd lit the gas grill, and billows of smoke were seeping out the sides. Whatever was roasting beneath the lid scented the air.

"You're cooking?" he said as he moved to the lawn chair beside her.

"Hello to you too! And yes, I'm cooking. I'm smoking a pork shoulder for dinner. It should be done in another hour or so."

"It smells good."

"It does, doesn't it?"

Brennan smiled. He'd missed her. He'd been worried about her. But he didn't say so. He hoped she would know without him telling her. Because he didn't have the words to say what he wanted. Nor could he, given the circumstances of their situation.

"I had a good day," Stella said, as if reading his mind. "How about you?"

"Not as productive as I would have liked, but then some days are like that."

"Aren't you tired of babysitting me?" Stella said. "I imagine you'd probably like to go back to your own home and life by now."

"My job is my life, and I'm perfectly fine right now. Making sure you're safe is a priority for me."

"Well, I'm glad I give your life some purpose," she said teasingly.

Brennan laughed. "Anything I can do to help with dinner?"

Stella shook her head. "Just stay out of my kitchen so I can show you how real professionals do it."

With a nod of his head, Brennan stood back up. "In that case, I'm going upstairs to take a shower and change."

"I hung your clothes in the guest room closet," Stella said. "And I did your laundry. If you plan to stay, there's no reason for you to live out of your suitcase."

His eyes widened. "Thank you. I didn't intend for you to—" he started to say.

Stella interrupted him. "Don't make a big deal out of it. I just know the sacrifices you're making to be here. I just wanted to show you my appreciation."

Brennan dropped his hand to her shoulder and gave it a light squeeze. Moving back into the home, he didn't have anything else to say.

DINNER WAS DIVINE! As Brennan filled his plate for the third time, Stella had to praise her own cooking. As her late father use to say, she put her foot in that meal. The meat was perfection, tender enough to cut with a plastic fork and melting like butter in your mouth. She'd sliced it thin and served it with baked macaroni and cheese and turnip greens. It was a Sunday-after-church meal, the likes of which reminded her of her family's Southern roots. It was comfort food from the first bite to the last.

Brennan hummed his appreciation. "If I eat another bite, I'm going to burst," he said. "This is so good!"

"Thank you. Save some room for dessert though. I made banana pudding."

"I don't think I've ever had banana pudding," he said. "Well, maybe I have. The kind that comes in a box."

"This is homemade. With vanilla wafer cookies. There's no box involved in my banana pudding."

For the first time that day, Brennan was relaxed, and Stella could see it on his face. He had showered and changed into sweatpants and a T-shirt. The casual attire fit his personality, and she liked that he had made himself comfortable in her home.

She changed the subject as she lifted the empty dinner plates from the table. "The Henleys called me today. Well, Mr. Henley called me."

"What did he say?"

"He just wanted to check that I was doing well. They'd gotten my thank-you note for the work they did on the house."

"Mrs. Henley still hasn't warmed up?"

"She said hello. That's about as warm as she'll ever get."

"They're both giving the mayor hell about the investigation. They think other cases are taking precedence over finding their son's killer. They're breathing down her neck, she's breathing down the FBI director's neck and the director is breathing down my neck."

Brennan had risen from his own seat to help Stella with the dirty dishes. She washed and he dried, the duo standing side by side at her kitchen sink.

Stella nodded. "You can understand their frustration. I want the case closed too. And I know exactly what you're going through trying to find his killer."

"And keep you safe from this monster," Brennan added.

Stella smiled. Quiet descended over the room, and each fell into their own thoughts. When the dishes were washed and put away, she pointed him to the family room. "*Family Feud* is about to start. Turn up the television while I get us some dessert."

Brennan shook his head. "Really, Stella? *Family Feud*?"

"Don't criticize. Just turn on the TV, please. I like Steve Harvey."

"You and every other woman."

"That's not true. Some women don't appreciate Steve's relationship advice."

"Why?"

"Because a man who's been married and divorced multiple times isn't the relationship guru he'd like people to believe he is."

"Tell me more."

"Nope, I just want to watch mindless TV and relax. If we start talking relationships, you'll probably get your feelings hurt, and then I'll have to deal with your emotional fallout."

"My emotional fallout?"

"You men can be especially sensitive when we say things you don't like."

Brennan laughed and Stella laughed with him.

Minutes later the two were sitting side by side on the sofa, bowls of warm banana pudding in their laps. Brennan hummed with each spoonful into his mouth, and Stella giggled at his enthusiasm.

"I think we should open a restaurant," Brennan said. "We'd make a fortune if you cooked like this."

"Why do I have to cook?" she asked.

"Because I could never recreate this and have it taste half as good."

"At least you know it," she replied. "But let's not share it with the world. It'll be our little piece of heaven here at home."

"I'm saying let's just share it with the five boroughs! We can take on the world next year!"

Stella grabbed his empty bowl and rose from her seat. "Do you want more?" she asked.

He shook his head. "Maybe later. I couldn't eat another bite right now."

Turning, Stella moved into the kitchen. She washed the dessert dishes and was wiping down the kitchen counter when Brennan's cell phone vibrated. He'd left the device there when he was drying the dishes and putting them back into the cupboards.

She called into the other room. "Your phone is beeping! Do you want me to bring it to you?"

"Yes, please!" he called back.

Picking up the device, Stella glanced down at the screen. An incoming text message was chiming for his attention. She carried the phone back to the family room, handed it to him and sat back down. She reached for a lightweight cotton throw that rested on the sofa arm and draped it over her legs. She watched as Brennan pushed buttons and then scrolled.

The change in his temperament flipped so quickly that it surprised her. Stella didn't expect his reaction as he suddenly shifted forward in his seat. His jaw tightened, the lines in his face hardening like stone. His eyes narrowed into thin slits, and for a split second, he looked like he was ready to spit venom.

"What's going on?" she asked, shifting her body closer to his. "What's wrong, Brennan?"

He shook his head but didn't speak. Rage seeped from his eyes.

"You're scaring me," Stella said, her voice dropping an octave.

Brennan passed her his phone, the two exchanging the briefest of looks. Putting the device into her hands, Stella read the message on the screen.

Shouldn't you be out looking for me, Agent Colton? Instead, you're shacking up with a murder suspect. I thought you Coltons didn't like killers since that one who got to your dear old daddy? I'm still out here, Agent. I'm headed to the theater. See you on Broadway!

"What's going on?" Stella said. "Who sent this to you?"

Brennan tossed her a look. He took a deep breath and then he answered.

"The Landmark Killer."

Chapter Eleven

It wasn't an hour later before Brennan's team was crowded into Stella's living room. She had brewed a large pot of coffee and plated the last bit of banana pudding. His cousin Sinead and the NYPD's lead investigator Wells Blackthorn had arrived first. Brennan's fraternal twin, Cash, arrived next, followed by his brother Patrick and Rory Colton. Ashlyn Colton arrived last, not at all happy to have been pulled from a date with a hedge fund manager. Waves of anxiety flooded the room, the wealth of it like an electrical current flowing from one to the other.

"This son of a bitch is playing games with us," Patrick Colton snarled.

Stella turned to stare at the man. He was angry, hostility spewing with every word. The family resemblance was strong, although his hair was browner than Brennan's, she thought. And she hadn't ever seen Brennan rage like that.

"He knows us," Brennan snapped. "He knows too much about us."

"Well, it's personal now," Rory said.

"It's been personal," Sinead replied, the two women glancing toward each other.

"Clearly, for him to know this much about all of you, he has access to your personal records," Wells said calmly. "One of our agencies has a mole."

"Or he's efficiently stalking us all," Ashlyn countered.

"It has to be someone we work with," Brennan said. "How would he know where I am if he wasn't with one of our offices?"

"So, you think they're NYPD?" Rory asked.

Brennan shook his head. "I didn't say that. It could easily be someone at the FBI's Manhattan office. We don't know, but we need to figure it out and figure it out fast."

"Who've you pissed off lately?" Patrick asked, lifting his brow as he tossed Brennan a look.

"You'd get a shorter list if you asked him who he hasn't pissed off," Cash interjected.

Nervous laughter filled the room. Stella took the opportunity to interrupt their conversation. "Can I get anything for anyone?" she asked.

All eyes were suddenly on her. She gave them the slightest smile. "There's no more banana pudding, but I've got cookies. Chocolate chip."

"Thank you," Sinead answered. "We're good. And that pudding was to die for. I'd ask for the recipe, but I know I won't make it."

"It was good," Ashlyn said. "And we apologize for the intrusion. It's nice to meet you though. Our big brother is quite smitten with you."

"Shut up, Ashlyn," Brennan said, his cheeks turning a deep shade of fire-engine read.

They all laughed.

"Well, it's my pleasure to meet all of you," Stella said.

Cash turned the conversation back to the topic at hand. "Whoever it is, him throwing our father into his sick games is going to get him hurt," he said, still seething.

Heads nodded in agreement.

Wells interjected again. "Let's toss out some names at both departments. People you're close with. Anyone you've had run-ins with. Let's see if we can narrow it down. And let's focus on Sinead and Brennan first, since they received the first two messages. Any other cases you two have in common? Anyone you two both worked with or had issues with?"

Like a fly on the wall, Stella sat back and listened as the family did what they did best. It was interesting to watch them analyze information and bounce ideas off each other. It also made her realize how much she missed her own work. How she would like to be on a case, doing the investigative work to tell a story no one knew. Finding the details that blew something wide open and shone a spotlight on something relevant. In that moment, she realized it was past time for her to get back to work. She made a mental note to call the senior editor the following morning to plead her case.

Sinead stole a glance at the clock on the wall. "Wells and I need to get home," she said, "before the sitter calls child services on us for abandoning our baby."

Wells laughed. "We haven't abandoned our baby. The sitter knows how this works."

"Well, I miss baby Harry, and I want to snuggle him one last time before he goes off to sleep."

"Isn't it past his bedtime?" Ashlyn questioned. "Babies go to sleep early, don't they?"

"She will wake him up to put him back to sleep," Wells said with a shake of his head.

Sinead laughed. "I am not that bad!"

"He's such a sweet baby," Rory said softly.

Wells leaned in to give Sinead's sister a hug. "You're welcome to come and visit him anytime," he said.

Sinead smiled. "Especially since we might need a new sitter if we don't get out of here."

Patrick waved his hand excitedly. "I volunteer!"

Brennan looked from one face to the other. "We're all going to be available if we don't get some answers soon."

Cash nodded. "I can't do diapers!" he said, wincing. "Diapers terrify me."

Laughter rang warmly as they all headed for the door at the same time. Ashlyn moved to Stella's side and hugged her warmly. "We're glad you're doing okay. You had us worried there for a while."

"Thank you."

"When this is all over, let's do lunch or something. Get to know each other better."

"I'd like that."

Ashlyn winked an eye at her and exited the home. Brennan watched as his family went their separate ways. When the street outside was quiet, he waved at the patrol car parked across the way. A plainclothes officer waved back. Brennan shut the door and secured the lock. When he turned back to the family room, Stella had already collected the dirty dishes and had tossed them into the dishwasher.

"You're using the dreaded dishwasher?" Brennan said, surprised that she wasn't handwashing them.

"We're both tired. And I still have questions," she said.

He gave her a look. "Questions?"

They moved back into the family room and sat down. Stella turned to face him, folding her legs beneath her as she sat cross-legged.

"I'd like to know more about your father and why the mention of him was so disconcerting for everyone."

Hesitancy crossed Brennan's face like a dark cloud billowing in front of him. His jaw tightened, and the light that had been shining in his eyes dimmed.

Realizing she'd hit a nerve, Stella reached out and touched his arm. Manicured fingers tapped lightly against the soft flesh. Concern washed over her expression. Concern for his well-being and curiosity lifted her gaze.

Brennan pulled himself from her touch. The gesture startled them both, and he saw a look of hurt seep from Stella's eyes. He grabbed her hand, contrition furrowing his brow. "I'm sorry. It just…" He heaved a deep sigh, emotion stealing the words from him. He apologized a second time. "I'm really sorry. I didn't pull away because of anything you did."

"It's okay," Stella said. She shifted her body back ever so slightly, putting a hint of distance between them. "I just wanted to understand."

He took another deep breath. "You have a right to know. I'm just surprised, though, that after all these years, it still hurts as much as it does." A gust of air eased past his thin lips as he continued. "My father was Mike Colton. Michael Patrick Colton. He was a dedicated police officer; a beat cop who proudly walked the streets in the Bronx. When we were kids, he was brutally murdered. By a serial killer. Ashlyn was still a baby at the time. She never even got to know him the way Cash, Patrick and I did."

Stella reached out and touched him again. "Brennan, I'm so sorry. I didn't know." He didn't pull away as she trailed her palms against his forearms.

He closed his eyes, settling into the warmth that flowed from her fingertips. His voice was soft and low when he spoke. "Things were hard for us after that. Our mother, Mary, never got over the loss. She did the best she could raising the four of us alone, but she couldn't get past our father being gone."

"Did they ever find his killer?" Stella asked.

Brennan hesitated before answering. "It took years before they captured the man that murdered him," he said finally. "Everything about my father's case was why we all went into law enforcement. We wanted to uphold dad's memory through our work in the justice system and get as many criminals as we could off the streets. My father's killer was on death row when he got into a fight with a prison guard and was killed."

When he opened his eyes and lifted them to hers, Stella was staring at him intently. Compassion dampened her lashes, and her stare was like the sweetest balm.

"When you started calling me, I thought you were doing a story on my father's case. Over the years, we've had a lot of reporters wanting to interview us. It's not a story I was interested in sharing with the public. I didn't want to revisit the details of the case, and I didn't want my mother to have to relive dad's killing over again."

"No," she said. "I didn't know any of this. I called because I was hoping to get a lead on the Landmark Killer case. Something no one knew that could set my story apart from the other stories being written."

"A journalist through and through. I respect that." He trailed his hand down the side of her face, outlining her profile with his fingertips. He brushed a loose strand of hair away, tucking it gently behind her ear. The intimate gesture gave them both pause.

"Don't be facetious," Stella said, her voice a loud whisper.

Brennan's bright smile washed over her, lifting her spirit.

"I know you said your mom is in Florida now. Are you two close?" she asked, wanting to know as much about him as she could discover.

He nodded. "I adore my mother. We all visit her a few times during the year, and I speak with her weekly. When I'm going through something, I might call her every day just to hear her voice."

Stella smiled. "That's a blessing. I miss hearing my mother's voice."

He pulled her hand into his and kissed the back of her fingers. "I told my mom about you. When you were in the hospital, I kept her updated every day. I was afraid that I might lose you. I knew that she would pray for you when she went to Mass, and she did. She's still praying for you. And for us."

Stella lifted her brow, surprise painting her expression. "Brennan, I don't know what to say," she whispered.

He shrugged his shoulders. "You don't need to say anything, Stella. I just wanted you to know…" he started to say.

Before he could finish his comment, Stella lifted herself up and wrapped her arms around his neck. She pressed her mouth to his and captured his lips with her own. She kissed him hungrily, every ounce of feeling she had for the man exploding in a kiss that would forever leave them tied to each for an eternity.

It would be the first of many kisses. The connection so magnanimous that both could feel a cosmic shift of sorts, pulling air and space into a single thread that only they shared. Brennan knew he would never again be kissed by any woman with the level of desire he and Stella had for each other. He needed her. Badly. Like he needed oxygen and food. She became all his needs and his wants; the intensity of what was happening more than he could have ever imagined.

Stella tasted like a sweet syrup with a hint of banana from the pudding they had shared. Her mouth was sugar and heated, burning like a freshly lit torch. He wanted to hold her close and never let her go, and yet the intensity of them together was so exhilarating, he thought he might cry.

Time stood still. Sound was nonexistent, save their breath as both panted heavily. Her hands were hot, as were his, and they trailed paths across each other's body that burned every hope and dream each had into bare skin. Brennan pulled at her clothes, his own already lost to the floor. He pulled her against him, desperate to feel her bare flesh atop his own. He wrapped his arms tightly around her, his limbs like vices locked into play.

Stella moved with him in a seductive dance that left nothing to the imagination. She was dynamite exploding through nerve endings. She was snow melting on a mountain top. Stella was love in its purest form, and everything about her left Brennan whole and broken, confident and scared, forceful and timid. He was suddenly a contradiction of emotions, and he was famished for more.

Their kisses intensified, tongues easing past parted lips. Darting back and forth in a game of touch and treat. Kisses chased hands that led the way across skin damp from perspiration. Fingers pulled and pinched, and palms caressed and kneaded tissue that was soft and hard to the touch.

He kissed the curve of one breast and then the other, and suckled at nipples that had hardened like rock candy beneath his touch. Stella gasped. Or maybe he did. One echoed the other in a whispered mating cry. Every muscle in his body hardened, his blood vessels taut with anticipation. Stella sheathed him with a condom that seemed to appear out of thin air. Her touch, soft fingers wrapping around his hardened appendage moved him to quiver and shudder with anticipation, seconds from his entire body erupting like Hawaii's Mauna Loa volcano.

She eased above him and plunged her body down against his. Someone cried out in pure ecstasy, the sound like music wafting through the late-night air. Brennan bit down against his bottom lip to hold back the tears. They met each other stroke for stroke, a give and take so delicately balanced that no one and nothing could have torn them from each other.

Stella came first, murmuring his name over and over again as if in prayer. She pulled him with her as she plunged off the edge of ecstasy into a cavern of sheer bliss. Brennan screamed, his toes curling, his limbs cramping with pleasure. Everything between them exploded, firing fragments of sheer happiness through nerve endings. They were pure, unadulterated joy.

Their loving took them from room to room throughout the house. They made love in the kitchen, on the staircase, in the shower and on the guest room floor. It finally led them to Stella's bedroom and her king-sized bed.

Their sensual exploration lasted most of the night, occasional naps only coming as long as it took one or the other to catch their collective breath. When all was done, nothing else to learn and discover before the sun rose and reality swept in like a tidal wave, Stella lay her head against Brennan's chest. He wrapped himself tightly around her and held her close. Sleep tiptoed in, determined to reclaim its time as both drifted off into the sweetest dreams. Stella closed her eyes, her breathing and heart rate syncing in time with his. Brennan whispered her name, and then he said, I love you.

STELLA HAD NO idea the time. When she eased out of the bed to go to the bathroom, she only knew that it was still dark outside. Brennan was snoring softly beside her, and he rolled away, claiming the bed with the entirety of his body. She smiled at the sight of him, his wiry frame sprawled haphazardly against the pillow-topped mattress.

She like him there and that surprised her. She hated when a man thought he should spend the night in her bed after a sexual encounter. There had been shame when she had roused a lover and sent him on his way. Now, she hated the thought of Brennan leaving, and she realized that was a conversation to be had when all their bad business was behind them.

With an empty bladder, Stella eased back into the room, settling down against the side of the bed. She had wrapped the length of her hair around her head and slipped on a silk bonnet to protect the strands. She was still thinking about what Brennan had said as they'd fallen off to sleep. Wondering if she had heard him correctly, or if her own wants and wishes had teased their way into her dreams. Because she wanted him to love her, and she wished things between them could always be what they were in that moment. When neither was crazed about their careers and no one was trying to kill her or cause him and his family harm.

Chapter Twelve

Brennan had broken every professional rule that had followed him since the day he'd gone into law enforcement. He'd been standing in the doorway for a while, watching as Stella slumbered. He still didn't know how he'd managed to get out of the bed without waking her, period. They had been entwined so tightly around each other that he could barely tell when her appendages ended and his began. But he had, rising from the mattress without disturbing her rest.

He closed his eyes and leaned against the door frame. He'd been there to protect her. Instead, he'd crossed the boundaries his job and her case had demanded of him. What he had done was cause for dismissal, and there wasn't anything he could do if the director called him on his behavior.

Brennan pounded his fist against his forehead. Crossing the line had been one thing. And then he'd added insult to injury by telling her that he loved her. He had known better, but the words had slipped off his tongue before he could catch them.

Despite all the things they had discussed over the past

few weeks, the two had never talked about his aversion
to a permanent relationship. He had no interest in marriage or anything that resembled it. Brennan had always
been committed to his work, setting his personal life on a
back burner to those cases that required his total focus. He
had purposely dated women who were only looking for
Mr. Right Now, no interest in a Mr. Right. It made things
easier when he'd been ready to walk away. He had always
kept his head in the game, successfully ensuring he kept
his heart out of his encounters. Now, Stella Maxwell had
a vicelike grip on his heart and his head, the woman stealing into every wakening thought he was having.

They had spent their time together, becoming fast
friends and that friendship had him seriously considering what forever could possibly look like. Brennan didn't
know how to handle all the emotions flooding his spirit.
That damn text had thrown him completely offsides, leaving him angry and frustrated. Reflecting back on those
memories of his father and that time in life when he and
his family had been most broken, painful and sad. Sharing all of that with Stella had left him feeling vulnerable. Then a simple touch and a heated kiss had opened
his heart to emotions he had never experienced before.
He was feeling like an unholy mess, and redemption was
nowhere to be found.

Taking a step back, Brennan closed the bedroom door.
He stood for a moment to consider his options, and then
he grabbed his bags and headed for the front door.

WHEN STELLA WOKE NEXT, the sun was shining brightly
through her bedroom windows. The temperature had

risen, warning of a hot, blistering New York day. The bedroom door was closed, and Brennan was nowhere to be found. She wished he'd woken her, but she knew he still worried about her getting enough rest.

Rising, she headed toward the bathroom and the shower, anxious to be with Brennan after the incredible night they'd had shared. An hour later, she bounded eagerly down the steps, calling his name as she moved into the kitchen.

"Brennan! I was just thinking..." she started to say, expecting him to be standing as he did every morning— with a cup of coffee in his hands as breakfast awaited her. But there was no sign of him. No coffee brewed. No eggs or pancakes plated atop the stove.

She peered out to the rear patio first, then peeked through the front blinds. A patrol car remained parked in front, but Brennan's car was gone. Without giving it a second thought, Stella bounded back up the steps and into the guest bedroom. All things Brennan were gone, nothing belonging to the man to be found. Moving back into the hallway, she slid down the wall to the floor, pulling her knees to her chest. Her stomach flipped, threatening to spew even though she hadn't yet eaten.

Brennan had left without even saying good-bye. There wasn't a note or a sign that what had happened had meant something to him. She'd been played, and she hadn't seen it coming.

BRENNAN HAD HIDDEN in his office for most of the morning. He felt like a complete schmuck for leaving Stella the way he had. He kept looking at his cell phone, hoping she'd call to cuss him out, but she'd gone radio silent.

He considered calling her but knew he couldn't begin to explain how he was feeling. He knew Stella would have had no interest in hearing how he was relationship shy. Instead, he called the patrol team staked out in front of her home. Once they confirmed she was still there, inside and safe, he was able to breathe easier.

A knock on the office door pulled at his attention. He looked up as his brother entered the room.

"What's going on?" Cash asked. He dropped into the empty seat in front of the large wooden desk. The two men exchanged a look.

"Nothing's going on. Why do you ask?" Brennan answered.

"Because you haven't been in your office since you took on that other case. Now you're here at the crack of dawn? Something's going on!"

"Why are you here so early?"

"Don't change the subject, big brother. What happened?"

Brennan shook his head. Contrition was like a heavy mask on his face. He didn't need to say it out loud. Twin intuition said it for him. The two men held a silent conversation, everything spilling over in their facial expressions.

Cash shook his head. "What the hell were you thinking?"

"I wasn't thinking. I was responding and it just happened." Brennan's voice was low as he spoke, concerned someone might overhear their conversation.

"How does Stella feel about it?" Cash asked.

Brennan shrugged. "I didn't talk to her before I left."

His brother's eyes widened. "Did you at least say goodbye?"

Brennan winced.

"Dude! Are you trying to purposely ruin things?"

"It's complicated."

"You ran. That's not hard to figure out. But I'm trying to figure out why? Clearly, you have feelings for Stella. We all saw that last night. You care about her. That's not complicated at all."

"Why are you really here? I know it's not to discuss my personal life."

Cash shook his head. "That text you received originated from a burner phone. The transmission signal was roaming from someplace on the West Coast. We can't track it. Whoever this is, he's good. His technical proficiency puts him a caliber above Ashlyn's, and that's saying something."

"Have you been here working on that all night?"

"Most of it. I didn't have anyone to canoodle with, so I worked."

Brennan gave his twin a look and chuckled softly as Cash shrugged his shoulders in jest.

"What do I do?" Brennan asked, looking completely befuddled.

Cash shook his head. "My only serious relationship crashed and burned big time," he said, reminded of the divorce that had broken up his family. "I'm not sure you should be asking me that question."

"Well, I am asking," Brennan replied.

"Talk to her. You will never get anywhere with her if the two of you stop communicating."

THE STEREO SYSTEM was playing loudly through the home's speakers as Stella changed her clothes. She was singing along with the King George tune "Keep on Rollin'." She considered it her personal theme song, the lyrics saying one setback would not impede one's progress.

Her voice was crystal clear as she sang loudly.

She thought back to those days when her parents had danced to different songs, the two laughing as if neither had a care in the world. Those had been good days. After her mother died, her father would sometimes play a classic song as he stared out the window, the memories lifting his dark face into a slight smile.

She would never admit it out loud, but her heart hurt. Brennan had fractured it, leaving her feeling tattered. She'd fallen for the man. She had allowed him in, and he had left her devastated. Stella also knew the best way to come back from that kind of hurt was to throw herself into her work. So, unless the *New York Wire* was prepared to officially fire her, Stella was done and finished with her leave of absence. She was going back to work.

She continued to sing.

BRENNAN AND CASH were still talking. His cousin Sinead had joined them. Reviewing all the details of the case for the umpteenth time, they were plotting their next steps. His phone ringing interrupted the conversation.

"Agent Colton."

The speaker's response was muffled, but Sinead and Cash shot each other a look, Brennan's expression cause for concern.

"Yes… When? Did she say where she was going? Thank you," he said, disconnecting the call. Frustration looked like bad makeup across his face.

"Stella left the house and blew off the security team," he said.

"Why would she do that?" Sinead questioned.

"Yes, Brennan," Cash said facetiously, "why would Stella do that?"

Brennan glared at his twin. Sinead looked from one to the other and back.

"What did you do?" she suddenly asked, resting her stare on Brennan.

"Let it go," her cousin answered, rising from his seat.

Sinead looked at Cash, who eagerly answered her question.

"He slept with her. Then he snuck out of the house like a thief. He didn't even say good-bye to her. Just packed his bags and left. He hit it and quit it!"

Sinead glared at Brennan. "Please tell me you did not to that to that woman! How can you be such an ass?"

Brennan stood up. "I really don't need this from you two. I need to go and find Stella."

"Did they know where she was going?" Cash asked.

"No, but I think I do," Brennan answered. He fell into thought. He knew Stella well and would have bet his last dollar that she was headed to her job. He needed to meet her there to apologize and to convince her to go back home, where she was safe.

A knock on the door stalled his thoughts. Xander opened the door and peered inside. He was breathing heavy, as if he'd been running.

"You okay, dude?" Brennan questioned.

"I took the stairs," Xander said with a nod. "Sorry to

interrupt, but a call just came in. There has been another shooting. You all are up."

"Where?" Cash queried.

"The Capstone Theater. The victim is a man named Landon Stone. NYPD will meet you there. They've sent you the location."

"Thank you," Brennan said, scrolling through the messages on his phone. "The victim is still alive," he said as he grabbed his suit jacket. "I'm going to meet Rory at the hospital."

"I'll run point here," Sinead said. "Just keep me in the loop."

Cash nodded. "I'll head over to Broadway to check out the crime scene."

"Damn!" Brennan muttered as they all rushed from the room. "The Landmark Killer has dropped another body in our laps. He's gotten his L for Maeve O'Leary."

"I'll update Director Chang," Xander said, calling after them. Then he closed the office door as he watched them disappear into the field.

"Ms. Maxwell! It's good to see you!" The senior editor for the *Wire* was a man named Brian Price. He was lean and lanky, like he'd played basketball his whole life. To hear him tell it, though, he had no aptitude at all for sports or anything athletic. His youthful appearance, sun-kissed complexion, blue-tipped hair and playful exuberance belied his sixty-plus years.

He jumped from his seat to shake Stella's hand. "We've missed you around here!"

Stella gave him a wry smile. Brian was notorious for

blowing smoke at his employees. "And that's why I wanted to see you," she said. "I'm ready to return to work."

"You've been through a lot, Stella. Are you sure it's not too soon?"

"I'm certain. I need to get back to my desk. I need to be writing."

"It's my understanding that you are still under police protection. Is that true?" He leaned forward in his seat, meeting her stare with a narrowed gaze.

"Where did you hear that?"

"An Agent Brennan Colton called about you a short while ago. He was quite concerned about your safety. It almost sounded personal," Brian said, the comment edged in curiosity.

Stella bristled. The nerve of him, she thought. Was Brennan trying to totally ruin her life? She took a deep breath. "I assure you, Brian, I'll be fine."

"But what about the other employees? There's already been one tragedy surrounding you. Can you assure me the rest of us are safe?"

Stella took another deep breath, blowing it out slowly. Unfortunately, she couldn't give him that assurance since they still had no clue who had targeted her. She'd been so focused on her own hurt that she hadn't stopped to consider that her being out and about could potentially put others in danger. She said, "I can easily work from home until there are no concerns. You can key me into meetings electronically, and I can still give you the stories I know you're looking for."

"Even the Colton story?"

"Excuse me?" Stella's brow lifted, his question throwing her off-kilter. "What Colton story?"

"I recognized Brennan Colton's name. He's one of the FBI agents working the Landmark Killer case. I also did a little research myself, and his father was murdered by a serial killer years ago. You can't tell me there's no story there. It could be an amazing human interest piece. And from the way he spoke, something tells me that you might have inside access. Imagine that story being scooped!"

"I'm not sure..." Stella started. Her eyes darted back and forth as she considered what he was asking of her. She might be mad at Brennan, but she would never consider betraying him or his family that way. Sure, there was a potential headline with the Colton family history, the details surrounding the patriarch's murder that led them all into law enforcement, specifically tracking down serial killers and the current murders being investigated. It could potentially be a huge headline for the right reporter. She would have gladly written that story weeks earlier. But now...now she had to consider the consequences of doing such a thing. Bottom line, even if Brennan Colton was a complete and total jerk, she loved him and would never consider doing anything to cause him harm.

"Let me help you make a decision," Brian said, grinning at her sheepishly. "We got a tip in that the Landmark Killer is sending anonymous text messages to the FBI team. The Coltons specifically."

"When did you hear this?" Stella asked. A deep frown pulled across her face.

"Someone sent that message to your inbox earlier today. Obviously, you not being here, I intercepted it. But I'm willing to give it back to you to chase down. Find out if it's true, connect it to the Coltons chasing down a killer and spill the tea on their personal connection. It's a hell of a story, Stella, and if you want to come back to work, it's all yours."

"And if I don't want that story?"

"Then you don't want this job," Brian said matter-of-factly. "But I'm willing to give you some time to think about it. Not too much though. Let's just say I'll need an answer in twenty-four hours."

With a quick nod, Stella exited the office, feeling out of sorts by the conversation. She suddenly wanted to be home, where she could shut herself off from the world. Her friend Garrett was standing outside her former cubicle waving at her excitedly.

"Stella!"

The two friends hugged, jumping up and down in each other's arms.

"It's so good to see you, Garrett!"

"Honey, I have been worried to death about you."

"I've been good actually."

"How did it go with Price?"

Stella rolled her eyes skyward. "Some things don't ever change. That son of a bitch is blackmailing me for my job."

"Price would auction off his firstborn for a story!" He leaned in, taking a quick glance to see who might be eavesdropping on their conversation. His voice dropped to a loud whisper.

"Word around the office is the new kid is gunning for your cubicle. He's been chasing down those stories you would normally do. If there's a story Price wants, you can bet he's already promised it to Junior Mafia thinking you wouldn't be around to take it."

She giggled. "Is that what you're calling him, Junior Mafia?"

"His name's Carmine Something or Other. He's a nice Italian boy whose grandfather supposedly worked for the Gambino crime family. Price hired him because he claimed he could dish about the mafia family's current enterprises."

"Has he?"

"He's chasing your stories, Stella. He has nothing of his own to share!"

"Well, I'm trying to come back to write my own stories, but Price is being a real butthole."

"How can I help?"

Stella sighed. "Not sure anyone can help me with this one," she said.

STELLA APPRECIATED GARRETT taking time from his own schedule to sit and have lunch with her. She'd missed his crude jokes and laughter as they gossiped about others in the office. Although both kept looking over their shoulders for unaccompanied packages or ninjas driving paneled vans, it was a good time. The break from her usual routine also allowed her to clear her head and figure out what she wanted to do.

She dialed Brennan's number and waited for him to answer his cell phone. He picked up on the second ring.

"Stella, are you okay?"

"Please don't act like you really care."

"Stella, I'm sorry and I do care."

"I just thought you should know that someone emailed me at the *Wire* about the anonymous text messages from the Landmark Killer that you and your cousin received. My boss intercepted the message."

"How in the hell…?" Brennan stammered.

"My guess is whoever sent the messages is tipping off the media. My editor knows there's a story there, and he is sniffing hard to find it. Apparently, after you called to discuss me and my current situation with him, he did some digging into your past and found out about your father."

"You and I need to talk," Brennan said.

"No, we don't. You said everything you needed to say when you left this morning. It's no big deal."

"It is a big deal, but now's not a good time to have this conversation. And definitely not over the phone. There's been another shooting. The victim is still alive. I'm headed to the hospital now."

"Well, good luck with that," Stella said.

"Stella, please! I can meet you home as soon as I'm done here."

"You may be there most of the night. And I have things to do."

"I need to explain."

"Not necessary. We just had sex and then you booked it. You didn't even bother to thank me for the good time or say good-bye. There is nothing that you need to say to me now that I'm interested in hearing."

Brennan's voice dropped an octave. "First of all, we did not just have sex. I made love to you. It was so much more than some casual fling through your sheets."

"I wouldn't know. The way you packed up and took off didn't feel very loving."

"Dammit, Stella! I don't need this right now."

Slamming the phone down in Brennan's ear gave Stella much satisfaction. She refused to be moved, and she didn't care what he was in the middle of trying to resolve. They were done. She'd been nice enough to give him a heads-up about the information that was leaked. As far as she was concerned, she didn't owe Brennan Colton another minute of her time.

BRENNAN WAS PULLING into the hospital parking lot when Stella disconnected the call. His frustration was palpable and he considered calling her back. Instead, he found a parking space and headed for the emergency room entrance. The New York Police Department had cordoned off the area, and as he approached the door, he flashed his badge. The rookie officer looked him up and down before allowing him to pass.

"Where can I find Detective Colton?" he asked another uniformed officer who was standing at the reception desk.

They pointed him toward the waiting room, the space bustling with activity. Rory stood off in a corner, texting messages to her team, who were still on sight.

"Hey," Brennan said as he moved to her side. "What do we have?"

"White male, midthirties, took a bullet to his left side, currently in critical condition. They just took him up to surgery."

"Are we sure it's our guy? Was there a note?"

"No note. He got spooked. Another employee heard the shot and interrupted him. The perp was standing over the body and took off running when she cried out for help. One guy gave chase but lost him in the crowd."

Rory paused, texting on her phone before she refocused and continued, "As soon as the doctors bring us that bullet, we'll run the ballistics for confirmation. Right now, though, everything is pointing toward our killer."

"If he's the L. And why is this guy going out of order if he's spelling Maeve O'Leary's name? Unless it's just to fool with us?"

Rory nodded. "Unfortunately, whatever's going on, Landon Stone's name didn't do him any favors. So now we have to wait and pray he pulls through."

"What about the woman who walked in on them?"

Rory looked down at her phone. "Cash is there interviewing her now. Her name is Gail Cooper. She told my guys that the killer wore a mask and had on a hoodie and baggy clothes. She didn't notice anything else. She said it was dark. Someone had shut down the stage lights, and Landon had gone to check the fuse box. That's why he was back there alone."

"If there's something more, Cash will get it from her."

"That's what I was thinking."

Brennan stole a glance toward his watch. Rory turned to take a seat and he followed. "We have another problem," he said as he made himself comfortable.

Rory's eyes lifted questioningly. "What now?"

"I just spoke to Stella. She said someone's tipped the *New York Wire* off about the anonymous messages Sinead and I received."

"Are they going to run it?"

"I don't know. I'm not sure if Stella knew anything either."

"She's a journalist. You don't think she wouldn't run the story?"

The question gave Brennan pause. He wouldn't think Stella would do something like that, but their circumstances had changed. And she was angry.

"I don't think so," he said finally.

"You do know you might not be able to trust a woman who you've royally pissed off, right?"

Brennan's head snapped in his cousin's direction.

Rory chuckled. "Don't look surprised. You know it's hard to keep secrets in this family."

He shook his head. "I don't know what to do. She won't talk to me."

"I wouldn't talk to you either. When did you become such a big jerk?"

He tossed up his hands in frustration. "I screwed up! I just want to make amends."

"What happens if she's not interested? Are you prepared to let her go?"

Shifting forward in his seat, Brennan dropped his head into his hands. With every question Rory asked, things were beginning to look bleaker and bleaker. He hadn't wanted to consider that things with him and Stella were over. He clearly hadn't been thinking at all.

Chapter Thirteen

"Stella? Stella Maxwell? I thought that was you!"

Tensing, Stella looked up anxiously, surprised to hear her name being called. She hadn't expected to run into anyone in the Duane Reade Pharmacy. As Pamela Littlefield sauntered in her direction, she felt her entire body relax, realizing just how tense she had been.

"Pamela, hello!"

"How are you?"

"I'm doing well, thank you. How about yourself?"

"Busy as always. I'm so glad we ran into each other. I'd been planning to call you after that horrible incident at Rockwell's vigil. I hated that that happened to you." Pamela's smile was wide.

"I appreciate that. Things happen, though, when emotions are running high."

"Don't I know it!" Pamela said, waving a dismissive hand. "Things were crazy there for a while. I hear you had it rough too. That someone tried to blow you up? It was all in the news."

Stella shrugged. "Yes, it was."

"You'd think you being a reporter and all that you

could do something about the stuff they write about you."
Pamela's head was waving anxiously from side to side.

"You'd think," Stella responded. "Well, I need to finish
my shopping and get going. It was nice to see you again."

"You didn't ask me what I've been doing," Pamela
said, a hint of attitude in her tone.

Stella blinked, her lashes batting up and down rapidly.
She took an inhale of air before she spoke. "Didn't I? I'm
sorry about that. So, what's new with you?"

"The campaign keeps me busy, and you know what a
tyrant Tobias can be. It's exhausting!" Pamela paused to
take a breath. "Here," she said, reaching into her purse.
"Have a campaign button!"

Stella held out her hand as Pamela dropped the button into her palm. "Marshall Tucker? That was quick."

"That's politics!" Pamela chirped. "But what I wanted
to tell you is that I got engaged!" She held out her hand
for Stella to see the engagement ring on her finger. It
was a thin band with a petite stone, and it flattered her
small hands.

"Congratulations! How exciting!"

Exuberance wrapped itself around Pamela like a wool
blanket. "We haven't set a date yet for the wedding. I
think we should wait until after the election, but my fiancée doesn't want to wait."

"I'm sure you'll both figure out the perfect time."

"It's so sad that you and Rockwell never got engaged.
But things happen for a reason. Right?"

Stella gave her a polite nod, wanting to cut the conversation short. "Well, I'm glad we could catch up. But

I really do have to run. It was good to see you and hear your good news."

Pamela smiled widely a second time. "It was. You take care, and I look forward to our seeing each other again soon. Maybe we can do lunch?"

"I'll keep that in mind," Stella said. "Maybe when our schedules aren't so busy, especially with the election and all."

"You're right. But soon, okay?"

"Okay! Bye now!" Stella grabbed her basket and headed toward the register. She could feel Pamela's stare still locked on her. She was curious to know what the woman was doing in that neighborhood but decided that to ask would take more time than she had to spare.

For a brief moment, she considered calling Brennan to tell him about the encounter but remembered their relationship wasn't like that anymore. By the time she'd finished purchasing the tampons, clear nail polish, deodorant and face cream she'd selected, she'd decided there really wasn't anything for her to be concerned about. She and Pamela had never had a problem with each other before. She couldn't imagine that anything had changed.

Minutes later, she made her exit, heading toward the subway station. Pamela stood on the corner, hailing a yellow cab. She waved and called out good-bye one last time. Stella waved back and hurried in the opposite direction. She couldn't get home fast enough.

HOURS LATER, STELLA was pacing from room to room. She'd been there long enough to check the locks at least a half dozen times and had actually checked them a dozen times more. It surprised her that she was as anxious as she was. Going out had seemed like a good idea that morning, but as she had come to realize how exposed she was, that good idea had felt wholeheartedly foolish. She was kicking herself for acting so irrationally simply because her feelings had been hurt.

She moved into the kitchen, trying to decide what to make herself for dinner. Suddenly, the prospect of eating alone felt like a challenge. She moved to the wine chiller, grabbed the first bottle she touched, popped the cork and took a swig. Leaning back against the refrigerator, warm tears suddenly misted her eyes.

She hated that she had grown comfortable with Brennan. Hated that he had made her feel safe. She found it galling that she had actually thought there was something special between them, and it infuriated her that she'd given herself to him and that she hadn't protected her heart.

Now her own shadow was scaring her. Bumping into old acquaintances felt sketchy, and she no longer trusted her own judgment. In the blink of an eye, she felt as if she'd been taken advantage of. Brennan had used her, and she had let him.

Stella had started her day happy and hopeful. Minutes later, it had gone straight to hell. Now she hurt, someone still wanted to cause her harm and everything she'd believed in felt lost to her. Taking another swallow of wine, Stella leaned across the counter and cried.

BRENNAN WAS CERTAIN he'd worn through the soles off his leather shoes with all the pacing he had done. It had been a long afternoon waiting for news on the latest victim. Waiting to see if the man would survive was physically draining. It had left him with nothing else to do but think. And with no new leads to follow, all that was on his mind was Stella.

He still couldn't believe he'd walked out on her the way he had. She had trusted him, and he had failed her. He couldn't blame her if she never wanted to have anything else to do with him. If she refused to give him a second chance, he wasn't certain he even deserved one.

Brennan would never be able to explain how he was feeling because even he didn't understand the wealth of emotion that was suddenly so consuming. All he knew was that he wanted to go home. Home was wherever Stella was, and he'd managed to burn down the walls the two had built together.

He loved Stella and he had told her so. If he could tell her again, he would. But Stella wasn't having any of it, and now he worried for her safety. Worried about her being well, and he was petrified things between them had ended before they'd had a chance to let the relationship bloom.

Rory suddenly called his name, interrupting those thoughts. She gestured toward the doctor who was headed in their direction. Both shifted their focus, giving the physician their undivided attention. Rory flashed her badge and introduced them.

"How's Mr. Stone doing?" Brennan questioned.

Dr. Ralph Brett nodded. "Under the circumstances, he's doing amazingly well. He's a very lucky man. The bullet just missed his lungs. An eighth of an inch in either direction, and things would be very different for him."

"We're going to need that bullet," Rory said.

The doctor nodded. "I bagged it. We just need your signature on the paperwork for the chain of custody."

"Not a problem," Rory replied.

"When can we speak with Mr. Stone?" Brennan asked.

"Not before tomorrow. He's just gone down to recovery and will probably spend the night in the ICU so we can keep our eye on him. If things go well, you should be able to talk to him in the morning."

"Thank you, Doctor," Rory said.

The two stood and watched as the man walked away.

"I swear," Brennan said. "We can't catch a damn break!"

Rory shrugged. "I'm going back to the crime scene. Let's regroup here in the morning."

Brennan said, "Sounds like a plan. Let me know if anything else comes up. I'll also give Cash a call to see if he got anywhere."

"Will do," Rory replied. "And Brennan...?"

"Yes?"

"Go make things right with Stella!"

BRENNAN HAD BEEN standing on her porch for at least ten minutes knocking at the door. Stella was conflicted as she peered at him through the front window. She wanted to let him in. And she wanted to tell him to go to hell. She watched as he moved down the steps to have a conversation with a uniformed officer standing on the sidewalk.

Their exchange was brief before Brennan came back to the door and rang the bell again.

Stella took a deep breath and moved to the entrance. She opened the door slightly and looked out. "What do you want, Brennan?" she asked, attitude wrapped around every word.

"I wanted to make sure you were okay."

"I'm fine."

"We need to talk."

"Say what you have to say."

"Can I come in, Stella?"

"No."

"We need to have a conversation about your case. You're going to lose the security team after tomorrow. We've finally hit that shortfall in the NYPD budget. We should talk about other options, maybe consider private security for the time being. At least until we can be certain you are safe."

Stella winced. After the day she'd had, that was the last thing she wanted to hear. Her anxiety rose a level.

Brennan persisted. "Stella, please, let me come inside!"

"I don't want you in my house. I can't trust you," she said.

Brennan blew a soft sigh. "That's fair and I understand, but we can't fix this if you don't give us a chance."

"We? Us? I'm sorry, I didn't walk out on you. I was here for a conversation this morning. You weren't. I don't need to fix anything, and clearly, *we* never existed."

"I was scared, Stella. And I made a mistake."

There was a moment of pause, and then Stella said, "That's not my problem."

A heavy gust of warm breath blew past Brennan's thin lips. He took another breath and held it deep in his lungs before exhaling again. "What do you want from me, Stella?" he asked.

"Not a damn thing!" Stella answered. "I don't want one damn thing from you, Brennan Colton!"

"Please, Stella…" Brennan started to say.

Eyeing him one last time, Stella shook her head, then closed and locked her door.

BRENNAN RETURNED TO the office to clean up some paperwork. He had hoped to be spending time with Stella, making up for his transgression. He would have cooked a special dinner, let her pick a movie for them to watch and massaged her feet as they lay on the sofa together. It would have been relaxing and joyful, the two continuing to discover each other's eccentricities. He had really wanted things to be well between them. He'd practically been desperate for it.

Stella however had no intentions of making it easy for him. And that was okay, he thought. He was willing to work as hard as he needed to if it meant things between them could be well again. There was just something about her that made him happy. Even in the midst of so much sorrow and frustration, Stella Maxwell was the sweetest ray of sunshine. Even when she was being surly and giving him a hard time.

He packed away the folders on top of the desk, and when it was clear, he made his exit, turning the lights off behind him. The office was quiet at that hour, only a few agents still working out problems or finishing up paperwork. As he headed toward the exit, Xander waved him down, hurrying out of the director's office.

"Brennan, I'm glad I caught you! For some reason I thought you'd already left."

"I did. I went and grabbed a slice of pizza for dinner and came back. What's up?"

"I received a call this afternoon from a reporter at the *New York Wire*. They wanted a statement about you and your work. They asked questions about your past, as well as your record here with the bureau. I told them no comment and then referred them to the bureau's public communications department. They handle all that. I just thought you should know."

Brennan hesitated as he considered the consequences of the media digging into his life. When his father had been killed, they'd been relentless, harassing his mother and them like blood hounds running after a catch. Then there had been the daily headlines and strangers staring at them like they were exhibits at the zoo. School had been the worst, other kids relentless with the questions and bullying. What had happened to his family had been emotionally debilitating, and he'd be damned if he allowed it to happen to them again.

"Thank you," Brennan said. "I appreciate you looking out."

"Just doing my job. You have a good night!"

"You too, Xander. You too!"

BRENNAN NEEDED TO clear his head, so he walked. Why he'd chosen to walk Broadway remained to be answered. But he loved the city at night. It grounded him, and there was actually something magical about the late-night atmosphere. The lights were abundant, casting shadows across the streets and buildings, and most people out that time of night had either left a good time or were heading to one. Rarely did he ever run into anyone who wasn't simply minding their own business, not bothering him as long as he didn't bother them.

The consequences of what he'd done had slapped him broadside. It had been in the look Stella had given him, the harshness of her tone, punctuated by that door closing in his face. He'd been taken aback, believing that an apology would have been enough to make amends for any of his actions. But he now realized that his actions had cut deep, and there was still an open wound that hadn't even begun to heal. He'd messed up, and Stella didn't mind making sure he knew it.

Brennan crossed the street to walk the other sidewalk. His mind wouldn't rest. Two killers were out here still able to wreak havoc when they least expected. If there was nothing else he was certain of, he was certain that they would strike again. He hated feeling like he was being toyed with; a puppet of sorts who could only react when something happened.

With each step, he revisited one case and then the other, going over what they knew again and again. The Landmark Killer's last victim had survived. That added a new dimension to the case. They had to consider how he'd respond. Would he go after Landon Stone a second time? Would he pick another victim to kill, determined that he stay on task with his body count? What would he do? And when?

Rockwell Henley's killer hadn't surfaced since the bombing. Had their obsession with Stella changed, or were they waiting? Sitting back knowing that time would be their friend and she would become comfortable again, no longer wary of people. Did the unintended deaths of the postal worker and the patrol officer strike a chord, playing on their sensibility? Did they have regrets that pushed them to let their obsession go?

The thoughts in his head were circling much like he was walking from New York block to New York block. His late-night stroll would inevitably come to an end as he made his way home or back to the office, depending on his mood. But the noise in his head had taken up permanent residency, and there was nothing that would change that except solving both cases efficiently and effectively so that convictions were guaranteed.

STELLA BOLTED UPRIGHT in her bed. A loud bang had sounded through the room, pulling her from a light sleep. She sat for a moment and listened for any other strange noises before throwing her legs off the side of the bed. When her feet hit the floor, her toe slammed into her iPad, and she realized she had knocked it off the bed and onto the floor as she'd slept. A wave of relief flooded through her.

Rising, she eased down the steps to peer outside. The patrol car was still parked out front. Learning that would soon end had left her jumpy. She wasn't ready to admit that she was outright scared. She tried hard to pretend that she was okay after watching two men be blown up in front of her. She'd successfully convinced herself that a masked gang trying to drag her off to no-man's-land was no big deal. Just a single bad day in a line of ordinary days. She knew she wasn't fooling anyone, but it helped to pretend like she was.

After grabbing a glass of water, she eased back up the stairs and settled down in her bed. Pretending she didn't miss Brennan felt harder to pull off, because she would have given anything to have him there with her. Curling up against him to fall asleep would have been a dream come true, and she no longer believed in happily ever after.

The *New York Wire* wanted a story about him and his family and their connection to so much bad business. They wanted her to write it, and Stella would if it was anyone but Brennan. Or could she? Would it be better coming from her, a woman who knew him intimately or some random stranger who didn't care about him? And what if she refused? Where would that leave her career?

Being angry with him was proving to be harder than she'd imagined, and she had never before had a problem walking away from relationship that wasn't working for her. But she didn't want to walk away. She wanted to give him a hard shake and then make love to him like that first time.

Everything was complicated in a way that Stella didn't know how to resolve. Who hated her so much that they would go to such lengths to harm her? Why wasn't the puzzle falling into place, the whodunit ending on a high note, like in the movies? How much longer could she pretend not to be concerned? And why wasn't she certain about how things with Brennan would play out? Could they continue to be friends? Friends with benefits? Or was it possible that love would be everything the two desired? Or even more disturbing, what if she couldn't get past the hurt for things to be well with them again? What if she wrote that story and he hated her for doing so? What if this stall was just the beginning of one serious crash and burn?

Chapter Fourteen

When Stella stepped out of the elevators in the *New York Wire* building, Garrett was there to greet her. Her friend grabbed her arm and pulled her down the hall toward the administrative offices.

"What's going on?" Stella asked, her eyes wide.

"I just want to wish you luck and prepare you. They plan to dangle a promotion in front of you for the inside scoop on that Colton family. And one of those fools down in marketing started a pool for everyone to bet on whether or not you'd do it."

Stella rolled her eyes skyward. "These people make me sick!"

Garrett smirked. "Full disclosure... I did put in my twenty dollars. The pot's almost a thousand bucks right now!"

"What did you bet?"

"I'm not going to tell you. I don't want to influence your decision. Just don't disappoint a friend!"

Stella laughed. "You make me sick!"

"Hey, I like to think that if anyone around here knows you, I know you best."

"You're lucky I love you, Garrett, because I'm not in a good mood this morning. I really don't want to have this conversation. I just want to come back to work."

"It'll be okay. You've got this," Garrett said. He leaned to give her a hug. "I've got an interview, so I need to run. I'll keep my fingers crossed that it all works out in your favor. I miss having you around."

Garrett gave her a wink and headed in the opposite direction. Taking a deep breath, Stella headed toward the senior editor's office.

"STELLA MAXWELL!" BRIAN'S grin was Cheshire-cat wide as he popped up out of his chair to greet her. He pumped her arm up and down excitedly, then pointed her to a seat. Returning to his own, he leaned across the desk, his hands folded together in front of him.

"I knew you wouldn't disappoint me! So, what's you're angle on the story?"

"I have no angle," Stella said. "In fact, I'm only here to tell you that it's not a story I'm interested in writing."

Brian looked surprised, his wide smile falling into a deep frown. "How can you not be interested? This could be an award-winning piece, and with your personal connection to Brennan Colton…"

Stella bristled, a wave of surprise washing over her complexion. "What do you mean, 'personal connection'?"

"I mean, he's practically living with you, right?" Brian smiled again. "We've been getting some interesting information. I'm sure with everything you know and my tips, it'll fill in a lot of blanks and connect the dots."

"Who's giving you these tips, Brian?" Stella questioned.

"That's on a need-to-know basis, and you don't need to know if you don't plan to work here."

"Brian, I can only reiterate how much I love my job. And I'm good at it. In fact, I'm one of the best journalists to work at this rag. I'm ready to come back. But I will not write the article you want. I don't think there's a story there. At least not one that our readership will be interested in. I think there are other stories and angles I can get behind that will be far more lucrative for the paper."

"But that's the only headline I want," Brian said snidely, "whether you write it or not. We're here to get the news out, Stella, not protect your boyfriend. You need to decide what's more important to you—this job or that man."

The silence that suddenly descended over the room was thundering. When Stella finally spoke, her voice was low and even, just the faintest hint of hostility in her tone.

"Brian, I'm a journalist. I report news, not gossip. That *man* and I have no personal connection. He is *not* my boyfriend. But what's most important to me is maintaining my journalistic integrity. Because whether I work here or somewhere else, my integrity will follow wherever I go. Clearly, you should want to do the same. So my answer is still no."

"Then why are you here?" Brian snapped. He leaned back in his seat and crossed his arms over his torso. His jaw had tightened, and a blood vessel in his neck was pulsating as if it were preparing to burst.

Stella hesitated, seeming to drift off into thought as she considered his question. Finally, she lifted her eyes to meet his stare. "I'm just here to pack up my desk and say good-bye," she said, rising from the chair she'd taken a seat in.

"You'll regret this, Stella!" Brian yelled as she moved to the door and made her exit. "Trust me when I tell you, you will regret this."

"Not nearly as much as you will, Brian" Stella replied.

Stella had quit her job. She was still stunned that things went as far left as quickly as they had. Clearly, Brian hadn't been interested in her ever returning to her job, and that told her everything she needed to know about working for the *New York Wire*.

She blew out a soft sigh. Garrett helped her pack her few belongings as a security guard stood watch over the computer. He'd been giddy about her turning the assignment down, having wanted the office pool to fall in his favor. But he brought her to tears with his good-bye, reminding her why she loved her job and would miss seeing him on a daily basis.

"You're not getting rid of me that easy," Garrett said.

"We have a standing lunch date every Thursday at one o'clock. Thai...until I get tired of it, and then we'll pick a new spot. So don't be late."

"What if I get tired of Thai food first?"

"We'll talk about it. But I'll still have a job to go back to. Things will need to be convenient for me."

Stella laughed. "That was low! Even for you, Garrett."

"But it made you laugh!"

She slid the photograph of her parents into the container and slid on the lid. She took one last glance around the space and nodded. "I won't be bullied or blackmailed," she said, the comment not directed at anyone in particular.

Garrett nodded. His voice dropped an octave, and his tone changed, the joviality waning ever so slightly. "I'm proud of you. They don't deserve you, Stella! So, when you get that job working for the *New York Times*, remember who your friends were. I might need you to put in a good word for me."

She smiled. "What if I go to the *Washington Post*?"

He chuckled heartily. "Forget you know me. I have no plans to ever leave New York City!"

Stella winked her eye at her friend. "Neither do I!"

BRENNAN AND RORY stood outside of hospital room 413 waiting to speak with Landon Stone. Their entry had been barred by a nurse, whose petite frame made her look like Tinker Bell, but with her attitude, she came across like a sumo wrestler, larger than life and potentially deadly. Brennan had learned early in life not to mess with women like that, and even Rory admitted to being slightly intimidated.

"Did she snap her finger at us?" Rory asked as the door closed in their faces.

Brennan nodded his head. Not only had she snapped her finger, but she'd also given them a look that could have melted ice.

"Should I knock?"

"I don't think so," Brennan said. "Do you have the doctor's direct number in your phone?"

"That won't be necessary," a stern voice said, interrupting their conversation. "Mr. Stone is ready to speak with you. But don't take too long. He needs his rest," the nurse said, peeking out the door at the two of them.

Brennan smiled. "Thank you."

The nurse opened the door to let them enter, and then she exited the space, closing the door behind her.

Landon Stone looked like a man who'd just been shot and undergone emergency surgery. He was hooked to multiple monitors and lay back in the bed with his eyes closed. His complexion was ashen, not an ounce of color in his cheeks. But his blond hair had been brushed neatly into place, and when he did open his eyes to look at them, they were a brilliant shade of radiant blue.

Rory took the lead. "Mr. Stone, my name is Detective Rory Colton. I'm with the NYPD, investigating your attempted murder. This is FBI Special Agent Brennan Colton, and we're both with the team investigating your assault. We apologize for disturbing your rest, but it's important that we ask you some questions."

Landon Stone nodded, looking from one to the other. He cleared his voice before he spoke. "I don't know what I can tell you," he said softly, his voice a loud whisper.

"Can you tell us what was going on before you were shot?" Brennan asked.

Landon closed his eyes again, his breathing slightly labored. They waited until he was ready to speak. It was only a few seconds, but it felt like forever. Brennan took a deep breath when he finally opened his eyes.

"We were…finishing up…rehearsal," he said, "when the lights…went out."

He took a deep breath and then continued, "I knew… where the…the…fuse box was. So I volunteered…to go check."

"Was it dark back there also?" Rory asked.

He nodded ever so slightly. "The back door…was open, and there was light…coming through."

"Is that door always left open?" Brennan questioned.

"No."

"What happened next?" Brennan said.

"I saw…something move. And…when I looked…there was a man."

Rory shot Brennan a look. "You're certain it was a man?"

Landon nodded his head, his blue eyes closing and then opening again. "Yes. But he had on a mask. And dark clothes."

"Was he large? Small?"

"He had on a…a mask. A carnival mask…like for Mardi… Mardi Gras."

"Did he say anything? Or speak to you?"

"He said a name… May…or Mary…"

"Could it have been Maeve?" Rory asked.

"That's it…and the last…last name was Irish. O something…like…like O'Malley."

"Then what happened?" Brennan said.

"He shot me!" Landon gasped, and when he did, one of

his monitors beeped loudly. At the same time, the blood pressure cuff around his arm activated.

"Do you remember anything after that?" Brennan said, persisting.

Landon paused. "He had...nice...nice shoes."

The room door swung open, and Landon's nurse stormed inside. "Time's up. Mr. Stone needs to get his rest."

"Why did you notice his shoes?" Brennan asked, ignoring her.

Landon waved a weak hand. "I was... I was...lying on the floor...and he...was standing...next to me. They were leather...and expensive..."

"I said—" the nurse started to say.

Rory rolled her eyes at the woman. "Thank you for your time, Mr. Stone."

Seconds later, the two had been shuffled back into the hallway. Nurse Pain in the Ass was standing at the nurse's station eyeing the two of them, venom shooting from her stare.

"I need a distraction," Brennan said.

"What are you...?" Rory started to say, the words catching in her chest as he glared at her with a narrowed gaze.

With a shake of her head, Rory moved to the nurse's station, asking questions that pulled the woman's attention from him. When the two were focused elsewhere, he moved back into the room to Landon Stone's bedside.

"Landon, I have one more question," he said, rousing the man from the lull of sleep.

Landon opened his eyes, a hint of curiosity peering up at Brennan.

"I need to show you some images. Would you let me know if you recognize any of them?"

Landon nodded his head slowly.

Brennan pulled seven photographs from the inner pocket of his suit jacket. One by one he showed them to Landon. One by one Landon shook his head no.

"Thank you," Brennan said. "I'll get out of your way this time. I promise"

"Just catch him," Landon said, his voice slightly stronger.

Brennan nodded. "Yes, sir. That's my goal."

Stepping back into the hallway, Brennan appreciated that Rory was still chattering away. The nurse was clearly beginning to lose her patience. He gestured for Rory's attention and turned, heading toward the bank of elevators at the end of the hallway.

"What was that about?" she asked when they were inside the elevator.

Brennan passed her the stack of photographs. "I was hoping he might have recognized someone."

The images were staff members from the 130th precinct and the FBI office. They were persons the team had named when they were last together at Stella's house. Potential suspects who might be killing to honor Maeve O'Leary and taunting the Colton family for the hell of it. Landon not recognizing any of them was disheartening.

Rory flipped through the lot of them, and then she burst out laughing, pulling one in particular from the pile. "Did you really include a picture of Cash?"

"Why not?"

"What if he had picked your twin brother out of the stack?" Rory said, still giggling.

Brennan laughed. "Then we'd really have a problem!"

"Where now?" his cousin asked. They had exited the building, heading to the parking area.

Brennan paused, considering their options. The conversation with Landon hadn't given them anything new to work with. They were still at a complete loss. He turned to give Rory a look.

"Let's go to Rikers. I want to talk to Maeve."

STELLA HAD A lengthy list of things she needed to do, starting with finding a job. Running through the numbers in her head, she knew she was good for at least six months. More if she was exponentially frugal. She'd amassed a decent savings, and if she watched her spending, she'd be able to pay her bills without pulling out her hair.

She knew of multiple freelance opportunities that she could take advantage of, and most of them were for social media. It would be spare change to help with the bills until something more permanent came along. As she considered all she could do, Stella mused that the timing might have been a blessing in disguise. She had been considering her options for a while, so maybe now was as good a time as any to send out her résumé and writing samples for consideration.

She'd made it to the subway station and stood in the center of the platform waiting for the train. As usual, there was a decent crowd waiting with her. She shifted her box of belongings from one hip to the other, finally resting it on the concrete at her feet as it began to feel heavier and heavier.

A stranger caught her eye, and only because he was staring at her so intensely. He was young and there was something about him that was familiar, but she couldn't put her finger on what it was. She was certain they had never met before but equally sure that it wasn't her first time seeing him. Something about the look he was giving her was off-putting, and she felt her anxiety level rise to an all-time high. He frightened her, and despite the fact she was standing shoulder deep with a crowd surrounding her, she didn't feel safe. She didn't feel safe at all.

Taking a deep breath, she shifted her body so that she was facing him directly. She tilted her head just so, ensuring he knew she was watching him as hard as he was watching her. His head lifted and his stance straightened. The hint of a smirk pulled at his lips, and he extended his arm to point his index finger at her. At that moment the train pulled into the station, and there was a rush of bodies to get on board. He smiled and took a step forward, and before she gave a second thought to what she doing, Stella lifted her cell phone, engaged the camera and took his picture.

Before he could reach her, she was running to the steps, climbing back out to Forty-Second Street. The box with her possessions was abandoned on the platform, and she hoped someone with the transit department would find it and take it to Lost and Found. As she flagged down a taxi and climbed inside, that man burst onto the sidewalk, looking for her. The smirk on his face had shifted into pure rage. He caught sight of her as the taxi pulled away from the curb. As she stared back at him, Stella could see his anger explode, and he screamed like a wounded animal.

Minutes later, she was safe behind the locked doors of her own home. The alarm was engaged, and she was starting to breathe easier. She sat staring at the photo she'd taken, determined to figure out who that man was. She was drawing a complete blank, and the situation was eerily frustrating. Every few minutes she'd run to the windows to peer outside, but there was nothing there that raised any concerns.

Knowing she'd never be able to find the answers on her own, Stella knew what she'd have to do, and it struck a nerve that didn't sit well with her. But she wasn't left with any other choices.

She dialed Brennan's cell phone. It rang and then went to his voice mail. She hung up and dialed again. On her third try, she left him a message, sharing what had happened. After hanging up, she sent him a text message and attached the photo so that he too had a picture of the man she felt was intent on doing her harm. Glancing out the window one last time, Stella sat and waited, hopeful that Brennan would call her back soon.

THE BACKUP ON the Triborough Bridge to Queens eastbound along the Grand Central Parkway took longer than anticipated. Just as Brennan's irritation was rising, they made it to the exit at Astoria Boulevard. Bearing left, they headed straight onto 23rd Avenue then left to 82nd Street. A right at the next block, and then another right turn put them exactly at the parking lot of Rikers Island prison.

Rory had called ahead to preregister them for an appointment with Maeve O'Leary, and when they reached the entrance, they were met by a guard. They were relieved of their personal possessions. The contents of their pockets, their cell phones and their government-issued weapons locked away in a courtesy locker.

They traversed the halls to an interrogation room, where they were left to wait for Maeve to be brought down to speak with them. It felt like it was taking forever as the two paced the room from wall to wall. Minutes later, a guard escorted Maeve O'Leary into the room.

Rory backed her way into the corner, her arms folded around her torso. Brennan stood by the table, waiting patiently as the guard connected her handcuffs and chain to the metal ring secured to the table. With a slight tug of the chain, guaranteeing she was secure, he gave the two of them a nod and exited the room.

"To what do I owe this honor?" Maeve questioned, eyeing Brennan curiously.

Brennan moved to the chair opposite the woman and sat down. Maeve O'Leary was nothing like he expected, despite having seen her image flashed across ever major television network. She was a beautifully stunning woman, tall and slender with delicate features, a warm tan and blonde hair that had been whitewashed by the sun. She was notorious for the many disguises she'd worn to keep herself from being captured by law enforcement.

Maeve was the Black Widow. She was awaiting trial on the murder of her last husband. And the one before him and the one before him and the one before him. Six husbands in all who had fallen for her charms, married her and then had died under mysterious circumstances, leaving her financially wealthier. Maeve was accused of being a serial killer for profit.

"We'd like to ask you some questions," Brennan said after introducing himself and then Rory.

"Questions about what?" Her voice was smooth and rich, like sweet molasses.

Brennan smiled. "You have an admirer. Someone who is killing blond blue-eyed men in their midthirties. The first letter of their first names spells out your name. We were hoping that you might have some idea who that might be."

Maeve laughed. "I was always a good wife. I shouldn't be here. This has been a horrible misunderstanding."

"Your dead husbands might not agree," Rory muttered from her post in the corner.

Maeve never looked in the other woman's direction. Instead, she smiled sweetly and batted her eyelashes at Brennan.

"I'd love to tell you how I met my last husband. Do you have time, Agent Colton?"

Before Brennan could answer, Maeve leaned up on her elbow and began to talk about her life. It would have been entertaining had they nothing else to do and maybe a drink or two to dull the monotony of her stories.

"Really, Maeve," Brennan interrupted. "We're trying to stop anyone else from being hurt. You really need to tell us something."

Maeve smiled sweetly. "Will that pretty girlfriend of yours write about me in that newspaper she works for if I do talk?"

Brennan recoiled, shifting backward too quickly in his chair. "Excuse me?" he snapped, the chair hitting the floor with a dull thud.

"It's the *New York Wire*, isn't it? The newspaper that she works for? I hear tell she's quite the writer. I'd even consider giving her an exclusive interview if she'd like to come talk to me in person."

Maeve flipped the length of her blonde hair over her shoulder. If she hadn't been wearing the requisite institutional uniform and the shackles around her feet and hands, she would have been a perfect model for a shampoo commercial, Brennan thought.

Rory had moved to his side, her hand resting on his forearm. She didn't speak, and her silence soothed the rising ire that he had wanted to spew. He stepped back as she moved in front of him.

"Mrs. O'Leary, we need to know who you've been talking to. Who's been talking to you about Stella Maxwell? And what do you know about the Landmark Killer cases?"

Maeve waved a dismissive hand at the woman. "It is time for my afternoon constitutional. A girl has to get her beauty rest!"

"Maeve, we need you to answer our questions," Brennan interjected.

"You know what would be nice," Maeve replied. "A down pillow and comforter. Just a few little conveniences from home would make a very nice gift, and very nice gifts might inspire me to tell you what I know."

Brennan shook his head. He knocked on the door and called for the guard. The visit had been total waste of time, because Maeve O'Leary was only interested in self-preservation at any expense.

The guard returned shortly after. "Is there anyone else you need to see, Agent? Detective?"

Brennan shook his head. "No, but we do need to review her visitor logs and any mail she's received."

"I'll need to clear that with the warden first, sir."

"Do whatever you need to do. A man's life is depending on it."

BRENNAN AND RORY RETURNED, having struck out yet again. The prison records didn't get them any closer to discovering who was supplying Maeve with information, and she wasn't talking. But she knew enough to mention Stella. Brennan was still kicking himself for reacting. Had he been playing poker, he would have shown his hand.

As Rory called the rest of the team to update them, Brennan ticked off everything they knew. The list was short and sweet, not a single detail to move the case any further along. It was infuriating, and all of them were frustrated. Having the killer taunt them with details about their family was galling in a way not easily explained. Cash especially fumed over their father's name being bantered about, no respect given to the circumstances of his death and the trauma suffered by his family. Knowing whoever they were looking for possibly worked with them or sat in their inner circle made their situation even more difficult.

"Let it go," Rory said as he pulled up in front of the police station, returning her to her office.

"What do you mean?"

"You need to clear your head. Go home. Watch some television. Read a good book. Do something other than think about this case. Come back to it tomorrow with fresh eyes."

"I wish it was that easy," Brennan said.

"That's an order," Rory stated. "And I get it. I completely understand how you're feeling. But if we're going to win this war, we need to get through the small battles. And we can't do that if we can't focus."

Left with nothing else to say, Brennan waved her away. Before pulling back into traffic, he checked his cell phone. The device was dead.

Chapter Fifteen

Brennan's phone ringing woke him from a deep sleep. He'd been dreaming about the entire team being on an extended vacation to celebrate the trial and conviction of their father's killer. He was just a kid, the age he was when his father had died. His mother was serving freshly baked cookies, and the laughter was thick between them. They were in the old house in Bay Ridge, and they were happy. Happier than they had ever been, right up to the moment the home was surrounded by reporters clamoring for a story. Reporters who were hiding out in the lush bushes, sneaking behind trees with cameras, and jumping out at them from behind parked cars. Reporters calling them by name and asking questions that weren't fun to answer.

It was a bright and cheery dream until it wasn't. And when the phone rang, he was snatched from the first inklings that his dreams were about to become a nightmare.

"Hello?" His voice was low and groggy.

"Are you still asleep?" Sinead questioned.

"I'm not now. What's up?" he said, greeting her

warmly. "What time is it?" He squinted his eyes to try and see the clock.

"I need you to stay calm."

"What's going on, Sinead?"

"The *New York Wire* ran a story this morning. It's not pretty. In fact, it's worse than we thought."

Brennan sat upright in his bed. His heart was suddenly racing, and he felt like he'd been punched. "Is it online too?" he asked, catching his breath.

"Yes, I'm sure it is, and Brennan," Sinead hesitated, her nervousness reverberating in her voice.

"Tell me, Sinead."

"It looks like Stella wrote it. Her byline is attached to it."

Brennan cursed, the air punctuated by the harsh vocabulary.

"If you need to call me after your read it, then call. We should all get together later and decide how we want to handle it," Sinead said.

Brennan nodded into the receiver as if she could see him on the other end. "Thanks for calling me," he said.

After disconnecting the line, it took no time at all for Brennan to find the news article. It came with old family photos that had run with the original story when his father had been killed. Pictures of his parents, him and his siblings, and their family home. There were details that only a few were privy to, things he had shared with Stella, trusting they would stay between the two of them. Details she had promised would not be shared. There were also details about the investigation of the Landmark Killer that both the police and FBI had kept to themselves. The story made it seem like the family was acting emotionally, wanting to enact revenge for their father's murder. That those emotions were interfering with them finding the killer. Sinead had been right. It was far worse than he would have ever imagined.

By the time Brennan had showered and dressed, he'd fielded calls from Parker, Ashlyn, Rory, FBI Director Chang and a few close friends. The only person who had not called had been Cashel. Brennan couldn't help but worry about how his twin brother was taking the insult. Having the details of his marriage and divorce play out publicly surely didn't bode well. Stella had violated their trust and attacked their character. She'd made them look foolish, and that was hard to process. His family would need to lean on each other more and consider how this story being out would impact their ability to do their jobs. The Colton family had been attacked, and not one of them was prepared to take that lying down.

Brennan stole one last glance at himself in his bathroom mirror. It would have been different had Stella just came after him. But she had gone after the people he loved most. He had worried how things would play out between the two of them. Now he'd gotten his answer. Stella had shown him her hand, laying all her cards on the table. Sadly, he thought, it was a game that they had both lost.

STELLA WAS ENJOYING her second cup of coffee that morning when there was a loud pounding on her front door. She hesitated the first time it sounded. The second time, Brennan called her name, screaming at her to open the door.

Moving to the entrance, she was taken aback by his forcefulness. He hadn't returned any of her calls, and she found herself worried that something tragic had happened. Or maybe that stranger was closer to harming her than she'd been ready to believe. Whatever it was, Brennan wasn't happy, which meant she wasn't either.

She snatched the door open and stared at him. "What's going on?"

"Why don't you tell me?" he snapped as he pushed his way past her, moving hurriedly through the entrance.

"How dare you!" Stella snapped back, thrown off guard by the aggression. "I didn't give you permission—"

"And I didn't give you permission either," Brennan said. He held out the early morning edition of the *New York Wire*. "Why, Stella?" he asked. "Just tell me why?"

She snatched the newspaper from his hands and unfolded it. She inhaled sharply when she saw the headline on the front page.

"Law Enforcement Family Hell-Bent on Revenge." Stella's byline and headshot followed.

Confusion washed over her expression. She gave Brennan a quick glance as she began to read the article. There were photos of him that she had never seen before, details of his father's case and a host of information that she would have never included in any story. Personal information about him and his siblings. It had Brian Price's handiwork all over it.

"Brennan, I didn't do this." She shook her head emphatically.

"Don't lie to me, Stella. After everything that happened between us, please don't lie to me now!" He was shouting, and that unnerved her.

Stella took a step back. "I am not lying. I don't lie. And I would never lie to you. I didn't write this damn story!" she shouted back.

"The *New York Wire* says otherwise."

"I don't care what they say. I don't work for them anymore. I quit yesterday. Brian gave me an ultimatum. This story or you. So I gave them my resignation. I would never have agreed to write something like this. What kind of person do you think I am?"

"Isn't that the million-dollar question? Clearly, you're not the woman I thought you were. I understand you were angry at me, but this article hurt my entire family. Not only did you stab me in the back, but you gutted them as well."

Stella shouted again. "I told you! I did not write this article! Not one single solitary word! And I didn't give them my permission to credit me for the story. The senior editor has to be behind it. I wouldn't do that to you!"

"You've told me a lot of things, and we see where that got me. And here I was trying to make amends for my own screw-up so we could move forward, and the entire time you were plotting against me."

"I swear to you, Brennan. There is no way I would do something like that to you."

"I don't want to hear it. Clearly, what you were willing to put on paper says otherwise."

"You need to listen to me. We need to fix this."

"Well, you've been right about one thing. There was

never any *we* in this relationship. Is this why you were calling me yesterday? To warn me?"

"You didn't read my texts?" Stella's eyes widened, and something like fear washed over her expression.

"No. I deleted you out of my phone. Blocked and deleted! I don't want to see or hear from you ever again."

"Brennan, please!" Stella felt her entire body tense as she pleaded with him. She took a step forward and he backed away.

Brennan moved to the door and stepped back over the threshold. Turning to give her one last look, Brennan shook his head. Tears glazed his eyes. "I can't believe I fell in love with you," he said, his words laced with every ounce of hurt and disappointment he was feeling.

"Brennan!"

"Good-bye, Stella."

STEPPING BACK INSIDE her home, Stella slammed the door closed. She was still holding that newspaper, and she flung it across the room. What Brian had done was vile, and she would deal with him later. First, though, she had to figure out how to get through to Brennan. He had to know her better than that. She refused to accept that he would think so poorly of her. She understood his hurt, and she knew pain like that would leave anyone angry with the universe.

She also needed help with her stalker problem. If he had not listened to her voice mails or read her text messages, then Brennan didn't know about the man who had chased her. Stella stood ringing her hands together anxiously. If Brennan wouldn't listen, she knew someone else who would. Rushing up the stairs, she hurried to shower and dress. She needed to get to the 130th precinct for help.

WHEN BRENNAN ARRIVED at the FBI building, Cashel was waiting for him in his office. He and his brother exchanged a look, holding a silent conversation between them. He didn't have to tell Cashel how he was feeling. Cash always knew. Just like he felt it as deeply when something pained his brother.

"Did you talk to Stella?" Cash asked.

"We exchanged words."

"I bet that was entertaining. I would have liked to have been a fly on the wall."

"You didn't miss anything. She insisted she didn't do it. I called her a liar. Now she hates me even more, and I'm still in love with her. But the relationship is over, and we really didn't have a relationship. Hell, we barely knew each other! Then I left before I cried."

"I'm sure that was a sight to behold."

"Lucky for me, I was able to get out of there before I embarrassed myself further."

"Do you really think she did it?" Cash asked, his gaze laser-focused on Brennan's face.

Brennan stared back at his brother. The question wasn't at all what he expected. As he pondered his response, still hesitating, Cash continued.

"I mean, have you really thought about it? This woman meant something to you. So much so that you have been pining for her since things between the two of you went south. You've been making a fool out of yourself over this woman! Would a woman you care that much for do something like this to you?"

"Stella was adamant that she did not write that story. She says her editor at the paper published it and used her name without her permission. In fact, she claims she quit the newspaper yesterday. For that very reason."

"You and I both know anything is possible. People are dirty. We already knew her job was on the line."

"I honestly don't know what to believe. Everything has me on edge. Between her case and the Landmark Killer case, half the time, I don't know if I'm coming or going."

"You have a lot on your plate, which is why you might be reacting without rationalizing."

"I'll be honest with you, Cash. I'm broken right now. Completely broken. Which is why I can't understand how you are managing to be so damn calm. I just knew you'd be ready to break someone's neck."

"Trust and believe, I am not that calm. But something about this just isn't sitting right with me. There were things in that article Stella had no way of knowing. Things I don't believe you would have told her. I'd bet my last dollar that you didn't talk to Stella about my marriage and my divorce. Or that me not wanting kids was an issue.

"Or how our father's death impacted Ashlyn. Or the problems Patrick faced. There were details in that article that only someone with personal knowledge of each of us would have. Or that someone with access would find in our personnel files. Things that would have come out during our required psychological evaluations."

Brennan's head snapped up as he and Cash locked

eyes. "Stella said that email the other day about those anonymous text messages that Sinead and I received set off the newspaper wanting to do an article."

Cash nodded. "And is it possible that whoever sent that message didn't also feed more information to someone else there?"

"I really think we need to pay her editor a visit."

"Is this visit on the record or off?" Cash queried, a slow smile pulling across his face.

"Oh, this is definitely off the record. And it won't be FBI-sanctioned either."

STELLA HESITATED AT the top of her steps. She looked left down the block and then right. It was relatively quiet for the midmorning hour, not much activity stirring things up. She had called and left a message for Detective Rory Colton, but she hadn't called her back yet. She couldn't help but wonder if the entire family was furious with her, believing she had betrayed them.

She'd left a message with an Officer Davis, wanting Rory to know that she was headed in that direction. She didn't add that she was scared, but deep down inside, Stella was petrified. She was still debating whether to call for an Uber or take the subway. She hated that she was starting to feel like a hostage in her own skin. And it infuriated her that some nameless, faceless person had that much control over her life.

She took a deep breath, her decision made. Easing down the steps, Stella lifted her head, her chin high up. Pulling her shoulders back, she took one more deep breath and began to walk toward the subway station.

THE TWO BROTHERS walking into the offices of the *New York Wire* looked like movie gold. They seemed bigger than life: tall, handsome and determined. As they glided by, people paused at the sight of them. Their jawlines were set like stone, and the look in their eyes was pure fury.

Brian Price's eyes widened nervously as they stormed into his office unannounced. He'd been sitting back with his hands clasped behind his head and his feet up on the desk. He'd been thinking how well his day had started, watching the growing website numbers. People were weighing in with their opinions on the front-page story about the Colton family. To suddenly have two of the brothers standing in front of him was disconcerting.

"You don't have an appointment," he stammered, looking from one to the other.

Brennan moved to the man's left side and Cash eased over to his right. Brennan sat down on the desktop, nudging Brian's legs to the floor.

"What do you want?"

"We need to speak with Ms. Maxwell about her story this morning," Brennan said. "Is she in yet?"

Brian cleared his throat. "I can't have you trying to intimidate my reporters."

"Will she feel intimidated?" Cash asked.

"I feel intimidated. You have no right to try and strong-arm me."

Brennan smiled. "That's not at all what we're doing. We just have some questions. We're going to give her the opportunity to answer them here. Now. Or in court, when we sue."

Brian coughed. "I'm sure every fact was checked and verified."

"Are you sure about that?" Cash asked.

"Why don't you call her in so that we can verify that? She did write the article, didn't she?" Brennan asked.

Brian stammered again. "I…we…she's not…"

"What, Brian? Spit it out!" Brennan said, his voice raised slightly.

"Who supplied you with the information?" Cash interjected.

"I can't reveal my source!"

"You can't? Wasn't Stella your source?"

"Her source…" he muttered.

"We passed Ms. Maxwell's desk on the way in, and it was empty. That doesn't look good, Brian. It looks like she quit or was fired. Which is it?"

"She…we…it's not…"

"You write so creatively. I'm surprised you're having a hard time getting your words out."

"This is unacceptable," Brian shouted.

Brennan leaned back, humming contemplatively. "I sure hope she still works here, Brian. And that you can verify it. If not…"

Cash leaned in and whispered into the man's ear. "In the business, we call that identity theft."

"Fifteen years max, with heavy fines if the victim faced financial losses," Brennan continued. "Legal fees, perhaps."

Brian's eyes darted between the two men. "You're bluffing."

Cash shrugged. "Alternatively, you could clear this up now and give us your sources. What's it going to be?"

Brian was not at all happy about his current situation. He pointed to the bottom drawer of his desk. Cash pulled it open and pulled out a large manila folder that rested on top. The Colton name had been neatly typed on the side tab.

"Get out of my office," Brian snapped. "That's everything I have."

"*Did* Stella Maxwell write that story?" Brennan asked.

Brian didn't voice the answer out loud, only glared. That was all the confirmation Brennan needed.

"Pleasure doing business with you," Cash called back cheerfully.

"I'll be filing a complaint with your superiors!" Brian shouted.

Brennan paused in the doorway. "You do that. We look forward to it. Have a good day now!"

The duo returned to the elevator and waited for it to reach their floor. Brennan smiled. She didn't write the article. Now all he needed to do was to find Stella and grovel for forgiveness.

Chapter Sixteen

Stella was just six short blocks from the police station when she saw the man from the previous day. He stood on the other side of the street dressed in a black hoodie and matching sweatpants. He stood out because the day's temperature was pushing ninety degrees, and he was dressed for a winter snowstorm. There were enough people on the street that she didn't feel like she'd be an easy target, but then she thought about her delivery man and the police officer. They hadn't seen her as an easy target either, not knowing that they were directly in the line of fire. Stella would have been devastated if one more person was caught in the cross-fire of someone trying to get to her.

She came to an abrupt halt as she weighed her options. He was smoking a cigarette, leaning against the wall of an office building. They traded gazes as he seemed to be waiting for her next move. Which is why she stood still, her feet frozen to the sidewalk as she in turn waited for him. She refused to show him any fear. If he was coming for her, she fully intended to give him one hell of a fight. She prayed that the expression on her face showed him that.

She watched as he took a step forward. He dropped the cigarette butt to the ground and smashed it beneath the heavy steel-toed boots he wore. His gaze moved down the block, and he stared before turning back to give her a smug glare.

She shifted her gaze to where he had looked, and her breath caught in her chest. Crossing the intersection was another man who looked identical to the guy across the street. He too was dressed all in black with a hoodie on. Twins, she thought, the reality of her situation beginning to take hold. Not one potential villain out to get her but two. Suddenly both men were headed in her direction.

Stella turned, moving forward. She had just reached the corner and was crossing the street when she caught sight of the third man. *Triplets?* She suddenly felt outnumbered, and the police precinct was still five blocks away.

A horn blowing drew her attention, and when she looked over, a GOP campaign truck was pulling up to the curb. The outside had been repainted with the image of the new candidate, Marshall Tucker for Governor, in bold black print. Pamela sat behind the wheel, waving at Stella excitedly.

Grateful for the bright smile shining on her, Stella glanced behind her and rushed toward the idling vehicle. She jumped into the passenger seat, slamming the door shut and locking it behind her.

When she turned toward Pamela, the other woman was still grinning excitedly.

"Everything okay?" Pamela questioned as she pulled back into traffic.

Stella glanced back at the trio of ninja-suited strangers. They were standing together, staring after the van. Stella eyed them through the side view mirror, her gaze frozen in place until they were out of sight.

Sitting back in the seat, she breathed a sigh of relief. "Thank you. I'm good now."

She turned back to Pamela whose smile had waned substantially. It was that very moment when Stella realized the mistake she had made. The man from the previous day had seemed familiar, and she now saw the resemblance as if someone had painted the picture for her. It was their eyes. Pamela and the stranger had the same eyes.

Stella feigned a smile and pointed out the passenger side window. "If you can just drop me off around the corner here. I have an appointment with the detective on Rockwell's case. She's expecting me."

Pamela shook her head as she made a left turn at the light, heading in the opposite direction. "I don't think that's a good idea, Stella," Pamela said, losing the cheery tone to her voice. "I think you and I really need to talk."

"Really, Pamela. This is important, and I don't have time for your games!" There was a nervous edge to Stella's voice, the sound foreign to her own ears. She turned back to give the other woman a look, and that's when she realized Pamela was pointing a gun right at her.

"STELLA DIDN'T WRITE that article!" Brennan exclaimed as he entered the conference room at FBI headquarters.

The team had all gathered to discuss what had happened and update each other on anything they might have learned. He moved to the seat at the end of the table.

All eyes turned to give him a look. Amusement wafted from one to the other.

Patrick spoke first. "You seem especially excited about that."

Ashlyn nodded. "Almost giddy. Like you'd actually believed she'd done it before."

Brennan shrugged. "I had concerns."

His sister turned to Sinead. "Why are men such asswipes?"

Sinead laughed. "I can't answer that. My man is a gem."

"So, who wrote the story?" Patrick asked.

Cash answered the question. "Stella's boss. Our mole fed him information about all of us. Practically told him the story he should write. He gave us his documents, and based on what he had, we were able to get a warrant for his computers. The digital forensics team is examining them as we speak."

Patrick gave him a high five. "Good job!"

The conference room door suddenly swung open. Rory, Wells and Director Chang moved into the space. Rory shot the twin brothers a look. Wells eyed them also, rolling his eyes skyward. The director's glare was edged in criticism, and the entire team could feel a reprimand coming. Rory took the seat beside Brennan and kicked him under the table.

Detective Chang was tall and exceptionally lean. Her straight black hair was in a short pixie cut that complemented her dark eyes. She wore silver-framed glasses and a black silk suit that hugged her petite frame. Her expression was serious, and she was known for being straight-forward and painfully direct.

The room went quiet as she eyed them one by one, her stare pausing on Brennan and then shifting to Cash. "Can someone please explain to me why I've spent the last hour fielding a civilian complaint about two of my agents harassing a newspaper editor?"

"We did no such thing," Cash said.

Brennan nodded. "We were asking him about information he'd received, and gave him some friendly legal advice. Then we left."

Detective Chang shook her head. "I'll need written statements from you both," she said. "And there's to be no further contact between you two and anyone at the *New York Wire*. Is that understood?"

"Yes, ma'am," Brennan said.

"Where are we with the Landmark Killer case?" she asked.

For the next hour the team updated the director on all they'd been able to accomplish and where they were still hitting a brick wall. She reiterated the importance of them closing the case as quickly as possible. Reminding them the mayor was breathing down her neck, and she would continue to put pressure on them when he was making her life miserable.

When the conversation was finished, the director looked at her watch. "I have a plane to catch. If any of you need me, Xander will know where to find me."

A chorus of appreciation and well wishes rang through the room.

"Thank you, Director," Brennan said.

"Safe travels," Cash interjected.

When the door closed after her, the two blew sighs of relief. Laughter rang warmly through the room.

"I can't believe you two," Ashlyn said.

"Believe it," Rory countered. "The fool editor has been on the rampage for most of the afternoon. He wasn't happy with the two of you."

"He's pond scum," Brennan said. "What little attention he deserved from us is done and finished. He just wants another fifteen minutes to redeem himself for being an idiot."

"There's no saving idiots," Cash said matter-of-factly.

Parker rose from his seat. "I'm headed down to forensics. I'll call you once I see if they're getting anywhere."

"Thanks," Brennan said.

Rory was listening to her cell phone. Her expression changed, the easy glow shifting to something dark and serious. She held up her hand, moving them all to quiet down as she jotted notes onto the notepad before her. When she was finished, she paused to text a message, promptly hitting the Send button when she was done.

"Have you heard from Stella?" she asked turning to give Brennan a look.

He shook his head. "Not since I spoke to her this morning. It was before I learned the truth, and I was angry."

"Check your messages. She said she sent something to you yesterday."

Brennan suddenly looked contrite. "She told me that too. I lied and told her I had blocked and deleted her and her messages. The truth was my phone died and I hadn't had a chance to review them."

Rory shook her head. "Well, you being an idiot may well have just gotten her killed," she said, rising swiftly from her seat. She played the voice mail on her phone, putting the device on speaker. Stella's voice came through clearly.

"Detective Colton? Rory? This is Stella. I really need help. I'm sending you a photo of a man who came after me yesterday in the subway. He'd been watching me, and he chased me out. I think it might be the man you're looking for. The man who killed Rockwell. He's familiar to me, but I don't know where I recognize him from. I've tried to reach Brennan, but he's not answering me. He's mad at me. But I'm mad at him too, so we really are of no use to each other. I've sent him the photo also. I'm headed to the precinct now. I should be there within the hour."

Rory tossed Brennan a look. "That was four hours ago. Check your messages!"

Brennan picked up his phone. There was a single missed call and voice mail from Stella. He put the phone on speaker and pushed the Play button. There were two voices, and both were muffled, but there was no mistaking that it was Stella in conversation with someone. Somehow, Stella had managed to hit the redial button on the last call she had placed.

"Stop talking!" a woman was saying, exasperation filling her tone.

"You need to let me go. You don't need to do this."

"Don't tell me what I need to do."

"Then just explain it to me. Help me understand why. Why did you kill Rockwell?"

The woman laughed. A deep bone-chilling chortle that made the hairs rise on Brennan's neck.

Stella persisted. "Why did you do it? And the bomb? What were you thinking?"

"Make her stop talking!" the woman shouted. "I have to think!"

Stella suddenly cried out, her scream cut short as if she were suddenly choking. And just like that, there was silence.

Brennan pushed the Stop button and began to scroll through the text messages that Stella had sent the day before. His eyes widened as he read them. Then he saw the photo, and he too had a sense of familiarity that he found unsettling. He was squinting as he tried to make the image larger on the screen.

Ashlyn snatched the phone from her brother's hands. "I'll be right back. I'll get this enlarged and printed out."

Brennan nodded. He'd gone cold, his blood feeling like ice water pumping through his heart. He'd been angry and had gotten so caught up with finding out the truth about that damn article that he'd forgotten about her messages. He'd screwed up royally, and now Stella was in serious trouble. He didn't know if he'd be able to recover if he failed her again. He suddenly felt helpless, and he had no doubts that it showed on his face.

"We'll plug into all the city cameras between her house and the precinct to see if we can find her," Parker said, racing from the room.

"Her phone's off," Rory said, trying to call her. "I've got my guys tracing the last cell tower it pinged."

"Grab your files," Cash said, his tone calm. "Let's go through everything you have to see what we might have missed."

"I've gone through them a million times," Brennan muttered.

"You haven't reviewed the last one I tossed onto your desk. My office only left it there this morning, and we took off shortly after."

"What file is that?"

"You requested everything I could find on that campaign woman."

Brennan nodded just as Ashlyn moved back into the room. She'd enlarged the photograph, capturing a clear image of a young man wearing sweats. He was smirking, the look he was giving the camera feeling like it could burn a hole in concrete.

"We're running it through facial recognition software right now," his sister said.

Brennan was staring at the image, his mind on overload as it worked like an unhinged computer. Why was that face familiar? Where had he seen that man before? It was beginning to drive him crazy, most especially because his remembering could be the answer to finding Stella.

When he looked up, Cash and Sinead had split up the files on Stella's case and were beginning to go through them. His brother pushed the folder labeled with Pamela Littlefield's name across the table toward him. And then it clicked.

Grabbing the image of Pamela Littlefield and the photo of their unidentified perp, he held them both up, side by side. He looked from one to the other, back and forth. The resemblance was undeniable. It was deeply embedded in their eyes, their gazes identical, his equally as beautiful as hers.

Chapter Seventeen

"Pamela Littlefield was a quadruplet, the only girl and the eldest in the set of four. Parents were Leona and Eddie Littlefield. Mom died during childbirth. Pamela was delivered safely, but complications left the three boys compromised. They were deprived of oxygen and suffered maturation deficits after birth. According to the report, that part of the brain that controlled speech was affected, and none of the boys has ever spoken. It was believed that they were mentally challenged, and they were committed to a home care facility at a young age where treatment and care meant handcuffing them to beds and locking them in cages. Pamela was raised by her father until his death when she was sixteen. At the age of nineteen, she petitioned for guardianship of her brothers and won."

Sinead looked up from the document she'd been reading. Her expression was telling.

"What?" Brennan questioned. "What does it say?"

"The father died in a house fire. They weren't able to prove it, but Pamela was suspected of starting that fire."

"Well, that wasn't her last rodeo," Cash said. "That was not the only person murdered where Pamela was a suspect. And the brothers have lengthy criminal records. But she always manages to get them all cleared. It seems her political connections have come in handy." He passed a document to his brother, who read it and passed it back.

"It's been her the whole time," Brennan said. "And her brothers have been helping her."

Silence swept through the room. Without saying it out loud, they were all thinking the same thing. Stella was in serious trouble.

STELLA HAD NO idea where she was. She believed they were somewhere in the South Bronx, remembering them exiting off the Bruckner Expressway toward Hunts Point. Pamela had driven the truck through bay doors, coming to a stop inside a warehouse. From what she'd been able to ascertain, the warehouse was home for Pamela's brothers.

She shook her head. Pamela had introduced her family as if she expected them and Stella to become fast friends. Owen, Charlie and Miles had only stared at her as if she were an albatross they couldn't wait to be rid of. They weren't happy about her being in their space, and Pamela seemed completely oblivious to that fact.

Pamela was off in her own little bubble, narrowly focused on the problem that was Stella. Trying to figure out how to eliminate Stella and get away with it.

From where they had forced her to sit, Stella had a front-row view of the room and the family. One of the brothers, the one named Owen, Stella thought, was hunched over a table, playing with wires and boxes and batteries. Every so often, he would chuckle, seemingly pleased with whatever he was working on.

The brother named Miles was with Pamela, seemingly distressed over something. He sat cradled against Pamela's lap as she stroked his back and rocked him back and forth. Charlie had disappeared, nowhere to be found. Not knowing when he might pop up or where didn't give Stella any comfort whatsoever.

They had found her cell phone, turning off the device and throwing into a trash dumpster blocks away. She wasn't confident that her last calls had gotten through. Whether or not Brennan or any of his team would come for her felt unlikely. She was alone, and if she were going to survive this, she would need to remain calm.

Pamela suddenly rose from her seat. She was yelling at Miles and then she slapped him. Hard. He reacted violently, sending everything atop a desk in the room to the floor. Pamela stood with her hands on her hips, chastising him until he finally calmed down.

At least an hour passed by before Pamela shifted her attention back to Stella. She marched across the room, halting abruptly in front of her.

"Are you hungry?" Pamela asked. She gave Stella a bright smile. "I can send one of the boys to pick you something up. Any requests for your last meal?" She laughed as if that were funny.

Stella shook her head. "No. Thank you."

"Suit yourself," Pamela said. She turned to cross back to where she'd been earlier.

Stella called after her. "Pamela, please tell me why you're doing this. Please!"

Pamela smiled. "Because I can!"

"Why did you kill Rockwell?"

"To make the world a better place, of course!" Her expression was stunned, as if she couldn't fathom Stella not making sense of it all. "Rockwell wasn't' always a nice man. You know that."

"I don't understand. You and Rockwell were friends."

"No, we weren't. Rockwell's mother was his only friend."

"But why set me up to take the fall?"

"You were supposed to die too. It was supposed to be a murder-suicide, but Miles messed up. He sent you the message too soon. If he had waited, I'd have been able to slit your throat and leave you for dead beside Rockwell. And it had to be you. It just made sense. Your fingerprints on the knife would have sealed the deal!"

"How did you do that?" Stella questioned. "Put my fingerprints on the murder weapon?"

Pamela jumped excitedly. "We saw it on television one night. On that show Matlock! It was so cool. You take a piece of clear tape and press it down over an original fingerprint. Then you transfer the print to another item. I got the knife from Rockwell's kitchen that night we were all there for pizza. And I lifted the fingerprint from your water bottle after you and Rockwell left me to clean up. He had walked you to the subway station. As soon as you got on the train, he went to meet Rebecca. She wanted to reconcile, and I think he did too, but you were in the way, always being pushy with his time. His mother said you were a problem, and I'm good at getting rid of problems."

"But his mother didn't want Rockwell dead. That

doesn't make any sense!" Confusion washed over Stella's expression.

"It makes sense because that's how we wanted to play the game. We decide who lives and who dies. We decide how and when. We always make sure whoever is supposed to be guilty, looks guilty. Always! This would have worked if we had killed you both in your house like I suggested, but it was one of the boys that wanted to see if we could pull it off in broad daylight. But he got the timing wrong, and now I have to clean up the mess."

"You've done this before?"

"Of course, silly!"

"Why the bomb?"

"The boys again!" Pamela said, her singsong tone irritating. "Owen tried to make things right. But you got away again! Now I have to do it. Charlie wanted a turn, but he tends to be messy. And messy makes law enforcement want to figure out what happened. Charlie would have tried when you were in the hospital, but he could never get past that cute Agent Colton. So now it's my turn. Your dead body floating in the Harlem River can look like an accident. Or a suicide. No mess. No blame. Game over."

"You're going to get caught. The Coltons are going to figure this out."

Pamela's tone was saccharine sweet and condescending. "You want to believe that. I understand. And that's okay. But I know, you're going to die, and then I'm going to a fundraiser for our new candidate. And tomorrow, my brothers and I will pick someone new to play with!"

BRENNAN STOLE AWAY to his office, closing and locking the door behind him. His head throbbed, and his heart felt like it might burst out of his chest. He knew he needed to step back and calm down before he gave himself a stroke or a heart attack.

They'd been searching for Stella for most of the afternoon. It was as if she'd disappeared off the face of the earth. A patrol car had been parked back in front of her home, and he'd gone there himself to check that she wasn't lying hurt or dead inside. The team had pulled together to help search for her and the Littlefield family, who were all looking like serial killers who had flown so far under the radar that no one would have ever considered them suspect.

Sinead had attributed at least twelve murders to their handiwork, with twenty other unsolved crimes she liked them for. The more that was discovered about them, the more fire they were able to throw on a host of cold cases. But Brennan couldn't focus on what they had possibly done in the past. He was only concerned with what they might do in the future. What harm they might bring to Stella if he couldn't find her soon.

Tobias and the Henleys had been brought in for questioning. The Henleys couldn't fathom Pamela being able to do such a thing. Mrs. Henley had accused him of grasping at straws to make a case. That he was making everyone a suspect because he wasn't good at doing his job. She earnestly believed that Pamela could never do Rockwell any harm. Discovering that Pamela had three brothers had stalled any further comments, the couple admitting that maybe they didn't know the young woman as well as they thought they did.

Tobias knew the family's history. He acknowledged the brothers had always been problematic, but rarely did he see them. According to him, Pamela never talked about her siblings at all. Unless, of course, she needed help to keep one of them out of jail. He didn't seem at all surprised to hear that she was suspected in Rockwell's death. Brennan found that strange. When he asked Tobias if he had ever been concerned about Pamela working for him, he'd been dismissive, believing that as long as she needed him, he was good to go. Tobias had been asked if he had any idea where Stella could be found, and he had denied any knowledge of her whereabouts. Brennan found that hard to believe. When he considered the time Pamela spent lost up her employer's backside, following him around, nothing Tobias said sounded reasonable.

He remembered Stella thinking Pamela might have been in love with Tobias, and he had asked him about that as well. He'd responded with a dismissive shrug and a wry smile, like Pamela was one of many women who fawned all over him.

The Henleys and Tobias had shared as much information as possible before being escorted back to their homes.

Before retreating to his office, Brennan had left his sister and cousin to follow up on the leads they'd been given. Each of them was putting in extra hours to get things done. He didn't have words to express how much their efforts meant to him. Finding Stella was going to take all the manpower they could muster, and doing it all on his own was never an option.

Brennan pulled open the bottom drawer of his desk. He pulled a bottle of bourbon and a small shot glass from inside. He poured himself a quick drink and downed it without blinking an eye. For ten more minutes he sat inhaling and exhaling deep cleansing breaths. When he began to feel more like himself, he stood up and stretched. Deep down in his midsection his gut instincts had kicked into high gear, and there would be no ignoring them.

Brennan hurried back to the conference room that had become serial killer central. He rushed through the door shouting orders. "Let's do a deeper dive on Tobias. Something tells me his connection to Pamela isn't as casual as he would like us to believe."

STELLA COULDN'T BELIEVE she'd actually dozed off to sleep. She woke with a start, unsettled as she remembered where she was and why. She had no clue how long she'd been there or what the others had been up to. As her eyes adjusted to the dim light, she jumped, fright spiraling up and down the length of her spine.

One of the brothers was sitting in front of her, watching her closely. His head tilted slightly to the side and his eyes widened when he realized she was awake. Stella made herself smile, unsure what he was doing or why. He just stared, his body down in a low squat.

"Hi," she said, her voice low. "You're Charlie, right?"

He didn't answer, only shifted his head to the other side as he kept staring.

Stella tried again to engage him in conversation, but she got nothing. As she thought about it, she hadn't heard one of them speak. Not a single word since she'd been taken. Pamela had been their voice, telling them what the other was saying. They didn't sign, nor had she seen either of them write a note to communicate. Pamela seemed to be their only link to each other and the outside world.

As if the devil had heard her thoughts, Pamela called her brother's name. "Charlie! What are you doing? Get away from her! It's not time yet."

Charlie began to rock back and forth. When Pamela called him a second time, moving in their direction, he stood up straight and rushed past her, dodging a blow as she swung a fist in the direction of his head.

Pamela stood where Charlie had just been resting. "Have you no shame?" she snapped at Stella, a look of disgust on her face.

Stella glared up at her. "I just said hello to him."

"I see how you flirt. You always need to be the center of attention. That's why I picked you. Charlie didn't want you to get tagged for the game. That's only because you have him snowed too. Like you did Rockwell."

"You are seriously delusional."

Pamela bristled, but she didn't respond.

"Why don't they talk?" Stella asked. "I haven't heard your brothers speak."

"They talk. They talk to me and they talk to God. They don't need to talk to you or anyone else. It's our gift. We were blessed with it when we were all together in our mother's womb. It's why we're special. We've been chosen for great things. I hear all their thoughts. They don't need words for me to know what they want to say."

Stella shook her head and muttered under her breath. "Like I said, delusional!"

Pamela screamed, the sound like nails on a chalkboard. Stella's eyes widened, her heartbeat beginning to race. She shifted back against the wall, sliding closer to the corner. Pamela continued to scream, seeming to unleash whatever emotion she might have been feeling. Behind her, the brothers barely blinked, their sister's tantrum not even registering an ounce of emotion from them. Stella shook her head.

"What are you going to do with me?" she asked as Pamela finally paused to take a breath.

Pamela smiled, collecting herself as if nothing had happened. "I'm not going to do anything to you. You are going to overdose on pain medication and fall into the Harlem River. You've been distraught over being accused of killing Rockwell and then having someone trying to kill you. It was more than you could take. I told you, Stella. We have to make the details fit the story!"

STELLA PULLED AT the zip ties that secured her hands and tied one ankle to a steel rod that ran from floor to ceiling. She been trying to work herself free when she thought no one was looking, but soon discovered one or more of them were always looking. Pamela had slapped her the last time, something like rage gleaning through her fingers and palm.

Time seemed to be standing still, and Stella was grateful for it. Pamela appeared to have her own schedule of doing things, and she would not be moved from Stella dying at precisely the right time. That had bought her an extra hour or two for Brennan to figure out where she was so he could come save her.

Stella had all the faith in the world that Brennan Colton would save her. She imagined him and his team working to put all the puzzle pieces together until they exposed the criminals from everyone else. He would work things out, and those details Pamela was so proud of would inevitably be her downfall. At least, that's what Stella was praying for.

She missed him. She would have given up a firstborn son, the family cow if they'd had one and even an appendage to be able to press herself against him one more time. She wanted to feel him so close that it would be like they were conjoined twins. She wanted to apologize for pushing him away. She needed to make things right between them. She had salvaged rage that was not his and had tried to drown him with it. She'd not given him a second chance, and that had come from dating way too many men who hadn't deserved one. She prayed that there would still be time for her to make things right. Because all she wanted to do was to tell Brennan that she loved him.

Chapter Eighteen

"Bingo!" Ashlyn jumped from her seat. She rushed to the printer and pulled a stack of papers from the receptacle tray. She waved them high in the air for everyone's attention. "Tobias Humphrey was born Tobias Tyson Hodges. Legally changed his name ten years ago after graduating from community college in New Jersey. In his high school yearbook, he was voted the student most likely to succeed. I bet you can't guess who his prom date was, and your first two choices don't count."

"I'll do you one better," Sinead interjected. "At least six of the deaths we believe the family is responsible for are individuals with connections to one Tobias Humphrey. It was believed the last couple died in a home invasion gone wrong. The husband was campaign manager for an opposing candidate. Another victim was a college professor who gave him a failing grade. It looks like they were eliminating people Tobias had problems with."

"And that's why they targeted Rockwell and Stella!" Brennan exclaimed. "She wasn't making things easy, and Rockwell had continued to support her. Getting rid of them both allowed Tobias to start over."

Everyone was nodding. "And didn't I see something in your notes about her having a boyfriend named Tyson?" Rory asked. "Tobias and Tyson are one and the same!"

"Where would they take Stella?" Brennan questioned. "Did we get anything on the city's camera feeds?"

"This is so your lucky day!" Patrick chimed. "A campaign van was seen in the vicinity of police headquarter around the time Stella made those calls. We were able to track it to Queens. And for the topping on that cake, her phone has been pinging off a cell tower that's close to the last camera sighting. And I can unofficially say those calls are coming from Tobias's phone."

"Why unofficially?" Ashlyn asked.

"Because it's not information we're supposed to have without the appropriate warrants. But I have friends!"

"What's in Queens?" Brennan asked.

"We're still looking. We're searching public records to see if Pamela owned any property or is connected to any business there."

"Let's add Tobias to that search as well."

Rory rose from her seat and gestured in Brennan's direction. "There's a fancy campaign fundraiser tonight. I say we take this show on the road and go pay Ms. Littlefield a visit."

Wells suddenly moved toward the door, pushing buttons on his cell phone before he reached the entrance. "I'm calling the district attorney. We're going to need warrants for both their homes, campaign headquarters, all cell phones, and you're going to need warrants for their arrest. I've also put out an all-points bulletin for Stella Maxwell. We'll find her!"

Brennan nodded, giving Rory a look. "Let's dance, Detective Colton!"

PAMELA AND ONE of her brothers were dancing a bossa nova toward Stella. Or rather, Pamela was dancing and pulling the man along with her. She had changed and was now wearing a floor-length gown in a vibrant shade of emerald.

"Don't you look nice," Stella said casually. Her stare was suspicious.

"Thank you. My fiancé picked it out. Tyson loves this color on me, and he says we need to make a grand appearance at tonight's fundraiser."

"Will he be joining you here?" Stella asked.

Pamela stared at her, and then she laughed. "He doesn't need to join me here. I'll be going to him. But good try, Stella Maxwell!"

"You need to let me go, Pamela. We can fix this."

"It's already been fixed. Unfortunately, I have to shift to plan B. That boyfriend of yours has gotten too close, and Tyson says we need to cut our losses while we can still get out of this." She pressed a hand over her bosom. "It hurts my heart too! But we always knew this day might come."

"I don't understand," Stella said, confusion teasing her expression.

The dress Pamela wore had pockets, and she suddenly pulled a cell phone from inside. She read the screen and then she shook her head. "The things we will do for the men we love!" She turned, walking back to the other side of the oversized room and small office against the front wall.

Stella watched as the brothers followed her inside. Pamela wrapped each one in a warm embrace before kissing their cheeks. They retreated to their respective corners, the simple good-bye seemingly an innocent display of affection.

Pamela moved back to her. She carried a small bottle of water in her hand. Charlie followed on her heels, and when they reached Stella's side, he squatted down next to her. Pamela smiled that bright smile of hers.

"Share your candy with Stella," Pamela said.

Charlie opened his hands to show Stella the small white pills inside his palms. He suddenly shoved a handful into Stella's mouth, forcing her to swallow them. Stella gagged, feeling like she might choke as they slid down her throat, and then she coughed, spitting the taste of them out of her mouth. "What the hell did you just give me?" she snapped.

Charlie had swallowed his pills and was drinking the last of that bottled water. He began to rock back and forth, his eyes closed.

Pamela knelt down to kiss his forehead. "It won't be long now, Stella," she said softly. "You'll just drift off to sleep and everything will be glorious! See," she said as she pointed toward the other two brothers.

Owen sat in a recliner in front of a small television. He'd fallen to his side as if he'd drifted off to sleep. Miles sat at his worktable, his movements unsteady, until he too slipped down to the floor.

Stella felt a layer of fog descending across her brain. Her eyelids had gone heavy, and she struggled to keep them open. "What…what…did you give us?" she stammered, her voice barely a whisper.

"It doesn't matter," Pamela said. "I just needed to make quick work of the cleanup."

"They'll…they'll find us," Stella said, her whole body feeling as if every muscle had suddenly gone limp.

"They will," Pamela said. "Maybe months from now. I doubt there'll be anything left of you though, except maybe your bones. I don't think the rats eat the bones." She genuinely looked confused as she considered her own statement. "Just sleep, Stella. Don't fight it. Just sleep and you won't even know when it happens."

Charlie had curled himself against Stella's side. A single tear rained out of his eyes and down his cheek. Stella leaned over him, no understanding of how Pamela could harm her family. She closed her own eyes and felt her breathing begin to labor. Everything around her went quiet. In the distance, Pamela was humming to herself, and then the roar of a truck engine echoed out of the bay door. Pamela had left them there to die.

THE CAMPAIGN FUNDRAISER for the new candidate was being held at New York's Helen Mills. The venue was a stunning four-thousand-square-foot space with a beautiful thirty-seven-foot-long hand-crafted bar and a multi-seat theater. Some three hundred people had been invited for a cocktail-style reception.

Brennan and Rory entered the venue followed by a team of ten NYPD uniformed officers. He held the arrest warrants in his hand and eagerly searched out Tobias and Pamela. He found them huddled together in a corner, Tobias looking upset by something. Pamela caught sight of them first, and she waved them over, the exuberant gesture unsettling.

"Special Agent Colton, to what do we owe this honor?" Pamela said, her tone too cheery. "Have you come to endorse our candidate?"

"Where's Stella Maxwell?" Brennan said, firing the question at her. "And your brothers? Where have they taken her?"

Pamela looked confused. "Stella? I haven't seen Stella in ages. And what does this have to do with my brothers?" She cut an eye toward Tobias.

Tobias took a protective step in front of the woman. "What is this about, Agent? Why are you and the detective here?"

"You're both wanted for questioning in the disappearance of Stella Maxwell, as well as multiple unsolved murders here in Manhattan," Rory said. She took a step behind Pamela. "Put your hands behind your back," she said.

"This is ridiculous!" Pamela exclaimed.

"If you want to make this difficult, you can try," Rory said. "But it will not end well for you."

Two of the uniformed officers stepped forward, their hands perched precariously on their guns.

Pamela gave them that gummy smile. "Now why would I be difficult? I'm sure this is a simple misunderstanding." She pulled both arms to her back side, flinching ever so slightly when those handcuffs clicked and locked.

"You have the right to remain silent. Anything you say can and will be used against you in a court of law…" Rory began to Mirandize the woman.

Brennan had already snapped handcuffs on Tobias, and he did the same. "…You have the right to an attorney. If you cannot afford an attorney, one will be provided to you. Do you understand the rights I have just read to you?"

Tobias nodded, his eyes rolling skyward as if he were annoyed and bored.

"This is just so unnecessary," Pamela quipped.

"With these rights in mind, do you wish to speak with me?" Brennan questioned. "Are you ready to tell me where I can find Stella Maxwell?"

Tobias chuckled. He answered, "I'd like to speak with my attorney."

Pamela shook her head. "So sad that she would suddenly disappear like that."

Tobias repeated himself a second time, staring directly at Pamela in a silent conversation meant only for her. "Attorney!"

BRENNAN WAS WATCHING as Tobias and Pamela were placed in the back of two patrol cars headed to the precinct for processing and questioning. Although there was a level of satisfaction knowing they'd just gotten two serial killers off the streets, his anxiety over not knowing where Stella could be was at an all-time high. He desperately needed to find her. And he needed to find her safe and well.

Rory moved out of the building onto the sidewalk.

She tossed Brennan a look, seeming to understand what he hadn't verbalized. He nodded his head and gave her a slight smile.

"You good?" Brennan asked.

She nodded. "I'm good. I'm headed to the station to get them processed."

"Don't let the bobo twins interrogate them, please?"

Rory laughed. "The bobo twins?"

"Those two you let interrogate Stella. Frick and Frack. We don't need to lose this case on their stupidity. And those two," he pointed at Tobias and Pamela. "Those two are cunning! With them already lawyering up, we'll have an uphill battle to bring them to justice."

"Rest assured, only Wells and I will be interrogating them. This is way too big for any of us to be messing it up." She pressed her hand to his back as she eased past him, heading to her own ride. Watching his cousin walk away, Brennan felt assured that whatever else followed would be a walk in the park.

The cell phone in his pocket vibrated for his attention. He didn't need to look at the screen to know it was his brother calling, the ringtone designated specifically for him.

"What's up?" Brennan answered.

Cash didn't hesitate to reply. "We found Stella. I've texted you the address."

Chapter Nineteen

Brennan barreled toward Hunt's Point in the South Bronx with his sirens blaring. He exited the Bruckner Expressway, running parallel with the Bronx River. Property tax records showed an old warehouse near the food distribution center owned by Tobias Tyson Hodges. Cash had taken an FBI tactical team to investigate the premises and had found Stella restrained inside. His brother hadn't said she was okay, so Brennan was desperately trying to prepare himself for the worst.

As he pulled into the lot, FBI agents and local police were spread out over the property, checking every nook and cranny for evidence. The coroner's truck was parked near the bay doors, and a single ambulance was close to it. He took a deep inhale of breath, then jumped from the driver's seat, slamming the car door closed behind him.

He hurried toward the interior of the building, flashing his badge as one patrol officer after another tried to stop him. As two body bags were carried out past him, Brennan felt himself begin to shake, his legs threatening to give out and send him to the floor. He took another breath and came to a standstill as he struggled to catch himself.

Cashel called his name, and when he looked up, his brother was standing at the entrance, waving him forward. "She's in here," he said.

As Cash turned, Brennan hurried after him. He still had no idea what he would find, and though he convinced himself he was prepared to face whatever, his confidence was completely shook.

EMS personnel hovered beside Stella. She lay on an ambulance stretcher, and when her hand moved, her fingers pushing at one of the technicians to leave her alone, Brennan released the breath he'd been holding.

"Is she okay?" he asked shooting a quick glance toward Cash.

"She's dehydrated and a little banged up, but they say she'll be fine. They had to give her a dose of Narcan to get her breathing again though. It seems Pamela gave them all an overdose of opioids. The brothers didn't make it."

Brennan could only begin to fathom what Stella had been made to go through as he glanced around the room. He and Cash exchanged one last look as the twins slapped palms. Brennan pushed his way to Stella's side. He leaned to wrap an arm above her head. His other grabbed her hand and kissed the back of her fingers. Her eyes were closed, and tears had dried against her cheeks.

"Hey, you still mad?" Brennan whispered into her ear.

Stella's eyes opened and she smiled. "Are you?" she whispered back.

"Yeah!" he said. "I'm mad as hell!"

"Me too!" She pressed her hand to his cheek, drawing

the pad of her thumb along his profile. "I was so scared," she said. "Pamela has some serious issues! You need to catch her. It was a game, Brennan! A sick, evil game!"

He smiled. "She's already in custody. So is Tobias."

"But her boyfriend was..." she started to say.

Brennan shook his head. He leaned to press his lips to hers, kissing her ever so gently. "Shh! Don't let it worry you. We have it all under control. Let's get you home and healthy, and then I'll catch you up on everything you missed."

Stella lifted ever so slightly to kiss him a second time. "I have to tell you something," she said, shifting against the pillows behind her head.

He shook his head, tapping her lips with his index finger. "You just rest. I'm not going anywhere. I promise, you're going to have a really hard time getting rid of me."

Stella smiled. "I love you too," she said, and then she slowly drifted off to sleep.

WHEN STELLA WAS headed toward the hospital, Brennan moved to the other side of the room to catch up with Cash. "What'd you find?" he asked, his brother dictating instructions.

"We hit gold! Their entire lives were stored here in this warehouse. And Pamela kept meticulous records of every kill. Some go back ten years or more."

"Unreal!"

"And they collected trophies from their victims. We can tie them to the murders, and the DA should have no problems getting a conviction," Cash said with a nod. "That's one more down and many more to go. Our work never ends, but a win like this sure makes what we do worth it."

"Yeah," Brennan said, "but I like it so much better when the universe just drops them into our lap."

"Well, this case was clearly a slam dunk. I don't think any of us anticipated this outcome." Cash led him to the makeshift office area. There was a toaster oven and hot plate that sat on the surrounding counter. Someone had a real liking for strawberry Pop-Tarts and Little Debbie honey buns. Boxes of them had been stored in a cupboard over the counter. Bottled water was stacked in one corner. Paper littered the floor.

Cash passed him a pair of latex gloves, wanting to preserve as much of the evidence as they could. They were already battling layers of aged dust and dirt. The composition notebook was labeled with a woman's name. When you flipped open the cover, an image of the victim had been glued to the inside. Meticulous notes followed, weeks and months of surveillance until everything about that person had been discovered. Then came the plot to kill them. The how and why. Plans changed as every single solitary detail was weighed and measured. But every correction had been duly noted in pen and ink, sometimes accompanied by little scrolls and arrows.

It was bizarre in a way that gave Brennan pause. Surprisingly, it felt exactly like Pamela: disturbingly happy and joyful, and morbid in the same breath. She was proud of each project, wanting to commemorate that person's death with a yearbook of sorts. That last rah in their hurrah.

Each notebook was dated and adorned with pretty

stickers, and ribbons in assorted colors were tied in lofty bows to keep them closed. There had to be at least two dozen or so lined neatly on a shelf. Brennan shook his head. He rested the book in his hand back onto the table. As he turned, something caught his eye. One last notebook that hadn't been completed. On the cover, Stella's name had been printed in a delicate calligraphy.

STELLA OPENED HER eyes to find Brennan sound asleep in the medical recliner beside her bed. He had leaned himself back, and his head was rolled to the side. His mouth was open, and he snored. Loudly. It made her smile, and she imagined that it was the first decent night's rest that he'd gotten in some time. She was sure that knowing he was close by and she was safe had done wonders for her.

When she'd wakened earlier, she'd requested copies of the morning newspapers. Someone had obliged her with the *Times*, the *Daily News*, the *Tribune*, the *Post*, and of course, the *Wire*. She and the Coltons had made the front pages yet again. This time the family received well-deserved accolades for the work they'd done in bringing down a family of killers. The mayor had pledged to honor them for a job well done and had reminded the community that they were working as diligently to bring the Landmark Killer to justice.

Brennan snored ever so slightly, and it made her smile. They still had far to go with their relationship, but the prospect of having him in her life and never again letting go of what they shared was pure joy. She was excited to learn things she didn't yet know, and the thought of them growing together as they reached for mutual goals made her heart sing.

Stella would never again *not* fight for them when it got hard, she thought, and Brennan had pledged the same to her. With a deep sigh, she closed her eyes and drifted back into the sweetest sleep.

"STELLA!" BRENNAN CALLED her name for the umpteenth time standing at the bottom of the stairs in her Harlem brownstone.

"I'm coming!" Stella yelled back. "Just give me one more minute!"

He shook his head. From the living room sofa, Rory and Cash both laughed at him.

"Leave that woman alone," Cash said. "She knows we're here."

"Yes, I do," Stella said as she bounded down the stairwell. "And your brother knows I was not dressed for company."

"You weren't dressed," Brennan said as he pressed a damp kiss to her lips.

She kissed his back, then turned away as she pulled the length of her dark hair into a ponytail that hung down her back. "Good morning, family," she said, moving to hug Rory first and then Cash.

"Good morning," Rory said with a laugh. "How are you doing?"

It had been three weeks since the FBI had found her left for dead in a local warehouse. She'd spent a few days in the hospital, then had come home to complete her recuperation. Brennan had been by her side the entire time,